What others are saying about THE LAST ARCHIDE

Chad has created a vivid and incredible world with *The Last Archide*, and has only begun to tell a tale that can easily be described as "epic." Set in a futuristic era where the technology has advanced to the point where the rules of warfare had to be rewritten, this masterful tale enthralls readers. Due to the invention of an impenetrable armor, armies are reduced to hand-to-hand combat to once again raise the stakes of war. Out of these high stakes rises a hero for the ages.

—C. Trebus, *Service Coordinator & Technical Writer*

An intriguing tale of a boy who becomes the ultimate warrior and leader of men. He asks for no quarter and gives none in return.

—Daniel Lyn, *Biology/Human Physiology Instructor*

THE LAST ARCHIDE

THE LAST ARCHIDE

THE WARLORD OF NAVARUS

CHAD R. ODOM

Tate Publishing & *Enterprises*

The Last Archide

Published by Tate Publishing & Enterprises, LLC
127 E. Trade Center Terrace | Mustang, Oklahoma 73064 USA
1.888.361.9473 | www.tatepublishing.com

Tate Publishing is committed to excellence in the publishing industry. The company reflects the philosophy established by the founders, based on Psalm 68:11,
"The Lord gave the word and great was the company of those who published it."

Cover illustration by Ashley Delgado
Cover design by Marianne McShane
Interior design by Chris Webb

Published in the United States of America

ISBN: 978-1-61663-439-1
1. Fiction / Fantasy / Epic   2. Fiction / Fantasy / General
10.06.10

ACKNOWLEDGMENTS

Special thanks to Ashley, Will, and Candice, who put so much into making this book what it is. To my parents, wife, and children: Thank you for your love and support. Without you, this would have never happened.

TABLE OF CONTENTS

Prelude

It was a frigid night. The cold winter air raced sharply through his nostrils and into his lungs. A steady breeze rustled the branches of the evergreens, which stood like sentinels all around the camp. It would snow soon. There was an electricity in the air that brought with it the promise of precipitation to come.

He had fought many battles before this one. Each brought with it its own emotions. There were new surroundings. He had fought in grass-covered fields, on sandy shores, and on the scorched earth of harsh deserts. Some days it rained; some were fought under an azure sky. Some, he and his men battled the elements almost as much as their enemy. Each new battle brought with it new wounds, new scars, new disease, and new death, but the end result was always the same: victory.

Somehow, it was more than the snow that made this battle different. There was a feeling here. There was a premonition of future events that the warrior could not place. The weight of the incursion before him weighed on his mind. His rifle was slung over his shoulder. He carried his helmet under his arm. His handcrafted and custom-designed blade rested against his hip. He was just as ready as he had been a hundred times before. Why was this different?

The warrior breathed in again, letting the bitterly cold air enter and then leave in a slow controlled mist from his lips. He crouched low to the ground, removing his helmet from under his arm and placing it in the already fallen snow. With a glance over his shoulder, he observed the life that existed only before a battle. Lights glowed from each tent. The men talked amongst themselves of victory and bravery. They shared stories from previous battles of their brand of heroics.

Others were more introverted, praying to whatever god they worshiped for a safe return and victory. There were those who sang songs. There were those who quietly slept. All ranges of human emotion and ritual existed here. At no other time and no other place could you find such a display. The warrior had seen it many times. For him, he required solitude, and that is what he sought.

Before him was a large hill. Before the snow had obscured its slopes, they were covered in short grass, laden with various sizes of stones. A few of those rocks still peeked just above the white blanket.

He reached across with his left hand and removed the glove from his right. The winter temperature bit at his fingers instantly, but he took no notice. He reached for the ground, slowly running his fingers through the snow. Their warmth melted four individual paths through the thin layer of ice and into the softer stuff beneath. The soldier withdrew the digits from the frozen ground and looked at the snow still stuck to each one. It melted quickly, leaving only traces of cold water running into his palm. His hand gripped the droplets in its fist, and then he returned the glove to its proper place.

He stood to full height, picking up his helmet as he did. Arrayed in armor and ready for battle, the specimen was an impressive sight. He was the most feared man in the world, and even he knew it. Thousands had fallen by his hand alone. He was the best that had ever lived. He feared nothing.

There is an uncertain fate that awaits me. This battle is unlike any that I have heretofore fought. I go, not into victory, but into the very mouth of the lion. I go to court my doom.

The warrior placed the helmet firmly on his head. One more short breath came and was exhaled abruptly. He was ready. His time had come. For the first time, he was stepping into a future he was not sure of, but he faced it with courage and with the knowledge that fate had guided him this far. Whatever it was, it awaited him at the top of the world.

BEGINNINGS

In another time, in another corner of the universe, a hero was born. He was not born a king or a prince or a ruler. He was not born into wealth or in any position. His birth was not miraculous, nor was it heralded by a heavenly chorus or a celestial sign. It was ordinary, and it was common. In fact, like so many great lives, it was marked early on by tragedy.

He was born a slave. His mother was stricken at his birth with an infection that she would never fully recover from. By the time he turned four, she was gone and he was left to be raised by his father. They had nothing except each other, yet his father knew he was destined to be more than a slave. It was in his blood.

His father, Armay, was born in another nation. Armay was born into a military family, and he lived up to his birthright. When he was only eighteen, he was made a general. At twenty, he was leader of all the armed forces of the kingdom of Gondolin, answerable only to the king. He held his position for twenty years. His devotion to his country and his family cost him nearly everything, including his home, his wife, and even one of his eyes.

Armay's son, Oryan, grew up fast and strong. He carried his mother's traits in empathy and compassion. He was hard, but full of understanding. He could learn anything he was taught immediately, but he was not arrogant in his intelligence. He was loyal, and his sense of duty and honor came to light early on in his life. He would be a king were he born anywhere else. This haunted his father.

Still, he was his father's son. He was a warrior, and no skill, no trade, no knowledge was absorbed more quickly than that of combat. He was a brilliant tactician. He excelled at all sports, whether they demanded his mind or his arm. There did not seem to be a challenge great enough for him in his world of slaves. He began taking on the older boys and soundly winning. The fire, his father's fire, burned like red coals in his blue eyes.

He worked as a mason with his father. The labor kept his body strong since there was no formal training allowed for slaves. Secretly, his father taught him everything he knew about combat in the shelter of the trees behind his home. The training went fast, as he was a model pupil.

On a night like any other, the pair walked home from a long day's labor. They traveled in silence, both thinking deep thoughts they could not articulate to the other. They passed through the chain-linked gate, barely acknowledging the guards who were stationed there. The lights on the posts above the gate glowed blue when the door opened, and with the click of the lock and the hum of electricity, they returned to their normal red.

The boy and his father traversed the familiar paths to their domicile and had made it nearly there when Oryan broke the silence.

"Do you miss Mom?" he asked.

Armay stopped, fighting back hard emotions, and searched for the appropriate answer. He missed Kathrine, his wife, and shared his feelings about her little, though he spoke of her often. Oryan stopped as well, searching his father's face.

Armay's answer was simple. "Every day, son; every day."

"I wish I could remember her," Oryan said. "I think I dream of her."

"Oh?" said Armay, feeling sorrow and joy all at once. "Tell me about it."

"I dream often of a girl. She is beautiful, and she makes me feel ... *at home*."

Armay smiled. "What does she look like?"

"She has soft dark hair with brown eyes. When she smiles ..." The boy paused. "When she smiles, it takes me away from here to a faraway place, away from these walls and this life. When I dream of her, I never want to wake up."

Armay kneeled next to his son and placed his hand on the boy's shoulder. "Hold on to her. Keep her safe, if only in your dreams.

She is not your mother, but maybe your mother sent her to you. Whoever she is, she must be an angel."

"Do you dream of Mom?"

"Every night, and I fight hard never to forget her. I fight to keep her safe." Tears began to roll down his cheek though his voice remained strong. "If only in my dreams.

"Some things are worth fighting for," Armay continued. "Some things are worth dying for. But you must always remember that you must fight for something more than yourself. There are greater forces and greater ideals out there than this childhood arena. If you will but devote yourself to something more, to a vision greater than yourself, greater than the stars in the sky," his voice became powerful and passionate, "if you can only do this, you will become more than a man, my son. You will become more than a hero. You will be a legend. A hush will fall over the world when your name is spoken. You will stand among kings, and they will kneel at your feet. You will fill a destiny unlike anyone before you."

Oryan was filled with emotions he had never felt before. His father was a large man, but his size was amplified by his nobility. Now, with Armay on his knees before him, he seemed larger than life itself. Armay's vision was lifted to the heavens; he seemed to whisper something to the numberless stars though it was not audible. A son sank next to his father and wrapped his arms around his neck.

"Father," he said after a long silence.

"Yes, my son?"

"What is worth fighting for?"

Armay turned to his thoughts, searching for the right words. He knew the answer, but it was a lesson he was not ready to teach.

"You have to find that answer for yourself. Live every day to its fullest and always progress. Never stop striving to excel. Be the best at all your endeavors and, above all, live for others. If you do these things, your destiny will be laid before your feet. Don't be afraid to walk it."

His gaze was finally moved to his son's face, and he lifted the boy's chin until their gaze met. "But, beware! If you choose to look only inward, you will fall. And great shall be the fall of such a bright star. It will rend the heavens and shatter the earth. The only sound that will be more sorrowful will be the cry of anguish within my heart. Beware pride! Beware ego! They are so tempting and so seductive. The world will chant your name. Do not do the same."

Armay embraced his son. He felt as if, for the first time, he was holding his child. Not his student, his tool, or his prodigy. He held his little boy, and Armay knew this was all he could ever hold of his beloved wife. Nothing could replace her, but his son made him whole.

At this moment, he was back in his garden in Gondolin with his Kathrine, the smell of roses and fruit mingling with the springtime air. He was home. The dark night was lifted, and he was transported to the tall spires and rounded domes of the palace in his kingdom. The sun was shining radiantly, and he could feel its warmth on his face. At this moment, he suddenly knew his highest calling. Not general, or friend, or even husband. It was father. *That* was worth fighting for.

Oryan looked at the stars above his father's head. They were the same stars he remembered from a thousand previous nights, but something had changed. Not the stars themselves, but the way he perceived them. For the first time in his young life, he marveled at their beauty. They shimmered and winked at him, a billion points of brilliant light. All he wanted now was to shine among them, to play his part in their intricate dance. That was his calling. For the star that shines brightest, shines for the least amount of time. Just to be numbered among them was enough. Somehow, he found his center in those celestial orbs. Somehow, they offered him a small measure of peace.

From that day on, his training took on a whole new life. He was trained in combat, in games of strategy, and also in the ways of valor. He was shown what it was to be valiant. His father began to instill in him the need to use his great gift only as a last resort, when words and peaceful actions were not enough. His competitions with the other boys became less intense. He knew the names of each opponent and shook their hands at the end of every event. Though his new teaching had taught him sportsmanship, he still never lost. Despite his father's teachings, humility was a lesson he struggled to learn.

His skill in the mason shop was unmatched. By twelve, he could outperform many of the men. Only his father worked harder or longer. They smiled coming into work and patted each other on the back when the day was done. If any passerby had seen the two of them, they would never have been aware they were anything but free men enjoying the fulfillment of a hard day's labor and each other's company.

Over the years, his body continued to become stronger. His deep blue eyes and physical prowess earned him the attention of the girls. He would show them kindness and affection, having a few flirtatious relationships here and there, but he found them to be more a distraction. The formalities of holding hands, kissing at the appropriate times, and saying the right things were taxing to him. His heart belonged to the girl in his dreams. No one else compared. When he found her, he would belong to her forever.

He made many friends of all ages and was generally considered to be a worthy young man. His willingness to do most anything for others had endeared him to almost all. However, with his vast popularity came bitter enemies. Some of the older boys held hard grudges against him. Some had been defeated by him and felt embarrassed by his kindness afterwards. Others felt that his constant time in the limelight was ill deserved. Though they did not openly oppose him, they watched with green eyes of jealousy. One in particular stirred the simmering pot of envy.

Each day, Oryan and Armay would arise with the sound of the work bell and head to breakfast. From the food lines, they left the gates and fences of their confined existence, passed the guards, and went to their assigned post at the shop. This had been the routine for as long as he could remember. Now, at sixteen, he knew it would be the routine for the rest of his life. It troubled him immensely. Though he never admitted it to anyone else, he hated the confines of this prison. Though he loved his father and the people he lived with day-to-day, he dreamed of something more. Were he asked, he could not say what he was looking for, just *something* else. His dreams could not be contained within the walls of this place.

One morning, when the bell sounded loud and clear, Oryan started to dress for the day. He finished and rounded the corner to see his father still in his bed. He was breathing hard and his pillow was soaked with sweat. Oryan placed his hand on his forehead and felt the fever burning through him. Armay looked at his son and afforded himself a small smile. "It has kept me up most of the night. Just a bit of dinner that didn't agree with me, that's all. Don't wait for me. I'll be fine. Get to work. I will be here when you come back."

There was a long moment of silence as the two studied each other closely. Oryan looked long upon his father's face. His temples were red with fever. A sleepless night had deepened the lines on his face. Oryan was painfully aware of his father's age.

Armay beheld his son. Years had passed since he cradled him in his arms for the first time, but he could still see his little boy. He was the perfect image of youth and innocence. He would do anything to give him a better life than this. Armay knew, however, that it was his own actions that had brought them both here. Soon, he would have to let him go. No matter the cost to himself.

Oryan turned to leave but felt compelled to look one more time at the man who had sacrificed so much for him. "Thank you, Dad. Thank you for all that you've done for me. Someday, I will make all things right."

He turned and walked to the door. As he was about to leave the small archway, he froze. A sense of foreboding and dread held him at the doorway as strong as if he had been bound to it by steel chains. Never in his life had he known this hesitation. Something was going to happen today. He could feel it. For good or ill, a storm was coming. This feeling was not directed at his father as he felt no urgency in his condition. It was something before *him. It was fear.* He had never known it before, but now, it groped at him with cold, steely hands.

"Remember, courage is moving forward when fear would have you turn back," he heard his father say. Oryan looked back at his father to see him unmoved. He was still lying in his bed, wrapped in a blanket, fighting the fever. He began to wonder if he had actually heard him speak. "You can never fear change," he said to himself, "and change is coming."

With that, he stepped into the world. The effort, for such a simple feat, had exhausted him. He left his home behind, but the fear was eager to tag along. It dragged behind him, making each step labored.

He went to the food lines but did not eat. He ignored his usual friends and sat alone, trying to pretend that today was a day like any other. The dreary skies did not help. A distant rumble of thunder sounded in the distance. The cold wind rushed across his face and brought with it the promise of rain to come.

No matter. It has rained on other days.

He passed the lines of broken brick homes that lined the narrow streets. There were no yards, no color, save that of faded red kissed with silver steel. They were all slaves, the emperor's work force, so they were only afforded discarded building materials. Past the houses rose a line of trees. They were tall and mostly bare. Above the treetops stood watchtowers filled with snipers and spotters who monitored his world constantly. Most days, he gave these things no notice. Today, he soaked in every detail.

He filed into the lines heading to the various trades and factories. The electronic scanners herded the masses by their Sig Cards to their appropriate gates. Today, his was gate four. The gates were not designed to keep enemies out. They were simple deterrents meant to keep the residents in. They were chain-linked fence with razor wire lining the tops. Each section of fence was held together by a thin steel pole capped with horns that would sound various tones to alert guards and captives alike of the events of the day.

What kept the prisoners at bay was the fear of the guards. Most were military police, stationed there because that was their job and it kept food on the table. There were, however, a handful of the guards who were bullies at heart. They had joined the force simply to be able to throw their weight around in a uniform that held some authority. They were the head-breakers. Some were drafted in. They resented their service completely, and so they felt others' lives should be just as miserable.

They were not dressed in the armor of defensive troops, nor were they suited for the fast pace of open-field combat. Their dress was simple: gray jackets with gold buttons fastening off-center to the left side of their chest. Their rank was displayed on their right arm and on the top right of the chest. The pants were the same color and material. Boots, belt, baton, and firearm also adorned their persons. No helmets, only short-brimmed hats.

The sky lit up with a streak of lightning, and the thunder boomed behind. A light sprinkle began to fall. The cold water felt refreshing on Oryan's face. He looked upwards to greet it. It was a cool, clean shower that cleansed his mind of present circumstances. The fear retreated. He thanked the heavens for that.

"Hey, Oryan, where's your pop?" cried the guard at the gate. The sound of his name shook him from his trance. He knew most of the guards by face, but slaves were not allowed to know their names. Once, when some of the slaves had rioted at the gates, this particular guard had received what would have been a fatal wound had it not been for him and his father. Armay had waded into the chaos, retrieved his broken body, and carried him to the facility's physician.

"Home. Case of food poisoning, he thinks," Oryan answered.

"Shame." The guard pulled him aside and spoke to him under his breath. "If he needs anything, you let me know first, aye."

"I'll tell him you send your regards."

A smile crossed the guard's lips as Oryan walked back into his line.

As he walked away, the fear crept back up his spine. It had only suppressed itself for a few moments. Now, it was quickly building with each new step. It was a predator, stalking its prey. Had he and the guard been paying attention, they would have noticed the scanner bulb glow red indicating that a worker was headed through the wrong gate. That fact having been missed, there was no warning to what was about to happen.

Oryan passed through his gate. He looked to his left, watching the guard disappear behind him. Then he looked right at the herd of people there. Nothing suspicious in front of him either. *What was this?* Fear was closing in on him again. Each step was harder than the last. It was as if it had venom that paralyzed its victims before it devoured them. It was coming for him now to finish what it had started, and he was helpless to stop it. His eyes darted this way and that, looking for any signs of trouble, sweat mingling with the cold rain.

He had left the perimeter fence, leaving the drab black and white world, yet it seemed to him this day that the outside world was more colorless than the one behind. It seemed this was another side effect of the venom.

Then, all at once, it happened.

Fear lunged at him for the final kill. But it was no longer the same fear he had on his doorstep. This was different. It was calming. It heightened his senses, made him all too aware of the rain that splashed around him. The sound of each drop was deafening. He could feel the cold sting like daggers on his skin. His eyesight was sharp, enough to notice each line of woven fabric on the person's clothing in front of him.

The sky unleashed its fury, and heavy sheets of rain began to fall. He could hear the torrent on each inch of ground. Each inch, that is, except the ground directly behind him where something was blocking it from reaching its destination. Whatever it was, it was moving fast and straight at him. He could hear the object displace the falling water as it moved. It was larger than he, but not as fast.

The fear was gone. He recognized this new sensation: it was combat. Only combat did this to a man. Fear had been new to him because every time he fought before had been a controlled environment, one with rules and adults to enforce those rules. This, however, was true combat. His actions now were the result of a thousand lessons that no one else had been taught. This fight was over before it started.

His weight shifted to one foot, and he pivoted hard to face his adversary. They would collide in less than a second. More than enough time. He rotated his torso to avoid the lunge and thrust his fist soundly into the boy's temple as he passed. His attacker's head snapped sideways, the eyes going dull and the body going limp. It fell with a thud to the ground.

The second attack was equally predictable. From what was now his left, the second one came on. This one was more cautious than the first and stopped short of his target. He raised his arm and threw all his energy into a single punch.

Foolish amateur.

Oryan let the punch slide past his face. He could hear the rain parting around the blow. He grabbed the boy's wrist, rotated hard, and secured the arm near the shoulder with the other hand. Using the poorly aimed punch's momentum, he threw his victim over his shoulder and onto the muddy ground. With a splash, he landed, and a swift elbow delivered to the fallen foe's nose sent the attacker into unconsciousness.

The third attacker was a surprise. How he missed him, he did not know. He stood up, and as he did so, a flash of metal slashed through the rain and opened his chest. It was a long, deep wound that left its mark from shoulder to stomach. The wound stung, but he did not acknowledge the pain. The rain diluted the blood, but it was not long before his clothes were a dark crimson. The edge of the weapon was sharp, but not sharp enough. It was not a clean cut. The flesh around the opening was ragged and frayed. This was the first blow he had ever received from an opponent.

His heart went cold. All the lessons he had learned about dignity and honor vanished in a flash of steel and muscle. Every word of his father's about mercy receded into the deepest portion of his brain as if they had never existed. When he finally laid eyes on the person who had done this to him, he turned completely inward. No one would ever wound him again. He would never again see his own blood so long as he lived. And this man, this one exception to that rule, was about to find what the cost would be for being the instrument of this infraction. He would pay for it. *One drop of my blood spilt for every ounce of his.*

The second blow was on its way. The sound of the guards' horns faded into the background. The shouting of the people around him was as good as silence. He stepped aside again, dodging the thrust directed at the center of his chest. His grip was like a vice on the hand carrying the knife. The boy lost his grip on the weapon, and he shrieked in pain as Oryan crushed the bones in his hand.

Oryan moved incredibly fast as he spun into the blow and across the inside of the boy's arm. The arm that did not grip the wrist came up with deadly force. With a sickening twist and the strike from beneath, this enemy's elbow shattered, and his shoulder was violently removed from its socket.

Oryan's feet were just as fast. His boot came down with a crunch on the front of the attacker's knee. With a snap of tendon, bone, and muscle, the young man fell to the earth like a stone. He screamed a deafening scream that was almost as nauseating to hear as it was to listen to the injuries themselves being inflicted.

The sound of the chilling scream faded as a shock-induced coma took the boy. Oryan stood over his victim like some ravenous bird ready to tear apart the helpless prey. His senses were still sharp, listening for the next attack, but it did not come. Instead, the only sound he heard was the sound of the still pouring rain drumming on the wet mud. All the people who were witnesses of the attack had formed a semicircle around him. Their faces were frozen in a picture of horror. Even the guards had stopped in their tracks.

Only two pairs of eyes looked at the situation with any other emotion than shock and terror. One pair belonged to Oryan.

The other belonged to the captain of the guard. He had watched the situation from the start. He had watched the younger boy discard three older ones with proficiency and skill unsurpassed by anyone he had seen.

Where Oryan saw victory, this captain saw opportunity. Where the guards saw a bad situation made worse, this man saw talent. Where the onlookers saw bloodshed and violence, he saw a profit.

From Slavery to Bondage

Oryan woke up from his bed in the infirmary. They had given him a large dose of anesthetic, and he was not sure how long it had lasted. Had he been there for a few hours? It could have been weeks. There was no way he could be sure. All he knew was that after the fight, his attackers had been taken away very quickly and as discretely as possible. They had rushed him to the infirmary, and he had been there ever since.

A few small things puzzled him. There were no guards and no motion sensors at his doors to sound the alarm if he tried to escape. He had never been placed in restraints, nor had he seen a single physician from the medical facility that was nearest his home. This place was very sterile, and the walls were bleached white. The smell of *real* medical care was everywhere. All of these departures from his reality made him very alert and very wary. He had to be ready for anything.

The strangest of all occurrences was the dressing of his wound. Under normal circumstances, when a slave was cut, the physicians came in, administered a shot to numb the pain, and cauterized the wound. It was fast, and it took no time to stop the bleeding. That procedure was not a guarantee, as many times they would fuse too much or sometimes too little. Infections were common, and sometimes death followed. This was not the case for him. His cut was professionally cared for. No laser scars or the smell of burnt flesh. When he pulled away the garment he was wearing, he could see that the cut had been very carefully stitched. The stitches were small and very close together. It was also apparent that the wound had been efficiently cleaned and that surgical glue had been applied to aid the stitches in healing. This meant no infection and minimal scarring.

There were no windows in his room, so he had no gauge of time. Now that he was fully conscious, he wanted answers, and there was no one around to give them. In fact, there was no one around at all. He had heard that in normal hospitals there were ways to call for help that did not include screaming, but he saw no such thing here. With the exception of his bed, the equipment to monitor his health, and the door, there was nothing here at all. Very curious.

He sat up in his bed. Surprisingly, small pressure-sensitive hydraulics pushed the bed up as he rose. This was as close to luxury as he had ever known, but he had no time to enjoy it. He was fit and healthy now, and there was no time to lose. The wound had been superficial and should heal nicely. He felt no more pain, so he was ready to get back to work, ready to get back to his routine, ready to get back to his father.

His father! That thought was almost painful. How long had it been? Was he all right? When he had left, Armay was sick, too sick to come to work, and for Armay that was unusual. He had to know.

"Hello?" he yelled at the empty room. No answer.

He removed the monitoring sensors on his head and chest, threw the sheet to the floor, and sprang out of the bed. His bare feet hit icy-cold tile, and he was now faced with a stark truth. Aside from the gown that covered front and back, he was naked. This would not do. If he was to get out of here, he would first need clothes. No problem; easy fix. He grabbed the sheet from the floor and tore a strip free from the material. He cinched the sides of the gown together and tied the thin strip of torn cloth around his waist. Good enough.

He walked to the door and pressed his ear to it. There did not appear to be anyone on the other side. He could hear no sound of voices, no jingling keys, and no heavy trudge of footsteps. Still, caution was needed. He kept listening. Oryan knew that although he felt better, he was not at top performance yet. He reached for the doorknob. He would inch the door open and visually confirm what he had heard. Then, he was gone. He had to see his father.

His fingers reached the knob, and he slowly turned it until he knew the door would open soundlessly. He moved his head in position to peer out. Just a pull on the door and he would be a free man. Then, he heard voices coming down the hall! One was apparently a doctor, using all the right jargon, and the other sounded much more gruff and matter-of-fact. There was a heated debate taking place. Apparently, according to all official records, Oryan was never to have been treated here.

This information would be useful for any escape attempt.

They were nearing his door, but it was too late to get back into the bed and pretend he was still asleep. He had no idea how the sensors worked or where they went on his body. No one would miss the torn sheet either. So, he did the only thing he knew he could do on short notice. He made himself as small as possible in the corner of the room beside the bed, opposite the door, and waited. They would not see him at first, and that would give him an edge.

They were right outside the door.

"Yes, I know that you have paid good money for this one, but the hospital can only make so many exceptions; *I* can only make so many exceptions. Do you know what would happen to this place if they found out we were sheltering and giving this kind of care to slaves?"

"I don't think you realize what we've got here. This boy will be something we haven't seen in years. He will be a *champion*. Remember what that was like? You're a gambling man. When the time comes, I'll be able to tell you where to put your money, and it'll be on this kid. You will be rich beyond even your imagination." There was a moment of silence as the gruff one let the last statement sink in. "For now, he never existed and I was never here. Have the video and audio surveillance erased, and never speak to a living soul about this again. Trust me."

"I've heard that one before."

"This time I mean it." The door opened. "You just—" The door was completely open, and the two surveyed the scene before them: torn sheet, no boy.

"I knew he had removed the sensors; all his vitals had gone flat, but where has *he* gone?" asked the man whose voice Oryan had identified as the doctor.

The two men looked around, knowing there was no place in this room to hide for long. The doctor went back into the hall to check with the orderly, and the other man continued to look around. There were very few places to actually check, so he did what anyone would do: knelt down to check under the bed. After all, kids always hid under the bed.

No child there either.

"Where did the little bas ..." he began to ask. He began to stand up only to find he was staring face-to-face with the person he was looking for. Not under the bed, but on top of it. *This kid was quiet!* The child's eyes were fixed on his. Normally, he would not be intimidated by a boy so young, but this was different. He had seen what this boy was capable of, and he knew that despite his size and strength advantage, he would be in for a fight. This kid was lightning fast. Two of his last victims had ended up dead, and he had barely broken a sweat.

"The orderly says that he—" the doctor began another sentence that went unfinished upon returning to the room and seeing the present situation. The patient was crouching on the bed like a viper ready to strike. For a very brief second, the doctor wished he would. He would be rid of that troublesome man, but then he would be faced with two bodies to hide and more tales than he felt he could spin to cover his tracks.

The second man slowly held up a hand to the doctor, signaling him to keep his distance. He wore a military uniform, but not like the guards that Oryan was used to. This man was clothed in a very sharp black dress uniform. It looked as if he was here to visit a diplomat or some high-ranking official. His sandy brown hair was clean cut, and his green eyes stared at Oryan closely. He had recently shaved, but the shadow was returning quickly. This was a solid man, not fat, but not muscular, and all that bulk was on his right foot. His opponent was right handed. In his position, expecting an attack, a person would free up his more dominant arm, in case the worse was to happen. Oryan sized him up quickly.

"Why am I here?" Oryan asked.

"My name is—" he began.

"Not your name. *Why* am I here?"

"You're here because we wanted you to get better. And for that, we needed all the proper medical care," responded the doctor, who had taken some bold steps into the room. The second man still did not flinch.

"Where is here?"

"You are in a professional hospital, one far away from the Slave Quarter. You have never heard of this place before or the city it is in. It's best that you never know, and for those reasons, we will never tell you," said the doctor.

Oryan watched the eyes of the second man. He was obviously waiting for a violent reaction to the last statement.

"I want to see my father."

"That can be arranged," replied the officer.

"Now."

The doctor stopped his progression into the room. Something in the boy's tone made him freeze. This kid was a threat to him, and so far he had not given the answers this boy wanted to hear.

"My name is Halgren," said the man at his bedside.

Oryan's head did not move. He simply shifted his eyes to meet the new voice that was addressing him.

"I am the captain of the guard at your facility. Your father is fine. He sends his regards."

"Answers," said Oryan.

"You are understandably curious," said Halgren, finally standing to his full height. Oryan shifted back to the far side of the bed and sat on his haunches should he still need to defend himself. "Where to begin? I can see that you are a very to-the-point young man, and I respect that. I'll be blunt. I saw you fight. Where did you learn that?"

Silence.

"No matter. Do you know what a Centauri is?" Oryan did not answer. "I didn't think so. I did some checking on you while were asleep. It seems you are something of a legend. The people say that you are a tough kid and that you compete in lots of sporting events. They say you are the toughest kid in the entire quarter. Impressive."

"They say a lot of things."

"Agreed, but you have not denied them. Nor should you, or would you. Your talent is something to be proud of. You should never be ashamed of who you are." Halgren paced the floor, one hand behind his back, the other at his chin. He was searching for what to say next.

"For being blunt, you take far too long to get to the point," Oryan quipped. There was something about him that he could not place. The man was arrogant for all the wrong reasons. He fancied himself a soldier, but the absence of battle scars and the poor way he handled himself in front of a potential enemy proved he was no such thing. His words were silken and filled with lies and half-truths. This man was an opportunist. Opportunists were not known to be men of their words.

Halgren allowed a small smile.

He was quickly beginning to dislike the ungrateful brat. Though he never spoke them aloud, he cursed the boy a thousand times. "A Centauri is a sportsman. They compete in the ultimate sport, a sport that would be perfect for you. Better yet, that *you* would be perfect for! One that could bring you the fame and admiration of the entire civilized world! One that could make you a legend, with your name shouted from the stands! You would have your choice of the girls; in fact, they would flock to you. Ever been with a girl, son? Nothing quite like it. This sport would make you famous!"

"And you rich."

A wave of contempt passed over the captain's face. This boy was trying his patience.

"It could make you a free man. Your father too," he lied. "The world would be at your command. Whatever you ask for, you would have."

Oryan perked up at this last temptation. How much truth was in his lies? He did not know and could not be sure, but the look on the face of the doctor confirmed the last statement. Although riches, fame, and women did not sway his judgment, the idea of seeing his father a free man was worth putting some trust in this less-than-reputable character. His father sacrificed everything for him. Maybe he could give something back. Besides, he was always good at sports.

"I'm listening," he said.

Halgren and the doctor stopped sweating and smiled.

The exit from the hospital had been fast and secretive. They had laid him on a bed, covered him with a thick sheet, and sent him into a transport that was waiting outside the loading dock doors near his room. He did not see anything but white sheet for several hours. Eventually, the bland surroundings became tiresome. Curiosity finally took hold, and he sat up.

His transportation was not much to look at. The trip to the hospital had been in a very nice, smooth-moving craft. He had been surrounded by doctors, machines, and white light. This was the exact opposite. In here, it was dark and musty. The narrow hold had dark gray walls with no windows. Even though the vehicle did not touch the ground, each discrepancy in the air cushion beneath it caused a bump or a jolt in the trip.

Oryan felt alone, but not scared. He finally had a chance to wrap his mind around the events that had so quickly been thrust upon him. He was not to see his father until his "training" had finished, though he was not even sure what that meant or how long it would last. Halgren's answers had been short and cryptic. That conversation had turned unproductive as it was obvious that neither man wanted him in that hospital anymore. Oryan knew that the only way he would get any answers was to speed the process along.

He felt no deception from what facts he had received. He had to sift them out from the lies, but the doctor's face was as easy to read as a children's book, so he could tell when he was being fed a line. Halgren had been evasive about the subject of his father, and there was something else behind his voice. He was hiding something, but Oryan could not place the suspicion.

Whatever it was at this point did not matter. At this point, he was still a commodity. A valuable one, it appeared, but a commodity nonetheless. He was smart, and he was fast, but he could not outsmart or outrun a bullet. Escape would come to him one way or another. He knew now that it had to be more opportune, as any rash or ill-conceived attempt would cost his father's life as well as his own. He was patient, and his time would come.

Oryan felt the transport reduce its speed. There was a gentle rock as all motion stopped and there was a soft shift in elevation as the vehicle lowered itself to the ground in order to let passengers out. He heard footsteps outside the thin metal walls. There was a fumbling of keys and then the sound of a lock being opened. The keys dropped to the ground with a curse from Halgren, and then one of the doors opened wide. Light streamed into his hold, bright and momentarily blinding. It was early morning, and there was not a cloud in the sky.

Halgren moved out of the way of the door, signaling to Oryan that he was to get out. Oryan moved to the back of the hold and jumped out onto the ground. It was dusty and hard. His feet landed on small rocks, but he was accustomed to such things. Halgren shuffled him off to a small, run-down shack near the vehicle and shoved him inside.

"Here," he said, handing Oryan a small gray bundle tied shut with cheap twine. He unrolled the mess to find shoes and socks that had been rolled into a jumpsuit. "Put it on." The socks were a blessing, though the shoes were too small and the jumpsuit's legs only reached his shins. Still, it was better than the hospital gown and torn sheet.

Halgren led him down a flight of stairs and then a long corridor. The building had not looked nearly this big from the outside, so Oryan ascertained that they were now underground. It was very drab in this place as well. There were no windows, no pictures, or even paint. It was a solid concrete structure with poor lighting and the occasional wooden door. They bustled along for about two or three hundred yards before Halgren stopped outside one of the doors.

"Sit here," he said, pointing to the ground. "You may not see them, but there are guards all over, and they wouldn't give a second's hesitation to killing you on the spot. Don't run."

Halgren turned from him and opened the door. Oryan briefly caught a glimpse of a dungeon-like office. There was a small desk in the middle with a portly man sitting on the other side of it who barely noticed Halgren's entrance. The door shut quickly behind him, and Oryan slid down the wall until he was seated on the floor.

At first, the silence was deafening, but as his ears became accustomed to the lack of sound, he could hear the conversation taking place on the other side of the door. There was something about a huge event. Something about a man named Ratajek and his exploits as a Centauri. Then Oryan caught parts of the conversation regarding shame in conjunction with this man. More disturbing still was that he heard his name as being even better than whoever Ratajek was. What was he being forced into?

He had to know more of what was being said, so he crawled across the few feet that separated him from the room. He placed his ear close to the small gap between the hard pavement floor and the bottom of the door. The conversation, which before had been fragments, now took on a whole new life.

"You're last few rejects from the Slave Quarter have proved less than impressive. As I recall, the very last one didn't even survive the training! Now you want me to believe that you have brought me the next *Ratajek*? You've only seen this boy fight once. It could have been sheer luck."

"I'm telling you, this one's *for real.* You didn't see this fight. These other boys were twice his size. They were older, stronger, had weapons, and he still beat them. Two didn't even survive the assault, and I don't think he was *trying* to kill them!"

Oryan's heart sank. He felt his head spin, and his stomach flooded with nausea. They were dead. He had taken from them what he could not give back with a handshake or good sportsmanship. Their families would never see them again. Living in the Quarter, family was all anyone had. He felt the vomit begin to rise. His heart was beating so hard it shook his whole body. *What have I done?*

Then something else entirely took over. His conscience hardened. *They attacked me. From the looks of things, they meant to kill me, and would have if I had let them. I only defended myself. They should have known better. Now is not the time for remorse!*

His attention turned back to the Halgren's conversation. He forced the memory of their contorted faces and dead eyes in the back of his brain. He had to survive.

"Come on, didn't you get the security footage I sent you? It's all there!"

"Thirty seconds of recording. For the most part, all I could see was the crowd and the rain. That proves nothing." Oryan could tell that the man had seen more than he let on.

"The report from the guards and the doctors on call that night at the Quarter should have!"

"That is the only reason I agreed to see you. If he is the killer you say he is, he'll bring you a pretty penny in royalties. More than my competitors would offer. But I want proof more conclusive than your word and this recording. It's a risky business we run here. If the empire finds out we're pedaling their slaves ..."

"I am well aware of the consequences. There won't be any holes to compromise this one. I made sure."

Oryan understood. He was being sold to the highest bidder. He was still not sure for what, but this was getting deeper all the time. Strangely, Oryan felt more interested in what holes Halgren was filling than the fact that he was being bartered. Freedom, it seemed, came with a high cost.

"Bring him in."

Oryan scrambled away from the door and sat against the far wall as if he had been there the whole time. Halgren opened the door wide and motioned for him to come into the room. Once he was in, the door was shut behind him and both men stared at him curiously. The room was as featureless as he had originally thought. With the exception of a light on the ceiling and one on the desk, there were no definable marks to this place. It was probably meant to be that way, indistinguishable from a thousand other rooms.

The fat man sat back in his chair and eyed him in silence. Oryan stared back, making sure he knew that he was not what he seemed. He felt no fear in their presence. There was something else to this new stranger. He could not place the warning.

The man was dressed very similar to the way he was, a gray jumpsuit with no extra markings or intricate details. The man's face was bearded, but his head was balding. It was quite apparent that he did not bathe often and that he took very little hygienic care of himself, if any. When he spoke, the teeth he did have revealed a similar disgusting truth.

"Strip," was all he said.

Oryan looked at Halgren suspiciously. He made no motion to interject. Halgren was a member of the dregs of society, but pedophile he was not.

Oryan removed the jumpsuit and stood naked in front of the

other two men. The fat man sat up and clumsily got out of his seat. This required great effort as gravity had far more control of him than he did of it. He walked around the desk and to the front of Oryan. He cocked his head and studied the boy's features from head to toe. Oryan was now painfully aware of the wound he bore from the attack. After a second, he began to circle behind him, keeping the same studying look on his face as he did. When he came around to the other side of Oryan, he asked a question. "You are sure that the Quarter didn't mark him for ID?"

"Do you see an ID tag? He was born a slave. They only ID those *made* slaves."

"And Records can't trace him?"

"Like he never existed until you say so."

"Put your clothes back on, boy," he said as he headed back for his desk. When he got there, he slumped heavily into his seat. It groaned heavily under its new, but familiar, burden. "I'll give you ten now and seven percent royalties."

Halgren's look was an incredulous one. "Fifteen now, *ten* percent royalties, and I get a voice in all career moves and sales."

There was a pause as the fat man stewed over the counteroffer. "Acceptable if we have the understanding that if he is not all you say he is, I seize whatever assets you have in order to recover your debt to me. Consider this a good faith loan until we can prove otherwise."

"Done," Halgren said and turned to leave the room.

"Oh, and one more thing," said the man as Halgren opened the door. "You better hope that he makes due on your loan. The first asset I will be after will be your lying tongue."

"Would I be any good at what I do if you had to remind me of that?"

With that, Halgren shut the door behind him and left. Oryan was once again alone with a man he had never met. He would just as soon remove what teeth the man had left as look at him.

"Come, boy. Training starts right now," he said with a sloppy smile. "You're gonna *love* this."

It can only be an improvement. I hope.

THE PERFECT SPORT

Modern combat required a soldier to know a wide variety of weapons and battle tactics. In an age of technology, where the latest war machines were ruling the battlefield, a simple scientific discovery made classic warfare cutting edge.

All armies still taught their troops to use such things as swords in order to make their hand-to-hand combat, when needed, more effective. Some soldiers were proficient with their use of such weapons, but they only used those skills in simulation and not actual combat. However, a group of combat engineers made a fantastic discovery while trying to invent a more cost-effective material to build their tanks and fighters that made the up-close-and-personal the only real way to fight a battle.

The empire of Navarus had made their weapons more effective by simple science. As their rounds left the barrel of the guns, they passed through an electrical charge which super-heated them without slowing down, changing direction, or damaging the weapon. The result was an extremely hot surface, which melted armor with no trouble, leaving the bullet unscathed to reap its desired effect. The only limitation to the round was that the coating eventually burned off, so at long distances, it was no better than a normal bullet.

The technology required a massive change to the empire's weapons, including a rechargeable and exchangeable battery to keep the electricity flowing, as well as advanced cooling techniques to keep the firearm itself from overheating. Despite the cost, the other armies of the world quickly stole the technology and made the appropriate changes.

Military scientists quickly began work on defense against the new bullets. It seemed that simply making thicker armor was no use. The amounts needed to make the round ineffective were both costly and cumbersome to both soldier and vehicle. After some time, researchers in Vollmar discovered an alloy that was lightweight and durable but came with a very handsome price tag. The discovery was at first passed off due to the expense, but the military suddenly discovered that it was well worth the cost. It did not simply absorb, but all together deflected, electrical current. When a hot bullet struck the metal, it neutralized the electrical current, making the round no more potent than a regular one. There was no charge known to the civilized world that could do more than scorch its surface. Even at that, after a little polish, the scar was hardly noticeable. They named it Tamrus, in honor of their king. It was not meant to deflect bullets, but the scientists were able to coat the existing bullet-resistant armor with a layer of Tamrus, and the desired effect was achieved. The Tamrus displaced the current-induced heat, and the armor slowed the bullet. Though not impregnable, the technology had an 83 percent combat effectiveness.

The legislature of Vollmar decided that the metal was too expensive to produce on all its combat machines. To retrofit all older models with the alloy on the scale needed would quickly exhaust the entire military budget. However, all new vehicles were to be built with the material.

Vehicles were not all that stood to benefit from the discovery. New body armor was developed using the Tamrus design. Over the course of the next two years, Vollmar dominated the battlefield and drove enemy forces far from its borders. They were able to take back many lost lands, as well as reinforce the battlements that were already theirs. The strategy developed around these seemingly indestructible soldiers was one that, at first, could not be countered. It also gave the troops a more medieval look that intimidated their foes. Once they appeared on the scene, swordplay and hand-to-hand combat were far more effective weapons than anything conceived on a factory floor.

The alloy itself was difficult to produce. Its exact contents and the formula needed to make the metal were kept top secret, known only to the scientists who invented it. Separate manufacturing facilities were made, each one responsible for a separate portion of the alloy's composition. The workers were not made aware of any of the details, and they were also not made aware of the locations of either of the other facilities.

Unfortunately, everyone has a price. One of the creators had been born within the boundaries of Navarus. His parents were sympathizers with the empire as their hometown was demolished by a bombing run gone wrong, orchestrated by an ally of Vollmar. Their complaints about their new government and the injustice that had been brought upon them eventually struck a chord with their son. When he was approached by agents of the empire with the promise of a new order and a very handsome paycheck, it was not a far stretch for him to sell all he knew.

When the use of classic weapons and combat skills became more prevalent on the front, a sport on the brink of extinction found a new appeal with soldiers and citizens alike. The sport was very much underground at first, allowed legally in only a few of the more uncivilized cultures, but as its popularity grew, it quickly became a spectator favorite and it was broadcast across the globe. It became universally accepted when the king of Vollmar endorsed and sanctioned it within his borders.

This sport held such mass appeal largely because of its brutality and its amazing displays of skill. Combatants were put into various terrains and then proceeded to initiate simulated combat before the eyes of the crowd. Sometimes the environments were real; sometimes they were fabricated. They fought with modified weapons and with individual combat vehicles in the air, on the ground, or on the water. It took place on open fields, on private stages, or on the grandest scale in huge forums erected to glorify these warriors.

The athletes wore special gear and uniforms lined with light sensors and pads to cushion direct blows. The suits were designed to paralyze the individual who had been struck. They became more advanced as the interest grew, and it soon became the standard that the suits had vital and non-vital sensors that monitored hits. If it was a shot to the leg, the contestant would lose the use of that limb for the rest of the session; a shot to the head meant complete paralysis.

The favorite of the masses was consistently individual combat. Two Centauri from diverse locations would meet to fight each other. Soon, children were pretending with their friends that they were the champions they had only heard about from the event. It was the most common conversation among sports enthusiasts as well as at shops, factories, and service stations across the planet. Women would lay claim to their favorite fighter for their fantasies. The heroes and villains of the sport were the most admired, or hated, of all celebrities. The better contestants were made wealthy, though no one was paid when they started. This was a volunteer event, most of the time.

This was the lifestyle that Oryan was introduced to. Halgren wanted to keep traceability low. He had been forced to shorten his last name from the customary *Armayson* to simply *Mason.* He was also informed that any mention of his past, any attempt to correspond with his father, or any attempt to escape meant the movement of his father from a forced labor camp to something far worse.

He had been sold to the fat man, who had taken him to the training facility located just a short distance from the underground complex where they had met. This training site was home to many volunteers but had a separate barracks attached for the runaways and orphans who had nowhere else to go.

It was as a runaway that Oryan was introduced to the instructors. They met him just outside the training grounds. The grounds themselves were surrounded by large, smooth metal walls, which was a harsh contrast next to the desert climate that stretched around it as far as the eye could see. There was a large chain-linked gate that appeared to be locked most of the time. A square, white sign with black lettering was attached to one of the gates. "No Entry except by Invitation" was all it said.

The two men were tall and lean. The swagger in their walks and the alertness to every detail around them showed Oryan that they were either retired soldiers or they had devoted themselves to the life of a Centauri. The sport, and his role in it, had been explained to him by his escort on his way to the grounds.

"What rodent did you bring us this time, Taj?" one of the instructors asked.

"A promising one. We caught him running from the authorities and putting a few of his friends from home in body bags. He's a winner."

"Are we gonna have a problem with this one?"

"Only if you try to fight him," Taj said with an antagonizing tone and a sadistic, toothless smile. "In your condition, I think he would make *you* the student."

An air of arrogance passed over the instructor's face. His stone features flashed with hatred for the disgusting creature insulting him. His expression said it all: *I could kill you where you stand.*

All the banter was over. It appeared to have its purpose, as Oryan found out later that not everyone was admitted to this school. The instructors stepped away from each other like sentinels granting passage to the halls they guarded.

"A pleasure doing business with you," said Taj. "You will find the contract details and the funding options on the Net. I'll be around."

"As little as possible," retorted the teacher, who had before been silent. Oryan seconded the sentiment.

Oryan watched Taj climb into his vehicle. The machine sank at least six inches lower to the ground as he entered it. Oryan smiled; his first smile for some time. That piece of transportation was comically too small for its passenger. Or, perhaps, Taj's girth made it appear so. Either way, he was happy to see it, and him, pull away.

He turned and looked at the two he had been left with. The one on the right was smaller and favored his right leg. Oryan was measuring the threat these two presented to him. He realized at that moment how often he had been put in that situation lately. He began to wonder if the rest of his life was going to be spent discovering the fastest way to disable or kill others. What a horrific existence.

The larger of the two produced a small access card from his pocket. He held it up to the gate, the sensor on the lock blinked green, and the doors slid silently open. The man turned to him.

"Better get inside. Locals don't know this place exists. Were you to try and leave now, we would kill you before the thought was finished running through your head," he said. Oryan shrugged off the not-so-warm welcome and went toward the uninviting gates.

Somehow, these few steps were very easy for him to take. When Taj had explained to him what his next few years of life would entail, it was like a piece of clothing hand-tailored to fit him. This idea was not at all foreign. His whole life had been directed toward fighting and combat. Why not put that to some more practical use? Now he was actually here and confronted with the reality of his circumstances. These gates and these guards simply welcomed him home.

As he passed the two men he had been left with, he observed their dress and features more closely. They wore sandy orange-colored uniforms. Their shirts were short-sleeved, neatly pressed, and made of a lighter material designed for movement and comfort. There was a small insignia above the right breast. It was too small to make out the details yet, but it was the same on both men. They had a black belt that featured a makeshift first aid kit on the left side and a pistol in a holster on the right. The pants were the same color as the shirts and had no defining markings. Their boots were black, shin high, and polished to a shine. There was discipline here, and Oryan was looking forward to it. As a slave, he had not had the opportunity to take pride in much. Even shined shoes were a welcome idea to him.

Once he was inside, the instructors followed, and as they did, the gates slid shut. The click of the lock was a reminder to him that he was now a permanent resident, though it did not change his elation at what he saw. He was used to locks, gates, and walls. To him, the scene before him was *freedom*.

The grounds were covered in combat exercise courses. There was boxing, wrestling, marksmanship, and weapons training all around him. The smell of sweat and blood was in the air. He soaked up every sound, smell, and taste. This place was *his* arena. He would dominate this place as he had the small tournaments in the Quarter. His senses were as heightened as they had ever been, and his eyes darted from student to student, analyzing them in an instant. There were challenges here. None that frightened him, but the kind that made his mouth water for the opportunity.

"When do I start?" he thought out loud.

"Eager, are we?" asked the taller instructor. "Don't you want to settle in first?"

"I'm settled. When do I start?"

The instructor looked at him curiously. Was this arrogance? Was the boy simply full of himself, or was that remark from Taj more than an idle one? Taj was always throwing insults around, but he had never sounded so confident in one of his finds. The instructor decided he would have to review all of Taj's notes on this one again. And he had never actually watched that recording of this boy he had been sent.

Most kids, even the older ones, who wound up here were not near as calm as this one. Some were terrified, some were thugs wanting to run away, some looking for something different, but most had delusions of either fame or toughness. Few actually were tough, and most did not make it through his course. This scrapper seemed different. He seemed dangerous, yet subdued. He was something special. The instructor could not place it yet. He had seen hundreds of youth pass his halls, but not like this. His instincts had been correct 100 percent of the time before. It was time to test those instincts again.

"So, you think you're ready now?" he asked Oryan.

The child's reply was positive, but his attention was not focused on the question. It was on the other students. This was promising. He scanned the boys who were training, looking for the right test. This one needed a challenge with some skill, but he was not sure how much he could handle yet. He didn't want the best, but this had to present a threat. After a few moments of silence, he made his choice.

"Rolen!" he shouted. All action stopped. The students stood as still as trees with their ears waiting for the next command. All but one. A student came running through the maze of the other boys and headed up to stand next to the instructor. He was lean and strong. The sweat on his face was lined with dirt. His eyes were keen and dark. He had paid no notice of Oryan when he had been called.

The entire fight was already mapped out in Oryan's head. This boy was his size, which was probably why he was chosen. The instructors probably thought this would be an even match. This person was more a threat to him than anyone had posed before, but he did not feel in danger. He was not scared or intimidated. Just ready.

"You start now," said the teacher. "Rolen, this boy here noticed you fight. He said you were clumsy and slow on your feet. Said you were weak. How long have you been here?"

"Four years, sir," Rolen said, gritting his teeth. "Fifty three fights, forty one wins. Twenty one combat sims and sixteen victories."

"This *boy* just stepped foot in here. Never had a day's training in his life. Thinks you're nothing. Is that true?"

"No, sir," he said, glaring at Oryan.

The teacher knew how to get under this student's skin. This one was afraid he really was nothing, and that made him hold back. Probably why he had lost so much.

"Prove it. Take him to the ring."

Rolen turned on his heels and walked toward the center of the yard. Oryan could see where he was headed. There were ropes sectioning off a circular area in the center about fifteen feet wide. The floor of sand was carefully raked. This was saved for special occasions, scheduled fights, and the occasional challenge battle. The students had to earn their right to compete in the amateur tournaments. From there, they could only hope to be noticed by the professionals.

Oryan analyzed the situation. Already, the others were gathering around the ring. There was no noise, no commotion, just a silent gathering of onlookers, vying for their look at the action. The larger, more experienced ones were front row. This was natural selection. Here, you either rose to the top or you fell to the back of the crowd. He smiled again. They did not know what they were in for. This was a show they would never see coming. Oryan reveled in it.

Rolen ducked under the ropes and stepped into the ring. Once he was in, he turned to face the other students. He filled his lungs with air, pushed his shoulders back, chest out, chin high and then he shouted, "Blood and tears!"

"Pride and strength!" shouted the others in unison. Their combined voices shook the air. It was menacing and full of false courage. They were all fighters, but Oryan wondered how many were warriors.

He stepped into the ring opposite Rolen. He calmed his mind

and let his senses take over. His gaze was slowly drawn upwards. It was still midafternoon, and the sun was high and bright, but in his eyes he could see stars. They were brilliant and inviting. He was about to join them. He was now harshly aware of the smell of sweat and sand. He could feel each grain as it brushed by his legs, carried in the wind. Above the chanting, jeering, and shouting of the other students, his ears were uniquely aware of the task at hand. He heard Rolen's heart pounding in his chest. He heard Rolen's feet displace the sand beneath them as he shifted his weight from side to side. His vision was suddenly not his own. It was as though he was observing everything from a third-person point of view.

Oryan began to sidestep around the ring, keeping himself on the opposite side as Rolen. He was waiting to see what Rolen's first strike would be. Rolen had training, but not like Oryan. Rolen had been taught to take one attack at a time, whereas Oryan was trained to combine all of his attacks and counters throughout the fight as one fluid movement. His mind was a machine calculating every possible combination of events that could happen. For every move Rolen made, Oryan had a predetermined response that he could execute instantaneously. He was always four moves ahead. Four moves were more than this would take. He had learned from his previous encounter. Put the enemy down fast.

Oryan heard the sand under Rolen's left leg suddenly grind more than before. He was planting his weight for a strike. *Here it comes.* Rolen sprang across the sand and covered the distance of the ring precisely when Oryan thought he would. When Rolen was about four feet from him, he planted his right foot and leaped into the air. His knee rose as if to deliver a kick, but his upper body twisted around and down to deliver a punch instead. Had Oryan been anyone else, he would have prepared for the kick and received a fist to the side of his jaw as a result.

Oryan was not anyone else.

It appeared to him that Rolen was moving in slow motion, and his feint was painfully obvious. Oryan put a knee to the sand and watched his attacker's blow fall well high of its mark. He reached a hand into the air and drew out Rolen's foot. With a jerk and a twist, Rolen crashed down on his side. The sand parted as if he had broken the surface of water. He had only enough time to notice the air leave his lungs when Oryan delivered a vicious elbow to his inner thigh. The pain was excruciating. It shot from his knee to his spine. The blow was followed by an elbow smashing into his chin. Rolen's world went black. In the future, all he would remember about the whole affair was what others told him.

Oryan rose from the sand. He was victorious once again. There was silence. His still-honed ears could hear every thud of every heart that beat around him. This was the same silence he had felt in the Quarter; except this time, the silence *was* what he wanted. He did not look for applause. This reaction was the perfect understanding from every student around him that he was the best. That his supremacy was not to be questioned or second-guessed. As far as they were concerned, he was in command. He met each of their eyes slowly in turn to further instill this truth.

In less than an hour, he was ruler of his new world.

Over the next year of training, he sharpened his skills. Though his dominance at hand-to-hand was never questioned, he had never touched a rifle in his life. The instructors taught him marksmanship, and soon, like all other forms of combat, he was second to none. He also perfected his endurance both physically and mentally. However, practice was always a must, and he would simply use the other students to build his stamina. He would run long distances and put his body through every grueling torture the instructors or he could invent with a sense of joy.

He soon took on the role of instructor and trained the others how to fight, move, and think as he did. Some caught on quickly and became close friends, though no one was as truly gifted as he. He was universally liked and respected by all.

The instructors soon gave up trying to teach him, letting him do his own training and letting those who could keep up follow. Their school became renowned worldwide in the Centauri community. It was finally given the official (and legal) title of Academy, and its existence was no longer a secret. With the help of both the minor and professional circuit funding allocations, it grew in physical size as well. Many of the older boys had gone on to the professional circuit, and those who made it to the amateur bouts were the headliners of their competitions.

As for Oryan himself, he began performing in the minors after four months in the Academy. He was their headliner. The Academy was known as *his* Academy. He recorded one hundred amateur one-on-one bouts with one hundred wins by knockout. In the combat sims, he was equally unbeaten. In his fifty simulations, he had commanded anywhere from one to as many as fifty other Centauri at one time. Whatever force he commanded always found victory. An even more impressive statistic was that in a time when 50 fifty percent losses at the end of a simulation were impressive for a commander, he was registering only ten to fifteen. When other commanders would imitate his formations, he would counter with new strategies. There seemed no bounds to his ability to create a seemingly endless supply of brilliant tactics.

He won all ten of the major tournaments he entered. In the final tournament of his amateur career, he only had to fight one match, as all of his opponents had withdrawn rather than fight him. He held every honor that could be awarded, including the title of Beta Centauri. This was awarded to any Centauri who won three consecutive worldwide tournaments. Before his induction into the professional circuit, he was given the highest honor that could be awarded to any competitor in the minors. It was called The Undefeated, and it had only been awarded to one other Centauri: the legendary Ratajek.

BOUNTY

His debut into the professionals was equally grand. It was held within the borders of the empire, and it should not have had the kind of turnout that it did. It was a small competition that featured no Centauri of notoriety. This was simply something to keep the interest up and to draw some extra money for the larger events. However, with Oryan as the headliner, the event was sold out. This was not uncommon when a Beta Centauri was featured, but for a newcomer to draw this kind of crowd was unheard of. It drew thousands who wanted a peek at this new and rising star. There were nobles, elected officials, and many big-time promoters of the sport who attended, but they were not the surprise spectator in the crowd.

The person that drew the most gossip and the most notoriety was none other than Lucius Kovac, the emperor's top military leader. To everyone's recollection, this was the first event he had voluntarily attended. He had paid top dollar for the suite he was in and even more to remain in solitude. Money was no object to him. He had more than enough for a small country, but even if he had none, it made no difference. From his point of view, if Oryan was as good as they said he was, he could spare the expense.

The stadium was of average size. It seated fifty thousand, and, for all intents and purposes, was not extraordinary in any way. Typically, inexpensive objects were strategically placed on the arena floor to be used as cover from oncoming fire as well as advancement markers. For Oryan's debut, a makeshift city had been built. It was designed to look like a small section of a city block. There were structures that stood some twenty feet high. Once erected, it would make for a unique venue for an indoor battle. To add to the effect, all the lights in the stadium were to be kept 40 percent lower than normal. This would give the combatants an opportunity to move without being spotted so easily.

Oryan's first sight of this place was disappointing. He had expected the arenas of the professional circuit to be much grander and larger than the amateur ones. This place was nothing new to him in both size or external design. The shuttle dropped him off alone in the back near the entrance, which was guarded by several large security guards. Once inside, he was directed where to go, and then he sat in silence for some time. He was starting to feel like a large fish in a small pond.

Hours later, Oryan waited in the entrance to the arena. He and four other men, who he had never met before, had been hurried into the lower dressing rooms and suited up. The introductions to the men he would be fighting with were brief. There was Tecton, Eash, Cargon, and Hargis. They had never fought with each other; they had only heard of him, and now they were expected to fight together. This was a disaster waiting to happen. They had spoken little to each other, but he had learned much of their strengths and weaknesses by the few words that had been said. It seemed that at least three of them were very happy to have him on their side, while the fourth felt he was merely a flash-in-the-pan who had made a reputation fighting the easier fights in the amateur circuit.

He and the others were dressed in thick, black jump suits that had yellow stripes running on one side from the top of his boots to the neck. The material was made to be flexible, mobile, and quiet. They all had belts around their waists that attached to a strap that extended from their left hip over their right shoulder and latched again to the back of the belt. They each carried a compact rifle that was light and accurate. The rifles fired pulses of light that could only be registered by the suits the Centauri wore. They recorded stats from the battle and the user had the option of making each trigger-pull audible (to imitate the sound or real weapons) or silent. Their helmets were plain with a glass shield in front that revealed the whole face and were equipped with communication devices.

On the viewing screens that Oryan caught glimpses of, he had seen the lines of people who were crowding the gates to see him. He could feel the electricity in the air. This was more the feeling he had expected when he arrived. As the hours dragged on and the preliminary bouts were fought, he soaked in the details. The crowd seemed more real and the sounds more pure to him. This was his world, and he had known that since that first day on the steps of an under-funded school.

There were three professional circuit events before his simulation. Two had passed, and the third was just beginning. It was an individual bout, and the names of the competitors were being announced. Oryan knew both of the fighters by reputation, so he knew that one had a clear advantage and, short of a miracle, this would not be a long match.

After the voice of the announcer finished his dramatic introductions, the roar of the crowd boomed. The sounds of combat rang through the air. Oryan breathed in the aroma. He drowned out the madness of the crowd, the vendors peddling their merchandise, and the sporting commentators discussing the events as they unfolded. There was only silence for him. He took a few more deep breaths and then began to listen.

First, the footsteps of the competitors on the floor became apparent. Like a highly choreographed dance, their feet drummed the floor. Then he could hear their weapons clash, then their voices. Like a masterful composer, the sounds continued to reveal themselves to him one layer at a time. Next came the announcers, then the vendors, even down to the ragged breathing of the four men at his back, each sound in its place, line upon line. Then he added the last touch: he singled out individual voices in the crowd one by one until they were no longer discernable independently. Each sound was like the roll of drums that led to the dramatic finale of his epic symphony. He opened his eyes and let every sound assault his senses at once. He could hear each sound by itself and all of them at once. It resonated through his body. It was as if the stars in the heavens were calling for him. *It was perfect.*

In the arena, the previous match ended. He took no notice and continued to relax his body and mind. Even when the stagehands bustled about constructing the false city in which he was to perform, he made no sign of awareness. The noise of the people had died to a dull hum of a thousand different conversations going on at once. The other four men with him were each preparing in their own ways. One stood like him, in silence, while the others were breathing rapidly, already sweating, and putting on a facade of toughness. How long this went on, he did not know, nor did he care.

The arena crew had made short work of their assignment, and Oryan could see the dark silhouettes of miniature wooden skyscrapers against the black stadium. "And now, draw your attention to the arena floor for the main event!" shouted the omnipresent voice. The crowd responded with roars of ecstasy. This was what they had come for.

He was standing shoulder to shoulder with the others. They were all seasoned and talented, but none were commanders. He knew this and took advantage.

"I'm new to this circuit, but this is not my first simulation. (*The fighting squad from Tal Erod led by Barrett Erker!*) You all know me and you know what I'm capable of. Keep your comms on and listen to my command. Whispers only. (*And representing our great empire…*) If you do what I tell you, when I tell you, we'll give them something they have never seen before. This is ours to win."

"*Led by the newest member of the professional circuit, our pride and strength, our next champion,* Oryan Mason!"

The thick, concrete floors could not contain this response. It shook the foundation. Oryan felt it in his bones, and it only fed the fire. Before the lights came back on, Oryan and his team had dispersed themselves into the arena. The lights, though dim, were lit, and the battle had begun.

The combat space was large, measuring thirty feet wide, seventy-five long, and fifty tall. There were five members of each squad. The objective was simple: disable all members of the other squad. The five men that they fought against were running from their tunnel, using the standard tactics for such a battle and taking up their positions. It was their intention to find as good a hiding place as they could and simply outwait their opponent.

Ten eyes scanned the floor, looking for any sign of movement. They were all proficient marksmen, and they felt confident that even this new so-called champion that the empire produced would have to stick his head out sometime.

The crowd had died to a dull roar. There were occasional shouts of enjoyment, but mostly, they were all scanning through the dim lights for Oryan and his men. Within five minutes, no sound was heard by anyone in attendance. Sports commentators calling the event were at a loss. Staff members checked the tunnel, the halls, and the training rooms wondering if, perhaps, the five men had missed their queue.

Ten minutes passed with still no sign of the Centauri from the empire. Each suit was electronically monitored, and as soon as each member of one team was disabled, it triggered the larger lights to come on and the horn to sound. Who could wait that long? The sponsors of the event talked in high box seats about whether or not to turn on the floodlights and cancel the competition.

The opposing team began to trade whispers between each other of their missing competitors. They signaled to the officials watching the match as to what they should do, but the men who usually had the answers had none.

The fans became restless. Some were filled with concern for the whereabouts of their heroes; others began to shout their disapproval as loudly as they could. Gradually, the aisles began to fill with fans disgusted with the lack of entertainment they had paid so dearly for.

Fifteen long minutes passed before nearly all of the officials were in agreement that there had been a terrible mistake and that this contest should end before a victor could be declared. As they decided their course of action, a strange thing happened. Throughout the arena, the victory horn blasted its single monotone note. Thousands of fans jumped, startled at the unexpected noise. Those still tracing their way to the exits paused and turned to face the arena. The lights slowly came back on, and as their eyes adjusted, they finally made some sense of it all.

Standing at the opposite side of their starting tunnel stood Tecton, Eash, Cargon, and Hargis. They had all removed their helmets and were all laughing amongst themselves. Officials, news reporters, spectators, and commentators looked at the four men in disbelief. How did they get there? Why had the horn sounded? Most importantly, where was Oryan?

The officials tried to contact the team from Navarus, but the men seemed to be using a channel that the officials could not find. There were no cheers, but a murmur began to sweep the crowd like a tidal wave. Their appearance caused a ripple effect across the body of fans.

As the results of the match were collected from the various weapons and equipment carried by Oryan and his men, they were posted on the electronic score board hanging from the center of the arena. It had many categories of statistics including kills, assists (which were shots that disabled but did not paralyze an opponent), shots fired, hits, and several more. The two columns boasted the numbers of the two competing squads. The column from Tal Erod was filled with zeroes. Even more startling was the results from the squad of Navarus. Five shots fired, five hits, zero assists, and five kills.

From the artificial battleground stepped Oryan, no helmet, weapon slung over his shoulder. There was still an anxious silence to the arena. It was as if all the people in attendance were holding their breath. Somewhere in the masses, a single voice shouted a single note that sparked the madness. Although they had seen none of the action, they were very aware of the result. Their men had won in decisive fashion. Never in the history of the sport had a team registered 100 percent hits to kills or shots fired to hits. Oryan and the four with him broke ground on a style of combat designed more for Special Operations Units, now brought to the thrill of the arena, and the crowd thundered their approval.

Oryan soaked it all in. The huge crowd had become a field of his stars, each one chanting his name. He was their hero, even though he had not given them the show they had expected. It was time to give them something in return. He raised his rifle in the air, saluting his fans. The noise grew deafening. His face was still emotionless, save a slight edge of gratitude for his audience. He turned slowly as if to make eye contact with each person. Once he had paid his homage, he and his triumphant teammates retreated to the tunnel they had issued from less than twenty minutes before. They waved their good-byes to the masses. Once in the archway, his team slapped him on the back and offered congratulations, drinks, and the promise to fight beside him any time.

Oryan's name was being chanted in the arena. He let the chant grow louder, allowing the anticipation to build. When even he could bear the wait no more, he jogged back into the arena floor.

The volume once again rose to deafening levels. Oryan was turning, saluting, and giving them the show they deserved. Suddenly, he stopped. His mood changed entirely. His heart fluttered, and his fingers were like ice. Of the thousands of faces in attendance that night, one caught his eye, if only for a moment. *It was her.* For an instant, he saw a woman—*his* woman, the one from his dreams. She was there, and, more importantly, she was real. But it was only an instant. He no longer saluted the crowd. His eyes were darting this way and that, frantic to find the angel that he was no longer sure he had actually seen. To his dismay, he could not find her a second time. He remained on the floor until the applause had died and the crowd dispersed searching in vain for her.

General Lucius Kovac looked on stoically. He had not moved an inch from the onset of the event. He had observed the whole thing with indifference. Even now, with the madness around him and the crowd intoxicated by this performance, he made no sign of enthusiasm or emotion at all. He *was* impressed, but no one would ever know. The one he had come to see had not been a disappointment, and he would have gladly paid twice what he had to see it again. Still, this was just a sport. *He is a gifted killer. Can he be something more? Or would he be another prima donna in love with his own legend? Time will tell.* One thing was certain: he would be keeping an eye on this one.

For the sport, the world was divided up into smaller and smaller subdivisions. The smallest was an area, usually the size of a small city, and its champions were called Area Centauri. Then there were districts, which were made up of multiple areas and best Area Centauri in the district was the District Centauri. Several districts made up a region. The best in the region became the Regional Centauri. Once you reached this status, you were allowed to compete in the global competitions so you could strive for the status of being a Beta Centauri. Some countries opted to host tournaments for all the Regional Centauri in their lands, and that person was known as the National Centauri. This was a prestigious title, but it was not recognized by the Board of Centauri, who oversaw the sport worldwide. Only one title was more profound than the Beta.

Every five years, the Tournament of the Alpha Centauri was held. Every kingdom from across the globe chose their finest Centauri to represent them at the tournament. In total, more than one hundred athletes came to compete in this ultimate championship. To win meant endless money, lifelong fame, and rights for the next five years to claim they were the world's best. It was the single biggest sporting event, bar none. The last tournament had been in a stadium that boasted seating for five hundred thousand, and it was filled to capacity.

One year before Oryan had found himself in Halgren's hands, the Tournament of the Alpha Centauri had been held. The next was still two years away. His first year in the professional circuit left him undefeated, and there was a growing unrest for the tournament to be accelerated so that he could compete while in his prime. The Centauri Board dismissed the idea utterly. That date would not be accelerated for any man.

It was after that motion the Centauri Subcommittee, which represented the interests of Navarus, was approached by two opportunists with a novel idea: since the board was uncooperative, bypass the board. These two knew the value of the empire's new superstar. They knew that to put him to the ultimate test would be the biggest moneymaking event in the history of the sport. They knew that it had limitless potential to finance the empire's massive military budget for the next ten years. More importantly, they knew it would make *them* rich in the process.

Since Taj still had the sponsorship rights for Oryan and Halgren was still making his under-the-table cut, they stood to gain as much as anyone. He had made them both incredibly wealthy, but it was not enough yet. They wanted one last big venture with Oryan to make more than they could spend in ten lifetimes and then sell him at the height of his success for enough money to last ten more. Once he won a big tournament, he would pick up a bigger imperial sponsor, and they would do better by selling at that point anyway. Why not go out big?

Their idea was simple: an imperial invitational. Each country represented on the committee was allowed to host as many invitational's as they liked as long as they did not call for a gathering of more than three Regional Centauri in any one competition. So, very simply, call for *none*. No Regional Centauri would be formally invited, but the empire would send a bounty worldwide.

"The empire of Navarus claims that they have an undefeatable Centauri," they propositioned. "Anyone who can defeat this champion in hand-to-hand combat will receive ten years' wage."

"Many tournaments offer such a prize," the Navarite committee countered.

"The empire still holds a majority vote on the board, does it not?"

"Yes."

"So we sweeten the deal. Anyone who beats Oryan wins the money *and* a guaranteed sponsorship from Navarus for the next Tournament of the Alpha Centauri. Nobody will be able to resist. They all know that they would get the bracket and the opponents of their choosing for the TOAC. Navarus always finishes in the top ten even when they don't deserve it. Everybody knows that. If Oryan wins, then the empire has just made a bundle of money and we sponsor the best Centauri in the world. *If* by some fluke he *loses*, well then the empire has still made a bundle of money and we get the best fighter in the world to represent us at the tournament. Either way, we are better off with this invitational in the books."

"And you think that the other Centauri would just leave their home countries and their allegiances at the door for the opportunity to fight for Navarus? Some of these men hate the empire and everything it stands for."

"Are you trying to muddy the water with *morality? Allegiance?* They would sell their mothers if it meant they fought for the empire at the tournament; patriotism isn't even a factor. Half of the Centauri weren't even born in the countries and kingdoms they fight in. They fight there because they got the best sponsorship from that place. Besides, if one of them takes the 'high road' claiming patriotism or moral standing or whatever, we shame them into coming. We make their own press and adoring fans boo them out of their own stadiums for missing the chance. This is a win-win scenario for all involved."

"The Board won't take kindly to the idea."

"Just because they didn't think of it first. Line a few pockets, and all is well."

"Are you suggesting we bribe them? We could lose our license to carry the sport in the empire."

"Won't happen. I'm just saying..." he started. "I'm just saying, be persuasive." Taj finished with a disgusting smile.

The committee retired to a separate room, and the idea was discussed in detail. This *was* a win-win situation for the empire. It would mean lots of planning and lots of publicity, but it would also bring in lots of tourists and Centauri enthusiasts. That meant money. Money meant power. And power is what drove everyone who held a seat of authority in the empire.

A bounty it would be. *The* bounty.

After long deliberation, they came back to Taj and Halgren with their decision. "We accept the proposal. We know you are an opportunist and a man who stands much to gain from this, Ratajek, but we also know what a loser you can be. We still remember your Tournament failure. See to it your boy does what you promise. If not, we will show you the scope of our... persuasiveness."

There was a shift of power in the conversation. Before, Halgren and Taj had dominated the control in the room. No longer. The committee members at this meeting had taken it all back.

"And what do you stand to gain by all this, Captain Halgren? You are an officer with an impeccable record and to consort with such rabble is beneath you. The empire does not take kindly to losers, and this one reeks of incompetence," one man said, his glare fixed on Taj, whose hatred could not be hidden at this conversation.

Halgren smiled. His answer was cold, calculated, and prepared. "The glory of the empire, sirs."

"Curious," was the only reply.

The preparations began shortly after the committee had agreed on their course of action. They sent personal invitations to every leader and sponsor across the globe before they even discussed the event with the board. This ruffled a few feathers but, in the end, the smell of money convinced them otherwise.

The empire could not solicit the idea directly to the Regional Centauri, but they knew that once the invitations were received, the news would spread like wildfire. They also used their connections with the gambling community to promote the idea. Once a date had been set, the bets rolled in and so did the money. The organizations handling the money counted record highs, but this was only the beginning.

The "Imperial Bounty," as it became known, was the biggest news story for months. Every form of media available buzzed with the predictions. Sports annalists furiously debated on which Centauri would go and what their odds were. Despite his popularity and dominance, Oryan was a heavy underdog.

Because of the mass hysteria surrounding the event, the empire spent very little time on its own promotions. The media gave them all the free advertisements they needed. They spent most of their time, energy, and money on the event itself. A vast arena was constructed just for this event. Tickets were sold out within minutes of their availability. Scalpers made fortunes selling tickets with the record for a ticket being well into the millions. That was paid by Lord General Lucius Kovac. That sum did not pay for the ticket, as he was guaranteed one of those; it did, however, buy him a private suite, with no others allowed. He would not miss this.

The empire was very reclusive about its preparations. An occasional conference with a committee member was held, at which he would slander those Centauri who were, as of yet, not on the scorecards. Enormous media pressure was placed on those men that everyone wanted to see at the tournament. Most buckled under the pressure; those who didn't were very quickly replaced by another who was willing. The number of competitors multiplied every day. That number grew so much that the invitational quickly became a multiple day tournament.

Months passed, and the simple idea of two swindlers had grown into the largest sporting event in history. It had become a fan and media circus. When the day finally arrived, more than three million people crowded the stadium, the courtyard, and any public facility with a monitor and the sports channel to watch the excitement. The empire had recouped the money it had spent for all its expenses not only for this tournament, but for all the others it had hosted that year before a single bout had been announced.

Through all the praise and demonization, through the hype and the disappointment, through all the love and the hate, Oryan remained calm. He had won two more tournaments in the time between the announcement of the bounty and the actual event. He had been superb at each, and to date, none of his opponents had landed a single blow. He had defeated a few Regional Centauri, but none of the more prestigious ones. However, this tournament boasted every name he had considered a challenge.

The Beta Centauri from Vollmar, rumored to be the best in the circuit, was placed on the opposite side of the bracket from him. They were popularly held in the number one and two seats. The bounty was expected to go to Agrion. This older, more mature opponent was to be the end to Oryan's perfect record.

The tournament had stretched into a four-day event, with the quarter and semifinals on the third day and the finals on the last. The first two were packed with bouts. Over three hundred matches took place, many going as planned with only a few exceptions. Agrion dominated his side of the brackets and Oryan his, winning all of their fights in decisive fashion. All the contestants gave each duel their all, which made for thrilling entertainment and extraordinary feats of skill. The crowd was getting everything they had paid to see and then some. Even Lord Kovac, though he watched with infinite complacency, soaked in the raw emotion in the arena.

Aside from Agrion and Oryan, no one had predicted the quarter finalists correctly. Those who had made it this far had put on their best for the chance at the bounty. All who watched the events unfold agreed that after this tournament, the Tournament of the Alpha Centauri would pale by comparison.

The quarterfinal round commenced to the largest audience ever assembled to view a sporting event. Media estimates were in the billions of spectators. No match was over quickly, and all who participated showed skill and valor never before seen and never to be duplicated. Agrion and Oryan moved closer to their much-anticipated bout by winning their individual matches. Oryan achieved his usual charismatic win. Agrion had his hands full with a very motivated opponent, but still won soundly.

The semifinals were equally entertaining, including a spectacular bout between Agrion and Tecton, who was with Oryan in his debut more than a year prior. Tecton managed to outscore Agrion through the first three rounds, showing a speed, adaptability, and a courage seen only in one other. He would have won the bout; however, that form of combat was exhausting and was nearly impossible to maintain. Eventually, fatigue proved as much of a threat as did Agrion. Tecton finally succumbed to the relentless attack of his opponent and was beaten by a decision of the judge's panel after ten grueling rounds.

Oryan had won his match minutes before this bout had taken place, and so he took the opportunity to observe these two. He had tutored Tecton whenever he had the chance, as Tecton showed more potential than anyone he had known before and was a willing student. Aside from him, if anyone had a chance against Agrion, it was Tecton.

Agrion had a very blunt and uninteresting style of fighting, which was a near perfect antithesis to the flashy fast fighting used by most fighters. Their style was more to put on a show and impress the crowd. It made for short, but fast-paced and entertaining bouts. Agrion was patient, and his style was meant more to wear down an opponent than to beat them. He used very little energy in his movements, simply deflecting and dodging attacks versus countering them or trying to altogether block direct advances. Frustration was his greatest ally. He would continue to use an opponent's momentum against them until they became so agitated at not landing seemingly perfect attacks they would become sloppy. Then, he made his move. Once an opening was presented, the match was over. Tecton was the first Centauri to finish the full ten rounds with Agrion in two years.

Oryan was fully prepared for Agrion. In Agrion's mind, his style was unbeatable. His arrogance in his countless victories had blinded him to the glaring weakness of it all. Pride was a weakness that could be exploited. *He'll never see me coming.*

After Tecton's match was over, Oryan retreated to the training room beneath the arena and waited for his arrival. He knew his friend well enough to know this was where he would come. Tecton was a champion, and champions train when others rest. He would be here soon.

Oryan could vaguely hear the remaining announcements from the arena floor and the crowd's response. He heard his name and Agrion's announced for the final match to be held the following evening. The crowd bellowed its approval. Shortly after that announcement, he could hear the countless footsteps shaking the pillars and foundations of the great structure as thousands exited the stands and headed to other destinations. Within a few minutes, he heard the sound he was waiting for: a lone pair of footsteps.

The training room was a small area that housed a number of exercise stations. In its center was a fifteen-foot-by-fifteen-foot mat for sparring and warming up before bouts. It was usually very brightly illuminated, but with the masses leaving and the maintenance crew starting their enormous job, only a few lights remained on. It was dimly lit, and the corners were hidden by deep black shadows. Oryan retreated to one of these corners and awaited the arrival of his friend. The footsteps became louder, and before long, a tall silhouette stood in the entrance.

Tecton slowly walked into the room and made his way to the near wall, just a few feet from Oryan, which held several storage racks filled with various training weapons. He pulled a wooden sword from the wall and retreated to the sparring mat. Once he reached its center, he stopped and lowered his head. He inhaled deeply through his nose and pushed the breath out through his mouth. This action was repeated several times. He was slowing his racing heart and putting that last loss behind him.

He spun on his heels, bringing the sword up over his head and bringing it down sharply in front of him. The blow should have landed on the same empty air that it had split, but instead it came down with a whistling crack on a staff that was held out in a defensive posture. He met the eyes of this uninvited stranger with many an unkind word on his tongue. When the realization of whom it was he was standing across from hit him, he stood up straight, with a genuine respect for his role as pupil to this master.

"You lost that match for all the wrong reasons," said Oryan softly.

Tecton stared at him. His build was average. Some Centauri were muscle-bound, some tall, some with tattoos from head to foot, and some had no defining qualities of any kind. Oryan was none of the above. He was strong and lean, but his strength was not in the size of his muscles. He was not tall, yet not short, and bore a long scar across his chest. A small chain of silver always hung from his neck. In the arena, he wore a loose robe or armor, depending on the situation, yet now he stood bare-chested as he always did for training. He had a tattoo that stretched from shoulder blade to shoulder blade, centering at his neck, bearing the emblem of the Undefeated from his time in the amateur circuit. More defining than that was his naturally snow-white hair. It was always neatly kept and hung to his shoulders. For the match a few hours earlier, it was braided ceremoniously and moved so as not to be in his face during the fight. The lack of color in his hair was offset by his crystal blue eyes.

He was handsome, and his features were gentle, but hard. He had the demeanor of a man who had infinite patience and could spend the rest of his life in peace. Yet Tecton knew he was the deadliest man alive and should the situation require, those soft features became horrifying in an instant. He had taught Tecton how to go from an average fighter to a magnificent one. Had it not been for his tutelage, Tecton would not have even been in this tournament.

"I was over-anxious at the beginning, and I wore myself down too quickly. I should have paced myself and not gone for the kill early on," Tecton admitted.

Oryan moved toward Tecton and began to slowly move the staff in mock attacks at Tecton. "You had him beat. He didn't know how to react to you. That shot you landed to the side of his head made him think twice. Could you feel his hesitation afterwards?"

"I sensed it," said Tecton as he parried a blow aside. "I should have capitalized."

"You should have, but then you would be fighting me tomorrow," grinned Oryan, "and we all know how that would've turned out. The audience wouldn't have had to show up."

Tecton advanced and made several fast blows at Oryan, which were easily deflected. "Yeah, I would've hated to be the one who ruined your perfect record. You would've ended up like Ratajek!"

Oryan stopped the sparring. In all his time as a Centauri, he had been constantly compared to Ratajek, yet he had only heard a few details. "What happened to him?"

"Your sponsor really does keep you in the dark. All this time, I thought you were just kidding. The Tournament of the Alpha Centauri happened to him. He had never been beaten, and he was a sure thing to win the whole prize. He got so caught up in the publicity and his own pride that he walked right into an opponent in the finals who had spent his entire career with one goal."

"To beat Ratajek," Oryan finished.

"Yep, and so he did. He took him down in the second round. Hit him so hard in the mouth that it knocked four teeth out despite the guard. That was about it for old Taj."

Taj! The name struck Oryan like lightning. It couldn't be the same person. The names had to be coincidence. "What does he do now?" he asked, bracing for the answer.

"He makes his money sponsoring Centauri. He's pretty shady. He never tells anyone who he actually sponsors, just fronts a lot of cash to other agencies and organizations so as to keep his involvement anonymous. Rumor has it he's a slave runner, which is why he wishes to remain anonymous. He would be in a world of trouble if that was ever proven."

Oryan's heart stopped. His face went deathly pale as his shoulders dropped. All the muscles in his body went numb. He was unaware of anything else around him at that moment. Even when he dropped his wooden staff to the floor with a loud clatter, he did not notice. This new bit of information sickened him. He had forgotten his past. *Who am I? Father!*

The name hit him like a blow to the stomach. He had fallen in love with the idea of himself. *The world will chant your name. Do not do the same.* His father had warned him. Guilt and anguish filled his soul. At first, he had been fighting for Armay. Then he was fighting for his survival. Now, he fought only for fame and gain. This was not who he was. This was Ratajek and Halgren. Not him. The thought of those two was repulsive to him. But he had become what he beheld. *What have I done? What of my father?* He had forgotten him. Armay was never far from his thoughts; though the sweet taste that his selfless example had been to Oryan had now turned bitter. Each time he would remember the words he had been taught, he would push them down into the deep recesses of his mind. It was what he knew he should be doing; yet, he was enjoying doing the opposite. Now all those memories flooded his mind and stung him to the core. *Where are you now, Father? I could use your strength.* He longed to see him.

"Oryan," said Tecton, who was standing above him. "You all right? You don't look so good, and you've been down there quiet as the grave for a few minutes now."

Oryan suddenly realized he was no longer standing. His head was spinning still, but he managed a dazed response. "Why are we doing this?" It was a whisper of a comment, barely audible, but asked in such a way that Tecton sat beside him and searched for an answer that would not come.

"All of us fight for something, but what? Is it the money or the fame? Is it the women? I don't know. I suppose that is what others fight for, but why do we do it, you and I? I know you well enough to know that none of those things are of any value to you either. Have we wasted all this time?"

"I fight," Tecton began, "to make a difference. I have a son. Didn't know that, did you?"

Oryan looked on his friend in a whole new light. A new respect grew, and he was suddenly envious of Tecton.

"I was always good at fighting. Only thing I really excelled at, ever. I was in the amateurs, full of pride and hope. She was young and beautiful. Anyway, he's five years old now. I've never seen him. She moves from place to place, so I only know what she tells me, and that is usually when she needs something. I want to be a part of him, though I'm never around.

"This is what I know." He looked around the room. "This is my universe. If by doing this it means that I make a difference to him, then I'll never stop. She may never tell him that I'm his dad, but I know it, and that's all that matters. I would give it all to see him in the stands."

Oryan felt tears welling in his eyes. At first, his pride forced them back, but he fought past the walls that pride had built and let a single tear trickle down his cheek. "You're here for something more than yourself. You may be the only one. Thank you." He stood up and walked toward the exit.

"Where are you going?" Tecton asked, rising to his feet with a sudden sense of urgency. A strange premonition swept over him directed at his friend. He knew Oryan better than anyone. He would not let his friend become the next Ratajek.

"Away. For a walk," replied Oryan sullenly.

Tecton nodded. "Be back tomorrow? If not, you mind if I come along for this walk?"

Oryan disappeared into the shadow of the doorway. Tecton could no longer see him, and he no longer heard footsteps. There was an anxious silence. Finally, a mournful voice spoke up. "Thanks, Tecton. You always were a friend. What's your boy's name?"

"Teeman," he responded.

"Good name. Stay here. Tomorrow is a long way away." With that, Oryan's footsteps trailed off until they were no longer audible.

"I'll be here," Tecton vowed to the darkness. "I only hope you are too."

An Interested Buyer

Tecton could not remember a longer night. He was true to his word and did not bother going back to his hotel. He hid when the closing crew came through the training room. Once all was clear, he tried to stretch out on the soft mat and sleep, but sleep would not come. Under normal circumstances, he would have been dreaming within minutes, but this night was anything but normal.

To his knowledge, he had never heard Oryan speak of any family. He had never mentioned a woman or parents. If Oryan had done the worst and he was not coming back, there would be no one significant to notify. He knew of no mother or wife to deliver flowers to. No father or brother to softly break this news to. There was no one. Tecton understood why the conversation about why they fight was a harsh one for his friend. His comments about his son must have been salt on an open wound. *I am sorry, my friend. I did not see.*

Minutes dragged on like hours. This night, it seemed, would never end. After an agonizing night of ragged sleep interrupted by vivid nightmares, Tecton was roused by the sound of scuffling feet accompanied by the lights flickering to life. He felt awful and must have appeared it as well. The man who came down the tunnel into the training room was more startled by his appearance than the fact that he was there in the first place.

"They lock you in?" asked the old man.

"What time is it?"

"Dawn," said the man matter-of-factly. He looked at Tecton from head to toe, filled with concern and suspicion. "You been here all night?"

Tecton ignored the query, focusing on his own thoughts. It was dawn. That meant that he had not seen Oryan in at least nine hours. A lot could have happened by then. Dark thoughts raced through his mind, followed by panic-induced solutions. He could tell the authorities or the committee, or the board. That would do no good. It would only create a massive search, which would only drive Oryan farther away. If he was to come back, it would be on his own. Tecton realized he had to wait it out and see what would happen. If the fight came and Oryan did not, the search would begin without his help anyway.

"My name is Tecton Colvitt. I am one of the Centauri competing in this tournament. I am here to meet Oryan for an early warm-up at his request. It will be a private sparring session. He will have no visitors or press. Go away." Tecton snorted, trying to act like the rest of the men with chips on their shoulders.

The old man was not moved by his name or the mention of Oryan's, yet the attitude seemed familiar to him. "Have it your way. You stay out of my way, and I'll extend the same courtesy, *Tecton Colvitt.*"

The old man's gait was labored. He was far too old to be handling the work he was assigned. Tecton felt wretched for sending the man away as he had, but it was the fastest method to send him on his way. He had to concentrate on his next step. He had to think like Oryan, or, rather, he had to think like Oryan were he not himself. This would not be easy.

Tecton debated a personal search, going to the board, or simply waiting here. Each had its pros, the first two being that it kept him busy and moving for a few hours. However, the more that he contemplated his next move, the more logical the last alternative sounded. It was the only way. As the mental debate lengthened, the decision to wait it out became more resolute. It would be a painful, emotionally draining wait, but maybe he could get a little sleep during that time. That would both mend a few frayed nerves as well as relax the muscles. He could use both. *Wait it is.*

Tecton found a dark corner, pulled the equipment in front of him to avoid being noticed, and closed his eyes. Sleep was almost immediate. His dreams were troubled, yet the rest was much needed. He could have stayed there for many more hours, but it was not to be.

After three or four hours, he was awakened by the sound of voices in the tunnel. At first, he thought the voices were only in his dreams, but when they roused him from sleep, he realized he was not alone. When he was fully conscious, he realized it was not multiple voices, rather just one conversing with a communicator. He could only hear one side of the conversation, but it was enough to fill in the blanks.

"All I know is that I was told that I was here to meet a very interested, very rich buyer," the voice said into his communicator. "Other than that, I was given no details."

There was a pause while the person on the other end of the comm spoke their piece. "Maybe this time, I won't cut you in! What do you say to that?" Another pause. "I always choose my bedfellows carefully; you should do the same!"

The voice cursed and spat; the conversation was over. Tecton had moved to put face to voice and was sadly disappointed. Before him was a fat slob of a man who did not appear to have bathed in days. He was mostly bald with an unkempt red beard growing on his face. The man was pacing the floor and continuing the conversation, only now he was speaking to himself. After all these years, the cocky stride had not changed. Tecton could spot it a mile away. He had heard the descriptions, and they were a spot-on match as well. It was Ratajek.

Slowly, Ratajek gathered himself. His red cheeks returned to pale, his shoulders dropped from around his ears, and he let out a sigh. Apparently the conversation had rattled him, but whomever he was waiting for was going to be here soon. Tecton decided to stay hidden and see where this led. *What does the biggest disappointment in this sport do with his time?*

Ratajek was going over the conversation that was yet to come in his head. He was making points and counterpoints, trying to make sure he had a seamless, prepared response for any query or remark. He did not like being caught off guard. The past few years of dealing with every kind of businessman from the very shrewd and dangerous to the slow and stupid had taught him much. When he received a call saying that there was someone interested in buying Oryan, he dismissed it. Very few people knew he held the sponsorship rights to the superstar. Halgren had tried to shake him up like that before, and he had no reason to believe this was anything more than one of his poorly executed, idle threats. Most who wanted him would go through his frontline sponsors, who would then contact him via a phony name on the Net that was bounced from server to server to discourage a trace. When the attempts to set a meeting persisted, he decided to do some tracing of his own. He had no success. It was impressive when someone could avoid his search. That meant they had some money to spend. Halgren was not wealthy enough to avoid being caught, nor was he that clever. This, coupled with the fact that they had directly contacted *him*, prompted him to set this meeting. He was hoping it was worth his time.

Halgren had been opposed, of course, *the simpleton*. He knew nothing of business. His only talent was to spot those with a knack for hurting others, probably because he was such a brutal, vicious animal himself. Ratajek did not like doing too much business with him. Halgren made even him uncomfortable. The things he *knew* Halgren had done were only rivaled by the rumors he had heard about the man. Fortunately for Ratajek, he had kept his contacts and operatives secret. Ratajek was Halgren's liaison to the black market.

For now, his conversation with Halgren was over and he must prepare for this buyer. He knew little about him except that he was obviously rich and well connected. This meant he was either black market, imperial, or, on some rare occasions, a little of each. Either way, Taj felt he was about to have his hands full.

He tilted his head back and breathed deeply through his nose. He could smell the sweat of the room. He could feel the energy that was here, though no training was happening. Even though he had not turned a second thought to Centauri games, save for profit, in years, his body still recalled the thrill. At times like these, he could feel the adrenaline return to his limbs. He suddenly felt lighter, able to move gracefully and deadly again. His mind and body were sharpening for an upcoming battle, even though the battle required no weapons or physical intervention. This was unequivocally more life-threatening than the arena had ever been.

Ratajek checked the time. There were minutes before this person was supposed to meet him. He would not let being stood up slide easily. If that was going to be his only outcome, no amount of trace blocking or redirecting would stop him from finding out whom this person was. Then he would let Halgren lose on them, and God help them.

At the exact second the meeting had been scheduled, a shrill, horrid voice filled with venom, and hate echoed from the tunnel. "Have you come alone?" it hissed. In the arched entrance stood the jagged image of a man. It seemed a shadow that had managed to relieve itself of its host. It was tall and menacing. Were it not for the flash of crimson from its armor and sword hilt, Ratajek would have convinced he was seeing an apparition. This could not be real, or at least, not *human.*

"It's good to see that my buyer is punctual," retorted Taj, trying not to show how startled he had been at the sound of the voice. He had heard and seen nothing approach, and, despite his putrid state, his senses were still very keen. He swallowed hard, choking on his own saliva.

"Though I am not your buyer, I represent him," said the voice again, cold and chilling. "And before he will show himself, you must answer my first question. I warn you, Ratajek, do not make me ask a third time."

Ratajek knew it was to be taken at its word. Hearing his own name from this thing chilled his blood. "I have come alone. Now let him come forward, and you step back! The arrangement was that we were *both* alone. If your master wishes to treat with me, let him speak, not one of his sniveling minions!" His dialogue was only a façade. This was a false face of bravery and courage. Ratajek tried to show his disdain at the present situation but also was attempting to mask a very strange feeling for him. *Fear.*

There was a hiss from the tunnel that could only be described as laughter. The shadow slunk away. In an instant, Ratajek was not even sure he had seen or heard a thing. Unease tightened his stomach. From the looks of things, he had most certainly *not* chosen a good bedfellow this time. Halgren may be right. But then again, he could possibly still talk his way out if this. A morbid curiosity drove him on when fear screamed at him to run. What manner of man would be heralded in such a way?

There was another wait. It was not a long period of time, but, given his present circumstances, Ratajek felt it an eternity. He noticed everything going on around him. His senses were peaked, waiting for that thing to come up from the ground or appear from air like some apparition ready to steal the breath from his lungs. He could hear the beating of a fly's wings from across the empty space of the room. His joints creaked deafeningly with each small shift of his bulk. Sweat had begun to drip down his brow; he was painfully aware of a single drop that was traveling down his forehead toward his eyebrow. More than all the rest, he could hear his heart pound in his chest. Each beat rocked his whole frame. To him, it resounded in his head like a war drum sounding before battle. Had he known what was to come, he would have obeyed his instincts, cut his losses, and run.

He tightened his fists and regained control of his senses. He would not be bullied like this! It did not matter who should come through that archway; he was *the* Ratajek. As his eyes and resolution refocused, he saw a shadow pass across the tunnel floor. It was huge, darkening the entire archway entrance. This was a daunting mass, but definitely a human one. That fact alone was a comfort to him. This man was tall and thick. His broad shoulders dwarfed even the large entrance he stood in. A black cloak draped from shoulder to toe. His face could not be seen yet. There was not much light in the entrance, and the hood that hung over his head cast deep shadows on any facial features. When this man came to a stop, his hands moved to his hips in a motion of prowess and power. He was in control of these proceedings from that moment on.

"You do not know me," said the intimidating presence. The voice was deep but smooth. It was commanding but not abrasive. It could be used for both great and dark purposes. One thing was evident from his tone: whatever his intentions, he would get what he wanted. "A clever man would have known my name by now."

"You have me at a disadvantage, Lord," graveled Ratajek. "It is easy for one to know whom he speaks to when he can see his face."

"Do you mock me?" Ratajek squirmed for an answer. This was a line of questions he had *never* prepared for. This new tone made the man seem even larger, or perhaps it made Ratajek shrink. Perhaps both. "Understand you are here by my leave. Each breath you take from this moment on is a gift that I have proffered you. Reflect on that, and choose your words more carefully in the future."

"I am truly sorry, Lord. It was not my intention to offend. I have a great respect for you, and I know you by reputation very well, *General.*"

As if in acknowledgement of the correct guess, Kovac stepped out of the shadows and stood tall in the light. His arms rose fluidly to his face and drew back the hood. As it fell to his shoulders, Ratajek gaped. He had seen pictures on the Net, and he held images in his mind, but nothing prepared him for this. The man's face was like stone. It was a chiseled image of perfection. He was handsome and attractive, yet terrifying and chilling. His skin was flawless; his features symmetrical. Black hair fell to his shoulders in perfect silken form.

This was the face that no sculptor could duplicate. It was the face that should belong to every fairy-tale hero ever imagined, yet the reality of this face was a far cry from a fairy tale. This was, in fact, the face of intimidation and superiority. Most who saw this face shrunk from it in fear like a scorned dog. It had become so universally feared that the mere mention of its presence would make even the most powerful of men shudder. This man's sheer presence had settled wars without battles.

More striking than his perfect features were his eyes. They were also jet black. His pupil could not be discerned from his iris, so dark was the color. They were cold and emotionless. Just as the voice never rose nor fell with contempt or contemplation, the eyes remained void of feeling. No one could hold his gaze. Those who tried were left with deep scars that would never heal. They were empty and lifeless, dead to all that was human. A lifetime of shedding compassion, love, fear, and hate had made them such. A sculptor could not form a more perfect aesthetic masterpiece, nor could they find stone cold enough to be more inhuman. Such was the being Ratajek beheld. Super-human, yet not *human* at all.

"I have come here to be reasonable. Though your reputation

speaks otherwise, I have chosen to see you because I believe you can be a reasonable man," said Kovac.

"Reputations often are very far from the mark. Men can form opinions of others without ever meeting them. You will find that I am reasonable as well as courteous," replied Ratajek.

"You speak with a forked tongue. Your silken words have more edge than a sword. I am no fool. I am not some cheap trader that you swindle and place in your pocket. I am here for a very valuable commodity, which you possess and I require. I know what I am willing to give. Speak your terms, and I will show *you* just how reasonable you can be." Kovac's face had not changed. His tone had been firm and commanding, yet had one not heard the conversation, they would think that pleasantries were still being exchanged.

Ratajek felt his knees weaken. This was not only a poor choice of colleagues, but the most dangerous one he had ever met. Next to General Kovac, Halgren was an idle school boy. He rethought his offer for Oryan in his head, trying to decide if it was indeed a reasonable one. Then the thought occurred to him: *Be reasonable. More than generous, even. Then sue for imperial protection for future ventures.* He summoned his courage, calmed his heart, and made his reasonable offer.

"Lord, I have an offer that is reasonable. My price was fifty million for the boy. However, your *generosity* has stirred me. I know that you are a man who takes what he wants and needs permission from no one. Rightfully so. I also know that you seek audiences with no business partner, no matter how great. That you are here has humbled me. I thank you for your kindness and offer you the sum of *thirty-five*." Ratajek knew this was as steal. Oryan was easily worth one hundred.

The general remained unmoved. His silence was terrifying. After only a few seconds, Ratajek felt his offer very unreasonable and was about to start making counter offers of his own free will. Then Kovac spoke. "I will give you my offer: twenty-five and imperial indifference to your little enterprise so long as it does not interfere with imperial affairs."

Kovac detested this man. If there was anything he hated more than spineless slave traders it was spineless slave traders who delighted in profiting from loss. This one was particularly disgusting. He used his former fame to drive up his market value and that of those he sold. He claimed that his "eye" for talent was unrivaled. Except for Oryan, he had been dead wrong. His so-called intuition must have left him with his pride when he became the most public loser in history. A true warrior would not have been able to bear the shame. Ratajek reveled in his. To Kovac, the creature before him was no better than swine wallowing in its own filth.

Still, this wretch of a man served a purpose. Although slave trade was illegal, it made the black market thrive. The market was completely run and overseen by the empire, of course, though few knew that. The slaves were cheap labor for both the empire and the market. With the empire acquiring new territory every day and forcing those who resisted into bondage, there was no short supply of them. If the market took a few here and there, they were welcome. The revenue that filtered in through the less-than-reputable channels was considerable. It was enough to fund most imperial social projects, leaving the taxes and levies to fund the military budget. It was a flawless system, and Ratajek was necessary, however revolting he might be. Besides, when scum like him thought they were getting away with something, it kept business thriving.

Imperial protection was a fantastic prospect for both people here. The empire already protected Ratajek so long as his exploits did not publically surface, and he was very good at staying out of the limelight. Ratajek was not aware that he was already under imperial jurisdiction, so he would think the offer a great asset to himself and his enterprise. It would embolden him for a time, but the empire would use certain black market channels to keep him in check. For Kovac, nothing here changed, save his accounts being a little lighter. It was only twenty-five million. He had the accumulated wealth of an entire continent in his personal portfolio. Though it held no real appeal to him, money was power, and he was a very powerful man.

Ratajek stewed over the counter-proposal. The money was nothing short of robbery. He had made triple that just for this tournament. However, he could not afford an enemy like General Kovac. He knew that he could do better on the black market, but he would either be bankrupt or dead before the day's end if he were pushy. The empire would seize his assets, freeze his accounts, and expose his entire operation within minutes of his refusal. Though the idea of losing that much money was not appealing, the thought of being dead, in prison, or worse, *destitute*, was more horrifying still. He had backed himself into a corner here, and the predator in front of him would settle for nothing less than his absolute compliance or every ounce of his flesh. He had been doomed from the moment he accepted this meeting.

"Thirty," he found himself saying. The sound of his own voice was small and weak. It had even surprised him to hear it. *What have I done?*

Kovac remained unmoved on the surface. The coals of disgust for this man raged into flame, but he kept it behind his steely black vaults. Still, the sudden attempt at boldness had its effect as well. While the fires raged, the general also felt a sense of levity. This little ant who he could crush at any time was trying to seem significant. It was just enough to quell the flame and save Ratajek's life.

"I do not negotiate terms. It would be unfortunate for you to think me unreasonable."

"Twenty-five," came the sniveling reply.

"You will receive the funds when the boy is delivered into my hands directly after the final match tonight. It will be deposited into your market account to avoid suspicion."

This last comment was an intentional stab to make Ratajek realize just how much the general knew about him. Market accounts were mythical. No one even knew they really existed until they had the money to buy one. Even then, only the account holder was supposed to have access.

"Very well, Lord. I will deliver him personally."

"Send him alone. This meeting never happened, and I never wish to see you again. Instruction on where to send Oryan will be sent to you on the Net. I do not need to remind you the consequences of revealing this transaction or this conversation."

"Of course, Lord. It will be done as you request. Thank you for your generosity and your patience. I can only hope to someday be as ... *skillful* a trader as yourself."

The general pulled the hood over his head and turned to leave. His footsteps were barely audible over the brush of his heavy cloak over the floor. He was amazingly quiet for such a large man. He had all but disappeared into the shadows when Ratajek called out again.

"What if the boy loses?"

The general stopped. Ratajek knew of all things this would rattle Kovac's cage a bit. This was the only uncertainty in the entire equation for him. The only thing he could not dictate or control. These were the things that General Kovac did not enjoy. Variables were something he eliminated at all cost.

"He won't," was the icy reply.

Ratajek grinned. It was not much, but he had won a very small victory with that last comment. It was a risky move, but he needed to see some leverage in his favor.

When he was sure Kovac was gone, he let out a sharp sigh of relief and slumped to the floor. The past few minutes of his life replayed over and over again. It was surreal. At first, he was just satisfied to be alive. Then, the thought that he would have to tell Halgren crossed his mind. This was going to be hard to explain. As these thoughts entered his brain, regret and anger began to set in. *I have been cheated! Twenty-five!* He had found his courage again, and had it been any other man, he would have followed after to barter a better deal. Not this time. Kovac was not known for bartering, and he was still not sure that shadowy creature that came on before was entirely gone.

That thought forced him to look into the dark archway and try to identify anything moving. His mind now focused on the positive side of these events. Imperial indifference. That was something in and of itself. In the long run, that would more than pay for the money he had lost today. He could handle Halgren for now. Then, maybe he could use that imperial indifference to put Halgren forever behind him.

He sighed again. When he woke up that morning, he never thought he would look death in the face and live to tell the tale. Not only that, but walk away from death a richer man. Slowly, he came to his feet. He patted himself on the back a few times for being good enough to live through it all and then headed for the exit. When he got to the archway, he hesitated for a moment and then hurried through like a child afraid of the dark. The outside world could not come soon enough for him this day. He was sure that the grass would somehow be greener and the sky more azure. He had a new lease on life. Who could he swindle with it?

As he bustled through the hallway, another shadow moved from its place inside the training room. Tecton stood where the two had been moments before. His mind was still wrapping around everything that he had seen and heard. He no longer concerned himself with the worry of Oryan showing up for the match in a few hours. Right now, it may be better off if he didn't. The only thing for certain was that his friend was in more trouble after this circus than before or during.

He had to find him! Had to warn him before it was too late. It did not matter *how*, just *how soon*. If he could not find him before the match, he would never get the word across. Once it was over, the media would not let him breath, and from there it was bad to worse.

Tecton ran to the exit and up the hallway toward daylight. There was no time to lose. He was in such a rush that he did not heed the terrible premonition that he was not alone in that place and someone knew he had witnessed the whole event.

As he ran past, a black shadow grew as if from the darkness and followed him up the hall into the world. Though he did not know it, Tecton was in more danger than the friend he was trying to protect.

A Legend Is Born

Daylight wore on, dwindled, and finally disappeared. The brilliance of the sun was slowly replaced by the harsh glow of millions of artificial lights. Transport shuttles, personal vehicles, and luxury crafts had begun delivering their passengers for the final event some three hours before the first ticket had been scanned. The line outside the arena was more than a mile long when the gate accepted its first patron. The media and press coverage was unmatched. Celebrities from every country, nation, and kingdom filed in for their VIP access. They were swarmed by media, giving opinions and signing autographs, then taking their front row or suite seats. Early estimates for this night had put the revenue through the doors, including ticket sales, in the billions. That was not only an understatement, but a gross miscalculation. One man paid just shy of one quarter billion for front row seats and an autograph from both of the combatants.

General Kovac had arrived around two hours beforehand with no media attention. He had been seen coming in and not seen again until minutes before the main event. There were several award ceremonies and various crowd-pleasing activities before the match had actually begun. It was all, of course, to draw out the moment, and also to make sure that the money kept flowing. The general had no interest in any of it, so he attended to other business while the riffraff subsided.

Only one important face was missing from the whole equation. It was possibly the most important one of the night. That face belonged to Oryan. Ratajek paced the training room floor anxiously waiting for him to come down the tunnel. It was only forty-five minutes from the actual bout, and the boy was still nowhere to be seen.

The last footsteps he had heard had been those of Tecton's, running down the hall, peering in the room and then disappearing. That was not a good sign. Those two were always together. It appeared that Tecton was just as anxious to know Oryan's whereabouts as he was.

The forty-five minutes turned into thirty and then twenty-five. The arena was restless. The fans had all packed into their seats; standing-room-only was overflowing. The lights had all been dimmed, and the props and equipment from the last ceremony were being removed by one crew while another brought out the flooring for the battle to come.

There were no announcements being made as of yet, but Agrion was already standing in his entrance, head down, shifting his weight from one foot to the other. Agrion was an impressive specimen. He stood over six feet in height, weighing almost two hundred and fifty pounds. His weight was all muscle. He did not often flaunt his physique, usually wearing a loose robe or full body suit of one kind or another for combat. His head was bald by choice, with a bright tattoo where his neck met his skull. On this day, the left side of his face near his jaw was bruised and swollen due to his encounter with Tecton the night before.

He was average with the actual battle simulations. His skill was all in single combat. Oryan had destroyed him several times in team simulations. He had so thoroughly humiliated Agrion in those sims that Agrion refused to meet him in team battle again. However, the night before as Tecton and Oryan were practicing in the training room, Agrion had made a public statement guaranteeing his victory. Most already had him picked for the win, but his last match had put doubts into all minds. The only thing for certain now was that they were all in for the greatest spectacle in sporting history.

Now, only five minutes remained to the event. The announcements had begun, and the anthems for both Vollmar and Navarus had been sung. Each country's flag hung from the rafters. Ratajek was waiting at the entrance closest to his seat but also nearest to the exits. If Oryan did not show up, he needed as much of a head start as he could get. The general was sure not to forgive this insult.

The floor was utterly black. No lights shone on it, save a single ray that illuminated the wooden flooring, which had been laid for the final event. Though the crowd was not cheering, the excitement that was there, coupled with the beyond-capacity numbers, made the noise level outrageous. The event was formally announced as about to begin. The loud speakers boomed the record of Agrion. They emphasized all the highlights they could from his stat sheet, his height and weight, his sponsoring country, and finally his name. Another light shot down from the ceiling to the entrance where he stood. He was wearing a very expensive robe that was mostly blue and white, the colors of Vollmar. All of his important medals hung from his neck. When he reached his corner of the floor, the light revealed a table covered in a Vollmar flag and decorated by all the trophies with his name engraved on their plaques. He turned circles, saluting and waving to the crowd, his face grim and determined. His last gesture was to look up at the flag of Vollmar and place his hand over his heart. He then lowered his head and began to shift from foot to foot once more.

Ratajek swallowed hard. This was it. The light was going to beam down from the rafters to reveal an empty hallway. There was going to be a great noise as the gasp of the crowd drew all of the air from the arena, and he was going to become the most hunted man on the black market. There would be a reward for him more substantial than all that he now possessed. The collar of his shirt was soaked with sweat. He knew now he was a dead man. Not even his most powerful of friends could or would shield him from the general.

Tecton too awaited the moment. The announcer began to read off Oryan's undefeated record. His heart ached for his friend. He had searched every moment he had. He returned to the arena only moments before they announced his name for one of the placeholders in the tournament. He should have searched more. Now, all he could do was wait in the dark for the announcements to cease and for the loud speaker to blast his friend's name.

When that moment finally came, Oryan's name could barely be heard. The roar of the crowd was so deafening that his actual name was drowned out. The light blasted from the rafters and lit up the entrance for him. There were gasps. There were screams. Above it all, there were cheers. Oryan, son of Armay, undefeated champion, stood in the entrance. He was the picture of resolute determination. He wore his usual scarlet and black robe. It was lined with gold-colored stitches and highlights. It was the same robe he had been given when he had been pulled from the minors by the empire. It was worth more money than the average person made in a lifetime.

When he appeared in the light, Ratajek's knees buckled under him. He did not realize until that moment that he had been holding his breath for several minutes. He stumbled to his seat as if exhausted from a very demanding physical labor. For the second time that day, he had looked into death's eyes and tempted fate. For the second time that day, by luck or destiny, he was still alive.

There was something different in Oryan. Usually, he jogged to his corner, saluting the fans that made him a superstar. This time, he slowly walked to the center. His face, usually pleasant and carefree, was hard and filled with concentration. He did not salute, nor wave, nor give any real acknowledgement to the madness around him. His gaze was only on Agrion.

It was apparent by his dress and appearance that he had done some preparation before this fight. His preparation had not been training or warming up at all. Agrion had a slight gloss of sweat that covered his whole body. He looked as one should before an event such as this. Oryan looked like a man who was preparing for his own death. His robe was very neatly cleaned and pressed. His white hair was clean and ceremoniously braided; it looked as if he was dressed for a far more social event. His face had been recently shaven, and it was apparent that he had thoroughly bathed. Save his expression, he did not look ready for a fight at all.

Most duels were designed to end when either one man was off his feet or by a ten-minute match, broken up into two five-minute halves, which were scored by a panel of judges. This one was set for three of those rounds, or if any man was off his feet three times in that fifteen minutes, or a knock out. Each combatant was allowed to pick his own weapon.

This was a highly debated duel. Oryan was a straight-on fighter. He came at his opponents hard and fast, usually ending a fight in minutes. Agrion was his antithesis. Agrion waited for his challenger to attack, defended, and waited again. When the man opposite him had worn himself down enough, he used his strong blows to weaken him the rest of the way. Everyone expected this to answer the question of which style was dominant. These fifteen minutes could very well determine the face of the sport for years. Whichever man won, athletes everywhere would begin to adopt those techniques. These two were, hands down, the best.

The rules of the match were announced when Oryan reached his corner. Agrion placed all his medals and trinkets on the table behind him, preparing for the moment to arrive. When the general announcements were over, the floor judge turned on his microphone.

"Centauri to the center," he announced for the arena to hear. They bellowed their approval.

Agrion and Oryan reached the center and faced each other while the floor rules were spoken. While this was going on, stage hands moved racks of weapons to their respective corners. "Each man turn and choose his weapon," the judge finished.

Agrion faced his corner and trotted to the weapons. He scrutinized the selection. Agrion knew that Tecton was a student of Oryan's fighting technique, so the decision finally fell on the dual wielding of swords. He picked up the weapons, which were slim, light, three feet long, and made of a very solid metal covered in thin pads. These weapons were designed to inflict pain, but they had no edge. They were not lethal, unless just the right blow was placed to just the right spot. They did, however, break many bones and left even more bruises.

Oryan chose a single weapon. He knew exactly what he wanted before he even was presented a choice. He moved quickly to his rack and removed the six-foot staff from the top. He had anticipated Agrion's weapon choice long ago. To carry two single-handed weapons was useful in the right hands, but it was a hindrance as one weapon was primarily used as defense. If the proper pressure was applied, that was all both weapons would be used for. Oryan knew all the pressure points.

Agrion was already at the center of the floor waiting for Oryan. He was no longer shifting his weight. He was standing perfectly still, staring hard at his opponent. Oryan was not impressed, nor was he intimidated. He walked to the center, rotating the staff and centering the balance in his hands. The crew outside the floor rushed the weapon racks back into the equipment rooms, and then they raced back to the floor's edge to ensure they too saw the action. They stood toe-to-toe with each other, both men knowing they would emerge victorious in a few minutes time. They looked directly into each other's eyes as if it would cause the other to show some weakness. In the unspoken battle, neither would give an inch.

The floor judge stepped back from the two men, preparing to watch every move they made. At this point, all he had to do was raise his hand in the air and drop it sharply down to begin the war. Agrion and Oryan had backed away a few paces from each other, but each still held the other's gaze. The judge raised his hand. The air in the arena thinned as all watching held their breath. The judge held it for a moment for dramatic effect and then sliced his hand through the air down to his hip. It had begun.

There was a plan that this bout was supposed to follow. Everyone knew it. There was not a soul watching this fight who did not expect Oryan to make the first move. Thousands of bets and millions of dollars were lost in the first instant of combat. Rather than attack, Oryan stood his ground. He circled clockwise around the floor, with Agrion mirroring, but he did not attack. His head was forward, but his eyes were keenly starring at Agrion. This was *his* plan, whether the crowd approved or not.

Agrion was a prepared man. He had been up all night studying footage of Oryan's fights. He knew the man. He knew what to expect. This was not it. Already he was thrown off balance. He was never confronted with a scenario of an opponent who would not attack him. He waited for the attack to come, thinking that boredom would set in for Oryan and he would strike first, but he just circled him. Seconds ticked past like hours. The suspense was terrible, even for a man as patient as he. To the displeasure of the crowd, three and a half minutes passed and a single blow had not even been attempted.

Oryan was the ultimate predator. He could wait forever. In this battle, he did not fear his opponent, but he learned long ago a physically beaten enemy would return when his wounds healed. A psychologically defeated one lived in fear long after the scars faded. Agrion would grow to fear him. So he waited.

Agrion was now drenched with sweat. Though he had done

nothing more than slowly circle his opponent, his body was reeling from the tension. His legs were like rubber, his heart raced, and his vision was blurred. Four minutes gone. Still nothing. To add to his discomfort, Oryan still appeared as calm and as pristine as he did when entering. He would gladly hit himself just to end the agony. Instead, he chose a far more painful option: he attacked.

Agrion moved fluidly across the floor. He shifted his weight gracefully from one side to another, trying to throw Oryan off center. The crowd erupted in ecstasy. Oryan himself had firmly planted his feet and stood in a stance ready for anything. Though Agrion rarely made a frontal assault, he was far from out of practice. His skill in this part of combat was equally unmatched. He came down with the weapon in his left hand toward Oryan's face. This was more a diversion for the blow coming from the right to his thigh. Oryan met the first blow with the top portion of the staff. The two weapons clashed together. The second sword came in sharply and smashed against the bottom half of the staff that Oryan raised for defense against that blow. Using his opponent's pressure against both halves, he spun the staff one hundred and eighty degrees, crossing Agrion's arms across his chest and sending him past Oryan like an amateur. That was luck. He only got one of those, but it served its purpose. Agrion was out of his element.

Now Oryan came on. His staff darted through the air, slashing down and up, thrusting fiercely like a spear in one hand and then the other. It was all Agrion could do to stop the blows from landing, but he was very skilled. He parried and twisted shots from finding their marks. He moved with speed and talent to deflect his opponent's attacks, but they were so fast and so strong he failed even to attempt to gain inside position. At this moment, he was happy simply not to have been hit. Just when Agrion felt his skill would not be enough to last any more of this onslaught, the first round ended.

They parted. Oryan immediately stopped his attack and turned his back to Agrion to retreat to his corner. Agrion held his pride and walked tall back to his corner. They both had thirty seconds to rest and evaluate. For Oryan, the evaluation was excellent. Agrion realized with horror that he had only withstood forty-five or fifty seconds of attack. He knew he could not keep this up for another ten minutes. Every muscle in his body burned. His evaluation was introspective. His usual defensive stance would do nothing for him, yet he could not withstand this man for long. It was time to take the fight to Oryan. If that did not better his situation, this fight was over.

The horn blared again. Round two was on. The judge raised his hand and dropped it immediately. No need for suspense now. The last round went to Oryan. Agrion was about to make this one his.

He rushed in, both weapons striking with lethal precision. His movements were agile; his strength was marvelous. It was just the right amount required for each blow. This series and combination was designed to level any opponent. It should have leveled Oryan. Unfortunately for Agrion, Oryan was still only letting him entertain the idea that he was doing well. Oryan dodged every blow, most of which he did not even use his staff to counter. He was so fast that few of Agrion's attacks even needed to be countered. Most fell on empty space, whistled past his head, or were never fully executed.

After two minutes of Agrion's advance, Oryan spun away, putting distance between them on the floor. Agrion turned to follow but found his muscles would no longer urge him on. Even his will, usually made of cast iron, was debating if another attack could be sustained. He took a more defensive stance and tried to make Oryan fight his fight.

Oryan had noticed the sweat beginning to form on his head. This game was becoming tedious to him. He had only this last challenge to prove and he could rest. Agrion was thoroughly off balance. His weight was on his heels now and off his toes. It was apparent he was done offensively. His guard was down a bit, and his knuckles were white. He was tired and just hoping to survive another two minutes. It was time to end this.

Agrion feared his oncoming attacker. This man was beating him in every way, and no matter where he turned, he could only see his enemy's determined face. Agrion knew he was about to lose. Like a cornered animal, he swung on his attacker, trying desperately to land any blow. The attacks were slow and clumsy. Oryan ducked beneath one, sidestepped another, and with a sharp lightning-fast move of his staff, he disarmed Agrion all together. In the same motion, he spun on his heels and brought all his power through his extended weapon, crushing into Agrion's left temple. Agrion buckled, bone cracked, blood splattered, and he dropped to the floor like stone.

His eyes rolled into his skull, and a pale lifeless shadow passed over his face. One leg was bent back under his thigh when he hit the hard wooden surface. If he was not dead, he was cheated. The life he would be living after this was pure torture.

Oryan stood over his body; the look of determination and the cold, hard emotionless eyes remained fixed on his opponent. Suddenly he realized, like the day at the Quarter, he heard no applause. He looked up from his victim. The capacity crowd was on their feet, faces twisted in horror at the scene before them. There had been no restraint and no mercy. This was not only out of character but unheard of in the sport.

Once again, he soaked up the silence. His eyes continued up from the wide-mouthed faces to the arena ceiling. It was transparent, and despite the light inside the building, he could see stars twinkle in the distance. How he longed to be there, so far away from this place. So unattached to all that made life complex. He wanted nothing more than to just observe this life with the world as his glass.

His eyes turned downward; regret and contempt for what he had become rose in his gut. He suddenly despised the rabble that had come to witness this barbarism. His father had held a dream of him that was beautiful and special. He had spat on it all for the amusement of the mob. He hated himself, and he hated them. If this was the highest cause he would ascend to, his life was an utter waste.

The staff dropped to the floor. No one noticed. They still stared on in disbelief. Oryan opened his arms and spread his fingers as if to show the audience the blood that stained his hands red in his mind.

He turned his back in disgust and marched toward the entrance he had come from. Doctors surrounded Agrion and moved quickly to stabilize him and move him to a hospital.

As Oryan disappeared into the shadow of the arena's underbelly, the crowd began to hum. There was conversation to be had by all for months to come. They all began to herd to the exits. This was enough for one night.

One spectator remained. One who had observed the entire chain of events with ultimate complacency. He had watched the savagery unfold, and he alone reveled in it. Lucius Kovac remained calm. His features were unmoved outwardly, yet inside he afforded himself the slightest smile.

This display was the perfect sign that he had indeed made the right decision. He knew the boy was talented, and from what he had seen from the Quarter, he knew the boy could be deadly. What he did not know until this moment was whether the boy could be deadly by choice. The Quarter was a forced issue. He was defending himself. If he had not killed those boys, he would have been dead in there. Agrion was a whole different story. If he lived through the night at all, living through the night remembering his own name would be nothing short of miraculous. In this case, Oryan had not been put into a position that he needed to kill. He had done it instinctively.

Kovac raised a hand and signaled to his Captain, who stood behind him. This was the leader of his Legion, his greatest student. The Captain was no longer human. Kovac had tempered it like steel so that now it was more deadly in Kovac's hands that any weapon forged by man. It was fiercely loyal, fast, efficient, and deadly. Its name had long ago been forgotten by everyone, including itself. It moved like a shadow and was dismissed just as quickly. It was the perfect scalpel for the world's cruelest surgeon.

However much Kovac enjoyed his Captain, it was, in the end, an expendable tool. Kovac could train another should this one fail. Next time, he could do it faster and iron out some of the kinks he had run into the first time. The second version was almost always better than the first. What he needed was a thinker. Someone who was every bit the weapon that his Captain was but who would take initiative. Someone who could command as he did and rule with authority. He needed an equal. He needed Oryan.

The Captain slinked forward and leaned over Kovac's shoulder. Its movements were seamless, as if it moved on air. It was not a natural movement, giving more weight to the rumor that it was in fact some creature that Kovac had raised from the dead.

"See to it that Oryan finds his way in here," Kovac commanded.

It nodded its head under the hood and vanished into the darkness. It was doubtful that anyone would even see it until it wanted to be seen. It was on its master's business and could not be disturbed. There was nothing short of death that could keep it from accomplishing even the simplest of tasks, if it even could be killed. Oryan would kneel at its master's feet.

Oryan was in the training room where he and Tecton had met the night before. He had wanted to leave all together, but he knew had he done so, he would have been so mobbed by press that he may have had to threaten more than one life that night.

Tecton had come. He had sat next to him and spoke to him about something. Oryan did not listen to the conversation. He knew his friend meant well, but a well-meaning friend was the last thing he needed at this point. After a few minutes, Tecton had left and fielded the media waiting outside the room. Oryan would someday thank him for that.

Oryan's thoughts dwelled on his father. His absence that day had been a quest to find information about Armay. He knew that his father would have wanted him to accomplish everything he could. Armay would have done anything to hear the crowd chant his son's name. He would have shed tears to watch Oryan, his only son, be the victor that could not be touched. For this reason above all, Oryan had come back.

Now it was all over. He had proven to the whole world that he was the best. He had made sure that there was no question. That display settled two things. One, it made sure that any enemies he had would think twice about their chances. Two, it assured that his career as a Centauri was over. If the Board let him keep his license to participate in the sport, there would be no opponent who would fight him. This was his plan all along. He wanted out, and this was permanent. Had he run, he would have been hunted down and placed back in the arena. He was still a slave, after all, and someone still owned him. He was not sure anymore if that was Ratajek or not, but he was still someone's property.

As if his thoughts had been read, Ratajek appeared in the entrance. This was the first time Oryan had seen him in years. He looked much like he remembered. Now that he saw him again, he felt that he was even more repulsive than their first encounter.

"Leave now," he began. "I'm out of your shadow. I have become what you only dreamed of being, and I don't feel much like sharing my glory tonight."

Ratajek slowly, mockingly clapped his hands together. "Yes, you proved your dominance. Sixty-eight professional bouts and not a single blow landed by an opponent. Impressive. My boy, you have made me rich beyond my wildest dreams. When Halgren brought you to me, I thought it was another one of his rejects. I guess he finally picked the right slave. I was fortunate to be the one he turned you over to."

"Yes, you own me. Does that make you feel more like a man? Something has to. It is not your personality or your luck with women. The only thing bigger than your bank account must be your self-inflated ego. I'm telling you again: Leave now, before I don't stop at just words."

Ratajek chuckled softly. "You are right on all accounts, my boy. All but one. I don't own you anymore. That's why I risked coming. There is a very powerful man who has taken the reigns from me. It's been a ride, but I must take my leave."

Oryan was now standing. A new owner was at least the promise of something different, though it still meant servitude. He had often tossed around the idea of buying his own freedom, but he had no real income. Ratajek kept all that to himself and only allocated to Oryan what he needed. The news of a new owner was not what had made him stand. He had seen that coming for some time. It was the hairs on the back of his neck standing on end that brought him to his feet. There was *something* here.

Ratajek paced back and forth, spewing some nonsense about business ventures and profit. He was apparently unaware of the presence in the room. Oryan drowned him out and reached for his stars. His senses became razor sharp. He could *smell* whatever this was. His ears picked up soft movement, but it was barely audible. He dug deeper for the right sense to locate this threat. He felt a chill creep over his right arm. It crawled along his flesh, making his fingers numb. It was right next to him.

In a lightning-quick movement, Oryan reached for the closest weapon and drew it across the throat of this shadow brought to life. It hissed behind sharpened teeth. It tried to draw its own weapon, but not in time.

Ratajek jumped back, terrified to be before that all-too-familiar horror. It was the same thing that haunted his morning and had been in the back of his mind all day. He could not shake its effect and had been constantly looking over his shoulder to make sure it was not there. How it had gotten into this room full of light unnoticed, he was not sure, but panic gripped him like ice. He cowered on the floor, watching every move he thought he saw it make.

"If you don't tell me what you are and why you are here, you will see, I assure you, that I don't need an edge to put this through your throat!" threatened Oryan.

The Captain had never been detected like that before. It was not sure how to react. It hissed again, realizing it was in a very compromising situation against an enemy that may very well be his match. "My master seeks an audience with your excellence," was the shrill reply.

"And who is your master?" retorted Oryan.

"All in good time, Centauri," it said. "I am but the escort. The message lies with him."

"He … he represents your buyer," said Ratajek, finally regaining an ounce of courage. "What he tells you is the truth."

The Captain's demonic eyes shot a sharp glare at Ratajek. Oryan did not feel the fear that Ratajek felt. He was always a thinker. This man, or semblance of a man, was just a tool. It was designed to put one in a state of unease. It was clever, yes; it's guarded and cryptic answers revealed that. It was an effective tool to be sure. No one had ever come that close to Oryan before without being noticed.

With a snap of his arm, Oryan removed the weapon from the Captain's throat. It let out a slight wheeze and then fixed its gaze on Oryan again.

"Will you come before him willingly, or must I be more … persuasive?"

Oryan scowled at this wraith. He was utterly disgusted by its presence and its lack of self-respect. "The only way you will see me to your master is by my choice. I think you lack the *diplomacy* to take me there otherwise."

It shrunk back slightly and let out a shallow hiss of breath. It knew it would lose if that was what it took, but it would die in the attempt before going back empty-handed.

Ratajek felt bold again, seeing Oryan handle this most irksome guest. He now leaned against a training bench, one hand on the blaster concealed beneath his clothing. "It appears you got more than you bargained for, *slave*! Your master's errand has found you in a very compromising spot, now hasn't it? Do you think he knew that before he sent you? Do you think he thought, 'If I lose one, I gain one better?' You're expendable!"

"And you are a fool," Oryan retorted, not taking his eyes off of the Captain. "Keep your toothless mouth shut! You'll benefit most from your own silence now, *slave-runner!*"

Ratajek scowled at Oryan. His pride was pricked. The fact that Oryan had chose to defend this messenger was insulting. Though his mind raced with curses and retorts to return at Oryan, he kept quiet. Oryan was in no mood to humor any arguments tonight.

Oryan studied this new player in his life. He observed every detail with calculating eyes. The Captain was doing the same. He toyed with the idea of saying no and taking his chances on his own in hiding, but he knew there was no future in that. The questions he had begun to ask that day needed answers. Whoever this new buyer was, he obviously had very deep pockets. To buy Oryan took more than just a small advance and good credit. Also, if this buyer found out what relationship Ratajek had in the whole sordid affair, he was probably well connected. Besides, to know that he was no longer property of the slob behind him was a relief.

"If I agree to meet this buyer, what guarantee do I have I'll get a better arrangement than I do now?" Oryan queried.

"He has given you no word to keep, Centauri. You simply have no alternative. You can come with me now alive, or you will be dead before you leave this building. He has many ears and many eyes. He will find you." Oryan could detect a cruel grin in that tone. The jagged yellow teeth showed through a bit more with the last comment. "My patience is thin. What answer do I deliver to him?"

At that moment, the lights shut off with a thud of power generators powering down for the night. The room went utterly black for a second. When the reserve lights flickered on, Ratajek found himself alone. The soft yellow halo of each bulb cast deep shadows on the walls, but no one was left behind them.

He started for the exit. As he walked to the archway, he turned a circle to make sure that some unholy pact had not been made between those two against him. Once he reached the archway, he did not hesitate as before. He ran as fast as he could for freedom. He was rid of Oryan and rid of that thing. The boy had no idea what he was getting into. It was probably better for him. After the insult he had received at Oryan's hands, he was hoping that the general would kill him for his insolent remarks.

The deal was finished, and he had done all he had promised. He would not soon forget this day. Of all the life changing turns he could have made, he only had one thought. *If I never see those two again, it will be too soon.*

The Price of Freedom

Oryan stood in an elevator that was transporting him and his foul friend to his new owner. It had been tricky following this thing through the dark corridors of the arena. The soft glow of the reserve lights had been just enough to see his escort disappear and reappear from shadow to shadow. They had come at last to a private elevator, which required a seven-digit code and key to activate. Inside the elevator was wide and spacious. It was very decorative, made to carry the most important of guests. Oryan noticed it even had a small supply of drinks and glasses just in case its passengers could not wait to get to their seats before beginning their merriment.

His mind raced to a thousand different conclusions. When situations like this one arose, his brain became a difference engine, weighing all possibilities simultaneously as well as individually. He had already deduced his buyer. This dark messenger, Ratajek's reaction to this intruder, and the amount of money needed to buy Oryan from his captor—these clues pointed to only one man. Oryan wondered curiously how much he had been sold for. He was willing to wager that Ratajek sold for cheap when he saw who it was he was trying to squeeze money from. He probably only cleared twenty or thirty million. That was a beautiful irony.

The only question that he had yet to answer was why someone like Lucius Kovac wanted him so much. Oryan knew that the General could have killed Ratajek for his ownership, but a man's dirty little secrets seem to find their way to the surface when he is murdered. He knew it was better to do business with the slave runner than kill him. That must have been torment for the General. The only logical reason for this was that Kovac wanted him for the army. He did not need the money, so to keep him in the circuit was of no real benefit. There would be many armies, mercenaries, and terrorist groups bidding for him now. The General had just made the first move.

The lift slowed to a halt. *May all your guesses be right*, Oryan thought to himself.

"If it is answers you still desire, follow me," said the Captain.

What a simple creature. Haunting and effective, yet mindless and expendable. This was a powerful combination. Kovac trained his troops well.

Oryan once again followed the shadow down a short hallway. It was elegantly carpeted with paintings and pictures in expensive frames lining the walls. There were a few empty food carts parked along the way. Each door they passed led to a suite designed with the height of luxury in mind. They were all sealed by a similar key pad to the one at the elevator, as well as a palm scan for extra security. As the pair rounded the hallway, Oryan noticed a door with one more security feature. Above the door was a series of wires, barely noticeable especially under the dim light. Those wires could only be one of two things: an alarm, or a weapon used for extra deterrent against intruders. The General was not one to be subtle with his enemies, so Oryan guessed the latter.

The Captain slithered beside the door. It reached for the keypad with long, bony fingers. The sharp nails tapped another seven-digit code; then it placed its palm on the scanning device. There was a click and a beep as a lock unlatched and the extra security disarmed.

"My master waits," it said.

Oryan stepped into the doorway. The suite before him was very impressive. It was wide and could have been filled with twenty or more very comfortable chairs. It only contained three. It could have been colorful and decorative with paintings and designs, but it was not. The carpet was lush and thick. The wall was painted a very rich dark blue, which looked as if it swirled and changed shade and hue when viewed from different vantage points.

The three chairs were placed in the front of the suite. In front of them was a rich counter top. It had space for food and drink, though it was empty now. The floor slanted down gradually and leveled out where the seats were. A figure that made the seats themselves look small sat in the middle chair. He was gazing at the arena floor as if some competition was still going on. Oryan entered quietly and stood a few paces behind the man. His dark escort filed in behind, shut the door with a soft click and a beep, then stood in front of it, barring any escape.

"An impressive performance tonight," said the figure. "Knowing your reputation as I do, I would have thought you were the last fighter to leave the crowd gaping."

"Every mob I've performed for thinks they want blood. It isn't until you give it to them they realize how wrong they are. As one who placates no spectators, I thought you of all people would appreciate the thrilling approval of silence, General."

Kovac was already impressed. This was going much better than his earlier business venture. He stood and turned to face his guest. He looked at Oryan for some time. This man was smaller than he, and in his dark robe he looked to be of average build. He posture was perfect, his eyes fixed on the empty arena as he had been moments before. His arms were behind his back, hands at his waist, ready for anything. The lack of visual information was a novel concept for Kovac. It meant there was some mystery left to uncover.

Oryan remained calm on the exterior. One thing the Quarter had taught him was to be like stone no matter the circumstances. When the General arose, every warning signal he possessed sounded in his brain. This man *was* a threat. So much so that Oryan felt that if the worst should arise, he might not be victorious. His mind was calculating hard to come up with a viable scenario that led to him living through an altercation with this enemy, but none came. This man was hardly man at all. He was a force of nature. Oryan felt in his presence like any normal man facing a hurricane or the eruption of a volcano. Nevertheless, Oryan knew that Lucius Kovac would always remember the day he fought Oryan, the son of Armay.

Oryan felt no fear. The fear he had known from the Quarter had been the fear of the unknown. He had nearly let the fear get the better of him. When Oryan had finally faced the fear, he had crushed it forever. Fear was weakness, and weakness could not be tolerated.

"You see much, Oryan. Much that is not spoken and rarely seen. Do you know why you are here?"

"You have purchased my life, which leads me to conclude that you have no lack of money as I know I am a very valuable commodity in certain circles, so it would be of no interest to you to keep me in the circuit. You bring me here in the darkness alone, with no witnesses but your puppet, so I know it is nothing that will ever be publically known. You also meet with me in person, which means you have a personal interest involved. My only conclusion can be that my life was bought to spill blood for you in the battlefield rather than here in the arena."

"Do you find this proposition undesirable?" asked Kovac.

"Given the circumstances, I don't see any alternative. My choices are dictated by whoever's profiting from the men I am killing at the time," retorted Oryan.

Kovac felt a bit repulsed. "I have no need to profit from you, boy. I do not wish to take anything from you. In fact, I wish to *give* you something. You see, I harness power. I take the power that others possess, and I show them how to unleash it, how to release it for greater purposes."

"By greater purposes, I assume you mean your own. Careful, lord of lords. Power unleashed can be dangerous, especially when the focus of that energy is opposite the focus you have tried to give it."

"The only focus I seek is to unlock your full potential, to show you what you are capable of. If what you say is true, the only thing you are in danger of is self-destruction."

"When I learn all that you have to teach me, I will have no more use for you. What then keeps me in your company? I wonder: were these same hollow promises made to your stooge behind me before you stripped him of his humanity? If that is all I have to learn from you, I will respectfully decline. Do with my life what you wish, but I will not be another one of your weapons, General."

Kovac reveled in this. He was not often fond of arrogance, nor was he light-handed in dealing punishment to those who disagreed with him, but this defiance was marvelous. He was perfect. He had made every correct move thus far. Ratajek had been a fool to release him for such an insignificant amount. Kovac knew he could be very well training his superior, but he no longer cared. He had to see what this boy was capable of.

It was in this hour that Oryan made the first mortal enemy of his life. The Captain stood as still as a stone. Its mind, however, was anything but idle. It had never heard its master speak to anyone like that before. There was praise in his voice, even a touch of pride. Few could detect any inflection in Kovac's voice, but the Captain knew each sound. Its master had given it praise, it is true, but never pride. Kovac was not often patient with rebellious speech, but he tolerated this peasant.

He had taught it much, yet held back everything. For the first time that it could recall, it felt a very real emotion. It worked hard, struggling to remember the sensation that in its previous life it had taken for granted. It glowered at this new enemy. This was another obstacle keeping it from its master's true power. What it was feeling now was the most powerful sensation it had felt in years: *envy*. This nearly forgotten feeling made the Captain feel very vulnerable, which made it hate the Centauri even more.

But, the Captain was patient. It could wait, bide its time until the moment was right to strike. If its master continued to take such an interest in this mere mortal, then he must be removed from the equation. Slowly, its mind twisted cruel designs.

"Quite presumptuous, aren't you?" the General asked rhetorically. "No one here has said that you will be *my* student. You are a gifted fighter, and you have given the empire a great display of various talents, but that means little for you and less for me. The threat of death is a powerful force. In your arena, death was never present except as you dealt it. I bought you because I want to see if you can deliver these same results when death is ever present, when it is your shadow and not at your fingertips."

"I do not fear death, and I do not fear you. I will not kill others for your amusement. I have nothing to prove to you or anyone else. I know who I am."

"Do you? I know you as well. Better than you think Oryan, son of Armay!"

Oryan felt as if he had been punched in the stomach. For the first time since he entered, his gaze shifted. He remained perfectly still and calm, yet his eyes shifted from the blackness of the arena to meet the General's.

"You know who I *was*. You have done your research and so you think you know me, but nothing could be farther from the truth. Trying to use my father as leverage is a futile effort, General. I already know his fate. Your intimidation may work on slime like Ratajek, but I will not be so easily swayed."

Kovac felt the anger rise. Had the boy indeed learned that his father was dead? Armay had been one of his most deadly adversaries. Had Armay not been betrayed, he may have been his downfall. He was noble in every sense of the word and a brilliant tactician. When Kovac had learned of his untimely demise, he felt that the last great hope for valor had died with him. Then he had learned that his son still lived. And here he was.

This conversation was becoming irksome. He felt fatigue set in. He had not been verbally challenged like this in some time, and the boy indeed seemed above threats, but the General had one more card to play. "Your life is yours. You may do with it what you choose. You can walk away a free man or you can listen to the alternative."

"What are you not telling me?" Oryan asked.

"Your life is your own; however, I feel that Tecton's wife and son would benefit greatly from you being more ... reasonable. The choice is yours."

Tecton, you fool! Oryan had known he was following him that day. He had seen him more than once and avoided contact. Did Tecton know that he was also being followed? The Captain must have done its research after following his friend. Now, he had to make a dreadful choice. Oryan knew he could defend Tecton and his family against any adversary, but even his great skill was not enough for the long arm that was Lucius Kovac. There was no where he could hide them that the General would not find. They would be hunted to the ends of the earth.

The Captain was feeling much more justified. It was its efforts that day that were now putting Oryan in such a difficult position. It had also enjoyed watching its master turn the tables so skillfully. That little pest was thinking he was getting the upper hand, but it was not so. Its ego was feeling far less bruised.

Oryan's calculating brain was working feverishly to postulate the best alternative for all parties involved. No matter how he altered events or weighed variables, the result was always the same. If he left now, he condemned innocent life. In the end, it was not his difference engine that gave his answer, but his conscience.

He did not care what Kovac had to say. Oryan was not in search of greater power or self-aggrandizement. After the events of that day, he had no more use in a search for a higher purpose. He just wanted to disappear and never have anything expected of him again. This whole time he had been testing the General. Though he did not know which path to follow, he still had to make a hard choice now. Before he gave his decision to the General, there was another matter at hand.

"You," he began, looking hard at the Captain, "understand this: I will do everything within my power from this moment forward to take away the only thing that matters to you."

The Captain hissed, for it knew that Oryan knew what it was seeking. Oryan turned to face Kovac.

"General, I will fight for you. I will make your enemies my enemies, and I will defend you from any foe, both without and," Oryan looked back at the Captain, "from within. I will learn everything you can teach me, and I will be your greatest student. Know that I fight only for you. Whatever banner you fly shall be mine; your armies shall be my armies, and your victories will be my life's only pleasure." He knew this speech was transparent. He did not care what the General wanted, and he had no real desire to go to war. All he wanted was to see the Captain in the same position he was in. To make it writhe in the agony that is the knowledge that it was about to be replaced. *You have made me surrender my life, so I will take yours.*

"Perhaps in time, you will mean those words," said Kovac. "For now, this will do. There is a shuttle waiting at the east entrance. Go there, and it will escort you to your lodgings. I will send word."

With that, the Captain slid aside from the door. Kovac nodded at Oryan and said no more. He turned his back to them all and folded his hands behind his back.

Oryan walked to the doorway, relieved to be departing so soon. Far in the distance, he heard clock bells chime midnight. This was the end to the most exhausting day he could remember. His life would never be his own. He cursed the day he had discovered his gifts. If only he could have been born someone or somewhere else, things would be easier. His inspiration was gone. All that he had longed to be was vanishing into the night with his so-called freedom. For the first time, he felt tomorrow could only be worse. Hope was bleak.

The Captain threatened under its breath as he passed. Oryan stopped and turned to face it. This thing he saw before him was his future, some groveling, putrid form of life with no purpose or destiny. He loathed the image before him, but loathed himself more. Pity ran through him for himself but also for the Captain. *Did you know what he was going to do with you?*

Then the pity hardened. It flew from compassion to rage. *You still made the choice! Even if he had forced your hand in the beginning as he has mine, you chose to do it to me! I have nothing left to hope for, so I will turn all my energy that was used for my hope to bitter revenge.* Oryan felt in some dark way that whatever emotion he could hold on to in order to remain human was a good one. He knew the cancer that was hate. He knew it ate at you daily, but it was the only emotion he cared to feel. Hate was so much more bearable than heartache.

The door slid shut behind him, and he began the long journey to the east entrance. The darkness before him was welcoming. He could hide in it and never be seen again. Dark was his mood, and dark were his thoughts. It was darkness he longed for and that he accepted so readily. When he reached the outdoors, the sky was equally black. But something happened then that dispelled the gloom. High above him amongst the blackest of skies were a billion points of light. Even the darkest of days could not dispel their majesty. Suddenly, hope rose in him again and choked the weed of hate that clouded his judgment, and he remembered again who he was.

I am Oryan, son of Armay, and I have much to live for!

The Captain was watching from inside the arena as Oryan looked up at the sky. What did he see there? Why was he so fascinated at the scene before him? Then it began to notice a change. It seemed to the Captain that Oryan's countenance was full of light, and it was suddenly not so confident in its ability to remain unseen. When Oryan looked down and scanned his surroundings, the Captain felt quite exposed. There was a light that radiated from his eyes, a light that could not be extinguished, and to attempt to do so was a futile. It was the light of honor and nobility. He was the personification of peace and harmony. The world seemed in balance around him as it had never seen in its master. Kovac was the lord of all that he desired, but this was greater still. In the presence of so awesome a force, it felt ashamed. It felt a great desire for redemption from all its dark deeds. It felt guilt. The pain was excruciating.

Then, it heard a familiar voice call to it from down the hall. It was its master, beckoning him to come. At first, it hesitated, resentment for the captor of its soul filling its lungs with each breath. Then, it succumbed to an easier path. After all, it knew that though its master was the cause of its downfall, in the end, he was all it had. He understood and accepted it, knowing all its transgressions, and so it once again turned from redemption and disappeared into the comfort of the darkness where all misdeeds are hidden.

Oryan was taken to a very expensive hotel only a few miles from the empire's arena. The garage and hangar were packed with vehicles from around the globe. Oryan was sure that this place had not seen this kind of business for a long time. Such was the draw of the previous night's event.

The shuttle slowed to a stop at the main entrance after a frustrated driver had circled several times looking for a suitable place to park. When the vehicle finally stopped, the driver quickly rushed out of the front and came to open his door in the back. He was a well-dressed young man who had obviously been paid a lot of money to keep his mouth shut and just drive. He said nothing to Oryan as he let him out, and as soon as he was out of the car, the young man rushed back to the driver's seat and began to circle the lot again.

Oryan turned to face the few stairs that led to the main doors. He could see the boy waiting behind the glass doors to greet him with the fake, plastered smile he was paid to give and then rush his bags to his room. Unfortunately for this tip-seeking employee, Oryan had no bags and no money. He stepped up the scarlet rug lining the stairs and approached the doors. They slid open soundlessly, and the boy offered his welcome, flashed his white teeth, and proffered a rehearsed greeting.

Oryan brushed past him trying to get to the front desk and find out which room he was in so he could lay down for some sleep. He could stay up all night drowning in his last few hours, but all he wanted to do now was rest. Whatever was coming tomorrow, he was sure he would be better suited to handle it with a good night's sleep.

"Sir, do you have any bags that I can—" the boy began. "You're, you're ... you *are* him! I can't believe it! I don't believe ... Can I maybe get your autograph? I mean, if you're not busy and if that's okay, that would be great."

Oryan had nearly forgotten his notoriety. Anonymity is not a privilege of those who just hours before had been the biggest news in sporting history since the invention of global communication. Seeing this kid stumbling over words to ask such a simple question had lightened his demeanor. He had also noticed that the attendant at the desk had stood when he heard the conversation and was immediately on his communicator informing others.

"Do you have a pen?" Oryan asked in response.

The boy stared blankly for a moment as if he had been asked the hardest question of his life. "A ... a ... a ... what? Oh! Oh, yeah a pen!" He patted his shirt and pant's pockets looking desperately for any form of writing utensil.

After a few moments, Oryan interrupted. "Why don't we go to the desk? I would like to check in, and I am sure they will have something up there for me to use."

"G-good idea," the boy replied.

At the desk, the attendant was equally starstruck, and so trying to get his key card and room number took an unnecessary amount of time. He signed autographs for all the employees that had come to the front and a few of the guests who had noticed the commotion and stopped on the way out. There were a few very attractive women wanting autographs in very unusual places that made for a fantastic distraction after everything else.

The crowd dispersed, and he headed down the hall to the lifts. His room was on the suite level, which made sense to help to avoid suspicion. Why would he stay anywhere else? No one needed to know that he was not there of his own accord. After that entrance, he was sure that the media would be notified soon. He wondered what had been done to get him this suite. The hotel was full, and he was quite sure no one really knew he was coming until the last minute. Otherwise, the fanfare at his arrival would have been far more dramatic.

He was beginning to feel his pride creep back into his soul. All the attention made him remember the glory of the spotlight and the thrill of a million fans screaming his name. One of the girls had offered to come back to his room with him, and even though he had declined the offer, it was flattering to know that he could gain such attention just by being who he was. Tonight, however, was not the night for female companionship.

The lift stopped, and the doors slid open. He walked down the wide hall to the suite that matched his key card. He waved the card in front of the sensor, and the double doors parted. What he saw inside made him wish he had brought that girl with him if, for nothing else, to share the moment with. He had never seen anything like this place before. It was as large as most of the houses he had stayed in. There was a huge bed with decorative sheets and a thick comforter. There was a full-sized bar in the corner with every kind of refreshment he could ever want to drink and a menu next to it for the food. The bathroom was equally grand with a tub that could easily fit twelve people.

There was another door that led to the closet on the far side of the room. He stopped here last as he had made his way around the massive space. It was truly a shame that he was probably only going to spend a single night at that place. The desk attendant had managed to inform him that his "personal effects" had been brought over just prior to his arrival. What that meant, he had no idea, and everything he had seen thus far was almost certainly the property of the hotel. Whatever it was that was now his was in that closet.

He slid his fingers along the pad, which opened the sliding doors and illuminated the closet. It was as large as his home in the Quarter had been and was mostly empty. There were clothes racks, dressers, shoe racks, and even a smaller closet in this place. A huge mirror adorned the far wall. For all its extravagance, there was not much more than empty space except on a lone hangar in the corner near the mirror. There was a black garment bag that hung there with the symbol of the empire embroidered on the outside. It was a very expensive bag in and of itself, which meant what was inside was probably equally as impressive. As he came closer, he noticed very neatly folded and pressed shirts and pants hanging behind the bag. On the shoe rack just beneath them was a pair of highly shined black boots that looked as if they would almost reach his knees.

He touched the zipper and slowly opened the bag to reveal its contents. When he saw what was inside, he held his breath. There was a sharp, black dress uniform hanging there, complete with rank insignias, company numbers, Special Forces emblems and the like. He recalled this same uniform being worn by General Kovac earlier that same evening. He also recalled being slightly envious of the apparel. It had looked bold and intimidating yet professional and attractive. It was a model of discipline, and he was sure that even Ratajek could not wear it without holding himself to a higher standard.

The temptation to put on the uniform was overwhelming. He would love to go back to the front desk wearing this and see what the response was. He was quite sure that a great sense of fear would abound but that their curiosity would overcome that. Then reality set in. This was no game, and it was certainly not a fashion show. The idea suddenly seemed foolish and immature. The press was probably here by now, and to flaunt this new garb would undoubtedly draw a lot if unnecessary attention to him. They would ask questions that he could not answer and start rumors that he could not quell. Best to leave the uniform where it hung.

When his mind came to its final decision, he felt the fatigue of the day set in again. He had been awake for nearly two straight days now, and they had been packed full of physical and emotional demands. It was approaching two in the morning, and he was not sure what time he would be getting his wake-up call. His eyelids became as lead, and he felt it difficult to stagger back to the large bed. He tried to throw his body on top of the lush comforter, but the energy was not there. He slid down the side, finally ending up propped upright against the corner of the bed and the wall. His vision went from gray to black, and he slipped into unconsciousness.

That night, he dreamed sweet dreams, the like he had never known before. They brought complete rest to his body and soul. They brought a reassurance that an unseen change was coming that was to be welcomed with open arms. They brought a peace that he had only known once in his life, and even then it was only a memory. He felt rejuvenated as if to begin a great journey whose reward was nothing less than the home he had always sought for. Something was coming, and it brought redemption in its wake.

Despite the turmoil of his life, all would soon be made right.

The Day After

He awoke with a start. Something was wrong. All his senses were on alert, his body poised for anything, and his mind keen and clear. There was something here that was amiss, but he could not place the feeling. He scoured the room looking for any signs of life, and there were none. He tore apart the furniture looking for cameras and recording devices. Here too his search was fruitless.

It was still dark outside. The balcony of his suite showed nothing but a dim light of the morning sun peeking over the trees. The scene was serene, filled with a sense of renewal that the oncoming day brings. So why the intense dread? There appeared to be no immediate danger, no signs of a trap or set up, yet something was out of place.

Oryan paced the floor, trying to uncover the source of his uneasiness. Part of his brain was rolling over reasons for his paranoia, part was staying alert to all that moved, and the other was mindlessly counting his steps as he wore a path in the carpet. Light trickled down over his toes and crept toward the edge of the balcony. He began to guess the shortening length of the shadows cast by his feet.

After a while, his head began to pound from over-analysis. He stopped, took a deep breath, and focused all his energy on relaxing his tense shoulders and knotted neck. His eyes were shut so as to soak in the quiet. He felt the first warmth of the sun on his back and soaked that in as well. The heat was welcome, for in his frantic state his fingertips and toes had become like ice as they always did when danger was close but not at hand. He waited for the warmth to creep up his back to his shoulders.

As he cleared his mind, he felt the blood flow back into his extremities, but they were not warmed. He searched again for the strengthening sun, but he could no longer feel its rays. His senses raced again. His whole body had become numb! Something was wrong. His eyes flashed open to his still empty room, but something had changed. Instead of the natural light of the sun a dim electrical glow illuminated his surroundings.

He spun around to see that the sun was not rising at all. It was, to his shock, sinking behind the landscape. He scrambled for something that would tell him the time and the date. He found his answer quickly from the overturned alarm clock that he had tossed in his attempt to root out danger. It was not morning at all. It was dusk of the same day, but the entire day was gone. He felt as if he had only slept for a short time, and his body still creaked and groaned for more rest, but he must have had at least fourteen or more hours of uninterrupted sleep. He had expected to only be allowed four or five hours of sleep before he was thrown into the next stage of his evolution. He could not remember the last time that he had that experience.

Suddenly, he had discovered the reason for the rude awakening. It was because there had been no awakening at all. No soft beep of the communicator, no overly bright lights, no knocks at the door, and no uninvited guests.

Although this new realization raised suspicion and doubt, his body relaxed having put a name to his anxiety. His thought now turned to food. Before this morning, he had not slept in some time; it had been longer since he had eaten. He sat on the bed and pushed the button to call for service. Seconds later, a very pleasing voice sounded harmoniously in his room.

"What can I get for you, Mr. Mason?" His ears perked at the mere sound of a female voice. It was alluring, and it almost immediately set his whole body at ease. The sudden desire for soft company made him forget even the reason he had called.

"Your name, my dear," he said with a smile. He was sure in some other room in this hotel there was a young lady blushing. She could be the most hideous woman he had ever known, but this was an edge. He could get more out of her now than he could have by being gruff or short-tempered.

The voice rang again with a giggle in her tone. "What would you like my name to be?"

"Any name I could choose wouldn't do justice to such a voice! I must have it so I know who to request to bring me what I want."

There was a long silence. He wondered if she was laughing with the other girls and trying to overcome her excitement before she responded. He knew he had her in the palm of his hand now.

"Perhaps I should keep my name to myself until we can meet face-to-face. Then you can say for sure that the name fits the beauty," she flirted.

Clever girl, he thought. "Very well, love. I should greatly desire some food, I would love to read the news, and above all, I should love some company," he returned the flirtation, but he was beginning to think more like himself. If she did come to his room, he would keep her there long enough for others to suspect, then send her away. Keeping the celebrity persona was the best course of action for him now. Besides, she had probably seen most of the people coming in and out, so she could inform him of any press that might be waiting or any military presence in the building.

He detailed to her the specifics of his order, making sure to order two so she would be properly accommodated. Their little affair lasted almost ten minutes; then she assured him she would be there with his meal as fast as was humanly possible. Oryan pulled off his robe, leaving only his pants on. He did not want anything physical, but there was no reason to look as if he had been in three fights, sold to the highest buyer, and asleep for the whole day. He straightened the room, showered, and made himself presentable just in time for the door to chime.

He had expected that there would be a prostitute waiting when he opened the door. The hotel may not run any brothels, but he was quite sure that they knew who to contact when the occasion called. The way he had made it sound on the intercom, he expected a rather expensive trophy to be at his door. He was wrong.

He opened the door to a silver tray filled to the brim. His eyes flowed through the maze of food, up the delicate skin of her arm, across her shoulder and the curve of her neck to her face. There he stopped. This was a face he recognized instantly; one he had seen a million times before. She was the face in the crowd so long ago. She was the comfort he reached for when the world was chaos. She was the very woman he had loved for so long in his dreams. Her brown eyes, her soft smile, her silken hair, it was all too familiar, and yet, she was a complete stranger. Until this moment, he had never seen this woman in his waking world. Everything about her was foreign. She was a complete mystery. She was more precious to him than the very air he had forgotten to breathe.

Her voice broke the silence like angelic choirs raising their songs to the throne. "Do you still want me to come in?" she asked, seeing his hesitation at her appearance and his mouth agape. It had taken her more than a moment and considerable courage even to come to his door, and now that she was here, she was compelled to never leave his side. She had been drawn to him since she first saw him, and when the call came from his room, she had to find out.

Her cheeks were flush, and there was a strain in her tone. It was apparent that she had tried to do her best to put on make-up and fix her hair. Her breathing was in short, quick breaths. The top few buttons of her blouse were undone, trying to reveal more flesh, and Oryan noticed her chest pound visibly with her racing heart.

"Where are my manners?" he stumbled over his response. He moved away from the door to let her past with the tray and closed the door behind her. Were the circumstances different, he would have admired her hourglass figure and all the other feminine qualities that made her attractive, but she held his eyes captive. As he followed her into the room, he began to regain his senses. He wanted nothing more than to sit in silence with her, but there was something bigger than his feelings going on here. He seized the opportunity of not looking in her eyes to refocus. He had brought her here to get an assessment of the situation beyond his doors. She was an employee of no real significance, so she would suspect nothing of his questions.

He followed her into the main part of the suite. She parked the tray at the foot of the bed and stood by nervously. She would not make eye contact with him; instead, her eyes shifted between his neck, bare chest, and the floor. She wrung her hands at her sides, and her feet shuffled nervously.

"Please, sit anywhere you like. Make yourself at home," he said, stepping another pace back from her to put her at some ease. He needed the both of them to be a little less flustered before he asked anything further. He walked past her, trying to gain control of the situation, but as he did, he caught a small hint of her intoxicating aroma. A wave of euphoria swept over him, buckling his knees. He fought hard to keep his focus on his survival and not on her, but he had never felt this way before. Controlling new emotions took time, and she had come at him faster than light.

She drifted to a few different chairs and sofas in the room but made no decisive action to reach one. "You can sit there if you want," he said, pointing to the bed behind her. "Don't be afraid," he said with all sincerity. He moved to the sofa that was diagonal from her and sat down, locking his fingers behind his head and closing his eyes. *Remain calm. Focus. Master yourself, and stay alive.*

"Mr. Mason, I—"

He stopped her with a wave of his hand. "Please. Please don't call me that. My name is Oryan."

"Sorry. Oryan." She felt her cheeks flush further, and he felt his heart skip as his name fell from her lips. "I, I've never done anything like this before," she said softly, cautiously trusting her weight to the edge of the bed.

"I'm sorry. You've never had dinner?" he asked innocently. "I find that hard to believe."

"No, I mean that I've never come to a man's hotel room before to do ... this."

This lightened his mood some and allowed him the slightest distraction. She was so nervous. It was apparent she was as unsure of her feelings for him as he was of his own. "And what did you expect *this* would entail?"

"The other girls, they sent me up here for, well, for companionship." Her cheeks flushed a deeper red that spread to her chest.

He was amused at her state of mind, yet he was drawn to her innocence even more. "And you are opposed to the idea?"

"Oh, no!" she exclaimed, standing up straight, afraid she had offended him. "That's not at all what I had meant! No, I think *companionship* is great with you. *Would* be great with you," she trailed off.

Oryan chuckled at her unease and allowed his guard to fall ever so slightly. Despite her beauty, she was as unsure as he.

He stood and walked to her. He lifted her chin so her eyes met his. Her gaze sent a rush from his heart through his chest. "You have nothing to fear from me. Despite what the others told you, sex is the last thing on my mind. When I told you I wanted dinner for two, that's all I wanted. I have spent the last few months in near solitude. I just don't want to be alone anymore." His brain sent shock waves through his body. *What am I saying? Why am I acting so foolishly?*

Her shoulders relaxed. She could see that this message was genuine by the look in his blue eyes just as well as he could read the fear in her brown ones. She sat down heavily on the edge of the bed, a great weight lifting from her. When he turned to bring a table between them, she fastened the buttons on her blouse.

Oryan moved a few pieces of furniture and began to prepare for their meal. After a few mere seconds of watching, the shock wore off her and she jumped to her feet. "I'm sorry, this is my job. Please, let me finish."

"Nonsense! Sit down and relax. Forget you're at work, and forget what you thought you came here for." He chose each word carefully. He did not want her to feel rejected, nor did he want her to think that a physical interaction was out of the question. Despite the turmoil he felt within, there were appearances that had to be maintained. When she returned to her station, questions would be asked, and the wrong answers would only raise more suspicion.

He chose from the tray an apple and an appetizing loaf of bread for his plate and then a few small samples of the more tender looking meats to fill his empty stomach. He poured them each some drink and sat down on his sofa. Once again, he cleared his mind, calmed his heart, and took control. "There's no need to be polite. Take and eat what you like. This is all I want. It would be a shame if the rest went to waste."

He had ordered an extravagant meal, one that he was sure it would take her two days' work to afford. She eyed the food and matched his choice: fruit in small portions, some bread, and even smaller samples of meat.

"So tell me," he began, biting into the apple. "Tell me about yourself. Have I seen you before?" He stopped abruptly, looking at her closely to see if she reacted to his foolish question. "Slow down, Oryan. I guess we should start with your name. Our meeting through the comm was not, shall we say, satisfactory."

She started slowly, revealing her name, Celeste, and then as he asked more questions, the answers became longer. As she spoke, she reached for more food, taking her fill of the more rich and exotic samples. He listened carefully, slowly eating. After an hour, she was feeling more herself and he was confident she would tell him what he needed to know, but he was not about to interrupt. At this rate, when he transitioned into what he wanted to know, she would give him every detail she could recall.

Two hours sped on this way. They each asked questions of the other. He had learned that she was not particularly interested in his sport, just in him. She had a crush on him, and so when the call came from his room, she dropped the other one she was on to answer it. Oryan told her little of himself outside his career and said nothing of his lifelong infatuation with her. He had begun to relax with her, but there was a growing anxiety in his mind. Somehow he knew time was short, but he could not bring himself to stop her.

As the shadow in his mind grew, he found a short silence with which to change the topic of conversation. "When did you learn that I had arrived?"

"When I came in this morning. My friend at the desk told me you came in last night and she knows what a . . . *fan* I am. I knew something was different with the number of media shuttles parked outside. There have been quite a few coming and going lately what with your tournament and all, but these were broadcasting from here. That's how I found out."

Oryan smiled. "The press follows me most everywhere."

"That must be hard, no privacy and all."

"It didn't stop you. By now, every media station across the nation knows your name, and I can regrettably assure you that you will have more than your fifteen minutes of fame when you leave here regardless of what was said or done. Did you hear of anyone else of note coming here, or do your other crushes stay at home?"

She blushed from both his comment and his question. She would be seen everywhere as "the girl in his room." "I haven't seen or heard of any other celebrities coming through, but I did notice a few that caught my attention."

"Oh?" he said, leaning forward in interest. He had found from their conversation that she was astute in noticing details, even when she did not realize she was doing it.

"On my way up here, I noticed a military escort vehicle parked in the garage." His ears perked. "When I saw that, I made a bit of a detour after I got you food through the lobby rather than through the back halls. It was a guess, but sure enough, there were some sharply dressed military types sitting out there."

She stopped reminiscing and looked at him curiously. She waved him to come closer. He scooted the table out of the way and shifted the sofa so that they were inches apart. "You know, when I went to bill your room for the food, a really weird symbol and a code came up. When I ran the transaction, it didn't print me a receipt or give me a confirmation number. I've seen that happen a few times on very high-level accounts, but that symbol was altogether foreign to me."

"Go on." Oryan became deadly interested.

"But as I was walking through the lobby, I bumped into one of those military men and I happened to catch a glimpse of the ID card on his belt. They weren't normal military, I think. More like undercover kind of people. But the symbol on the ID card matched the one on your account. He was very rude and would not let me pass. He just asked my name and then pushed the cart past him. I'm not a person who believes in conspiracies or cover-ups, but I think you're being watched!"

She was more than beautiful; she was observant. She was more than observant; she was smart. She was more than smart; she was *right*. In all her observations, she had overlooked one thing: it was only after the officer had her name that he touched the cart. Oryan was sure that man's hands were not empty. He eyed the cart suspiciously. The officer had been looking for her specifically, and now they were probably listening. He had to change the subject and fast.

His outward expression had not changed during the conversation. He knew now his folly. They were both in danger, she especially, and he had to change the course of the conversation now without alarming her or there was a chance they were both dead. He leaned closer to her so that she could feel his breath across her lips. Her body shuddered. "If that is the case, if I'm being watched, then so are you," he spoke, barely audible. He locked her gaze. "Maybe you know too much already and you're in danger. Maybe you need a cover story, something to explain the night away."

"I don't believe in conspiracies, remember?" she said softly, moving her lips closer to his.

"What a coincidence. Neither do I." She could feel his lips now brushing past hers as he spoke. "If someone *is* listening, maybe we should give them something to listen to." He was trying to distract *her*, but the touch of her lips against his, no matter how brief, made it impossible for him to pretend he was doing anything other than what his heart had been screaming for from the moment he saw her.

"I have never done anything like this before," she said, tilting her head slightly to receive her reward.

"What a coincidence. Me neither," he said and forced his lips against hers. It was intense passion, both from the anticipation of the night and the years of longing for each other. She was living out her greatest fantasy. Her hands searched frantically over his body as if she did not want to miss the opportunity to touch every inch.

He gave his body to the heat of the moment, but his senses were still focused on his surroundings. Deep in his soul, he felt cheated by fate. He ached for this very thing since she appeared on his doorstep, and now he had her, and all he could feel was the lingering sense of danger surrounding this whole evening. She was like silk to touch, and her body heat was intense. His skin noticed only her, but he could not give himself completely to her.

The situation progressed quickly, but something held him back from undressing her completely or letting her do the same to him. There was something else happening. Now, the anxiety he had a moment ago intensified to overwhelm his desire for her. His time with her and this moment of forgetting his past, his future, his bondage, and his grief was almost nonexistent. He longed to stay in this present for eternity, but like all pleasures and joys in his life, it was about to be taken from him.

The double doors slammed open and footsteps filled the hall. Oryan was off of her in an instant and ready to protect her from any danger. She scrambled for the sheets to cover herself. She was terrified and felt more naked than she actually was.

"The girl knows too much," said a gruff voice from the hall. "She doesn't leave."

The first thing to round the hallway corner was a rifle barrel. Then the hand that gripped it, then the arm attached to the hand. It came on quickly, eager to squeeze the trigger and finish the business it came for. Oryan grabbed the wrist, jerked the arm forward, and with a hard upward blow of his elbow, he snapped the assailants arm in two. There was a scream, and the intruder fell forward, Oryan still gripping the arm. He yanked the broken appendage behind the man's back and with another vicious blow from his palm dislocated his shoulder with a sickening pop of joint and muscle. His victim fell to the ground in a heap of agonizing screams.

The short hallway was filled with at least three other armed men. The man closest to Oryan gripped a rifle which Oryan grabbed just behind the barrel. The man tightened his fingers on the grip, which was what Oryan was anticipating. He twisted the rifle muzzle down hard, and the desired effect was achieved. The man's trigger finger twisted with the weapon and cracked in two. Another quick yank outward, and his grip was lost altogether.

Oryan brought the rifle into firing position and put two shots into the faces of the other two attackers before they realized they were in danger. The silencer made whispers of the gun shots as two bodies fell dead.

The man who was nursing his finger on the floor looked up at him in fear. Oryan lowered the barrel so that it was in line with the man's eyesight. They had all been wearing black helmets with black visors to disguise their identity. Oryan used the rifle to raise this one's visor. His eyes were red, and his face was streaked with tears, but aside from his labored breathing, he did not make a sound.

"Unless you want my face to be the last one you ever see, you will tell me who sent you," Oryan said grimly.

Celeste now sat on the bed. She was quickly buttoning her blouse, trying to make herself feel less vulnerable. She had seen Oryan disable the first man, heard the struggle and what she thought were gunshots in the hallway but was unsure of the outcome until she heard his voice. There was comfort in that for her. She was not disgusted by the violence; rather, a new passion grew for him as she now saw him as her guardian and her white knight. Though she was still in shock, she was not afraid. He would protect her.

"I will not ask again; who sent you?" she heard him say again.

Then she heard a new voice, one that belonged to no man in a helmet. "I did."

Oryan drew the rifle to his shoulder, glaring down its length toward the open doors. The man on the floor sighed deeply, thinking he had been more fortunate than the two corpses behind him.

"I am unarmed," said the voice from outside. "I was sent to collect you. Please lower your weapon." A figure stepped into the doorway wearing an officer's uniform. It was not as flashy or as decorative as the one that hung in the closet behind them. This was a plain field dress, black with no rank insignia, but still very polished and professional. His name was engraved on a small black name badge on the man's chest, but Oryan was too far away to make it out at this point. He held one hand behind his back, his elbow jutting sharply to his side. The other arm hung loosely, the fingers making a loose fist. He stepped over the fallen soldiers casually and advanced toward Oryan.

Oryan flipped the rifle backwards and swung the butt into the side of the kneeling man's head. He slumped to the floor in front of the others. Not dead, but he did not envy that man's next few days. Oryan snapped the rifle back to his shoulder and drew the bead so as to shoot to kill this new comer should the occasion arise.

"Such a hasty response to a very non-threatening situation, my boy. These two will never make it home, and the other two will never see active field duty again," said the man.

"Maybe I did them a favor," remarked Oryan.

"Come now, service is not all that bad. You don't even know me."

"I know you're a liar," said Oryan, glancing at the man's sidearm.

"Young man, in the past two minutes, you have fired your weapon more times than I have in ten years. Were I to try something foolish, I would be another corpse before my weapon cleared the holster. I assure you, I am as unarmed as that woman, and her beauty is most definitely more dangerous than I."

Though he did not lower his weapon, Oryan knew he was telling the truth. This man was a messenger only; judging by the small gut that protruded slightly from the front of his uniform, he had been just a messenger for some time.

The man moved past Oryan so he could finally read the name badge. Stanton. He was a perfect messenger. He was a run-of-the-mill individual. No defining marks or outstanding features. Once his job was over, a man would forget him immediately.

Stanton made his way to the side of the bed where Celeste still sat. He looked at her curiously. "She is a beautiful one, Mr. Mason, and you didn't even have to pay for her. Some men get all the luck."

"She has nothing to do with any of this. She can walk away from here, and even if she told the truth, no one would believe her," said Oryan.

"I have no doubt, but still, she has seen too much, and judging by your *conversation*, she can probably discern the details from there. She is a liability we cannot afford," said Stanton, looking at her complacently.

"I won't let you hurt her. You die first." Oryan fixed his finger on the trigger. "If she is to be harmed, I'll know and all gentleman's agreements are over."

Stanton looked long at him before cracking a smirk of a smile. "My boy, I should wish no such thing. I made my attempt, which you successfully thwarted, and so now her life or death is your burden. I would have just as soon seen her dead and make the decision an easy one, but you saw things differently. So be it. Be aware that attachment is as dangerous as any man or weapon. Never forget that.

"She will leave here with you; the two of you will leave quite separately from me or any other military figures. She raises the right kind of gossip. I would only create rumors that could not be crushed, and besides, your image needs to be maintained as the man's man. Such a jewel at your side will be the perfect ornament to solidify that fame."

Celeste stared at Oryan. Part of her wanted to bolt to the door, her life forfeit. A larger part wanted to pack right now. She wanted to leave everything behind and never be seen or heard from again except by his side. Her emotions for him had come so far that night, and she was sure his had blossomed for her.

Oryan looked back. He saw through her. "You can leave now if you wish. No harm will come to you," he said, looking back at Stanton as if to say, *No tricks.*

Celeste shook her head. "I will stay with you, if you'll let me."

Oryan's heart pounded at her response. He was hoping she would say that, but he also dreaded it. He had chosen his life, whatever it was, but she had not, and he knew she had no idea what she was asking for. He lowered his weapon.

"Ah, very good, it's settled then!" said Stanton. "I will have a few men come by soon to clean up the mess. We will be moving the two of you into the identical suite across the hall for the night. This blood will stain the carpet, so our containment crew will have to replace it," he said, pointing to the dead and mangled soldiers. "This way you two can finish your evening together without their presence. Sorry for interrupting earlier, my boy. You were doing so well. I only hope you can pick up where you left off.

"Tomorrow morning the two of you will leave this building at exactly zero eight hundred. There will be a red unmarked luxury shuttle waiting for you out front. There will be clothing provided for the both of you in the new suite. I took the liberty of scanning you when I placed the device on your tray, my dear. The clothes will be accommodating. You will be taken from here to a secure location known only to a few most directly involved. At that time, the lovely princess here will be assassinated. Better make the most of tonight."

Oryan drew the rifle to the ready again.

"Sarcasm is lost on you, my boy," said Stanton with a smile. "There is far too much killing in your heart. I told you, she will not be harmed. After all, a man who lives and fights for nothing is of far less use than the man who stands to lose.

"Thank you for the entertainment. I enjoyed it immensely. We will never meet again, but I wish the both of you the best no matter what happens." He turned to leave as the containment crew arrived. "And, Oryan! Don't forget your uniform. You'll need it before long!"

Oryan watched him leave and then looked at Celeste. She did

not look scared, but he could see her breathing heavily. She stood from the bed and stepped next to him, wrapping both her arms around him and pulling her body close. Her blouse was still only loosely fastened together, and the feel of her warm flesh once again put him at ease.

A member of the containment crew came to them and politely showed them to their new suite. He gave them a new key card in exchange for Oryan's old one. They walked in and turned to watch the man bow, wave with a smile, and walk backwards. He repeated the motion. It was clear that he was trying to be courteous, but there was an obvious language barrier. As the doors slid shut, Celeste disappeared into the room while Oryan stood at the door.

He was listening for any sign of danger outside. His usual internal alarms were silent, and he felt that the rest of the night would be just as Stanton had promised, quiet and uninterrupted. Still, he stood behind the closed doors for almost an hour listening and waiting. Had Celeste not intervened, he might have stayed there all night.

She came up quietly and slipped her arms underneath his and rubbed his chest with her hands. Her face was pressed against his back, and though she made no noise, he could feel her sobs. She was recovering, but the last few tears had not abated yet. He wondered if she had been crying the whole time. He guessed that was the truth as he was sure that no one could escape that without some emotional trauma. Even he, though becoming accustomed to ending life, lost a little of himself each time he did it.

He gripped her hand in his. *I'm sorry.* His soul spoke to hers without words. She understood and held him tighter. She was still so perfect. In a world of death and fighting, she brought him life and peace. He would certainly try to talk her out of leaving with him in the morning, but for now, they both needed each other.

He turned in her arms to face her and bent down to kiss her. As they did, he picked her up off her feet and carried her to the bed. On one point, Oryan would follow Stanton's advice. He would finish what he had started.

That night they would both forget. Celeste would forget the atrocities she had just witnessed. She would forget her mundane life and the rut she had fallen into and could never see out of. She would lose herself in him, and she knew now that she would never be able to live the same life she had been leading. The air would be sweeter, the world more beautiful, and life more glorious. This night would last forever. It would sustain her for an eternity no matter what else might come.

Oryan would forget all about death, forget about the arena, his fame, his slavery, and all that made his life unbearable. Of all the stars he had gazed upon seeking comfort, she was the brightest and the most glorious to behold. He knew that he would never be closer to those brilliant lights in the heavens as he was that night, no matter how many millions chanted his name. She was his angel sent from some higher power to show him that redemption was possible.

That night, they both forgot. Sadly, as with a million nights before and millions to follow, every night has its dawn.

REMEMBER

Armay was not yet a slave. He was a general in the kingdom of Gondolin. He had watched his king kneel at the feet of Emperor Navaro and saw the colors of the world's greatest evil fly above his home in homage to their superiority. *He* refused to slip quietly into the pages of history, just another stooge for the empire. If there was no one else, *he* would see justice to the end, or he would perish in the attempt.

There had been an audience with his closest friend the king. He was told the decision to submit rather than fight would save innocent lives. He was begged not to retaliate or try to form any rebellion for the sake of his beautiful Kathrine and for the sake of every living inhabitant of Gondolin. The king's words fell on deaf ears. Armay knew already what he must do. In the face of these impossible odds, he would fight back. He listened in silence, but he was already planning his strategy.

He sent a coded communication to his bravest captains and those who loved country and freedom more than life. The response was positive from all who he contacted, as he knew it would be. This group of patriots, of noble men and women, would lead the most successful and massive rebellion against the empire. They were the first to threaten the might of Navaro and to rally many others to their cause. The fatal hubris of the operation was, as it always is, human.

After almost three years of success and victory, thousands had joined the cause, infiltrating the infrastructure of Navarus and nearly crippling its military might. Their ranks were invisible and their strategy was perfect. The empire had only months before its final defeat. There were constant untraceable leaks of information, armies stranded with no supplies on missions never authorized, generals and commanders killed in their sleep by the most brilliant assassins, and the empire was powerless to stop it.

One man changed the face of the war. His betrayal led to the most sweeping and violent internal manhunt ever organized. He gave General Kovac and the empire names of undercover operatives, he fed them constant information about troop movements and secret plans, and he used his growing status in both the empire and Armay's rebellion to dispatch many of the high-ranking officers that served freedom. Those who were arrested were subjected to experimental interrogation and torture until they revealed their comrades. If the torture did not kill them, they were executed when they finally gave up their secrets.

Armay discovered the identity of the empire's informant. His anguish at this betrayal was matched only by his rage. He told no one when he unraveled the mystery, vowing to take care of this dark business personally. But, this man was clever and had many ears in his service. He was warned of the oncoming wrath, and so he deserted, hiding under the protection of the empire.

Armay, seeing that his numbers were too few and too scattered, knew that his glory was about to be extinguished. He made preparations and rallied what soldiers he could to his cause. Once assembled, his army numbered just shy of three thousand. He sent a hand written correspondence to General Kovac, challenging him to open combat for the first time since the rebellion began. Lucius Kovac sent the tongue, eyes, and ears of the messenger back to Armay in response.

Kovac met Armay on the battlefield with an army of half a million soldiers. The battle tanks rolled and the fighters screamed, but neither was capable of damaging Armay's forces. Nearly one hundred tanks found their way to the bottom of the river that Armay's men had channeled into the field, and the air force was demolished by the anti-aircraft weaponry that the rebellion had developed. When metal and machine failed, Kovac turned at last to brute force and superior numbers.

Kovac's hordes swarmed the fields, threatening to devour Armay's dismal force, but Armay had trained them well. Each of his three thousand was highly trained, and in the first day of combat, no troop of the rebellion lost their life. On the second, thousands more of Kovac's men fell, with only hundreds being lost for Armay. In his wrath, Kovac commanded all his remaining forces to swarm Armay at first light on the third day. The battle wore on for hours before Kovac sent what fighters he had left into the air. With no discerning friend from foe, they raked the ground with rockets and gunfire. By Kovac's command, death for his troops and his enemies was certain. Armay's men, fighting the enemy on the ground, were defenseless to stop it.

All but a handful of Armay's valiant troops were slaughtered. In return, nearly half of Kovac's force had been obliterated either by the swift and hard stroke of Armay or by his own air force. To Kovac, the ends always justified the means. The rebellion was crushed, its leader fled, and the remaining sheep would scatter without the shepherd. Kovac was pleased, but his conquest was not complete.

Armay ran long and fast from the field. His war was over, but he had made them pay dearly for it. Still, the anguish of the sacrifice made by his soldiers, his family, and his friends wounded him deeply. He knew that Kovac was coming for him, and so he had only one choice. He fled not out of cowardice, nor in an attempt to save his own life, but to see one more time what he loved more than life, more than country, and more than his own soul. He ran to save his Kathrine.

When he found her, they wept together for all that was lost. They held each other close, their souls finding a small measure of solace. Long they embraced, feeling their hearts beat as one. If this was to be his last night in mortal life, he wanted nothing more than this.

"Armay," Kathrine began. "Armay, I have loved you from childhood, and I have stood by you in all things. In return, you have given me life and hope and love. You are a man of honor and of valor. You are the bravest man I have ever known, and you deserve a hero's death, but I must ask something of you that will wound you more deeply than any injury in battle."

Armay looked upon his wife. He always knew that she deserved better than a soldier. She was a queen without crown or title; she was a goddess without a throne. He thought he had seen every emotion in her eyes that any human could give. The last few years had held every thrill and disappointment that life could offer in its noble cruelty, but as her eyes met his, he saw something different. He saw in her eyes the look he longed to see but had feared for a lifetime. In her eyes was the tender gaze of a mother.

"I know what you intend to do. I know that you plan to fight Kovac and die with all the venerable honor you deserve. I know that you have come here to say good-bye to me and make the sacrifice that so many of your men have made before you, but I beg you now, as your wife and as your lover, not to make so rash a decision, glorious though it might be."

"You know me well, beloved. You know that your plea to me as wife and lover will not sway my determination, but I know there is something else in your request that you have not spoken aloud. I know what your silence has revealed, but I want to hear you say it before I abandon my campaign."

Their voices had been no more than whispers, but now a long silence fell.

"I'm not asking you as your wife or your lover, but as a mother, to reconsider your decision. I beg you as the mother of *your* son to turn now from the path you have chosen." Tears welled in her blue eyes, and her voice strained to deliver her next message. Her eloquence and reason had failed when it never had before. She lost her noble reserve and fell to her knees. "I don't want this without you. This is all for nothing without you. Our son deserves his father. Please! Please, don't go."

His heart was broken for her. Moments ago, his vision of an honorable and valiant death had seemed so rational and logical. Now, the idea filled him with heartache that he had never known. If he could only live to hold his son, that was all that mattered. To see his child grow strong. To teach him all the things he could teach to no one else. That was all that mattered.

"My love," he raised her to her feet. "You are all that is best in me. I have always loved you, not just for who you are but for who I am when I am with you. I must do a thing now, and it may take my life, but if not, I will come for you and our child. We cannot run for we will be found. I must do a thing that could save us all. I don't know the outcome, but we will be together. Remember me not as I am now and not for the actions that are surely to come. Remember me for all that I once was."

With that, he left her. She watched him walk away, certain she would never see him again. He trailed off into the distance, his figure growing small before she cried out his name. She raced to him, throwing her arms around his neck and kissing him deeply. She reached from behind her neck and removed the necklace that hung there. It was a single line of silver bearing a medallion of their family crest clasped by a blue crystal. It was what he had given her for their wedding. It was something she had never removed since the wedding day.

"Remember me," she said to him, trembling and placing the medallion around his neck.

He held her hands for a moment and then turned once again to confront his unknown future. She remained there until dawn, despair clutching her heart. But, as it often does, with the rising sun came rising hope.

Armay traveled far into the heart of the empire. He endured every hardship known to man with Kovac at his heels. When finally he reached his destination, he was a shell of the man he once was. Nevertheless, he climbed the stairs of the emperor's palace and threw himself at his feet.

The emperor, mistaking him for a beggar, allowed him entrance. When his identity was revealed, the emperor's guards closed in around him, but he was not dead yet. He disarmed the man closest first, taking his weapon, and killed two more before they subdued him. As Navarro was about to pronounce his death sentence, a voice rang from the door.

"I have hunted this man from one corner of the empire to the other, and I find him here now at your very steps, Emperor," announced Kovac. He moved across the room to face Armay. He kneeled in front of him, seeing his adversary face-to-face for the first time. "Death is what you have earned here, my friend, but death is far too easy for a man like you. I have revenge to take upon you, and so I shall." Uncharacteristically, a maniacal grin crossed Kovac's lips. "You will find no death here."

The emperor knew not to question Kovac in matters of death and judgment. Armay begged for the life of his wife and unborn child, swearing anything to see them live. Navaro demanded the names of all his remaining operatives and made him announce their capture publically. Those who were brought to trial were found guilty, and it was Armay who was made to carry out their sentences.

Kovac sent him to the Slave Quarter, and it was demanded that he surrender all that he own. When the guards tried to take the medallion from his neck, two more names were added to the list of the empire's men to fall at his hand. Kovac intervened again, and it was agreed that he should keep this token in exchange for the only collateral he had. In a dark room away from the Quarter, they took his eye instead.

He labored hard under his cruel taskmasters, whose sole purpose in life was to break him, for months until he was finally reunited with his beloved Katherine and his small son. His joy at seeing her outweighed his guilt for all his sins. Such joy was not made to last as she lived under the yoke of bondage only a short while. When she died, he shed no tears. His son, his Oryan, was all he lived for now. In him was the shining promise of a brighter tomorrow.

As they kneeled at her body before the guards took her away, he turned to Oryan, only four years old, and placed around his neck a medallion on a tarnished silver necklace.

"Remember her," was all he said.

Oryan and Celeste had only spent one night together, a single solitary night.

Perhaps it was the circumstance that made this night what it was. Oryan and Celeste had both led strong lives, but empty ones. Their joys were full of punctures that turned onto gaping caverns of loneliness and pain when the joys of the moment faded into silence, but here, now, they made each other whole. Though the time they had together was a blink of an eye, it set the course for lifetimes to come. That night changed the world.

It may have been Celeste finally seeing her dreams become reality. She had never been given anything. Her whole life had been a struggle to make ends meet. Her parents cared for nothing but themselves. They did not, she was convinced, even love each other.

When she was old enough, she had left them and tried to make it on her own. Her looks had taken her to a certain point, but she was not one to use her body to get ahead. If she was to succeed, she wanted it to be real and not some superficial reality manufactured by a pretty face.

She had seen Oryan in the arena first when he was in the amateurs. Her then boyfriend had just received his first sponsor to fight in the circuit. His first match was against a rising young star that just happened to become the love and focus of her life. When she saw Oryan's face throughout the arena, she thought he was the most beautiful man she had ever seen. The other girls gossiped around her, giggling like school girls about what they would do to him should they find themselves alone with him, but she wanted so much more.

She began to follow his career. She watched him every chance she could. The rumors flew that he was a typical celebrity. She heard every attack on his character that anyone could manufacture. When she finally saw him after a tournament, she knew that all she had heard was false. He signed autographs for the children with a smile and a joke. He thanked his fans for elevating him so, and when the crowds left, she observed. He sat alone, staring up at the sky. She had often wondered in those long hours by himself what it was he was pondering.

Now she knew. That night, she had seen into his soul. They had confided in one another. She had told him things that she had never revealed to anyone before, and she was sure that the things that he told her were truths that could never be repeated. She learned of his father and of his heartache at the news of his death. They talked for hours as if they were the only people in the world. Their souls had been laid bare. When she looked at him, she could see how pure he was. She could see that she may never meet a better man were she to travel the world for eternity. In this time of utter truth and perfect trust, her affection grew from a simple crush to deep and abiding love.

Oryan stood on the balcony with her behind him. She had her arms wrapped around his chest so tightly he could feel her every heartbeat. Though she held close to him, her touch was still gentle, soft, and warm. At this moment, he loved her. He loved her with a perfect love. She was everything he needed now and everything he could have hoped for. She was everything he could ever ask for.

The cool night air kissed the sweat on his neck and chest. She made him feel so alive he could feel the blood course through her fingertips and throb in her palms. His senses were awake, but not because of danger. This was so different. It was so much better. His hands were flush and warm. His heart was calm, yet it pounded deep and hard for her. He felt everything around him amplified a thousand times. Each sensation was sweeter, each breath was richer, and then there were the stars. They were radiant like he had never seen them before. They shone in the night sky with far more luster and far more brilliance than ever before, but none were as bright as she.

He gazed upon those stars wondering how long they had been waiting there for him, waiting for her, waiting for them. Those stars were placed in their precise orbits long before they so shone. So, too, were they placed in their human orbits to shine and to dance together at this instant in time. The heavens became witness to the covenant made to each other. They were one, and if this was the only night they would ever share, they were one for all time.

He was suddenly grateful for everything that had happened to him in the course of his life. The remorse and self-pity he had languished in the day before at being dealt such a cruel hand by fate was all but gone. He was thankful for the victories, the sorrow, the heartache, and every second of his existence that had led him to this point. Were he to have changed even a single thing, he may not be with her.

He turned to her and held her close in his arms. He looked into her eyes, soaking in all that was there to be had. No words were spoken. None needed to be. The rhythm of their bodies together was all they needed.

Later as they lie together in the bed, Oryan finally spoke the first words that had been said in hours. "I am a slave. I was bought yesterday by the Imperial Army, and in a few hours, I will be plunged into a world in which I may never see you again in this life. I meant to tell you sooner, but..." his words trailed off, "I didn't know how."

She lay by his side, taking in his warmth. The news was hard, but she knew that it was coming long ago. When she first saw a glimmer of hope that his affection could indeed be a reality, she knew it would be fleeting. Whatever happened to them after this night, she was his forever.

"I have a confession too," she said quietly. "My name isn't really Celeste."

He looked at her confused only to see her innocent smile. "It's *Elesya* Celeste, but no one ever calls me Elesya."

He knew then that his past meant nothing to her. She knew who he was and who he had it in him to become. Nothing else mattered.

Her fingers gently danced over his chest and traced the scar that lined its center. "Who hurt you?" she asked.

Oryan struggled for an answer. He had not been asked that question for such a long time, and now, with her, he could barely remember. It seemed like those events had happened to someone else. "I was very young, and so were they," was all he said. He knew that she was already aware of what he was capable of, but it seemed so trivial a thing to tell her just how long he had been a savage. She was so innocent. He felt for a moment as if he had robbed her of that innocence, and he was painfully aware of his naked skin against her soft flesh. His unease grew, and he was ready to climb out from the bed to cover himself and his shame.

Then she moved. She leaned over him as if sensing what he was about to do and what he was feeling. Her fingers traced the scar again. He winced, not out of pain, but out of a reminder of who he was and that she deserved so much more.

"Whoever you were, whatever is to become of you, I don't know, and it doesn't matter. I *know* you, Oryan. Your fans may see you as their champion; your enemies may see you in their darkest dreams, but I know you. I've seen past it all tonight. This is you, and this is what I love. You may hold the weight of the world on your shoulders, but it's a burden you don't have to bear." Her words pierced him and echoed though his thoughts.

"I can't bear the world's. My own are condemning enough," he said, looking away from her. He did not feel pity for himself, but he knew always he had to hold himself accountable for his own actions. No one else would.

"Look at me," she said softly. His defenses melted, and he met her gaze. She ran her fingers across his cheek to his lips. "You don't have to bear them alone. Let them go. Wherever you go, I will be with you."

He could not find the words. Even as she spoke, he felt his heart become light. His anger and guilt vanished, and all that existed in his world was her. He kissed her deeply, lost in every second that passed. Through the night, he had only known her warmth. Now, as his universe came into perfect harmony, he felt the heat of the sun across his face.

Morning had come.

They had said their good-byes in the suite. No tears were shed. There were no attempts to run or pleas to stay with one another. They had dressed each other, and both looked elegant. Though they had no sleep, they had all the rest they could ever need. When they finally made it down the elevator and into the lobby to leave the hotel, they were greeted by the reality they were both eager to have left behind.

The press swarmed with questions and pictures. Hand in hand, they made their way through the crowd to the steps outside. The faces of the public swarmed to and fro in front of them, but they caught glimpses of the red shuttle that was parked just a few paces ahead, engine still running. A man dressed in black waited by the back door for them to come nearer to the vehicle.

When the door shut behind them, the world became quiet again. The voices outside had not stopped, but the deafening chaos had been muffled into a dull roar. They sat close, still not speaking, knowing that time was all too short.

The shuttle was designed for leisure and privacy. There was dark glass that separated them from their nosy escorts. There were long benches, trays filled with food, and drinks on ice. Neither of them had a disposition for such pleasantries.

In the corner was the military dress uniform that he had left in his original suite. A small note clung to the hangar.

I told you not to forget!
-Stanton

As the shuttle pulled away from the sidewalk, Oryan and Celeste relaxed a little. The magic of their night together was still upon them, though the crowd had diluted it briefly. Oryan left her side, undressed, and did his best to put on the attire he had been given. Celeste did her best to help, and when they had finished, she could see that Oryan actually belonged in such garments. Now, with the weight of his fate crushing upon him, Oryan knew there were words that had to be said. He found the control for the volume to the music playing softly in the background and turned it up to maximum.

"Celeste," he whispered in her ear so that only she could hear. "When this door opens, I will never see you again. I can't change it, nor would I want to. You must listen now, as this may be the last words I ever get to say to you. I will never love another no matter what happens. You gave me peace in a lifetime of chaos. I will always love you."

He looked upon her and her upon him. Tears ran down her cheeks, but he held his own back. He could not afford the appearance of weakness now. He could not let anyone else know how much she meant as his choices from henceforth no longer affected just him. She had to be protected. His defenses were building fast, and the doors he had opened to her were slamming shut. He must be ready, and no matter how much it hurt her, he must be strong.

"You will see and hear things about me. Don't heed them! No matter how harsh or brutal it may seem, remember me! Remember *us*! Remember this." He slipped the necklace off his neck and fastened it around hers. "This is a treasure beyond worth."

With that, he sat back in his seat, separating himself from her. She wept, but her sobs were silent. The journey from there was long and hard. Though the music and talk of the broadcasts boomed and cracked, there was nothing but a cold silence for either of them. She recovered her composure as Oryan hardened himself beyond what he thought was capable. He knew now that he could dismiss her to anyone and they would be none the wiser. That was what he needed.

When at last the shuttle stopped moving, he did not look back on her. He said nothing when the door was opened for him, and he left with a façade of complete ease. He was greeted by several other men dressed as he was. They saluted him and then walked him into the doors closest to them. She last saw the driver drop the small black bag that the empire had given him for his personal effects just inside the door, and then he turned back to the shuttle. He shut the door, enveloping her world once again with blackness and silence.

As they sped away, she tried to see some markings or identification on the building where they left him, but there were none. It was a gray military structure, exactly like a thousand more across the empire. She sat alone, already realizing how much she missed him. If they took her life, it made no difference. She had lived a lifetime in just a few hours with him. He had made her whole. She rubbed the medallion between her thumb and forefinger. She sank into the seat, feeling utterly exhausted. As sleep took her, only one thought lingered.

Remember you? I will never forget, my love!

The Rise of the Kentaurus Knights

"There are a few small details that we must work out before we can officially announce your status as enlisted," said Colonel Alexander. "First and foremost, we must erase your identity and give you a new one. We can't hide your celebrity status, but we do need to conceal your history as a slave."

He pulled open a cabinet and removed a thick file folder with the words *Top Secret* stamped on the front in dull red ink. The colonel, Lieutenant Phaff, and General Trebus, the officers that had greeted him at the gates, had mentioned this file more than once during the past hour of introduction. Only now did he actually see it. It seemed to be filled to capacity with many different sizes of paper.

He had listened intently to all conversation whether it concerned him or not. He had answered each question carefully giving them guarded answers that were just enough to keep them from digging any deeper. He showed no emotion, no fear, and above all, no weakness. These men were trained to ask the right questions and to study the right body signs. Oryan would not be trapped by them. It was a verbal game of chess, and he had kept them at a stalemate. That was no easy task.

"Your part of this is surprisingly simple. Study the documents we give you regarding your new past. It includes parents' names, place of birth, and the life you never had. You can fabricate any details and memories you would like, only you can never mention the truth. You can never hint near the truth, never confide in anyone, nothing. If you do so, you will be in breach of contract and we will carry out the full extent of your listed disciplinary action." The general's features were almost bored pronouncing these harsh terms. Oryan was impressed. He wondered how many years this man had spent in interrogation rooms.

"And what is the full extent of my disciplinary action, if I may ask?"

"You will be executed. As well as anyone you care about."

That's a short list. "So what do I have to do in exchange for such … generosity?" asked Oryan.

General Trebus shot the colonel a doubtful glance. "You will be given a field commission as a captain. Here at this camp you will train a force of five hundred soldiers to be an elite Special Forces unit. You have six months to do so. If you cannot accomplish this, you will be demoted to the ranks of infantry and sent to the front line where you will most likely never come back."

You don't know me very well. "No formal military training, no experience commanding troops in a combat situation, and commanding men who have worked far longer than I for the rank. Grabbing at straws, are we?" asked Oryan, trying to get a rise from someone in the room.

"This entire conversation is classified and off the record. When we leave here, this never happened, so I am free to speak my mind. You're no soldier. You're a cocky, arrogant son of a half-blind slave, and you will fail. The only reason I am even humoring this insanity is because I am a simple soldier and I have to follow orders too. I look forward to the day when I can spit on your unmarked grave." There was contempt in his voice but not on his face.

This was what he wanted. It was always better to be expected to fail. The general was right about one thing: he was a simple soldier. He just laid all his cards on the table at once. He admitted that he did not run things here. He also revealed that he had no desire to help. He would rather see Oryan fail. Oryan wondered if he would change his mind when he saw what he was capable of.

"If a conversation never happens, how can it be classified?" This question was another diversionary tactic. There was a silence and three scowls to show their disapproval. "I suspect that I report to you, then?"

"No. You are free of the chain of command save one. General Kovac's Captain, the commander of the Legion, oversees these facilities. If there are any requests or reports, they go through him. In twelve years in his service, I have never seen the Captain fill any request or file any reports. He cares less about you than I do."

This was a pointless conversation. No one in this room had any clue what was to be done, and they did not care. He would get nothing from them as they gave little and knew less. It was time to move on. Six months was short. "If we're all done here, I would like to see my men."

The officers looked at each other, asking silently if there was anything else. Alexander pulled a black nametag from the folder along with some rank insignias that were to go on the shoulder loops of the uniform. Phaff fastened the insignias, put the proper pins in their proper places, and fastened the name tag above the right breast. Oryan studied it curiously.

"Jeckstadt? Oryan Jeckstadt?"

"It's your family name," shrugged Alexander. "You are to tell anyone who asks that *Mason* was simply a stage name you used to keep your family history out of the public light. The Jeckstadt's are dead. In all reality, they didn't exist until we created them. They are only on paper and with enough eye-witnesses and false reports to make them a reality to anyone who goes looking. The name means 'hero killer.' After Agrion, we found it fitting. Don't forget it, Captain Jeckstadt."

Oryan stood and was saluted by the other officers. He returned the salute sharply, taking the others off guard. They were unaware that he could look the part so well. Phaff opened the door opposite where he had come in. He could see a covered walkway that stretched for almost a hundred yards. At the other end was a large building, three stories tall.

"The barracks are at the other end of the walkway. Once you're inside, make your first right, down the hall, big room at the end. Your personal effects are waiting for you there," said Phaff.

"They always are," commented Oryan.

He headed out into the open air. It had become a cloudy day. The air was heavy, a sure promise of rain. He noticed the strength of the wind and knew that it was more than just a sprinkle heading his way.

"We've arranged a meeting in the courtyard on the other side of the barracks with your troops in one hour. I will do the introductions. Do not be late!" called Trebus from the doorway.

Oryan turned and half faced the three men. "Tell them to come ready to fight. This son of a half-blind slave wants to show you what men are capable of, sir." With that, he turned and headed to his quarters.

Once Oryan was out of hearing range, the officers began to talk amongst themselves. "Do you think Kovac is right about this one?" asked Alexander.

"Doesn't matter what I think," responded Trebus. "I never question orders."

"Just a simple soldier, eh? You're more self-deluded than that kid out there," the colonel quipped.

"I never question orders. I carry out my duties to the best of my abilities. There are just some orders that should have never been given," said Trebus, sitting in his seat behind the desk.

"That *kid* will prove you wrong in every way, General," said Phaff from the corner of the room.

"So you can speak? What makes you say that?" asked Trebus, turning to face Phaff.

"You didn't get the order from Kovac. I did. There was something in his voice I've never heard before," said Phaff, remembering his conversation with the General.

"We all know you have had *so* much personal correspondence with his lordship that you know his tones," began Alexander incredulously. "Give me a break!"

Phaff was unmoved by the sarcasm. "You were also not here when the Captain showed up. Ask anyone; he did not like giving up this place, and he was more than a little *off balance*, you might say. I have been around *him* enough to know his moods, though I wish I couldn't say that. Every mention of this new commander made him jittery. He was as close to scared as I have ever seen him."

The other two looked at him silently. He had been at this station far longer than they had, and he had the most direct contact with the Captain when it arrived on base. Phaff was one of the few that might be able to vouch that *it* was, in fact, a *he*. He could not be sure, though.

"I hope you're right, son," snorted Trebus. "If not, there are five hundred boys out there with targets on their backs."

Oryan had made his way to his new quarters and found them very accommodating. There was a desk and chair in the main room. A small door in the corner opened into his bedroom. It was simple with a bed and a closet, which was full of battle dress uniforms, shoes, socks, a second less flashy dress uniform, ties, undershirts, any clothing a soldier could ever need. It was fitted to him, of course, so he grabbed the closets battle uniform and disappeared into the bathroom.

He found the bathroom clean to a shine and stocked with all the toiletries he would need for the next six months. It was apparent they intended to neglect him and leave him to his dealings as much as possible.

As he changed into his uniform, he could hear the rain begin to drum on his windows. The rain was dramatic, and it was the perfect mood to begin his relationship with his men. Oryan remembered how his father trained him and the stories he told about bringing his men "up to speed." The men would hate him at first, but that was the intent. Oryan would make them into the greatest soldiers in the empire. He would rival Kovac's force, and he would do it in six months.

Once he was dressed, he headed to the entrance of the barracks. He had studied the maps on his walls, and he knew which path he was going to take. There was only fifteen minutes left in the hour he had been given by Trebus before meeting his men. The hallways were empty, and the thud of his boots echoed loudly against the tile floors and the concrete walls.

His thoughts strayed for the first time since their parting to Celeste. He hoped she was all right. He hoped that he had not been double crossed and she was indeed alive as Stanton had promised. If he ever found out otherwise, his rage would be unstoppable. No force in the world could save Stanton and anyone responsible.

He thought of her soft face and the eyes he had drowned in the night before. As his heart searched for the peace it had known so briefly, his mind sliced reality through, reinforcing the danger that such thoughts could lead to. If she was alive, he had to do all that was necessary to make sure she stayed that way.

His resolution hardened to stone again, and he pushed open the doors to the courtyard. The rain sang all around. It came down in sheets that made the space in front of him look a hazy gray. Trebus stood under a pavilion at the end of the walkway with Phaff and Alexander. They turned to acknowledge him then turned back toward the troops, who stood in the open field below the barracks.

"Your new commander needs no real introduction. Though you do not know him from other units or time in the service, you all know his reputation very well. You have been selected by the Lord General Kovac himself to learn and to fight for this man. You all know him as Oryan Mason, *Alpha* Centauri."

Oryan stepped to the front of the pavilion. No one cheered. The mention of his name usually brought a mad rush of applause, but here he was met only by the heavy drum of rainfall. It was familiar to him. Silence was a thousand times more gratifying than applause.

"Here, you are not what you were born but what you have it in you to become," Oryan began. The men were standing in formation drenched in the rain. "Each man look to the men to your right and to your left. If either man fails in combat, you will die. This cannot be a unit of common men.

"As of now, you are mine. I own you. And as you belong to me, I will have you strong. Soldiers, you will be the best, or you will die. What we will do here will not be supervised by anyone but me, and you will receive neither quarter nor compassion.

"I have a passion for history. Thousands of years ago, there was a small city on the other side of the world called Kentaur. Some historians believe it is just a myth. The only records we have from this small city are about their soldiers. The Kentaurus Knights.

"The record states that they were the deadliest fighting force in the known world. It tells us something of their training regiment, and it describes their gift and talent for warfare. They were smart, cunning, and lethal. One poet boasts that one Kentaurus Knight was equal to one thousand of any other warrior *alive.*

"Since their fall over three thousand years ago, the world has not known such a force. As of today, they will again! Starting right now, the legend comes to life. Men, let's go for a run." He ran through the middle of the formation, soldiers filing in behind him.

He kept a pace that was comfortable for him, but within minutes, he could hear the heavy and labored breathing of five hundred wet and frustrated soldiers at his back. He fell back through the ranks. Any man he saw not giving his all was dealt with. They received a sharp slap or punch to the face that sent them tumbling out of the line. Some he filed behind and kicked their calves or behind their knees. In all, almost half his men were hobbling along the trail after he was done. The other half was properly motivated.

The miles passed by. More men fell out, many threw up, and some passed out. In a clearing some eight miles from the barracks, Oryan stopped his men. He surveyed those who could keep up. They numbered less than one hundred. They were all gasping for breath; some bent over holding their ribs others with hands on their head.

"Front lean and rest," he said. "Move!"

They threw their exhausted bodies to the ground and began to perform ragged push-ups. The ground was soaking, and their hands could not find much grip. If one fell into the mud, he was met with a hard boot to the ribs. If one refused to go down and tried to stay with arms locked, he received a brutal elbow to the spine.

"We push until the rest of the soldiers catch up! We stay together, or we all die! If any one of you is thinking you made a mistake, speak up! It only gets worse," Oryan taunted. He would be the cruelest and hardest man any of them ever would know.

"If anyone decided to use their heads and stop focusing on their own pain, feel free to gather fallen teammates and bring them here. When my head count reaches five hundred, we'll stop!"

Every man in the clearing staggered to their feet and headed back down the path to find those who had not made it. They searched through the driving rain, finding unconscious or wounded men in the mud or in the tall wet grass. Oryan joined them. In the hours that passed, he brought more men back to the clearing than any other soldier. When all five hundred had arrived, he spoke again.

"This will be home tonight. Those with substantial injuries, ask your fellow troops. There are no doctors here. Mend wounds, stitch cuts, set bones, all here. Figure out how to stay dry, and we will begin again in three hours' time. Gentlemen, welcome to my world."

For three months he drove them. Oryan pushed them to the limits of human endurance, each day setting a new standard of what it meant to be in his army. He starved them, left them sleepless for days, and violent force was his lash. Through it all, there was no exercise he would not join personally no matter how brutal it was. He knew that a commander leads first by example. As they improved, he taught them first individual combat. He taught them every weapon he knew, from the rifle and blade to rocks from the soil. They all became proficient in the art of death.

Then he taught them formations. They learned how to be fast, how to be hard; they learned to be invisible and to maneuver past any force without detection. Oryan showed them how to be weapons on land or in the water. They chose their own leaders, and in time, they were formed into companies and platoons.

At first, they all resented their training and their trainer, but as they reverted to the carnal and primal force that was in each of them, they began to love their torture and their tormentor. There was not a soul among them that did not at one time or another suffer broken bones, from fractured fingers or ribs to heavy breaks requiring bones to be set and flesh to be mended. They were all given time to heal, but not much. Most of them did not ask for it any more, not because they did not need it or because it was not painful, but because they refused to be left behind.

The men showed no fear and no pain. They had one occupation and one purpose in life, and that was to deal and inflict pain and death. The only higher calling was to each other. They fought for the man next to them, knowing that the man next to them was all they had.

Oryan fought beside them in every drill. When it came to physical prowess, he remained unmatched, but his men were beginning to catch up. They would challenge him daily, some trying to outrun him, some taunting him into upper body contests of strength and endurance. None dared to fight him hand to hand.

After three months of breaking them down to their most raw state, the real training began. He wanted them not only to be lethal weapons, but to be students. He wanted them each to have knowledge of battle tactics, weaponry, vehicles, and the history of warfare that extended beyond the practical application. They needed to be able to take a leadership role, if necessary, as well as a soldier's role. He began to set time aside for classroom work, making them study everything from schematics to maps to books. They had to take tests and file reports while at the same time still being pressed physically beyond their imagining.

Kovac had done a marvelous job of picking soldiers. It was clear to Oryan that Kovac wanted him to be a success. Oryan knew that the General was, in the end, a brilliant leader in and of himself and knew what it took to win. He had given Oryan every tool he needed to make his force the best that ever marched. Each soldier that moved with Oryan had the potential to be molded into greatness.

After five months, they were ready for their first real challenge. So, on a clear bright day, he did something unexpected. He gave them a day off. Most, not knowing what to do with themselves, trained on their own, and those who did not motivate themselves to do so were motivated by others.

Days before, he had sent a message to General Kovac via the Net asking him to make a personal appearance to the camp with his Captain. He assured him that it would be well worth the time and effort. After three days of no response, Oryan received a coded message stating that Kovac would be at the camp in two days' time.

When that day came, he left the training field and the dense woods for the first time in five months. He barely remembered what his quarters had looked like. He had slept, ate, and lived beside his men in every condition that nature could inflict. He was filthy, unshaven, and ragged when he marched the six long miles back to the front gates.

It was in this condition that General Kovac and the Captain first saw him since the night in the arena a lifetime ago. He approached them with no apologies and no excuses as to his appearance. He gave a perfect salute and offered his greetings.

"General. My Captain," he started.

"Captain Jeckstadt," said the deep and smooth voice of the General. "The Captain believes we are here to inspect your men, but I have reservations about that theory. Now, judging by your appearance, my surmise was correct. So tell me, why are we here? I do not see just anyone for whatever reason they see fit."

Oryan bowed his head slightly, acknowledging the General's comment. "I have a proposition for you. Actually, sir, more for *him*," Oryan responded, pointing to the Captain. The Captain hissed behind its mask but remained silent. It knew well that its master did the talking.

"It is apparent that my Captain still harbors no love for me. I have asked you both here today to give *him* the opportunity to take a small measure of satisfaction for whatever insult I continue to give that offends him so."

Their interest was high, especially the Captain who wanted nothing more than to beat Oryan at his own game on his own territory. Kovac held his emotionless gaze but wondered what Oryan had to gain in this. He could have ended the debate then, but he wanted to see what his new officer had in mind. The Captain was obviously entertaining the idea, and Kovac loved nothing more than to pit two great soldiers against each other.

"Go on," he said.

"I suggest that the Captain gather one half of his Legion, choose any location he wills, and his one thousand have a combat skirmish with my five hundred. It will be simple game of capture the flag. One team wins when the other team's flag is no longer in their possession or each member of their force is out of service."

"What do you require?" the General asked.

"Transportation to the location and the battle equipment used in arenas for Centauri combat. That's all."

Kovac understood why the both of them had been requested. The Captain would dismiss such an offer if Oryan gave it to it personally. Oryan also knew that should the Captain protest, he could pressure it into combat by shaming and embarrassing it in front of its master. Oryan was still brilliant.

Kovac looked at his Captain. He looked at it with the same gaze that a child might give an old toy that he no longer cared to play with. "What are your feelings on this opportunity, Captain? Are your men up for such a challenge?"

Though his face remained calm, Oryan was smiling. The General was chiding the Captain. He would get his contest.

The Captain stood up straight and faced its master like a scorned dog. Its pain at such an insult was replaced by anger, burning quickly to rage. Though it was just a pawn, it was a deadly one. It was still a deadly tool in the hands of the General, and it could not be taken lightly. Oryan knew that this adversary was a skillful and cunning warrior, but he also knew it was deceptive and preferred late night visits and secret plots to a straight on fight. He had to watch for attacks head on but expect to be stabbed in the back.

"I accept your *challenge*!" it spat its venom. "I will tell you in all fairness, *Captain,* I do not consider you or your men a *challenge.* I look forward to carving that smug grin permanently across your face!" The scarred and partially mutilated face of the Captain contorted with hate.

"I'll look for you on the field. We will see who smiles when this is over," responded Oryan calmly.

Kovac soaked it in. His pet had always had a quick temper. It had always preferred slashing throats to civilized combat. Without his heavy hand over its head to keep the peace, it would have been killed long ago by rash action against a prepared opponent. Still, there was something else behind its words. Kovac knew it would not harm Oryan in an exercise, but it was not idle talk when it breathed its threats. He had to watch it. Perhaps, it had learned more from its master than its master knew.

"Please have the information relayed to me through the sub nets. I only receive coded information in the field.

I thank you for your time and your accommodation of such an audacious request. I must return to tell my men what has transpired here." Oryan bowed low and then excused himself.

He was anxious to get the men prepared, but he did not run or even quicken his pace. The Captain would be watching every move he made. His men had to stay alert at all times. The Captain was overly sure of victory, but that did not mean that it would not take the opportunity to weaken its enemies by some infected food or water. They would live strictly off the land until the contest.

Oryan signaled his commanders and told them to have their troops collect, sterilize, and store water, enough for two weeks immediately. He gave them no reason or explanation, just an assurance that he would explain all when he arrived.

Oryan was glad that the Captain was so transparent. Were its enemies to know how easy it was to taunt, it would not be feared so much. He wondered what it was trying to conceal or what flaw it was trying to make up for by being so impetuous and ill-tempered. One thing was certain: it commanded the most fearsome force in the modern age. Even if his troops were a match, the numbers were all stacked against them. This presented a problem, but like all such trifles laid upon Oryan, he had a solution for this one too.

He began to jog, not to hasten the news, but to keep his mind sharp. He always thought better when he was active. He had at least a forty minute run ahead of him, and he needed a distraction. He needed something to focus on other than the problem at hand so as to bring the problem to its logical conclusion. It was early afternoon, so his stars were nowhere to be seen. So he reached for the distraction that no one else could share. He reached for Celeste.

As his mind brought to light her gentle touch and soft lips, he relaxed. *Father, I have failed you my whole life until now. I have a chance to prove who I am. I have found a higher purpose, and her name is Celeste. Watch over her and bear me no ill will.*

He ran on, letting himself be free again, if only for a moment. By the time he arrived back at the camp, it was out of his system and he could instruct his troops. They would be incurring very deadly wrath with this mock battle. It would make them more targets for internal reprisal than they already were, but he had known that all along.

He had intentionally jeopardized their lives just to prove a point. It was only right that he let them know.

Pawns and Kings

Oryan kept his personal communicator off most of the time while he was in the field. When he did look to see who had tried to contact him, it was brief and he did not acknowledge most. Orders from Alexander or Trebus, for example, were disregarded as fast as they were received. He knew he was free from answering to them; however, some of their messages would have been beneficial for him to pay attention to.

The empire had never formally declared war on any other sovereign country, territory, kingdom, or nation. Kovac's threats of unleashing the Captain and the Legion allowed the emperor to take virtually anything he wanted without force. The rare occasions when the Legion was let off the leash placed much of the world in a truce of fear with Navaro. There was virtually no war he could not win should he choose to begin such a campaign.

However, one kingdom had the potential to be a true match for Navarus. Some believed that if the two countries were to go to war, the final outcome was undecided. Any one weapon could alter the course of such an event. Even a single person could spell doom or hope.

Vollmar and Navarus had kept an uneasy truce between one another since the day that Navaro had decided to take his neighbor's land for his own. Many in Vollmar criticized the king and his counselors for not taking action sooner, thus letting the emperor control so much and become so powerful. Others felt that, since the two countries were on opposite sides of the world, their involvement was not in the best interest of the people.

Still, Vollmar fortified its cities and strongholds, strengthened its armies and fleets, and prepared for the worst. Tamrus, the king of Vollmar, was a man of vision and knew that no matter how well built, the dam was sure to break. His spies were infiltrated deep in the ranks of the empire, and he was given regular reports on any move the emperor made. However, Tamrus knew that Navaro had many spies in his service as well. The deadliest chess game any one could imagine had already begun.

Tamrus was very careful not to be the catalyst that would lead to engulfing the entire planet in war. He knew that the emperor longed for this great conflict. Any excuse to start fighting was a legitimate one for him. Every word he spoke to Emperor Navaro was carefully guarded and premeditated. All of his military movements were meant to reinforce and fortify, but not to even give the appearance of advancement. He placed his forces strategically in places that he knew would be of interest to the emperor and his general should they attack. Each had been moving his pieces for years.

Now the board was set.

Only days before Oryan made his proposition to Kovac and his Captain, an incident on the borders of a neutral city smashed what peace had been held. Vollmar had been eradicating a small terrorist organization for the past several years. Its leader was a man who was all but invisible. His connections in every location spanning the world kept him very well protected. In return, he kept those who kept his secret very wealthy.

Vollmar's intelligence units chanced upon scattered intelligence reports that this man would be making a trade in a building not far from the country of Mira, a city that flew its own flag and answered to neither Vollmar nor Navarus. Tamrus dispatched a small covert operations unit to the location to capture this man and kill all who resisted.

The operation met its objective, but upon obtaining the target, the unit then found itself in a firefight with terrorist forces. The intelligence reports had been wrong when describing the number of men and firearms that followed this man. Vollmar's special ops unit was trained for such incursions, and most made it out not only alive but with the package.

At first, it was hailed as a victory for Vollmar, but it was only after the news had been broadcasted across the Net that Tamrus realized what a horrible mistake he had made. The target was said to have been making some kind of trade, but it was not known who he was trading with. His contacts turned out to be none other than high-ranking imperial officers. During the raid, the only person to make it out alive aside from the covert team was the target. All others were killed.

The empire accused Tamrus of reckless behavior and of not verifying his intelligence reports. Navaro used this operation as a rallying cry for all those who stood for war in the empire. The advisors who preferred to keep the peace were quickly convinced otherwise under the enormous pressure from their colleagues, as well as Navaro's propaganda. Only three weeks after the incident, the empire formally declared war and made its first strikes against key military objectives.

Tamrus launched his counter-attacks as well as a huge investigation into the details of the intelligence that started this chain of events. Upon further investigation, it was discovered that the report came from the son of a prominent member of the faction of the empire that had been promoting war with Vollmar.

Oryan's skirmish was delayed due to the Legion being sent to the field. There were rumors that they had suffered their first real defeat trying to take a very heavily fortified, yet key, Vollmar stronghold. This only spurred Oryan's men on further. They drilled and trained as never before, knowing that the enemy they faced was not invincible. Just as they were feeling invincible themselves, the date was set and a new wave of humility swept over them. They were facing the Legion, after all, which was still the deadliest fighting force in the world. They may have lost, but it was to no army. It was to a fortification that had been reinforced and prepared for such an attack for years.

Oryan could feel the tension in the air. They were all hardened men. They were reborn into the harsh fires of combat's furnace. Their blacksmith had tempered and shaped them into the most lethal and efficient force ever assembled. However, they had not been tested, and to march against the Legion, who outnumbered them two to one, was a daunting start. It took Oryan to shake the anxiety.

The morning finally came, and their hour was close. When the shuttle arrived to take them to their location, they were still dirty and gritty. They had not bathed for days, they were unshaven, and, in all other ways, they appeared to be a disorganized and undisciplined unit.

They waited beneath the pavilion where they had first met their new commander. They had trained the humanity out of themselves by his side for almost five months. Every man had a wound or scar to show for it. There number was now only four hundred and ninety-one as some had been injured beyond the capacity for return. Each man that had gone had left swearing his loyalty and his prompt return.

The men were in perfect formation, standing deathly still and quiet. Oryan had disappeared into the barracks and had not returned yet. Their eyes never moved from their fixed points directly in front of them. Even without their commander's presence, they were a model of discipline.

After a few minutes, Oryan stepped onto the pavilion and made his announcement.

"The shuttles are on their way. I expect nothing but focus during the ride. Now is the worst time to lose your edge. We have all trained far too hard to destroy our chances this late in the game.

"Do not lose your reserve. Think. Move and adapt to whatever comes at you. I guarantee you have seen a more fearsome enemy when you faced each other on the practice field. The only difference is reputation. Reputations are nothing to fear.

"I expect victory." Though the men did not flinch, each was calculating their long odds. "This is not an arrogant statement. This is not a statement I've made to try and convince you of your superiority. They are superior. They are seasoned veterans of every kind of war known to man. We are not. I say this because we will be victorious. We will give them a war they have never seen before.

"They still boast that no force has defeated them on open field! Their pride will be among many things to fall. The rest of the world fears them! We will not. They outnumber us. Their numbers count for *nothing!* Combat is a game of chess where the pieces move themselves for the advancement of the team. There are no pawns here! No kings, or bishops, only *Knights!*"

Oryan's men began to be more animated, sensing that their

leader was rousing more than discipline in them. They sounded off. "Oryan's Knights!"

"Let them remember; let them never forget this day! They claim to fear no man! By nightfall this day, *they will know fear!*" His men erupted with their battle cry. All anxiety was gone. Their captain was right. No one had trained harder; no force fought so well or so seamlessly. They were the Kentaurus Knights reborn, and they would suffer no rival. *Bring them on!*

The shuttle arrived. They were prepared for several small transports; instead they got a train shuttle. It held all five hundred men and fit their gear comfortably in storage compartments under the shuttle itself. They were not the height of luxury; however, they were well kept. It was spacious, and, best of all, there was air conditioning. No one on that shuttle had felt relief from the heat and humidity in close to seven months.

The ride was long. Some men slept; others spoke to their teammates, and still others sat in silence, searching their souls for whatever reason seemed best to them. Oryan sat in the front. His eyes were closed, but sleep did not find him. He was preparing for battle. His mind searched for its solace, finally being illuminated by the stars. He watched them rotate through the night sky, and as they did so, he began to find the constellations he looked for in each season.

The constellations were a testament to the magnificence of the heavens. His mind connected the points of light to form their intended shape. Each body of stars told a story. The stories were sometimes tragic, sometimes heroic, and sometimes a bit of both. He knew them all. Today, however, he was not looking for a constellation, but a star. When he found it, he knew again what peace could be.

It was Celeste. Oryan had found a place for her in his night sky. It was a star that many missed because it shone only as the night faded and first light came on. It was visible only for an instant as the sun rose, but it shone like a torch in a sky of sparks for that instant. That was his Celeste. He sat on the shuttle, hours passing with no notice, just the sweet memory that would always be his and his alone. *I love you.*

When the shuttle finally slowed to a stop, he was ready for his next challenge. He had weighed his life in the balance, and now his mind was clear and sharp. His body would follow suit. That was a tried, tested, and proven fact.

His five hundred Knights exited the shuttle and collected their belongings within minutes, and they were standing in perfect formation as the shuttle driver pulled away, far ahead of schedule. Oryan had taught them to seek perfection in everything they did. There was always pride to be had in giving even the smallest of tasks full and complete attention.

Oryan stood in front of them again. He could have said many things, but only one seemed appropriate. "Knights, you all know what to do. You were born for this moment. If you give this day everything you have and hold nothing back, there is a reward on the other end that cannot be bought with money or fame. Leave this battlefield with no regrets, knowing you could not have given any more, and you will know that reward. I'll see you all on the other side!"

The cries went up again. They were ready.

A short man in an officer's uniform bustled from the gates to Oryan. He carried papers in his hand. When he was closer, he saluted. "Captain," he puffed.

"Catch your breath, Lieutenant," said Oryan, saluting back.

The man puffed and sighed before continuing. "You're early. The Captain regrets that he could not deliver these instructions in person, but he says that he has preparations to make and that you'd understand." He handed Oryan the paperwork under his arm.

"If you see him again, tell him that I understand perfectly. A true soldier can look his enemy in the eye. What is all of this?" he asked.

"The rules of engagement for this contest. Also, an aerial and topographical map of the terrain, as well as directions to the barracks where your equipment is waiting. Do I really have to tell him what you said, sir?"

Oryan looked up from his papers. *You must be joking.* "No, Lieutenant. Run back to your station, and while you're there, see if you left your courage with your breakfast."

The portly officer saluted and scurried away much as he had entered.

Oryan's men were divided into small, effective units. He had five platoons with close to one hundred men each who were divided from there into four squads of twenty-five. Each soldier had a role in the squad and each squad a role in the platoon and so on. Oryan called his platoon guides, as well as his squad leaders and his company commander, to him. There were several copies of the rules in his paperwork, so he handed one to each. There was only one map, so he would display it when they arrived at the barracks for all to see. He passed the command for his leaders to inform their men of the formal rules.

"We play by the rules," he told them. "That doesn't mean we play by *their* rules."

The company jogged to the barracks. Once there, they suited up in the static suits they were given. Oryan had explained how they worked, their limitations and weaknesses. He had told them how to exploit the suits and how to get the most performance they could from them. He knew these uniforms well, better than the Captain, and that was a very sharp, much overlooked advantage.

Oryan posted the map in the empty mess hall so all could see. It marked the position of their flag as well as the enemy's flag. Each man looked at the map, mentally photographed it, and moved on. When they had all had their chance to memorize it, he gave his last words before battle.

"You all know the way this is supposed to go. The rules have been explained. You have your weapon and the man next to you. That is all you need. Keep your headsets on, and keep the channels rotating. Each squad choose their rotation, and the company will use Rotation Charlie, understood?" They all acknowledged. He had taught them to never use the same communication signal for more than two maneuvers. They had rotations they practiced to ensure the enemy could not listen.

"All right, let's show these amateurs what Knights can do. Commanders, to me," he finished with thunderous response.

Oryan's company commander was his finest soldier. His name was Ethanis Thomas, and Oryan had promoted him to lieutenant in the field. The other men admired and followed him. He was a very natural leader who led first by his example.

"Mr. Thomas, I want you to get with your PG's and tell them to get me their finest from each squad. Not the squad leaders. I want them to see me here before we go into battle; is that understood?"

"Perfectly, sir. They will be to you in ten, sir," replied Lieutenant Thomas.

"Make it five, we haven't got long."

"Yes, sir."

Oryan knew how to win this contest, but it was going to take some ingenuity. He knew that the Captain feared him, and so it would focus his attack on Oryan, not knowing yet what his men were capable of. When it felt the sting of his attack, it would reconsider. By then it would be too late. Unlike Oryan's men, the Captain's were all pawns. The Captain would throw the best he had at Oryan early, and so he would decimate the heart of his enemy's strategy and strength in one blow. He needed some good soldiers to pull it off, though. No sooner did he finish that thought than those soldiers stood in front of him.

Oryan and his commanders stood face-to-face with the Captain and its leaders. The time of the battle had come; the only thing that remained was the formalities. The battlefield was ideal for such a contest. A five square mile block of land had been sectioned off for the event, and servicemen stood at the boundaries to disqualify any who stepped over them. Each end of the field was covered in trees and brush while the center was open with nothing but short grass for cover. This is where the leaders stood to make sure the rules were explained one last time.

The pudgy lieutenant that had delivered Oryan his paperwork was reading the rules to both teams. Kovac himself was sitting in an observation tower just outside the battle grounds. He was monitoring as much as he could through cameras placed on the field and his high vantage point. Though he would never admit so openly, he had been looking forward to this for some time.

Oryan stared hard at the Captain. It stood a head taller than him, its skull resting on a thin, elongated neck. However, it had broad shoulders that, combined with its body armor, made it an intimidating presence. Its arms were thin, but deceivingly strong and tipped with bony, vice-like fingers. Some of the more human parts of it had been replaced by metal and technology. No one knew why. It was amazing to Oryan that, despite its size, the Captain could be virtually invisible at will.

He knew the rules, so he paid the lieutenant no attention and just stared at the Captain. For ten long minutes, he never shifted his gaze to anything else but the loathsome creature before him. However, Oryan knew that the Captain was a creature easily provoked, and so he used this tactic more as a challenge and intimidation than anything else. As the Captain never returned the gaze for more than a few seconds, Oryan knew it was working.

When the rules were finished, the commanders of both teams bowed to each other and then turned to head back to their flags. When they were out of earshot of the Captain and its leaders, Oryan spoke. "Well, now that you have stood toe-to-toe, what are your thoughts?"

"They're mortal. They're nothing more than twisted men. All men, no matter how twisted, can feel fear," said Lieutenant Thomas.

"And bleed," added Sergeant Keenan.

Oryan nodded. "Pass that word to your men. They should know what we face here. They outnumber us, but only two to one. That means if each man takes two with him, we break even. I expect each man to take at least twice that many before he finds himself unable."

His commanders nodded their agreement. They understood now why Oryan was sure of victory. The reputation of the Legion made them seem larger than life, yet they were not so. They were a deadly force, but so were Oryan's Knights. Moreover, the Knights were fashioned to fight for the man next to them, and the Legion was only concerned with victory. The Knights could win.

The commanders began the run back to their flag. When they arrived, they handed down the orders and the strategy that Oryan had discussed with them on their way back. Oryan took his squad and gave them his specific orders away from the rest of the company.

"When the horn sounds once, we have five minutes. We cannot move until then. When the horn sounds twice, the game is on. They have everything set up for this thing to at least last one day if not more, but I say we end this today and go home."

His soldiers sounded their agreement. "Now, the leader of the Legion has a bit of a personal vendetta against me, and I'm sure he'll throw his best at me first, so expect to take the brunt of the fighting for a while. When they realize how much damage the rest of the company is dealing them, they'll reconsider, but you all have to be at your absolute best, understood?" All responses were positive.

"Now, third squad will be on our tails but not fighting unless they have to. They will be as invisible as possible, and it is our job to make sure they remain so. We are a diversion. Only one squad is staying behind to defend, so we have to watch for the enemy coming from our flanks. These things we are fighting are good at not being seen, so keep your eyes and ears open." As he said this, the first horn sounded.

"All right, men, we move! We never stop advancing! Make them pay for every inch of ground we take from them! No quarter, no mercy! Hurt them if you must, or hurt them for fun; I don't care which!" His men laughed and sounded their approval.

They filed in behind him and ran as fast as they could to cover as much distance as possible before the second horn rang. Third squad was on their heels within moments. The entire company, save the defensive unit, was very near the open field when the second horn sounded.

The battle was on.

"Recons one and two, shoot and scoot across the field; let's see if they made it this far," said Oryan through the comm.

Two men ran serpentine onto the field and dove to the ground some twenty feet into the clearing. No shots were fired. Two more men ran to another point and found cover. The first two men were up again and moving closer to the enemy lines. The pattern continued until the four men were just yards from the enemy tree line. Still no shots had been fired. Oryan was suspicious.

"Recon one and two, hold positions and keep eyes on until I give the command. It's too quiet," he began. "East and west squads, report."

"No activity from east," said one squad leader.

"None on the west, sir," said another.

"Company, attention! These guys are going to use the east and west as their attack focus for our flag. All center squads move forward quick and careful. We cannot afford to lose too many, especially in the opening minutes. East and west squads follow once center has reached enemy ground. You need to stay with us, but be as thorough as possible on your searches. Chances are they will not attack you first. My guess is they aren't here yet, but they're not far away. Move!"

The men carried out the orders with absolute perfection. Just a few short minutes later, all offensive Knights were in the enemy tree line. Still, all was quiet.

"This is a trap, sir," said Thomas.

"Yes, it is, Lieutenant. Let's spring it early," Oryan replied.

"All right, men," he said to his squad. "Let's do this. Stay on me; it's gonna get really hot really fast. Don't let third down!"

Oryan got to his feet with another soldier and then plunged into enemy territory. No sooner than the second group of his men crouched low to do the same than the shots rang out. The enemy was here, but they were not set. They were forced to reveal position and did not have time to surround their line as they had wanted. Oryan's forces had been underestimated. That would not be the last time, but they were sure to learn from their mistakes.

With the first barrage, one Knight had been immobilized, but the soldiers in his squad needed at least one sacrifice. Two more sprang up and used their fallen comrade as a shield. Blast after blast struck his body but had no effect on the soldiers carrying him. Two objectives were achieved: Oryan knew the location of at least thirty enemy troops. They were excellent marksman, but too eager to pull the trigger.

Bolts of concentrated light sang overhead as Oryan's Knights advanced. The advancement was slow and on their stomachs, but they lost no more. All around them, the Legion was falling. The Knights were moving more quickly than anticipated and forced them to reveal new positions with every inch of ground gained.

"We have heavy enemy advance on the east perimeter, sir! Multiple contacts, multiple incursion points! Hand to hand already encountered!" shouted a squad leader across the comm.

"Can you hold?" asked Thomas.

"We'll hold! They are trying to overwhelm by numbers! We have lost few, but they've paid for it! No promises on advance!" was the reply.

"Hold them there!" said Thomas. "Fifth squad, fan out and see if you can't pick off a few of the agitators on the east perimeter!"

"Copy, Commander," said fifth squad.

Oryan worked his way through the center. They had spotted him already, and his squad was facing the most concentrated and precise fire of the company, which was what he had expected. He had not lost any more men since the first, and he was sure at least fifty of the Legion had fallen by their hands.

His mind was working fast, taking in all the reports he could catch over the comm. He estimated that at least one tenth of the attacking forces were already gone, with minimal losses for his Knights. The enemy had tried to use their numbers and disregard their training at first, but he could feel the pressure of these elite troops more and more with each inch.

A report crashed across the comm of some of the Legion having broken through their lines unseen and heavy casualties ensuing, but another report sounded off announcing the demise of that group of invaders. Oryan had already lost at least ten percent of his own men too.

These odds were not good. The Knights were only performing at the two-to-one ratio they had begun with. This was not enough. Oryan knew if they did not break through soon that ration would take its heavy toll and there would not be enough of his men left to finish the mission.

"Jeckstadt to base," he sounded off.

"Base here. All quiet, sir," said the sergeant.

"Send snipers to the tree line ASAP! You will have perimeter breach in a few moments. Tell them to shoot anything that looks suspicious!" Oryan ordered.

"Copy, sir."

"Thomas!" Oryan shouted into the comm.

"Sir!" he replied.

"Have second squad spread thin! Tell them to start picking off some of the enemy that is pinning us down! We have to shake loose now!"

"Copy!"

Oryan rose to his elbows and made two more marks drop. Hundreds of beams of light blasted over his head in response. Each of his squad members did the same in turn and was greeted by the same outcome. One more took a shot to the mask.

Moments later, Oryan rose again, this time to catch a glimpse of his enemies fending off not only his attack, but the flanking maneuver of second squad. That was all he needed. "Knights!" he shouted to his squad. "Close range encounters! Sling rifles! Pistols only! Time for the secret weapon! We break through now!"

He and his men ran low, covering the ground between them and their attackers with shocking speed. The suits they wore had a thin plate of metal in the back of the uniform to protect against a hard blow from an enemy. They had removed these and carried them in their hands as a shield against oncoming fire. It did not cover much, but their speed and their ability to stay low coupled with these makeshift shields made them a virtually impossible target to stop.

The Legion blasted away to no avail, and before they could draw their own hand-to-hand weapons, Oryan's Knights were upon them. They fought with surgical precision, each shot or blow felling at least one enemy. Oryan was in his element. He was wading through the enemy like a storm. Ten then fifteen fell at his hand before any even tried to stop him. After a few seconds, the center action stopped. "Recon three and four, we made a hole! Center incursion is open. I say again, center incursion is *open!*"

A dozen men from other squads ran past Oryan's position and took advancing positions. The legion was astounded. They began to bring up more defensive troops from the rear, and their forward troops began to fall back to answer this new threat. The Knights made a slaughter of the attempt. By now, Oryan calculated the kill ration for his Knights was closing in on four to one. *Much better.*

Oryan knew that if he did not move soon, they would settle in again and they would be more prepared for a maneuver like that. He had to keep his positions advancing. "East and west, status!"

"East here! They thinned out some! We are advancing, but slowly! Still under a lot of fire!"

"West is about the same, sir!"

"East, you've got it the worst! I am sending a squad to reinforce! When they arrive, kick it in and make them pay! I want them to think they attack is coming from there! Lieutenant, make it happen!"

"Already on it, Captain!" Thomas replied.

Oryan's first objective had been achieved, now for the second.

The Captain had remained at base, listening eagerly for news of its slaughter to come. When the first reports came in from its front line, it began to feel very human. Jeckstadt's men were already across its lines. How could they have covered so much ground so fast? It was sure to look into this and make sure no cheating had taken place.

When word came that its soldiers had broken through, it tasted victory. Soon followed the report that all troops behind the enemy were gone; the sweet savor turned sour.

It received news of a squad reaching open field. Its mouth began to water, but doubt nagged at its brain. In seconds, doubt was all it tasted when word reached it that Jeckstadt's Knights were the finest marksman.

It was only when it was told that its own lines were breaking and that their numbers were swiftly descending to match their opponents that it entered the contest personally. It knew where Jeckstadt was and where he would be soon, so it took a small contingent of troops with it to take on this arrogant young punk.

It led its men to the heart of the fighting, and it began to see the true horror of the situation. The legion was losing ground every second, and now reports were streaming in that the enemy had again broken through on the east perimeter. Its contempt for the situation raged. It had sent its first attack to the east, and now the enemy had not only held them off, but was advancing.

It saw its soldiers dropping on its left and right. It beheld its great might and strength being beaten at that profession at which they were supposed to be unmatched. A handful of its own troops fell back and ran toward their base. It knew in an instant that this battle was over. The best it could hope for was a stalemate and that is what it would have. There was no way it would let this fool embarrass it like this.

The Captain wrapped its wiry fingers around one of its commander's throat. "What is going on here? Why are we losing ground? Fight them, *idiot!* Close the distance; stab them though the heart! Once the fighting is close range, order the reserves up from defense, and shoot everything that moves, friend or foe! *Do it now!*"

The commander barked the orders of his Captain over the comm, and the battle quickly sounded with the clash of flesh and bone rather than the ring of laser blasts. Though they had taken heavy losses, they still outnumbered their enemy, and with this new strategy, the odds were sliding back in their favor.

"Now call for the defenses to advance! All of them! Especially those *cowards* who left the front line!" cursed the Captain.

The commander relayed the orders and then turned hesitantly to the Captain. "My Captain," he began, "all commanders in the field have reported in claiming their troops as either unable to fight or fighting still. *There were no deserters.*"

The Captain felt its flesh crawl. If there were no deserters, then the troops he saw fall back were not its at all. Horror gripped its black heart. It had called all its defenses to the front line. The realization turned its boiling blood into ice. "You men!" he said, pointing the squad he had brought with him. "*With me!*"

Kovac watched from his omniscient location. He was close enough to hear the combat, but his best view was from the cameras. He had watched with complacency his Captain make mistake after mistake and his student exploiting each flaw perfectly.

He watched Oryan and his squad discard their own uniforms and strip the fallen legion of theirs. The suits were designed to become flexible again when they were removed, but they could only be removed from the outside. He was proving even more impressive than his father. His father had proved more than a match for the Legion but had ultimately failed. It was only fitting that his son should be the end of it.

The battle had been raging for a grand total of three hours. In that time, the greatest force the world had ever seen was being made fools of by a group of men who had never fought another enemy in their lives.

Beneath his dark, unfeeling eyes, Kovac turned to his dark thoughts.

Oryan, you will be my greatest achievement or you will be my downfall. Either way, I have great plans for you.

Oryan and his squad ran toward the enemy flag. When the few hundred remaining troops of the Captain's ran by them headed for the front line, Oryan and his men got out of sight. Oryan knew that the Captain had become desperate, and like an insulted child, it would take as many Knights with it as it could. Little did it know that its defeat would come before it would taste such vengeance.

Oryan and his men slowed when they knew they were close to the flag. If there were any stragglers, Oryan did not want to walk into an ambush. He would take out whatever guard remained and make his way back to base. Thirty minutes was all he needed. His Knights could easily give him that.

As they closed in, they came in sight of the flag. It seemed unguarded, but Oryan remained cautious.

"Okay, I'll take the flag, but it stays in no one's hands for more than two minutes, understood?" he asked over the comm.

There was no answer. "Copy last transmission!" he whispered again.

"There is no one left to copy!" hissed a cold voice behind him.

Oryan stood and turned to face the voice. "Captain," he said.

"Captain," it replied. "It was so close for you, wasn't it? Did you really think you had won?" It circled Oryan like a vulture waiting on its prey to die.

Two of the Captain's men had taken Oryan by the arms and held him still. The Captain removed a pistol from its belt and walked close to Oryan. It pulled the helmet off of Oryan's head, and its men forced him to a kneeling position.

"These weapons are not fatal. That's a shame. However, at point blank, it's sure to leave you a wound you'll not soon forget. Your little *diversion* has failed!" it said menacingly, bringing the weapon's barrel flush to Oryan's head.

"You think I can't beat your pawns? You think that they hold me now out of anything but my will that they do so? My diversion failed, did it? *Checkmate*," Oryan said, smiling at his nemesis.

The Captain felt the icy fingers of failure creep over it again. It lowered the pistol and walked around Oryan and its men. With absolute horror, it realized its most grievous mistake. Its revenge had been so perfect; its victory over this insect was sure, until now. Its blackened eyes beheld the sheer horror of its folly. *The flag was gone.*

Its shock turned to fury. It screamed a horrible shriek that was heard at the front lines. It hissed curses and spun to slit the throat of the man who had done this to it with its master watching. Its eyes fumed with the fire of a hatred brimming over with vengeance. The rules meant nothing to it anymore. Oryan would die today, and it would be the one to kill him.

When it turned, a pistol came in line with its face and sat firm against its forehead. Its troopers lay unconscious around it with only Oryan left standing, weapon in hand.

"These weapons are not fatal. That's a shame. However, at point blank, I'm sure it will imprint this moment in your mind for the rest of your life. But first, I wanted you to hear something." Oryan grabbed a communicator from his pocket. "Recon one?"

"In position, sir," came the voice from the other end of the communicator.

"Now," said Oryan, and the horn sounding the end of the contest boomed across the field.

The Captain's rage knew no bounds. It hissed and cursed under its breath, but for all its hate, it was still at the gunpoint of a very unfriendly adversary. It was like a cornered animal, and it was contemplating everything, including losing its own limbs to escape this predator, but it did not react fast enough. Oryan was, as always, two steps ahead of it, and aside from the click of the trigger, the call of its defeat was the last sound it heard for many days.

OPERATION KNIGHTFALL

Oryan's Knights celebrated their victory. Against all odds, they had succeeded where no other army had done so. They reveled in their superiority and ingenuity. They now saw clearly the reason that Oryan had pushed them so hard and why he had used the methods he had. They would follow him into death and hell with no hesitation.

It was only Oryan who did not relish the accomplishment. It was only after the contest was over that he was informed that this battle was kept more top secret than many Special Forces operations in effect for the actual war. No one knew. No one could cheer them on. Their reward was what he had become accustomed to: *Silence.*

He savored the defeat of the Captain who, as far as he knew, was still hospitalized for injuries received "in action." He understood that the empire could not afford to let it slip that their undefeated force was capable of being defeated. Its enemies would take it as a sign of weakness and use that moment to spur on their own forces. The empire's greatest tool was intimidation, and the Legion was the core of that weapon.

What troubled Oryan was the knowledge that every army, force, or team, no matter how well prepared, had to lose sometime. Even history's Kentaurus Knights were eventually defeated. Oryan knew that the victory of his men would be a quiet one, but not this quiet. He wanted the rumors to begin to spread. Not that the Legion had lost, but that the empire now possessed a force that was even more deadly a weapon than they were. He wanted to visit barracks and mess halls and hear the other men whisper of his Knights as if they were to be feared by even the empire's own troops. For once, whispers and rumors would have been more satisfying than thunderous applause or breathless silence.

The day after the contest, the Knights found themselves back on their familiar ground, training and learning again under the instruction of their magnificent captain. They all fought and trained with more vigor and purpose than they had before. The adrenaline and the desire to stay the best still lingered in their veins. However, Oryan knew such things were not meant to last, so he immediately petitioned to have his men sent into combat. After that highlight, there was only one way to stay sharp.

Oryan did not have to wait long. Summer was wearing on, and autumn was fast approaching. The lush and green training fields had begun to turn various shades of orange, red, and yellow. Oryan continued to train his men, teaching them to blend in with the changing surroundings and how to stay silent with the presence of fallen leaves and other seasonal variables.

It was dusk on a chilly day. The sun had all but disappeared behind the horizon, and Oryan was wrapping up the day's exercises. He had not pushed his men that day. He had let them dictate their own pace and their own training routine. After giving the command, he set off by himself for quiet and reflection.

He had found a rather isolated knoll and stood there watching the last few minutes of sunset fade into dark. When the sun had become only a sliver, he crouched down, elbows on knees, to allow his muscles to relax but not get too comfortable. He breathed deep, letting the cold air fill his lungs, and watched his breath, now visible, disappear into the oncoming night.

The scene before him was serene and peaceful, yet his mood did not match his surroundings. He could see far, observing the beauty that nature produced. Such rich textures and vibrant color schemes were laid before him. Nature had been and always would be the only real beauty in the world. Man's self-aggrandizing attempts to imitate such a work of art were nothing short of comical.

This day had felt wrong from the start. For whatever reason, his mentality was grim, dark, and full of hate. He despised the human race for all its foibles and did not excuse himself. He tried to recall all that he had accomplished on his own and all the extraordinary distance his Knights had come in such a short period of time. They were more than noteworthy accomplishments, but he felt them all a waste. He felt empty and hollow. When pride tried to rise up and quench the bitterness, it was strangled by the choking weeds of despair. All he had done seemed insignificant. Why?

Finally, he turned to Celeste. He tried to find her in the fading light, but her memory too was forced back and blocked from giving him comfort. Then he knew that his body was sensing something. It was warning him, the way it always did, that this new wind was bringing more than just the cold. There was a chill across his back that did not herald the onset of a deep night of sleep and a shadow that was deeper than those cast by the sinking sun.

His world was about to change again; he just did not know how. Oryan knew that it was no use letting himself become so tense over events he could not control. He had been in this position every day since the moment he opened his eyes at birth. All he had to do was focus, and the calm would come.

He let his weight shift to a sitting position and finally came to rest, lying on his back in the grass. It was cold but welcome to his feverish state. He watched the last light of the sun become replaced by the soft glow of the moon. The stars began to glimmer against the blackness of space. His heart slowed, his mind stopped, and his body relaxed. He watched a few mists of breath escape his lips and then closed his eyes.

As his soul found its peace and sleep was about to take him, he felt the hairs on his neck stand on end. His body remained calm, for he knew this feeling all too well. It was one he had felt a thousand times before, and before he even opened his eyes, he knew what to expect.

"No matter how silent you make your approach, I know you're there, and you're not one of mine. If your intent is to kill me, leave now, or the only corpse on this ground will be your own."

Oryan opened his eyes. Above him was just as he left it; only some of his view was blocked by the silhouette of a very large man standing over him. The man seemed unmoved by his threat. "I was giving you a chance, friend. If you knew me, you would understand the danger your silence carries with it. Speak!"

"Ah, but I do know you, Oryan, Armay's son," said a smooth

deep voice. "I know very well what you are capable of. In fact, my Captain just found that out as well."

Oryan began to rise from the ground. "I knew I recognized the footsteps however light they may fall. What brings you to this corner of the empire, sir?"

"Was it not you who requested my presence?" Kovac asked.

"I asked only for your orders, General. Yet, your presence here is most welcome. What would you have me do?"

The General turned a shoulder to Oryan. He brought his hand to his chin as if thinking and let his elbow rest on his other arm. "Your victory on the battlefield was impressive, Captain. What do you attribute the results to?"

Oryan was not sure how to respond. This could be a loaded question designed to test him in some way, or it could simply be a point of interest for this student of warfare. He gave the only answer that satisfied both possibilities: the truth.

"My opponent was overconfident in both their superior numbers and also their experience. They wanted to win, but they were unwilling to use the tools given to them to do so. My men simply exploited that weakness."

Kovac examined the answer. "A wise choice of words, Captain. Your answer was guarded, not too bold, yet still confident. If you really felt that way, if that was your real feeling on the subject, why do you not rest with your men tonight? Only a commander who is wrestling with something his subordinates cannot handle retreats to solitude. What do you really think of my legion?"

Oryan realized that Kovac was actually fishing for genuine opinion. Either his pride had been wounded at the defeat as well or he was seeking improvement without asking directly for it. "They are flawed, my lord," he responded.

Kovac lifted an eyebrow.

"Each of those soldiers is dead already. They know going into a battle that they will never return, and so they are void of fear. That's a powerful agent, but it suffers a fatal error. Any man who fears nothing loves nothing. In the absence of those two passions, one of two things takes their place: despair or indifference. Those men are indifferent. So much so that when faced with defeat, it's no different than facing victory. The humanity has been trained out of them in an attempt to make them *super* human. Unfortunately, our humanity is our greatest strength, and any army lacking such a vital artery is surely meant for its own destruction. It was only a matter of time, sir."

Kovac countered. "Fear is a weakness. It causes men to think irrationally and to make very serious errors in judgment. It causes men to run backward instead of advancing. The sooner it is purged, the better a soldier becomes."

Oryan's response was instant and precise. "Selfish fear causes men to retreat. Those who fight just to stay alive will run. If you fight only for yourself, then I agree. However, anxiety for the man next to you or your wife and family's safety stirs all the courage a soldier ever needs. Free men fight harder because they fear to lose their freedom. Slaves have nothing to lose. If the absence of fear makes soldiers better, the outcome of our little contest would have been different."

Kovac's ego was bruised. At first, his anger and wrath began to awaken inside him, but he had no reason to be so irritated. The boy was right, after all. Kovac was the best not only because he was determined to be, but also because deep inside he feared to lose.

On one point, Oryan still was incorrect. To fight for someone else *was* weakness. It made you vulnerable to intimidation and allowed an enemy an advantage that they otherwise would not have had. To fight only for one's self was true power. Each time that you emerged victorious from a confrontation, it instilled in you experience and the confidence that one can only find by looking inward. After all, when the battle was raging and death was staring you in the face, there was only one life that you were responsible for. If it was lost, then it made no difference who you fought for. You could no longer carry on the fight when you were dead.

"Your communications request for active duty is to be granted to your men," the General changed the subject.

"They've earned it, sir," Oryan responded.

"Your men are ready to die?"

Oryan expected such a response. "No, they're ready to fight. Those men out there *expect* to come home, but they also accept the fact that it may not happen. Is there a challenge worthy of their blood, sir?"

"There is a military target that thus far our forces have been unable to secure. I am sending you and your *Knights* to make sure that happens."

"What target are we to take, sir?" Oryan could tell there was something behind Kovac's voice that he was not saying. This target he spoke of was no doubt the same target that the Legion failed to take. Oryan was still not sure of the General's intentions. For a time it seemed that he favored Oryan over his Captain, but, almost like a proud parent, he had begun to defend his creation.

"It is a fort on the shores of Vollmar. As you know, we have been unable to get a foothold on enemy territory, and we hope that this operation will give us the break we need. It has many waterways that surround it, making it an ideal location to move resources and troops. It is also in excellent position to defend against inbound air strikes, as well as troop landings and invasion fleets."

"What kind of defenses are we talking about?"

"Seventeen foot tall, three foot thick concrete walls, heavy artillery, automated air strike force, anti-aircraft stinger sites, an underwater channel for ship-to-ship defensive and offensive attacks, five to ten thousand infantry, and armor to support."

Oryan's heart sunk. It was a suicide mission. Apparently, he had dealt the General a more serious blow than he thought. His own arrogance was about to cost his men their lives. "You want five hundred men to take and secure a place like that?"

"Not men. Knights. Are your men not up to the task?"

Apparently you aren't either. "The odds are long, General. My men will follow their orders no matter the outcome, but I expect none will return."

"A grim choice you would have then, if your assignment were to take the fort using only your brave five hundred," began Kovac. "Fortunately for you, Captain, it is your assignment to take and secure the beach there and to clear a path for reinforcement troops and armor to the fort. Once you have been deployed, you will have forty-eight hours to accomplish the task. After reinforcements arrive, you will take your unit and disable the air force and the underwater escape route. That is the mission."

This was far more reasonable but still held great risk. Vollmar would surely not surrender the beach or the ground between it and the fort without a fight. "I trust that intelligence has all the terrain maps, thermal scans, and the location of their forward defensive points. I assume that I will be briefed on those key factors as well as all other information that our military has on the fort itself, its commander, and the details of what resistance can be expected when we arrive."

"All the information awaits you in the ready room at the barracks. We have provided only the best of information for you and you gallant Knights, Captain."

"When does this operation happen, and who do I report to?"

"You have four days to prepare. It is a cover of darkness operation. We have a diversionary fleet docked at one of our naval bases nearby who will take you halfway to the deployment point. Once there, you will be taken the rest of the way in on our stealth troop transports. As you know, those transports are very short range, so you can expect that the fleet will be taking enemy fire and your men will see some ramifications from that.

"You report to Colonel Alexander and he reports to the Captain." Kovac watched Oryan's response at that last bit of information. "Do not attempt to circumvent the Captain. It would be unfortunate if I were forced to hand control of your men over to another command."

"A rather unfortunate turn of events for the Captain. Did they ever find out what he was doing at such close range with no helmet?" asked Oryan with the slightest of smirks.

Kovac was pleased to see that Oryan had not failed to bring his competitive edge and his sharp wit. "Unfortunately, the details were very hard to sift through. I am sure that he will be able to sort out the whole affair."

Not likely! The Captain would take that humiliation to its grave before it revealed what had actually happened. "Colonel Alexander will have my full report and readiness status in twenty-four hours. I look forward to the opportunity, and I know that my Knights are eager for it as well." He saluted to the General, who simply nodded slightly and walked away.

He came here personally to tell me these orders. I have made a mark. Whether it is a scar or not remains to be seen. Oryan knew this interaction meant one thing. If nothing else, the General was coming to respect his opinions and him. That meant a lot from a man who was no respecter of persons save himself.

It was time to return to camp. Come morning, he would have to prepare his men.

Oryan had given instruction to Lieutenant Thomas to prepare the men to move out back to barracks at dawn. Thomas woke the platoon guides and the squad leaders shortly before dawn. He told them to get the men into formation and prepare them for an early morning run back to barracks.

Ethanis Thomas had been assigned to this company from another Special Forces. His family did not hail from wealth or privilege, so the military was not an uncommon place to find a Thomas. His father had served, and two of his four brothers were currently serving in different positions across the empire. Thomas had always been the strongest of his brothers physically, and even though he was not the oldest, he was definitely the head of the household after his father had passed away.

When several officers came to his school, he was not surprised that his name was included on the papers they carried with them for active duty. He did not feel it a burden or an inconvenience. With the exception of sports, he found his schooling rather mundane and spent most of his time in the classroom with his mind elsewhere. He was very intelligent, scoring higher than most of his classmates on any subject, but he still found the whole ordeal to be a waste of his time and talents.

He had been in the Special Forces for almost a year and a half when the orders came down requesting his participation in a new and specialized unit. Any chance for a new challenge was a welcome prospect for him. Unlike many of the other Knights, Thomas did not resent his captain for his training methods. He finally found what he had been searching for in the military, and that was a commander who knew what it was to be the best. The Special Forces had pushed him, but not to his full potential. He had admired the Legion and their skill, but something about them always held him back from requesting the transfer. Now, he was glad he had waited.

Though he had been deployed several times since his enlistment, he had never actually seen combat. Sergeant Keenan was the most seasoned veteran of the company, and even his experience was limited. Thomas could tell by his conversation with Captain Jeckstadt that they were being deployed, but as of now it was only his intuition, not definitive proof, so he kept his premonitions to himself. Better to wait and be right than to err and lose the respect of the troops who depended on his judgment to stay alive.

After the men were assembled, they ran to the barracks in the chill of the morning. Now, they gathered in a dimly lit room, but the projection in the middle more than compensated for the absence of brighter lights. It was a round room with their benches hugging the walls and curving three quarters of the way around. The seats were tiered much like the stadiums that Oryan had fought in so many times as a Centauri. In the center was a huge metal table, some ten feet wide and fifteen feet long. Its top surface was flat, and along the edges were hundreds of small cathodes, each capable of a huge array of colors and lights. When they were turned on, they could produce any object, person, or terrain map with precise three-dimensional technology. This was the perfect way to show an army what they were facing when it came to a mission such as this.

Oryan began. "We have all trained and fought as men. However, all of the training and even the monumental victory we have taken from our brothers in arms is only a precursor to what we are about to face. We have been chiseled over the past six months for war, and war is upon us."

Though he resented the empire, for the sake of his men, Oryan played the role of the patriot. "As you know, Vollmar has begun a war that they do not intend to lose. However, they also do not know how to win. Those men fight and win and die by the voice of corrupt politicians who are trying to dictate a battle from halfway round the world. They are bound by the subtleties of crafty men who seek to use their lives or deaths for political gain and power. They are a nation divided, and we are a force united. Our mission will demonstrate the difference."

Vollmar had a king, yet that office was more a remnant of an age long ago. The man in that position was the final word on policy, yet a king could be voted out of office or could be forced to turn his control over to his counselors should the public demand support such an action. What Oryan had said was true that Vollmar was a kingdom where its king was undermined by idealists who knew little of combat and less of war. They used half truths and lies to seduce the masses into believing that the empire was no real threat and, at times, convincing them that this whole conflict should not be fought.

However, the emperor was a man with a heart of stone and a soul as black as night. He would stop at nothing to have that great realm. His lust for power was unquenchable, and although it was officially Vollmar who drew first blood, it was Navarus that gave them the knife. Navaro did not care what the people of Vollmar believed was right or wrong, and his operatives and spies fueled the fires of discontent to keep Vollmar's full strength from being unleashed. So long as the people's voices were divided, Tamrus was bound. And as long as he was bound, he was vulnerable. Though it was a source of strength, the democracy Vollmar practiced was its own worst enemy and one of the emperor's greatest weapons.

Oryan's men would prove this, but to what end? Their invasion would unite the people of Vollmar, and so the war would wage hot and bloody for some time. But how long would it be before the bloodshed would take its toll? How long before corruption and greed would again take the political reins of Vollmar's army and choke the life from their advance? With any luck, Navaro's campaign would only have to last long enough to make the division of opinions in the kingdom more violent than the war itself. Then he could use Vollmar's own dissention to turn them against their king and unite them under his banner. It would appear to all that he was some kind of savior, bringing order to chaos. His victory would be complete, and the world would be his. That may have been what he had in mind all along.

"We are to be the first of Navarus's forces to hold enemy soil. Our mission is called Operation Knightfall. Don't let the name deceive you; it does not refer to *our* fall, but the first time Kentaurus Knight will fall on their enemies in thousands of years. We will make it a memorable event." A murmur of approval rippled through the seats.

Over the next few hours, Oryan laid out the details of their attack. "Understand something, men. Once we hit the beach, we *do not* stop," he said slowly. "Our attack will not be as covert as we would like, and although the fleet will soften the beach for us, every second we waste will allow the enemy to fortify more and more ground. We cannot afford to give them that chance. Once our feet hit the sand, we can't let them breathe.

"Knightfall begins in four days. We are landing under enemy fire against a determined adversary on their soil. We wanted a fight; they don't get much better than this. We start simulations today. I'll see you all on parade grounds after lunch, which is waiting in the mess hall. Last hot meal in a safe environment you'll have for a while, gentleman. Take full advantage."

The training was intensive and covered everything from terrain differences to new evasive maneuvers and even their actual strategy for each step of the operation. Each man learned his part; each squad could carry out their orders in the blink of an eye and change one hundred and eighty degrees just as quickly. Oryan had given them the tools, but each man had made them their own. They all had to relearn combat, which was not always an easy process, but now they had so mastered the new style that it was second nature.

Oryan fought with them through each simulation on its first run-through but then took a step back to make commanders observations. Even he was in awe with what he saw. They moved so fast and so fluid it was if they were all a part of each other. Each member was a hand or foot or other part of a single body that responded immediately and instinctively to any situation, and Oryan was the brain.

Even as he observed his men, the counter argument came to his brain. If that was true, the rest of the world would adapt fast and his revolutionary combat would become standard. To make the Knights legendary, they had to continue to give their enemies battles they had never seen. That would be a difficult task, but they were all up for the challenge.

After a grueling two days of simulation, the men were granted their rest. Most of the men slept soundly on bunks they had not seen for some time. Some slept through until it was time to leave; others wrote letters to their loved ones over the Net; some prayed to whatever deity they worshiped.

Oryan took time to himself in his quarters. He logged onto secure nets, disabled any and all keystroke loggers, trace programs and other monitoring software he could identify, and searched for the one thing his heart truly longed to see. He searched for Celeste. She was the source of every gossip site he could find, but there was no word of her whereabouts. Either they got to you first or you were clever and disappeared. *I love you, whatever fate has dealt you. I will find you.*

Oryan slept deeply, dreaming heavenly visions of stars and galaxies. His body found its center and once again prepared itself for battle. He awoke at dawn on the third day, ran, ate a light breakfast, showered, and tried to take advantage of his last few hours of solitude. As he left his quarters, he was met by a man who was as close to a friend as Oryan had since Tecton.

"Lieutenant Thomas. What brings you to my dark corner of the universe?" he asked his commander.

"I have to know something," he spoke softly. "Before I follow you and before I lead your men into war and death, I have to ask you a question."

Oryan did not respond. This was a side of his lieutenant that he had never seen before.

"I know why I fight and I know why most of those men out there fight. Some for family, some for glory, some for duty, and some because they are just plain mad. I can see their motivations written all over their faces but not yours. What I have to know is this: Why are you here? I'll follow you regardless of the answer, but I will go no further until I have at least that."

Oryan remembered a conversation like this one from his past. It was different times, and he had only himself to worry about then, but the friend in front of him was no less a friend and no less concerned. He had to search his soul then to find the answer, and it was not a pleasant one, but he could answer now with more confidence in his answer.

"It's a just question and deserves an honest answer. I have no family, so that is of no concern. I fight for duty and glory, but that is not what drives me. I am here, I fight, for hope. I fight for hope that somewhere in this whole mess I'll find what I have been seeking for all my life."

"What is that?" Thomas asked.

"My soul."

There was a long pause. Thomas did not know how to respond, and Oryan did not care to further that conversation. He had given his answer, and it had indeed been an honest one, but now it was time to take the spotlight off of him.

"How are the men holding up?" he asked.

"They're ready."

"And what about you?"

"I'm ready, sir."

"You're ready to die?"

"No, sir."

Oryan smirked and let out a slight chuckle.

"Then you have come to the wrong place, my friend!"

Thomas was not moved by the attempt of levity from his commander. There was still more questions he wanted to ask.

"Something else, Lieutenant?" Oryan asked intuitively.

"What happens when the ramifications of our operation comes full circle? Is that worth fighting, worth dying for?"

Oryan had thought the same thoughts a dozen times over the last few hours. He did not have a perfect answer, so he gave his lieutenant the only answer that had satisfied that question for himself. "Do you know what makes a good commander and a great commander? A good commander values the achieving of his objective over the lives of his men. He will do whatever it takes to make sure his orders are carried out and that if no one returns, they all die knowing they did all that they could to reach a goal, even an unattainable one. A good commander receives decoration, praise, and medals. He gets his name on the Net as a hero. History remembers him until he is replaced by another good commander.

"A great commander is just the opposite. He does everything to make sure that his men come home alive. He puts their values and goals above his own. Above all, his life is meaningless without the respect and love of his men.

"If any leader can accomplish this mindset, it is those who love him that make him great. Each man out there will fight for me not out of fear or duty but out of a sincere desire to never see me fail. I know that in order to elevate myself, I must elevate them, and they know that to elevate me is only to elevate themselves. We all succeed together, or we all die together.

"A great commander's name is only known to his men. Whatever victory his men achieve is theirs and theirs alone. He is bound to them by a force that is stronger than any known to man. It can only be forged by ordeal and trial, but the great leader, his men, and their bond, never die. Only then do his men become truly immortal and when they are immortal, so is he.

"What are you, Lieutenant? Do you have it in you to be a great commander? If you are, the ramifications of our operation become pretty obvious."

Oryan walked away from him toward the parade ground where the men were gathering to board their transports. Thomas watched him leave but thought on his words long after he was gone. He thought on who he had been when he arrived and who he had become. He had come so far as a soldier and as a leader, but it was not enough. This was just the first step of a journey that could only end when he stopped himself or he was dead. Oryan had carried him so far, but it was time to get down and walk beside his mentor.

Operation Knightfall, Day One: Men and Metal

The moon was particularly bright. It hung high in the late hours of the night, illuminating the world with the soft glow of reflected light. It was bright for moonlight, yet the water around them remained a deep black, tipped with white foam as the waves lapped against each other and against the side of the carrier. The banks of their destination loomed in the distance. They could see palm trees and small shrubbery, but it was all devoid of color.

Oryan reflected on how peaceful the sea was at that moment. The jamming signals, new stealth technology, and a few bombing raids had rendered them undetected in their approach thus far. However, they could see the shore, and that meant it would not be long before the shore's defenses spotted them. For now, all was quiet. His Knights and the members of the carrier crew remained silent as the grave. With the exception of a few whispered orders, no one spoke.

The moon danced in the water, appearing first on one wave and then reappearing on hundreds more as each facet of water reflected its brilliance. The stars, too, surrounded the ship and cast countless reflections from the water's surface. Oryan absorbed the picture, knowing that in a few moments this harmony he knew would be anything but peaceful.

His men waited below deck for him. Their transports to the beach were fully submersible, so their initial approach would be underwater. Once the transports broke the surface of the water, there were no guarantees. Though he was able to observe these last few moments of calm, his men were undoubtedly below waiting on pins and needles for their captain.

"Captain Jeckstadt," whispered the admiral of this flagship. "The fleet is in position and we are ready to begin our assault. It's time."

Oryan gazed at the ocean for a few more long seconds before he turned to the admiral. "Very good, sir. When you begin the barrage, we will begin our approach. I will signal when we are in danger of our own fire."

"Captain, I still feel it best to deploy flares as an indicator for you. The night can wreak havoc on a man's perception and his bearings."

Oryan had fought an uphill battle with the admiral over this point. They had eventually agreed to disagree, but Oryan sensed a hint of defiance in the admiral's voice. Even with his objections, that man may just alert the enemy on his own. "You're right, admiral, flares would light our way. They would also mark our position for the enemy and cost us the element of surprise. I would prefer not to paint brighter targets on my men than already exist. The moon is bright; we know the terrain, and in a firefight, there is nowhere else to go but forward. Thank you for the concern, but this is my mission, and if you jeopardize the lives of my men with your presumptions of what is best, we will have more than words."

"I could have you on charges of insubordination where you stand!" grumbled the commander.

Oryan put a finger to his lips, reminding the admiral of the silence required, and gave him a smug smirk and arrogant wink. "I think you would be finding yourself manning a security tower in the frozen north before you finished filing the report, and you know it. Do watch who you threaten, *Admiral.*"

The admiral knew he was right. Captain Jeckstadt, his men, and his mission were protected from on high by powers that he could not comprehend. He detested the insufferable arrogance of this boy. He had never even seen combat, and he thought he knew better than the battle-hardened man that he had become. However, he valued his career and his life over that of this boy's. Chances were that none of his men would live to see the light of day. The admiral knew who would have the last laugh.

"Very well," he whispered behind clenched teeth. "I will wait for your signal."

Oryan saluted and walked past him. It was not easy to face the enemy before him, much less to know that things were not so friendly behind. He hoped that the admiral was not foolish enough to ignore his signal and keep firing to satisfy his own need for superiority or to prove a point.

He made his way to the lift, slipped his access card into the reader, and began the descent into the carrier's staging area, near the bottom of the ship's hull. As the decks sped past him, he wondered if there was anything he should say, if there were any further words of wisdom or motivation he should give his soldiers. When the lift reached its destination, he knew that words were a waste at this moment.

The doors slid open, and his men were gathered around to greet him. None spoke, but he could tell from their silence and anxious looks what it was they wanted to know. Every man was prepared for combat, fully suited with weapons slung, sheathed, or holstered. They were a sight to behold. The five hundred deadliest warriors on the planet, dressed in their camouflage battle dress. Each man had elbow protection followed by a high-tech mechanical brace on their forearms that instantly fed each man vital information at all times. The braces held schematics, intel on enemy troops and weapons, all the way to monitoring their life signs and keeping a count of how much ammunition they had left. Should one get hurt, sensors located on various parts of their armor relayed that information to the brace for a medic to interpret. They had black helmets which contained their communicator. Their knees and shins were also guarded. Tamrus armor was beneath the cloth of the uniform, which contained dozens of pockets for storage. There was a pistol that hung from their black belts near mid-thigh, and some men carried another pistol strapped to the thigh of the opposite leg. Each man carried a special sword across his back designed to penetrate both bullet-resistant and Tamrus armor.

The transports were lodged in their jettison tubes ready for their launch. Once initiated, the tubes would be sealed, filled with water, and then the hatch would open and propulsion would engage.

"Each man to his transport. Thirty seconds before the

bombardment begins, we will be released. You all know what to do from there. Keep your cool, remember your training, and I'll see you on the beach," Oryan spoke softly but with force. At that, the men donned their helmets and boarded their transports. Twenty men fit in one submersible, twenty-five subs total. Oryan was the last to board. Though he was the last to enter, he would make sure he was the first on shore. He sent the signal to the carrier that his men were in place; the mechanical hum of each tube sealing behind them filled the air. Once the noise stopped, red lights flashed in front of them as the tubes began to fill with water. When the next signal was received, the lights would flash green and the hatch would open. It was just a matter of time.

Sergeant Keenan sat across from his captain. He was the most seasoned veteran of the company, but that meant little as he had only seen combat three times. In all reality, he had only fired his rifle a handful of times, and he was not sure if any of his shots had found targets. He, like every man there, was nervous but ready. He would follow his captain barefoot into a live volcano confident of coming out the other side unharmed.

"What was it like, Captain?" he asked. "What was it like standing in front of millions, fighting the best Centauri the sport had ever known? Did you know you would win?"

Oryan smiled. "Why? Were you betting against me?"

Keenan smiled in response. He had somewhat idolized his commander long before he met him. He had always wanted to be a Centauri but had been drafted shortly after entering training. With Captain Jeckstadt, he had the experience of the sport and a hundred times over. He could not ask for more.

Oryan heard a voice coming through the comm inside his helmet. "Thirty seconds, Captain," came the admiral's voice. For Oryan, that meant he released his own clamps in twenty-seven to make sure that he was the first on shore. He closed his eyes and found his center. His body and his senses heightened as they always did, and he was ready. When he opened his eyes again, the voice spoke up again. "Five, four, three ..."

He pulled the ejection handle and sent his transport into the sea. Seconds later, all other transports released, and he watched behind him as they all shot from the carrier into the deep. It seemed like hours before they heard the steady drum of artillery fire begin from the fleet. Over the fleet comm, Oryan heard mixed communication about beach bombardment and anti-aircraft weaponry being used. Apparently, it had not taken Vollmar long to respond.

They all began to hear the watery explosions of enemy shells detonating on the water's surface. The transports shook when one exploded too close. A very loud boom rocked Oryan's transport, and a steady leak began to drip from one of the joints. He could almost hear the heartbeat of the men around him. His remained steady. He glanced at the radar on his arm, which displayed the depth of the water and their proximity to the shore. They were seconds away from deployment.

"Saddle up!" he announced into the comm. "We are hot in twenty seconds. When you see the green light, pop the hatch and move like you have a purpose! Every Knight makes it to shore! Tonight, the legend comes to life!"

There was no sound off, but his comment was felt and accepted by all. The subs slowed and then stopped. Oryan watched carefully; his eyes were fixed on the hatch with the go light in his peripheral vision. He kept a silent count in his head. With exactness, when his mental clock hit zero, the overhead lights went black, the go light beamed green, and the hatch silently snapped open.

Water rushed in, quickly filling the bottom of the transport. Only the top quarter of the subs were exposed as the tops were designed to be very hard to see against a watery backdrop. Oryan was the first out. The water lapped onto his mask, but between waves, he could see the distant flash of artillery from beyond the enemy tree line. When one of the fleet's shells exploded, he watched the sand burst over the water, landing in grains and chunks all around. The brief light of fire made apparent the smoke that hung near the tops of the trees from the weaponry of both sides. He could no longer see stars, moon, or sky. A small unmanned jet screamed overhead but did not make it far before it was struck from the sky by a nearly invisible missile. The plane rocketed toward the water, smashing into the sea only a few meters from where the transports were docked. Fire lingered on top of the rippling waves. All the while, Oryan and the Knights swiftly made their way to dry land.

Oryan signaled the fleet to stop their attack. The sand-filled eruptions stopped. He waited with each stroke and then with each step for the pounding of machine gunfire. He waited and waited, expecting to be shot at with each foot closer. When his boot sunk into the mud on the beach, the realization hit him that the only fire had been artillery shells trying desperately to stop the attack from the water. An unease gripped him, but he had to proceed as planned.

When all the men had made it to shore, they immediately began to deploy, each man and squad, to their respective targets. They were swift, silent, and deadly. Light firefights broke out in a few areas of the beach, but they were quickly silenced. Hand signals flashed, and silent commands were carried out with perfection. The first hour of their battle plan had been accomplished in minutes.

The beach was all but behind them when the first intense fighting began. There was a row of palm trees fifteen yards from shore that stretched for another twenty yards and then a bare strip of sand that ran between one row of trees and the next. When the Knights hit the end of the first tree line, gunfire blasted from all around. The landscape closely resembled the battlefield they were on when they challenged the Legion, which made their tactics the only familiar thing they had on their side. No one was lost in the first barrage. The squads moved slower, but they moved methodically across the sand, taking no prisoners and giving no quarter. Very little hand-to-hand fighting was required as almost every shot taken took an enemy life. The fighting lasted nearly an hour, but slowly, the defending fire from the trees ahead became thinner and thinner. When the Knights had reached the line, it was nonexistent.

Oryan and the Knights paused for a moment to tally their casualties. "Report," he said into the comm. It was the first word uttered since they had reached land. Each squad sounded off their numbers. There were eleven superficial wounds, nothing critical, and the body count was zero.

As they plunged into the trees, they found the ground littered with the bodies of their enemies. Tamrus was an effective metal for defense, but since the Knights aimed for weak points in the armor, such as faces and necks, it was of little avail. The heated bullets would sear through a human, leaving a cauterized hole about two inches in diameter wherever they struck. There was little blood, but the smell of fused and burning flesh was everywhere. Lifeless bodies hung from safety lines they had been wearing to prevent them from falling to their deaths from the perches above. The few that still squirmed were shot and killed, and those on the ground still alive were met with a similar fate. Nothing could be left to chance.

From here, two skirmish teams forged ahead, clearing murder and fox holes, heavy turret stations, scouting parties and lookouts. One more went out in search of booby traps and other less-detectable defenses. Beyond this two-mile stretch of trees was the real test. Tanks and lighter armor awaited them.

Oryan gathered his best two infiltrators and spoke to them alone. "I need that air force gone. I need it to be inoperative by the time we clear these trees. There are plenty of uniforms to choose from. Try not to get one with a hole in it," he said with quiet laughter as the response. "Once you're inside, make sure the damage is impossible to find unless you were the one to do it. Clear?"

They nodded their heads. "Once that is accomplished, hide in plain sight, but lie low. Ask no questions, follow all orders, etc. Understood?"

They responded the affirmative, and he sent them on their way. "Lieutenant, report."

"So far, so good, Captain. We stand now with the same number we came ashore with. We estimate the enemy dead nearing seven hundred. All three recon teams have reported the terrain clear, and we should be able to rendezvous in five. Sunup is in four hours. We can easily prepare and initialize our anti-armor tactics in that time."

"Well done, Lieutenant. Carry on." Oryan was visualizing the terrain maps in his head. He knew that there was no more cover beyond these trees. Until then, his men would be invincible, but five hundred men against five thousand and armor in open field was a daunting task no matter now deadly they were.

"Captain," came Thomas's voice again. "All recon squads reporting. It's time to advance."

"Acknowledged, Lieutenant. Rendezvous and prepare for armor assault. Comm silence until I signal. Out."

The Knights began to make their way to the forward positions that the skirmish units had cleared for them. Once they all held the same front line, the next stage of their plan began. There were no further attacks through the remainder of the night. The enemy made no attempt to retake the beach, and Oryan's men did not advance. When dawn came, they would see just how invincible they really were.

Oryan had supreme confidence in his men, but like all well-laid plans, there was always the danger of the unforeseen. He sweated and labored throughout the night to ensure that as many of those variables as possible were eliminated. The explosives were in place to clear a path for the reinforcements coming from the river. All remote weapons and stationary positions were set. The preparations were made as well as they could be.

When he finally reflected on the night's accomplishments, he once again weighed their lives in the balance. The odds were slim, and beach landing had given many delusions of an easy victory. The coming day would prove far more difficult and far bloodier for both sides. The enemy knew that during the night while Oryan and his men were dug in, any attack made to retake the beach was a futile gesture, and so they made their plans as well.

Thomas had spent the fading twilight entertaining the same thoughts. When he knew that he would not have the opportunity again, he left his solitude and sought out Oryan. He found him much as he had been. Knowing his commander as he did, he knew that the wrong words would turn him to stone on a night like this.

"Outnumbered, out gunned, armor, artillery and aircraft against us, a strong and determined enemy with better knowledge of the terrain, well rested and anxious to take back what we have claimed. Those are just the obvious problems," he said to Oryan.

"It all seems very simple sitting in that room at barracks, doesn't it?" asked Oryan.

He had chosen the right words. "The men are ready. If the operation continues to be successful, we will dispatch the armor with minimal loss. The artillery is not a huge concern. I would match these Knights one hundred to one against their soldiers."

Oryan looked at his lieutenant. "Brave Ethanis. An army unto himself. I admire your courage. I don't hold the trust you place in me lightly." He sighed deeply.

"With any luck, the air force will be the least of our aforementioned concerns. I have done my research on this man who commands here. He's no fool. He defeated the Legion on this same battlefield. The only real advantage is that he doesn't know who we are. Our swift victory on the beach will push the idea of regulars out of his mind. He will be thinking Special Forces; with any luck, he will be thinking we are the Legion. He has studied them long, and so our little trap has a good chance of success."

"What was it like, sir, fighting Agrion that day in the arena?" Thomas asked.

Oryan pondered the answer. "That is the second time today someone asked me that question."

"And ..." led Thomas.

"There were no variables. I knew my opponent, and I could see the end from the beginning. I felt no fear."

"But you feel fear now," said Thomas intuitively.

"I didn't know before I fought him that I would kill him. It happened that way and could not have happened any other. I don't fear today. I only wonder how many lives I must take before I find one that I do fear taking."

"Or losing," finished Thomas.

Oryan nodded. A cool breeze blew across his face. The smell of the water behind him filled his lungs. He looked down at his boots and watched the thin whips of sand race across the laces. He felt no fear. He felt nothing. It was as if nothing mattered. He recognized the mental blocks going up in his mind. *Men will die today. Some I will kill, and some of mine will be killed. This is war.*

He felt the breeze again rush over his neck. It brought new warmth that he had not felt in some time. He looked up from the ground to see the pale light in the east. Dawn had come.

"All right, Lieutenant. Pass out battery packs and ammunition. Tell the men to deploy. I don't want to see a single shot come from the same place twice. That artillery better not cost me a single Knight. Make sure of it."

Thomas nodded his head and silently turned to the business at hand. Oryan picked up his rifle and walked toward the tree line. He could not see his men dispersing amongst the trees, but he knew they were there. He had trained them to be ghosts, and he had trained them well. He knew full well that they were surrounding the fort with every passing second.

The defenses were the best that the military could produce, and the commander was supremely confident in their ability to ward off an attacker. His attack was efficient, methodical, and predictable. The strategy was simple. Hammer away at the largest concentration of attackers with the artillery, and then send in the armor to finish the job. It had made even the Legion retreat back to friendly territory.

When the word reached his ear that the beach defenses had been defeated in decisive fashion, he assumed the Captain and his men had returned for another round. He knew that Kovac's finest fought a siege the same way each time. When the attack came the last time, he did not even have to deploy the air force. He had planned for everything. He was more than prepared for the Legion to come a second time. He would not only be the commander to beat the empire's best the first time, he would be the first commander to defeat them every time.

He was prepared for anything. Except what was coming.

Light was creeping over the landscape, drawing long shadows across the ground. In the early morning, a fog hung low over the sand. The palm trees swayed gently with each sea-born breeze. Gulls could be heard farther down the beach, signaling the discovery of a treasure of corpses. There were no shouts, the thud of boots could not be heard; not even the steady breathing of the Knights surrounding the walls was distinguishable. Were this any other day, it would be the picture of serenity and peace.

Another breeze rolled in from the water and carried with it the sound of the birds from the shore. In one instant, the scene drastically changed. The docile glory that nature had provided was shattered by the penetrating violence of man. Artillery cannons boomed and cracked, belching forth their explosive projectiles. The palm trees that swayed gracefully a few moments before bent and erupted into a million shards with the impact of the shells. With each thunderous fire ball, the sand melted to glass or embedded itself into its surroundings. The face of the land was forcefully changing, but for all the destruction, no human flesh was included.

The Knights moved constantly around the fortification just out of range of the initial barrage. When the cannons stopped, they made their move. They had to move fast as it only took a few seconds to recalibrate the artillery to fall at longer distances. They opened fire, killing snipers and lookouts in the towers, as well as any who were stationed on the walls. It was accomplished so fast that the commander was very slow to replace their ranks. He was still focused on his assault on the enemy he had not seen. Except for the glowing shots coming from the trees, he could pinpoint nothing.

The second barrage started with much the same effect as the first. Oryan's men spotted the most forward cannons and, with a few well-placed rockets, eliminated the threat. Shortly after, the cannons stopped and did not resume.

The Knights waited for the next wave. Their strategy was based on the enemy making the first moves. A direct assault on the fort was almost certainly a fatal one, so the bait had to be irresistible. They knew that they would eventually have to give the enemy something solid to shoot at; otherwise, they would lose interest and become introverted. In a waiting game, they would certainly outlast the Knights.

Time was against both armies, as Oryan and his men could only last so long against the overwhelming odds, and the commander of the fort knew that his enemy's reinforcements were coming shortly behind so defenses had to remain intact. The question was, Which side could make the best of their time?

"Stay sharp, Knights," Thomas spoke his warning. "They will not give up so easily."

From inside the walls, the sound of jet engines could be heard. The unmanned fighters were small and easy to knock out of the sky, but Oryan's men carried very little in the way of surface-to-air weaponry, and by the time they could use it effectively, the anti-infantry weapons of the aircraft would tear them to pieces.

"Saddle up the SAMs, men!" Oryan barked. "We've got incoming!" It was obvious that his infiltration unit had failed. The two of them must be dead by now, which meant that the enemy knew he was not facing the Legion and that resources must be tight to attempt such a desperate maneuver. Both of those facts loomed very grim for their survival and the success of their mission. He cursed under his breath.

"Front gate opening, sir! We've got armor and infantry support coming our way! Awaiting command," came a voice over the comm.

He's going for the kill early on. This may work to our advantage.

"Hold the gate. Proceed with operation as planned! Execute!" Thomas commanded the frontline forces. "Do we have those SAMs up yet?"

"Two minutes, sir!" was the response.

"We don't have two minutes! Get on it!" Thomas was running to the gate, eager to see if their long night's work would pay off. It would only work once as the enemy would not be foolish enough to lose so much again so quickly, but it would send a very clear message. If it worked.

The aircraft roared to life and rocketed into the sky. Oryan listened intently to their progress as they left the landing strip. He had rushed to the Knights who were assembling the SAMs to assist and motivate. Every shot had to count. He could tell now that the jets would soon be clearing the top of the walls, and so he began scanning the horizon to locate his first target. The wait was not long as two small aircrafts burst into view at incredible speed. They were headed in the direction of the front gate, no doubt to clear the way for the tanks and infantry.

"Pick your targets! Get a good lock, and make sure you hit something flying that shouldn't be there! We can't afford to—" His words were cut short. He had been giving his orders, but his eyes had remained fixed on the aircraft threat. At least six more had been released that he could count, and the sound of high-powered propulsion could be heard out of his visual range. Without warning, a potential disaster turned into a bright torch of hope.

As the first two fighters cleared the wall, their burning red engines went black, the deafening noise ceased, and they spun toward earth, bringing indiscriminate carnage in their wake. The powerless aircraft slammed into the ground like stones. They crashed into their own forces, slicing through steel and flesh as they paved a bloody path through the ranks. Jet fuel sprayed from damaged tanks and in the ensuing havoc erupted into a brutal, unquenchable flame. Some tanks were decimated and others halted to avoid the same fate. Much of the infantry scattered; some were crushed with each hurtling meteor, and others burned in agony. It was too late to call back the aircraft that had already been launched as most of them were already reaching the walls at speeds that could not be stopped, so as a result, the scene of death and chaos at the front gate repeated itself wherever the jets had been deployed.

The images dancing on the sand were graphic and bloody. Such a horrific chain of events should never have to happen, and the loss of men and equipment was nothing short of tragic. Bearing this in mind, with all respect for his adversary, Oryan stood in the trees smiling from his elevated position. His men had not failed, and they had infiltrated the enemy ranks successfully. If he saw them again, he would wrap their medals around the drinks he would buy them. This was more than a good start. It was better than he could have hoped for. It was worth smiling about.

"Did we lose anyone in all that?" he asked over the comm. A few seconds passed while commanders made quick counts and reported casualties.

"As of right now, *zero* casualties to report, sir," came the enthusiastic voice of his lieutenant. Oryan was quite sure that Thomas was smiling too.

The smile disappeared in an instant, and Oryan made his next move. "It's over; time to move on. Thomas, lure them in. Execute." *Let's see if fortune truly is on our side.* He had heard that lightning never struck the same place twice, but that was because he was not the one throwing the thunderbolts. That was a hard act to follow, but the show, he knew, must go on, and the second act promised to be just as dramatic as the first. He headed for the gate.

At the gate, the Knights were making short work of the enemy infantry. After the fighters crashed in the midst of them, the soldiers had become chaotic and disorganized. They were running in all directions, taking no heed for cover or formation. Most were trying to avoid the heat of the fuel fires, others were trying to rescue fallen comrades, and some were just trying to make sense of all that had transpired. Thomas and the Knights at the gate were picking off the troops that strayed too close to the tree line while others were sending grenades and short-range rockets into the confusion near the walls.

The tanks had stopped their progress trying to avoid the wreckage. There were a few that had fallen victim to the crashes, but most were still operational, suffering only minor damage from the fires or shrapnel. For the Knights staging the frontal assault, this was a perfect situation. Before the aircraft disaster, baiting the tanks to come into the trees was proving a life-risking maneuver. Now, with the infantry dropping left and right, artillery proving useless, and the air strike a disaster, the armor had no choice but to advance on the assailing foe.

When the order to strike was issued, the heavy tanks maneuvered around the wreckage and did their best not to crush the bodies of the fallen men. Once they had cleared the debris, they accelerated toward the tree line, cannons and short-range machine guns blazing. The Knights offered little resistance, only turning to return cover fire, feigning the retreat perfectly. The tanks took the bait and, spurred on by a desire for vengeance, pushed their huge bulk to the limits of their speed.

Thomas led the men on; each man knew his part, running and finding cover in the defilades made the night previous for just such an attack. Three men at a time would retreat further in the trees, while three more fired back at the tanks from their cover. Had they been on open ground, they would have been overtaken quickly, but the massive war machines had trees and underbrush to contend with, which slowed their advance. The retreat was precise and deliberate. Small arms fire and the occasional rocket kept the tank commanders hungry for the pursuit. Cannon blasts exploded around them, most missing their fast-moving targets.

Once they had reached their destination, they halted and began to offer strong resistance. There were a few small squads working their way back, but the heavy fire from their fortified allies kept them safe for the retreat. Thomas was watching the last three-man group move from their cover and make for the last hold out.

"As soon as those men are back, give them all you have. I want smoke grenades and flares ignited to cover the path in front of those tanks!" he shouted.

A sudden explosion rocked their position much closer than the others. Thomas turned to make sure that all his men had made it back to the fallback point. As the smoke cleared from the last explosion, he felt the sting of the Knights' first loss. Where his men had been just a moment before, only a blackened crater filled with a few lingering flames and ash remained. Time stood still. Until now, they truly seemed immortal. Now the harsh reality of war wrapped its cold fingers around the hearts of the compassionate commander. One second he had near five hundred men; the next, three lives were erased from existence. It happened in a heartbeat.

Thomas's heart began to race, and his mind swam; a million doubts and sorrow taking their claim. These were the first men he had lost while in command. They were his responsibility, and he had failed them. In the heat of the moment, he lost focus until a familiar voice shouted the orders that saved the lives of the rest of the men fighting the battle.

"Lay it down thick, Knights! Give 'em everything you have! Fire flares and smoke grenades! Fire, fire!" Captain Jeckstadt shouted.

The men responded flawlessly, and in seconds a layer of smoke several feet thick blanketed the space between them and the oncoming tanks. Thomas was again awakened to his responsibilities and took control of the situation. Oryan had joined the ranks of the men firing mercilessly at the enemy on the other side of the wall of smoke. Trees were smashing down in front of them as the heavy treads pushed down the shallow-rooted palms. A few of the trees slashed through the smoke, revealing the threat fast approaching. Less than one hundred men now held an invisible line against more than fifty armored twenty-ton tanks.

The Knights stood their ground and kept up their seemingly futile assault. The tanks began to pierce the smoke cloud like apparitions in the mist. Their rumble shook the ground, and the sound was resonating in each man's ears. They were sixty feet away. Another blast erupted, and half a dozen more Knights were thrown lifeless to the ground. Now only fifty feet. Still the Knights held on, firing at the thick steel armor bearing down on them. Two more blasts and a handful more fell. Forty feet.

It seemed that the tanks would soon overtake them, their grills and treads appearing to be twisted mouths filled with metal teeth waiting to grind bone and flesh. The tanks' treads elevated slightly as they passed over a slight raise. As they came smashing down back onto level ground, the Knights felt their hope renewed and the sacrifice of their friends shined with valor and bravery.

The heavy bulk of the tanks splintered the weak bridge the Knights had constructed and camouflaged the night before. Below it was an eight-foot-deep, sixty-foot-wide trench dug straight down into the sand. The momentum of the tanks sent them headlong into the trench with no way of recovering. There was a tremendous crash as tons of metal smashed into the ground floor. The tanks ground their gears and spun their treads in a desperate search for traction and escape. Many tank commanders realized the futility of their efforts and began to climb from their stations. What a moment before had been a massacre of men became a grave full of metal corpses.

"Now!" shouted Oryan through the comm. On his command, the soldiers nearest the trench lit their flares and dropped them into the hole below, igniting the accelerant lining the bottom. The fire erupted where the flares landed and spread in both directions along the trench floor. The screams of burning men could be heard back to the walls of the fort. "Forward!" came his cry again.

The Knights rushed around the gaping hole, avoiding the tall flames and the protruding rears of tanks. Any escaping troops were forced back to their fiery tomb. The few stragglers that had avoided the trench were reeling, trying to turn and flee to the safety of the walls, but the narrow space and uneven terrain made the retreat a far slower process than they hoped. Oryan's men were on them before long. They climbed to the top hatches, dropping grenades inside to kill the driver and gunners. Timed explosives were stuck to the sides of others, and seconds later they were nothing more than a twenty-ton roadblock in the midst of the fallen trees. Minutes later, Oryan and his diversionary Knights returned to what once had been the tree line to finish the job.

The infantry followed the tanks into the trees. They supposed that a majority of the attacking force was scattered by the tanks, but they painfully underestimated their enemy. No sooner did they get past the tree line than the Knights who had remained hidden on the flanks of the tanks' approach surrounded them and went quickly to work with sword and hand. By the time that Oryan arrived with Thomas and the rest of the men, the Knights had carved a bloody path almost to the shadow of the gate.

There were no remaining functional tanks. The sound of a few exploding fuel tanks and engines could be heard from the trench that now lay behind them. Thousands of bodies carpeted the sand, singed by precision gunfire or hacked down with lethal proficiency. What men were still able ran back to the safety of the fort.

As the noon sun rose, the forces of Vollmar had lost seventy-three armored vehicles, twenty-one aircraft, and more than three thousand troops. The Kentaurus Knights had lost twenty-eight men.

Soon after Oryan and Thomas arrived at the gate, all of the troops that Vollmar had released were either laying on the battlefield or safely behind the protection of their walls. Oryan surveyed the damage, soaking in the utter ruin that had been left in the wake of his Knights. The morale of the enemy *had* to be battered beyond hope of repair. His men were nearly unscathed. He took a moment to reflect on the fallen Knights, but while he lamented the loss of life, he reveled in the sheer terror that these men had caused.

He looked back at the fort's walls, now only some thirty feet behind him. No guards remained on the tops. No tower had snipers or lookouts. He half expected to see white flags of surrender flying from the nests. He turned back to the men who were now standing amongst the dead and the flames. He searched for the right words, searching hard for how to tell them how he felt at this moment. This battle was not over, but there was little doubt who would emerge victorious.

The captain of the Kentaurus Knights raised his rifle in the air and did the only thing that seemed appropriate: he bellowed a single monotone sound from the depths of his soul. It was more fitting than words, and his men, filled with the same adrenaline, followed his lead.

For the enemy on the other side of the wall, hearing their

dominating foe make such a noise was like hearing the sound of the hammer driving the nail in the coffin that was to bury you alive. Men who had held their composure during the battle melted into tears of despair. From this battle, there was no hope. Some men found the strength to pluck up their courage and carry on, but most turned inward and began to mourn the families, friends, and homes they would never see again.

Outside the gate, Oryan gave new orders. "Those of you with accelerant tanks, douse the battlefield. I want this place incinerated."

"Sir, there are men still alive on the field," Thomas noted. He had been trained to leave none alive, but after witnessing his men die for the first time, a merciful end was all he could hope for any man.

"I leave it to you, Lieutenant," said Oryan. "Shoot the wounded before you burn it, but make sure none live and that the fire consumes the corpses. Send a small company back to the trench. We need to do some clean up there and prepare our dead."

Thomas acknowledged the order. "What do we do in case of another attack?"

Oryan doubted highly that they would come out from behind their walls, but there was only one answer to give. "Make it the last mistake they ever make."

He walked away from the gate. Once he reached the first row of fallen trees, a group of ten men came running behind. He marched them back to the still burning trench and ordered that the flames be left to burn. They searched the surroundings for their fallen, sometimes finding the men, sometimes finding only pieces. They gathered them to a place behind the trench and began to build pyres for each. Soldiers of the empire did not return to their homeland to be buried. It was cremation or nothing for them, their ashes being spread afterward.

The men worked with their captain. Soon, twenty-eight small fires burned, and the men watched their comrades find peace.

"You men," said Oryan, "take your rest. Leave one for a watch, and I will signal if you're needed." Though he expected nothing less than perfection, exhausted soldiers were dead ones no matter how well they were trained.

He walked back up to the gate. The sun had begun its decent. Oryan looked above him to see the cloudless sky. Still, the black smoke from fires in all directions deluded the sun's rays. As he walked, he once again took pride in the day's accomplishments. It had been a flawless battle so far. Even the losses suffered were not as great as he anticipated. Reinforcements were due in fifty-eight hours, and at this rate, there would be no real need for them. Oryan doubted that any real fighting would be had for the remainder of their time. He expected more artillery fire, but that was easily avoided.

His thought became cool and completely without emotion. The engine that was his brain began to take over, and it made him sharp for dealing death. There was only one real outcome to this battle, and that was that every man inside that fort must be dead. Oryan and his Knights would never take a prisoner nor let an enemy leave with his life. There was too much at stake. Mercy, compassion, and rules of engagement were second to their survival. The message had to be delivered dramatically and without question: to face the Kentaurus Knights was to face death. Any battle they entered they would end and make sure that the same fight did not have to be fought twice. Even the Legion would grow to fear their presence. To be hunted by the Knights would be any man's worst nightmare, only worse.

One of his men came running to him and saluted when he came close.

"What news, Sergeant? It the field clear yet?" he asked.

"Sir, no sir. The commander of the fort waits for you at the gate and asks for an audience, sir. Should we kill him?" asked the sergeant.

Though he did not smile outwardly, he felt the urge. This soldier had caught his vision. "No. I'll go."

The sergeant bowed slightly and walked before him to the gate. The Knights gathered there had formed a semicircle in front of their enemy. The men on each end held an unlit flare in his hand ready to ignite the ground at the first sign.

The commander of the fort stood alone facing the Knights. His uniform was clean and neatly pressed. His rank insignias and all his medals were perfectly polished and shone proudly. He wore a neatly kept beard that was turning slightly gray as was the hair that could be seen from under his cap. He was a stout man, a slight pot belly protruded from above his belt, but he held his head high. His shoulders were back, and his broad chest was out. His posture was perfect. Vollmar was full of officers—some willing and able, others just able. He fit both categories.

Oryan approached, by contrast looking very battle worn. His rank only shone as a patch on both arms. A mix of dirt, blood, and ash covered the uniform and his face. As he removed his helmet, a mess of tangled sweaty white hair fell to his shoulders. When he had seen the enemy commander, he had tucked the butt of his rifle under his arm and held it loosely at his side.

The fort commander stared long at the man who was leading these troops. He was young, just a kid by comparison. Had he been more interested in such things, he would have recognized Oryan from the Net as many of his men did looking from the walls. This boy was no older than his son, but this boy had also just handed him the most humiliating defeat he had faced in his time as an officer. He may be young, but there was something about him. This boy was a killer—a tried, tested, and unrepentant killer. The commander rightly judged that he must choose his words very carefully.

"I am Lieutenant General Nikroe, commanding officer of the fourth army, seventh mobile air unit, and tenth armor division, charged with the defense of this fortification." He bowed low. "I have come in hopes that we can discuss the fate of our forces as men."

Oryan scrutinized this man. His conscience was still locked in a mode of indifference. Those words, however eloquent and moving, penetrated Oryan no further than his ears. "My name is of no consequence. These men with me are Kentaurus Knights, and their fate is decided by action and not by words."

The name Kentaurus Knights was not unfamiliar to him. He was a great student of military history, and though he felt such a boast a bit premature, he would not dismiss the notion. "Surely, *Captain*," Nikroe said, identifying the rank on his arm, "surely there is some way that we can come to a mutual agreement that will help to avoid any more ... unpleasant confrontations. You and your men have fought a battle today that you should have never won, but despite the odds, you have turned death into a fighting chance to live. You are to be commended for such valor."

"General, I am quite sure you have not put yourself in harm's way to tell me what I already know. I am offering you nothing. What terms do you have?"

Nikroe nodded his head, knowing that he had overplayed his hand. This was no politician or diplomat here but a soldier. Words would not sway him. "I know that though your men are valiant, they are few. I know that despite my losses this day, I still outnumber your men at least four to one if not more. I also know that you have no armor support, which means that you are only a diversionary force, sent here to clear the way for stronger reinforcements. I underestimated you today, and so I have paid dearly for my mistake. Don't think me so foolish as to make that mistake again."

"You see much, General. You've drawn many conclusions, some that are accurate and some that aren't. You think that by your unspoken threats you will persuade me to cease my attack and withdraw or surrender to your custody. May I remind the general that this morning we were outnumbered *eight* to one."

"Captain, please. The Knights of old were legendary and made the world tremble for hundreds of years. If you truly believe yourselves to be a force of legendary quality, don't throw away your lives here, for if you stay, you will die. I offer you now just one chance to turn from here and leave. I will allow all of your men safe passage to the river. Please accept these terms."

Oryan's defiance rose. He stared at this man who seemed overly confident given the days events. However, he was right. Oryan knew that he would not be so foolish as to send his troops out again so rashly. He would sit behind his high walls and batter them with artillery. He would make it rain shells. He was right on more than one account. The Kentaurus Knights were legendary. Legends are only born by taking legendary action in legendary times.

"Your knowledge of history is impressive. If you are such a student, then you should know that the fighting skill of the Knights of old was only matched by their ferocity. I know what you plan to do. Do not think me so foolish as to not see through your words!" As he spoke, Oryan seemed suddenly to grow taller and more menacing, dwarfing his adversary. "Your terms are *rejected!* We need no mercy from you! Look around you, *Commander!* Perhaps you should take heed and consider *your* fate! Go back now and send word to your superiors that the Kentaurus Knights have come and before them goes *death!*" The men behind him chanted, "Death, death!" It echoed long and loud over the walls and to the shores. Oryan shot his opponent a parting glance and very coldly ended the conversation. "Go, General, before you burn with the rest of your dead."

Nikroe stood tall and tugged on his uniform to straighten any wrinkles. There was no changing of opinions here. They must agree to disagree until one of them was dead. Despite his superior numbers and his access to far more deadly firepower, he left his encounter feeling anything but reassured. Their reinforcements would come eventually. Tomorrow or the next day, they would come. Could his men last that long? He felt less confident in his advantages than ever before. This boy and his men had beaten his troops once, and so his men would not fight with the same courage again. They had defeated his air superiority without firing a shot. And his armor had proved all but useless. They may be out of tricks, but then again, they may not. He left that encounter feeling only one thing, and that was doubt.

Oryan walked away from their meeting and signaled the men with flares as he passed. At that moment he and his men were immortal. They were on their way to being legendary. His men each ignited their flares and threw them to the ground. The accelerant on the ground caught immediately and roared to life. Soon, flames reached as high as the walls themselves, carrying with it black smoke, the smell of melting metal, and burning flesh. Troops from Vollmar watched the flames rise, seeing their enemy ripple like specters in and out of view through the rising waves of invisible heat.

Throughout the rest of that day and long into the night, Nikroe pounded the trees with artillery more to destroy the Knights' cover than to destroy the Knights themselves. Oryan watched the fort's ghostly image as it danced in the flickering flames. As the fires died, he watched the artillery rounds leave the cannons. He could see the lights as the massive weapons lit up the sky. Shortly after the lights came the distant rolling boom of the explosions. The barrels must have been superheated as the night wore on. Eventually, he could see the individual super-heated shells rise and descend like falling stars against the black sky. It held its own beauty.

He had sat alone, sulking in his melancholy mood, knowing that his men had found appropriate shelter and were simply waiting out the night. Oryan took some comfort in the silence away from his men and the up-close carnage of war. He had ordered comm silence, dictating that all communication be done in person. While his thoughts strayed, he sensed a presence behind him. It had come silently, but it was familiar and he had no need to fear. "Lieutenant, what report?"

"After twenty-four hours, twenty-eight dead, nineteen wounded, sir."

Oryan sighed heavily. It was clear to Thomas that there was something weighing on his mind more than just wounded men. "This is only the first day. There may be a hundred more."

"Sir, reinforcements ..." Thomas trailed off as Oryan raised a hand to silence him.

"I received a personal communication from the fleet four hours ago. They say that no reinforcements are available at this time."

Thomas's heart sank; his mouth fell open in disbelief. "Wh ... Extraction?"

"They say that extraction is not possible at this time. We're supposed to hold out and wait for orders. They refused to say how long. As of now, we do not inform the men."

Ethanis Thomas suddenly felt very alone. In a battlefield of brothers, he had to carry this burden alone. In a world full of strong men, he had to be stronger than them all. He refused to believe this was reality. He shook his head slowly; even if they could manage to survive until reinforcements came, how long would that be? *They have sent us here to die.*

His mouth moved, forcing a whisper, barely audible to escape his lips. "This is only the first day."

Operation Knightfall, Day Two: Oryan's Wrath

"You had us all a little nervous out here," said Oryan into his communicator.

"Well, we quickly discovered that the programmers of these planes designed them to ignore any previous command given when it is superseded by a command given under the codes of a senior officer," replied one of the Knights who had infiltrated the fort.

"So had you told them simply to never take off, the command to strike would have overridden that line of code."

"Exactly. However, the programmers, for all their genius, made a glaring oversight. They designed the aircraft only to engage once they reached the target zone. It's a good idea in theory because it makes them identify hostiles from friendlies instead of just a direct attack."

"That's good news for us. So what did you finally program them to do?"

"We simply gave them a range. We downloaded the schematics of the fort, and it turns out that the airstrip is in the exact middle of the structure. So they were given an immediate shutdown order just before they reached the walls. That shut them down before the strike order could be given while still not overriding any previous command from a senior officer."

Oryan smirked. *Genius.* It was a simple command, one easy to rig and hard to find. If they covered their tracks well, that line of code would be overlooked. Knowing his Knights, that line of code was probably as difficult to find as a needle in a stack of needles. "Did you cover your tracks?"

"Sir, they would need more time than they have left plus some to find that one."

"Good. Make sure it stays that way."

"About that, sir, I think we've figured out a way to take out that artillery for you. It wouldn't take much, but it would save you a few headaches."

Oryan considered the proposition. "After today, they will be looking for you. The artillery is just an annoyance. There's no need for you two to risk getting made. Lie low and don't die. I may need you before this is all over."

"Sir, everyone in here is preoccupied with the hurt you put on them out there. Believe me; we had to put on an award-winning performance not to be the only ones celebrating today. I think we could pull this off and no one would blink an eye."

"No. Do not proceed. That's an order."

There was a dramatically long silence. "Acknowledged, sir. Out."

Oryan was near the front gate, making sure that the only attack they were facing was indeed the artillery. He paced the ground, thinking on his last command. He did not want to lose those men, but to dismantle the artillery would certainly force Nikroe's hand. Would it be worth two more deaths? He weighed lives in the balance. If he knew it would save the lives of the rest of his men, he knew the choice he had to make. However, he was faced with the fact that no matter what they disabled from the inside, they might all still die. For now, he had to rationalize to himself that he had made the right choice. If nothing else, those men might make it out alive.

Nikroe was a man of conformity. He defended his fort exactly as it was supposed to be done. Were they to write a textbook on defenses, they need look no further than General Nikroe for their inspiration. He was also a student of war. He was probably bred from war simulations and strategy games like most officers in Vollmar. He was trained to think one step ahead of his opponent. He was trained perfectly, by the book.

But Oryan was not accustomed to reading the same literature as the good general. He had already dealt him an unorthodox battle, and so now Oryan knew that Nikroe would call what commanders he had left and begin to figure out what the next unorthodox step was. He would be trying to write Oryan's textbook before Oryan could. So, why not use such information? Oryan was there as a diversionary force that had now become the *only* force, but Nikroe didn't know that reinforcements weren't coming. So now, what to do?

He could not hesitate for long or they would all be dead in hours. Though the artillery was guesswork and not very accurate against his fast and adaptive Knights, it would soon take its toll destroying all cover and slowly whittling away lives. He had to act and act soon. What was the next page in his book? What was the next page in the normal book? That was the answer! Nikroe is now over-thinking. He'll be expecting some new elaborate scheme hatched from deep within Oryan's brain, but why not give him the expected. If his Knights truly were a *diversionary* force, the next logical step would be to clear a way for the *main* force.

His mind became clear and sharp as the decision locked itself into place. He felt positive about this course of action. It would not guarantee success, far from it, but it would open new doors.

"Where are you?" asked Oryan over the comm.

The shells were landing hard and loud, flame and shrapnel scattered in all directions. Thomas could barely catch the tiny voice of his commanding officer through the tumult around him. He braced himself behind the remains of a tree, covered his left ear with his hand, and shouted into his comm. "I'm here, sir! It's pretty dicey over here; no time for updates! I'll report in when things cool off a bit, over!"

"What other commanders are in the area?"

"Sir, just a few squad leaders! I think I have Enktuya and Arinbold!" A blast shattered his cover and sent him sprawling face first into the dirt. He scrambled back to his hands and feet and threw his weight behind another tree trunk. His ears rang and his head throbbed. Once again came the small voice of a calm captain.

"Do you copy?"

"No, sir! I did not copy, over!"

"I said, Enktuya and Arinbold are both capable commanders. Give them charge and rendezvous with me at the gate, over."

Was he out of his mind? What was he thinking? "Sir, I am in a fight! With all due respect, my place is here! Request permission to remain at the front!" Another shell slammed into the ground near him, throwing sand like a thousand small darts against his skin.

"Denied! Turn command over to the squad leaders and report back here, double time, over and out!"

Thomas fumed. He could not know what was so urgent that it required him to be pulled away from combat like this. If those men were to die, he wanted to die with them. He felt that their survival here hinged upon his presence and to leave them now was to condemn them to certain death. Still, he trusted his captain's judgment. After all, Enktuya and Arinbold were very capable commanders.

As he left the carnage, the noise of the explosions became more distant and not near as constant. He jogged at a steady pace toward the front, but he began to realize how tired his body was. He felt fatigue creep up his calves and into his thighs. Then his shoulders sank, and his fingers loosened on his rifle's grip. Blood rushed to his hand and returned color to his white knuckles. The sound of each heartbeat echoed through his whole frame, and each breath was a labor-filled torture. He ached. Sweat had long ago drenched all of his underclothing, but until now, he had not noticed. He had not slept in forty-eight hours. He had been Ethanis Thomas, Lieutenant of the Kentaurus Knights forty-eight straight hours. For the first time in that forty-eight hours, he was feeling much more Ethanis and much less lieutenant.

He jogged on, knowing that if Captain Jeckstadt felt it necessary to pull him from battle it must be worth it. The curiosity drove him on. It revived his sore limbs and gave flight to his sinking heart. Perhaps, the captain had heard some good news. Thomas neared the gate. He could see Captain Jeckstadt giving orders to two soldiers and then sending them away. If he ached as Thomas did, he did not show it. He stood tall and proud, not even flinching when an artillery shell exploded too close for comfort. Perhaps he had good news or at least, some word of advice to brighten Thomas's dismal demeanor. He was now standing in front of his captain. Perhaps, he had hope.

"You look like hell," he said, looking Thomas over from head to toe.

So much for hope.

"So you want us to line the trees with explosives and proceed as planned? Seems rather pointless, don't you think?" asked Thomas.

Oryan shrugged. There was an air of nonchalance to him. It was as if nothing mattered anymore. "Gotta keep up appearances. He doesn't know no one's coming," said Oryan, pointing back at the fort. His eyes were staring off in the distance. Thomas was convinced he was looking at nothing, for there was nothing to be seen save trees and sand.

"Sir, he won't fall for the same thing twice. He's smarter than that," replied Thomas.

Oryan sat still and quiet for a moment. As Thomas observed, he felt for the first time ever that there was really no cognitive thought passing through his commander's head. Oryan, until this moment, always had the look of a man whose mind was in perpetual motion. It was the most perfect, well-lubricated, and smoothest-running machine he had ever witnessed, yet now it seemed dull and sleepy as if time and trial had finally taken their toll.

His heart took pity on Oryan. It was a strange emotion to have, and Thomas felt embarrassed and ashamed to feel such a thing toward his captain. He knew very little of Oryan *the man.* The only side of this person he had ever been privy to was Oryan *the warrior.* He had no emotion save it served him on the battlefield. He had no life before his service, and it would end just as soon as that term expired, by his will or no. To his men, Oryan had not been *born.* He had been made, designed in some war factory to be the ultimate instrument of lethal destruction. Their captain was what he had to achieve, and that was what made him seem beyond corruption. Oryan's determination was what made the Knights as great as they were. It was his will that drove them past the Legion, and it would be his will that determined their fates here. Until now, that is all that Thomas had ever seen.

Now, Oryan looked very young yet prematurely old. He seemed burdened with the weight of the world resting on his shoulders. His demeanor was harsh; dried dirt rested on all his features save the spots where his sweat had cleaned a path down his face. Here and there spots of dried blood mixed in with the mess. A few strands of matted white hair clung to his brow and temples. Though his face told the tale of these last few days, and ultimately his life, there was a glow about him. There was a hint of innocence, of life that rage and carnage could not extinguish. For an instant, Thomas could see the humanity in him. There was a past and a future here that was far more than the military. He knew compassion. He knew sorrow. He knew love.

"Do you ever think that some people are *too* smart?" Oryan asked. Thomas looked at him puzzled. "What I mean is, do you ever think that smart people are eventually doomed by their own intelligence? Eventually, there will come a problem that they cannot solve. They'll analyze it until no probable conclusion can be reached. Then they'll overanalyze it. At what point does their intelligence become stupidity? They can't wrap their brain around a problem with no solution. They've been programmed over the years to believe that to every problem there is a solution, so they keep trying. What happens when a solution does not exist?"

Thomas still was not grasping the point of this philosophical discussion. "Sir, what does any of this have to do with us? And surely you didn't pull me from my men for a lesson on the stupidity of men."

Oryan turned his empty stare to Thomas and shook a finger at him. "They're my men. Don't forget that."

His tone was not harsh, nor was it defensive in nature, yet it stung Thomas to the heart. He had overstepped his bounds. He knew trust was a difficult thing to earn, easy to lose, and impossible to regain, yet now he had to wonder if he would ever get it back.

"What this has to do with *us* and with your life and the lives of all of *my* men is simple. The man against us has spent his life uncovering ways to defeat his enemies. For every battle he encounters, there must be a solution. He is proactive in the respect that he has an automated response to anything that an enemy can throw at him. It keeps him from being caught off guard.

"What can we do to defeat him and make it out of this alive? I have been analyzing this question for hours. Then it occurred to me: there was no solution to that problem because us making it out alive or even defeating him was not the problem."

Thomas started to see where he was going, but the answer was still hazy for him. He held the silence, letting Oryan know that it needed further explanation.

"The problem is not life or death, winning or losing with this man. The problem is who can *create* a problem that offers the other no solution. He has been *pro*active to all that we do, so why not do what will make him *re*active."

Then it fell into place for Thomas. "He is expecting the unexpected, so if we give him the expected, he will respond in turn. Blow the trees, and he will try and plug the gap."

"Exactly, but he will not underestimate me again, so we have to force the issue. He won't just send his troops out into the trees just because we clear a path. So at the same time, we stop all advances, all attacks, and all movement. We allow his spotters to return to their posts on the walls; we allow this fort to regain a sense of normal operations."

It was a novel idea. Silence could be torture unto itself if used correctly. "It will be a small victory for them. They will begin to regain confidence."

Oryan nodded. "Yes, and we let them have it. Then, we shatter those hopes a bit. We don't have to fire a single shot; all we have to do is make them think. We send out a fake signal over the comm. It states that reinforcements are coming and that it will be soon. The same signal needs to be repeated and needs to be broadcast on a low-frequency, encrypted channel. We can't make the encryption too hard or too easy, but once they break it, they will prepare for the onslaught. Then, we make our next move and double the size of the path.

"They'll think that the force coming after them is enormous. That would intimidate me. And so we wait until he makes his move. He will want to plug a hole like that as soon as possible. I doubt he'll send his troops as he saw what we did to them last time. The air force is still shot; we know that, otherwise he would have used it by now. That might just empty the rest of his armor."

"Get on it, Thomas. We may be able to turn this around."

Thomas saluted, smiled, and turned to his duty. The distant sound of mortar fire could still be heard. Oryan watched him disappear into the trees and watched three Knights fall in behind him, appearing as if they were ghosts in the dark.

Oryan found his communications officer and instructed him on what signal to send, how often to repeat it, and what frequencies to use. From there, he headed back to the gate. He could see no Knights, but they were there. The artillery fell like rain for a moment and then ceased. Then he heard the same pattern echo from another front. He was listening closely, discovering the pattern to their fire. It was clear that Nikroe was now trying to conserve shells. Earlier, there were no safe places around the fort; now, three or four sides remained calm.

The shells detonated in front of him for nearly a minute and then trailed off to hammer another target. The fire was anything but random. His Knights had been still for some time, only becoming visible to pick off any soldier who felt a false sense of security and ventured to take a peek over the walls. Oryan listened again to the fall of shells. They were working their way clockwise around the fort. He began to keep count in his head how long the shells fell in one place and then how long before they picked up again in another. Before long, he had the routine mastered.

He listened as the artillery approached the right side of the fort. There were two more barrages, forty-six seconds each, and then it would return to the front. He counted slowly. The explosions ended. Twenty-nine seconds until the destruction began here again. *Fifteen, fourteen, thirteen*, he counted in his head. This had almost become boring. *Seven, six, five… Get small, Knights. Three, two, one…* silence.

Nothing happened. No explosions, no cannon fire, no nothing. Oryan waited for troops on the walls, he waited for the gate to open, he waited for a white flag, for *anything*, but there was only silence. It was puzzling to him. If they had indeed intercepted the false transmission, they would not have stopped. They would have instead focused more of their fire on the gate. They couldn't be out of shells. Even a foolish commander would conserve them long enough to hold out for weeks if necessary. So, why did they stop?

"Explosives set. Detonation in sixty seconds. Clear front gate," said Thomas over the comm. Oryan and the Knights slipped from their cover quickly and silently as shadows. Just as they were settling into new positions, Thomas detonated the explosives. The sound was quiet in comparison to what they had become accustomed to in the artillery shells, but it did the job for which it was intended. Rows of trees fell with a crash to the ground. A wide, smoking path was now laid bare from the shore to the fort. Oryan waited for the rhythmic pounding of the artillery to commence again, but the only sound heard from inside the fort was silence.

"Sir, I'm at a loss," said Thomas. "Maybe he's calling our bluff. Maybe he knows more than he lets on."

"How could he know..." Oryan began his thought, but the realization of the answer struck him as if in response to his own question. His men inside. They had been discovered. It was they who had stopped the artillery. Nikroe found them and pried the truth from them. Then another thought came to his mind. Those men knew nothing of the lack of reinforcements. Even under the greatest torture, they had nothing to tell.

Oryan's instinct reaffirmed that his intuition about them was true. They had been the ones to stop the artillery, but at what cost? He loathed the idea of the loss of two more Knights. Every man lost hastened their defeat. More than that, Oryan felt as if these men were his brothers. They were blood to him, closer than any family he had known since... He suppressed the memories of his youth. They may yet be alive.

Legendary moments are born from legendary opportunity. It was at this moment that a legend was born. As Oryan was stoking the fires of war in his heart, Nikroe supplied then fanned the flames. Like the fires spawned from the damaged fuel tanks, Oryan exploded.

A call echoed from the tops of the walls. "Captain! Captain!" it taunted. Fifty men appeared atop the wall above the gate. The men there cleared a space where two bodies were brought into plain view.

"Captain!" they called again. Oryan and the Knights knew who the dead men were, despite the disfiguration and mutilation done to the corpses. The leering soldiers dropped the bodies over the wall where they snapped stiff, hung by their necks. The jolt of the rope's tension finished the wound around one of the Knight's neck, and his head was torn free of his body. The limp corpse and severed head fell to the ground in a grotesque heap. The other Knight still swung to and fro on the end of his rope, ten feet from the ground.

Hate consumed Oryan. The other Knights gazed at him in awe. This rash action had left them all in a state of such shock that they stayed in their places, fearful they might wind up a victim of their own captain's wrath. His cries shook the foundations of the fort, and from deep within its walls, General Nikroe shivered in fear, hearing his death approaching.

The soldiers on the wall fired wildly at him. He was the symbol of death and revenge coming for them, and so their shots were in desperation. None found their mark. To the Knights, he was moving in slow motion; to the men of Vollmar, it was as if he simply appeared at the wall. In a leap, he grasped the bloody end of the rope where his man had fallen and began to climb as if he were a starving spider who had finally caught her prey. The bolts rained down at him, finding wall, ground, and air but no flesh. A few shots glanced off of his Tamrus armor, but the shock of their impact did not slow him. The men tried desperately to cut the rope that he was climbing, but he was simply too fast for them to accomplish their goal.

When he was only a few feet from the top, he looked up at the men who stood there. Their eyes were filled with a paralyzing fear. Many of them were so frozen that the ability to fire their weapons was lost. He sprang to the top, drawing his sword, and in his first stroke, two fell headless from the heights. He was amongst them, around them, everywhere but nowhere at the same time. With the edge of his blade, he moved like the angel of death through the men on the walls. Some leaped to their deaths rather than face him, screaming as they did so.

And so the legend was born. Hacking, dismembering, disemboweling, and beheading, he tore through them. Fifty-three men lay lifeless within three minutes of his ascension. Before he was done, the Knights had gathered at the base of the wall and the soldiers of Vollmar were assembled on the other side. Oryan stood on the wall between the forces, sword in hand, still and silent. He was covered in blood, but despite his appearance, none could escape the fires that burned out of control behind his crystal blue eyes.

There was an eternity of silence it seemed before he spoke. He bent down and took a head by the scalp, holding it to his men and then his enemies. "See now what you have brought upon yourselves! See now and bear witness to all the world that you face Death here! Go! Let every man among you prepare to meet your fate for tomorrow. The hell we send you to will be a paradise by comparison!"

Then Oryan focused on the soldier nearest the wall, the only one who looked at him with awe and reverence rather than fear. "You!" he said, pointing at the man. "Go and tell your *general* what has transpired here. Bear witness to him that he has sealed his own death and the death of you all. Give him this," he threw the head at the man, "and tell him *we're coming.*

With the last stroke of his sword, he cut the rope that held the other Knight hanging from the wall. With that, he disappeared down the wall and to his Knights.

When he set foot on the ground, his men stood in shocked silence. None of them had ever heard of such feats, and most remained in disbelief that their eyes had beheld such a spectacle. Oryan looked at each of them, his eyes still burning. "Clear the bodies. Then return to your posts," was all he said.

He walked away from the wall, and the Knights waiting there moved out of his way, starring and gawking after him for many minutes to come. It was Thomas who broke the trance. "The captain gave orders. Clear the bodies and find cover. We still have a job to do here."

The Knights carried out the orders, at first moving lethargically as if they had been rudely awakened from a deep sleep, but then with the usual speed and efficiency they had been trained for. When they had all regained their state of invisibility, Thomas turned his thoughts to his captain. No one had seen where he went, but Thomas had an idea. He knew Oryan, and so he knew that wherever there was open sky, there he would be. But what to say and how to approach him, he did not know. Only one thing was certain: it was going to be a wild night.

Oryan was indeed sitting alone under a starry sky, though he did not gaze upon them. The blood on his body had dried onto his skin and clothes. His sword was sheathed on his back with his rifle slung on his shoulder. He had laid his helmet at his feet, and his hair lay tussled on his scalp. His shoulder throbbed from a bruise that had formed from the shot that had struck the armor there during the climb. Just twenty feet away, black waves lapped the sand on the beach as the tide rolled in and out.

He did not know how much time had passed, though he did know that when he first found this position the sun was high in the sky and it had disappeared over the horizon hours ago. He had not moved in that time.

The rage that had driven him to such a violent act had subsided. He had killed men before in combat, by accident and for sport, but none had ever been with such malice. He had massacred those men, taken their lives with his own hands and at his whim. Once he made the decision to kill them, they were dead. Only a few men in history could make such a boast. He had sought solitude because for the first time he had *enjoyed* the very act of killing. Even now as he sat, replaying the grizzly images in his mind and knowing that he should be ashamed and remorseful, he was not. He tried to reach for the emotions of compassion or sympathy, but they were not there. All he felt was pride at the accomplishment and peace. These feelings were a great contradiction to him. Though they were familiar in isolation, they were utterly foreign when combined. He had tried to make sense of it all for many hours.

This is how Thomas found his friend. Thomas stood in the shadow of the trees, silently observing Oryan for nearly an hour. He sat covered in blood, yet the image before him was anything but shocking. This man seemed to be somber and pure, almost angelic. He wished deep within his soul that he could find such comfort and peace if only for a moment. He knew then that he still had much to learn from his captain.

"You have been there for some time, Lieutenant," said Oryan calmly. His voice was fluid; like music it was inviting, strong but not harsh. In hearing it, Thomas scarcely believed that the voice was his and so forgot entirely what it was that he had wanted to say. "I don't suppose that you've come for the view."

"No … no, sir," stammered Thomas, finally composing himself. "I came to give you the report."

"Go on," replied Oryan.

"They apparently found the rig for the artillery. It started back up about an hour ago."

"I heard it."

"The opening barrage cost us a few Knights. It was pretty sudden, and we were finalizing a few key strategic locations when it started."

Oryan finally met Thomas's gaze. "How many men still stand?" he asked.

"Three hundred and eighty-nine," said Thomas, his voice sullen and hollow.

Oryan closed his eyes and breathed deeply. This was tragic news. There was so much death. Every Knight that fell took hundreds with them, but it still seemed too heavy a price to pay for Oryan.

Thomas spoke again. "Forgive me, sir, but I informed the men of the status of our reinforcements."

Oryan opened his eyes and found Thomas's again. There was a struggle of wills for a moment, but only for a moment. Oryan looked away and nodded his head. "That was the right thing to do. They needed to know," he whispered. "How's the morale?"

"They are ready, sir. Ready to follow you to the end; whatever end that may be."

Oryan looked back on the river. He took notice once again of the mists of water that gently touched his face as the breeze brought in the waves. The water was still black, nighttime water, and Oryan wished for the morning. The sun would bring much in its rays.

"He knows now," Oryan stated, his resolve hardening once again. "He knows by now that reinforcements aren't coming. He knows that there were only five hundred of us to begin with and that there can't be that many remaining. Even after this afternoon, he knows he's won. He'll whittle away at us all night like this. In the morning he'll send everything he has at us and finish us off. That's what I'd do."

Thomas nodded his agreement but kept his silence. He knew that Oryan was right, but with that acknowledgement came the realization that he and the others had mere hours of life left to them. It was a moment of reflection for him. Through all the training and all the success, they would be defeated on their first mission. What a waste. He thought on the things that could have been accomplished with such a force. They could have been legendary.

Now, they faced the end so soon after the beginning. Thomas did not fear death, and neither did the Knights. They would make their stand, and it would be a valiant one. If the tale was ever told, it would certainly be a thing of legend. The last stand of Oryan and the Kentaurus Knights. The world would speak of it for years to come.

Similar thoughts flowed through Oryan's mind. A glorious final confrontation, driving the enemy back again and again, then watching them reform again and again. His Knights fighting bravely, giving one-hundred fold what they took. He could envision his force falling one at a time until only two hundred remained, then fifty, then ten, then one. A more honorable death no soldier could ask for; however, therein lay the problem for him. Though he, like his lieutenant, did not fear death, he was not ready to die.

Oryan picked up his helmet and tucked it under his arm as he stood. His eyes began to burn again from tranquil to defiant. Thomas felt his courage and hope rise as his captain did.

"Tell the men to be ready. We will last this night. In the morning, we make our stand. This isn't over. We're not finished. Tell the men this is not the end."

Operation Knightfall, Day Three: The World Changes

General Nikroe had spent most of his night discussing strategy with what commanders he had left. His best had lost his life at the massacre on the wall. It was that commander who suggested the audacious hanging as a psychological message to their enemies.

It was the captain of this attacking force that intrigued Nikroe. He was a man unlike any he had ever encountered on the battlefield. In Nikroe's experience, there were two kinds of commanders. There were field commanders, those who could inspire by action and who you entrusted the lives of your men to when the battle began. Then there those who were far better looking at the big picture. They could take the vital statistics of the armies on the field, a map, and coordinate a strategy that would produce the best possible outcome for victory with the fewest risks. He felt himself the latter of the two, which is why he chose field commanders as his subordinates.

But this man whom he fought against now seemed to be flawless at both. The general had known many commanders who had a feel for both sides of this equation, but each one seemed to favor one side or another. Not this man. He seemed to perform perfectly on the field while keeping a view of the entire battlefield in his mind at all times. Each move he made was the start of a chain reaction that rippled through the rest of his men. It was like they were all part of the same larger organism whose only instinct was war.

He had used the name Kentaurus Knights. Nikroe knew the name, and since he had met with their commander on the field the previous afternoon, he had spent hours looking through military history books learning what he could about the Knights of old. At first, he had thought the captain presumptuous and arrogant. Now, after seeing the kinds of things they were capable of, more importantly, what their commander was capable of, he began to think that title was more than fitting.

However, Nikroe was still in the better position. He still had at least thirty tanks at his disposal as well as two thousand more men. At best, his enemies had four hundred men left, no siege weapons, and no armor support. He had feared a larger force to follow, but it was clear now that it was either delayed or not coming at all. This meant it was only a matter of time. No matter how good those who stood against him were, no men could last that long in open combat with those odds.

His artillery barrages had been mildly successful, killing only a few enemy soldiers. Still, it was a safer move than to march his men to death or risk losing more tanks. The men who had infiltrated the fort had done a wonderful job dismantling his air force. If they had been his men who pulled that off, he would have placed medals around their necks instead of ropes. Until the previous day's events, he had been comfortable in the thought of weathering the storm from the inside. However, all distress messages sent over the comm and those sent on foot had been intercepted and had never reached any help. Now he knew that he had to act soon or die slowly behind twenty-foot concrete coffin walls.

He had ordered all remaining ordinance to be loaded and that every inch of tree within range be demolished during the course of the night. When daylight broke, he would send everything he had, leaving only a skeleton crew to the defense, to finish off this captain and his men. It was time he finished this battle the way it should have begun: by *his* rules. He would end these new Knights before they too could become celebrated legends on history's pages. If he could not, he feared there would be no stopping them. This course of action was the best to take; yet in the back of his mind, doubt gnawed. It was the best, but was his best enough?

Dawn broke. The sounds of desolation ceased for the first time in eleven hours, and an eerie silence fell. Smoke clung to the ground even as it rose to the heavens. The few mangled trees that were left groaned under the stress of their failing support. Small fires danced everywhere. There was no movement. Charred, black corpses lay strewn in pieces across the sand. Soldiers of Vollmar and of Navarus were indistinguishable in their ruin.

From inside the fort walls, a horn blew long and clear. After its call, the sound of great doors opening on weather-worn hinges could be heard. The ground began to rumble as engines roared to life. The first of Nikroe's tanks rolled from the gate just as the sun had fully cleared the horizon. Minutes later, twenty-three of the machines formed a solid steel line in the sand beyond the protection of the fort. They stopped there, engines idling, while two thousand soldiers filed into formation behind them. If the Knights were in front of them, the tanks would certainly rouse them from their hiding. If they were behind, the troops could made light work of their infantry. Less than one hundred men stayed behind.

Upon the signal from their commander, the tanks lunged forward, plunging into what was left of the trees nearest the fort. The troops jogged behind, waiting for the first signs of battle to begin. The memories of watching their friends die the day before were still fresh, so they kept low and wary as the tanks rumbled on.

As the army approached the ruins of the palms, the pace slowed. Even the tank drivers were leery of the unknown before them. Beyond this point, none of them could be sure they would ever return. Like an unarmed man entering a lion's den, they plucked up their courage and proceeded to the point of no return.

There was little left of the hundreds of trees that had once surrounded the fort. The army crawled along the sand, methodically searching for the phantoms that had haunted them for these past few days. Once the tanks reached the end of what had been the first grouping of trees, the mood changed. There was no sign of the Knights anywhere. They all began to step a bit lighter, quickening their pace to the beach.

With each step, their spirits rose. Perhaps the army arrayed against them had indeed left. Maybe they had received the word that their reinforcements were not coming and so they had fled back to the safety of their own lands rather than face the coming storm. Just maybe all of them might live to see another morning.

Finally, they all reached the beach. There were footprints still visible in the sand heading out to the water. Several packs and some of the heavier equipment had been discarded near the trees as well. There was no sign of a living Navarite soldier. Nikroe surveyed the signs personally, his suspicions remaining very high. The men began to talk excitedly of victory and life. A ripple of hope swept through the ranks, cheering all. When most of the trees had been searched, the beach had been cleared for miles in each direction, and Nikroe was sure that the signs were correct; he allowed hope to enter his heart as well.

The soldiers began to cheer and sing, joyful to know the precious value of a new day. They climbed onto the tanks, hailing their victory, boasting of their defeat over both the Legion and these new Knights. Who could the emperor possibly send against them now? They shouted the praises of their general and his commanders who were brave and valiant until the end. Soon, they had all but forgotten the last few days. The visions of death, the sleepless nights, and the utter despair were all but swept away. Here, under this new sun on a beautiful tropical beach, they celebrated the gift they had been given.

Nikroe smiled and congratulated his commanders. He had also let his fears pass. The captain of the Knights was as wise a man as he was brutal. He valued the lives of his men more than victory, and so he had saved those who remained. That was the sign of a great commander. Although he had achieved victory this day, Nikroe knew he had only lived to face that adversary again. The next time he may not be so fortunate.

The general made his way through the crowds of celebrating men to find his communications officer. "Hail the fort, and get a status report. Then prepare the men for a moment of silence in remembrance of those who fell to give us this day," he relayed his orders and began once again his merriments.

The moment of silence was announced over a tank's loudspeakers.

Almost immediately, the men removed their helmets and bowed their heads. There was much to be thankful for, but there were many who had not made it here to enjoy the thanksgiving. All the men remembered their friends who gave their lives. "Though they do not stand here, they will always be with us," said the chaplain into the speaker.

While the men reflected, the communications officer sought out General Nikroe to give him his report. He found the general near his commanders discussing quietly their report back to the capital.

"Ah, Lieutenant," said Nikroe as the officer approached. "Did you deliver our good news back to the fort?"

The usually confident officer looked bewildered. He would make eye contact with no one, just stood open mouthed and shaking his head. "I made contact, sir," he finally admitted, "but this was the only response that I received." He held the communicator in his outstretched hand and clicked on the speaker.

Nikroe's face went deathly pale. His knees buckled, and he swooned as if to faint. His officers held equally horrified looks. One vomited; another wept openly. All good will and light-heartedness vanished. The general listened to the sound from the communicator, unable to listen to anything else. He was in a trance, the whole world suddenly becoming very small. He could see nothing though his eyes were open, and he could hear nothing save the sounds that were chilling his blood. How could he have been so blind? Such a grievous oversight! His folly had sentenced them all to death.

From the communicator came the voice of another one of his men. "Private Doan A. Wilson," said the voice through tears and sobs. "And I don't wanna die." The transmission ended. After a few moments of silence, the comm cracked to life again. "Name and rank," said a harsh voice. "Artemis Doyle," was the response from another emotion-choked soldier.

Nikroe fell to his knees, tears streaming down his cheeks. The finality of death was sinking in. He still made no sound. The men nearest to them had heard the sound, and now dozens were crowding the communications officer. Nikroe could hear their hearts beat, and he could feel their fear. It saturated and permeated him like rain on a deep winter's day.

General Nikroe raised his hands to the sky, admitting silently defeat and pleading for mercy for his men at the same time. As his mind desperately searched for solace and refuge, his ears received the last sound they would ever hear. It was a noise he was all too familiar with, and it was normally one that reassured him of a fighting chance to live. Now, it kept his mind focused on the grim status of his last moments on earth. Above the lapping water and the mournful cries of his men, he heard the sound of automated fighter aircraft engines carried on the wind.

And death was in their wings.

Three days later

The Captain stood on the deck of one of the empire's flagships. There had been no report from Oryan or his Knights since they were deployed. To it, the silence was like sweet music to its wretched ears. General Nikroe had defeated it and its legion, but that was not near the humiliation it had faced at the hands of Captain Jeckstadt. To share the same title with Oryan was revolting. *Putrid, unworthy slave!*

That is why it had sent them on this mission first. There were dozens of battlegrounds where they could have been of better use, but it did not want them to be of any use. It wanted them dead. Better yet, to die in the humiliation of knowing that they never won a single battle. It could not have been more pleased with the results. It was so pleased it came with the convoy sent to find the Knights personally. It wanted to spit on Oryan's corpse.

As the small fleet approached the banks of the river where Oryan and his men had landed nearly a week before, a crooked smile remained etched on its twisted mouth. Smoke still rose from the fort. The black cloud was thinning but could visibly be seen from the river. Somewhere amongst the casualties of these fires was the body of its nemesis.

"Captain," said a sniveling midshipmen standing behind it. It acknowledged only by stiffening his neck to hear the rest of the sentence. "We are going to deploy the boats and the rescue team to go ashore. Will you still be joining them?"

Of course I will. I wouldn't miss it.

It turned and faced the soldier, hunching over him and staring with venomous eyes. It leaned in close, so close that the young man could feel each breath it took through its jagged teeth. He shook, knowing the Captain's reputation and concerned with his own life. He wondered if there was some etiquette or protocol that he had been unaware of and missed when addressing the Captain. This thing slunk to his side, still focusing its glare on his face. It stopped, hesitating for a moment, and then brushed by him. A shiver ran down the man's spine and not from the chill morning air. He was relieved he was still alive. He was even more relieved that it was gone.

The Captain made its way to the rescue boats and boarded the first one it came to. Most of the team was still bustling about, preparing their things and moving supplies to the boats. After a few minutes of waiting for the team to be fully prepared, the Captain grew impatient. It marched off of the boat it was on, grabbed several of the larger team members by the back of their necks, and hoisted them into the ship.

"The time has come," it hissed. "There are enough supplies on this vessel. Release the clamps, and let us be off!"

One of the men hesitated. "Sir, we have orders to wait for the rest of the team, and the supplies are not—" The Captain moved across the boat and dug five long fingers tipped with sharpened nails into the soldier's neck. It drew the twitching man close to its face.

"My authority *supersedes* all previous orders given. Perhaps you should have reconsidered your objection," it snarled. The helpless soldier gasped and tried to fight. His limbs began to twitch and jolt as the Captain's grip tightened. There was a loud crack and a splash as it snapped the vertebrate in his neck and dropped his lifeless body into the water. It looked back at the men who were still preparing the other boats. All movement had stopped, and they stared on in horror.

"You!" it spat and pointed to the soldier nearest the boat. "Get on board!"

The soldier climbed into the ship as fast as he could, though he was still in considerable shock. "Pull the lever and get us moving!" the Captain demanded.

One of the team members jammed the lever into the release position, and as the boat pulled away, he looked back at the other members of his unit who were still paralyzed in disbelief.

As they approached the beach, they began to see the original transports now fully submersed below the waves. A few remaining bodies still floated on the water's surface. The beach itself was still smoldering. The sand was littered with tanks and corpses filled with holes, charred black from explosives or high-heat bullets. A few of the more intact yet still inoperable tanks had begun to be swallowed up in watery sand as the tide had come in and removed solid ground from beneath their treads. Nothing was unscathed. Closer to the tree line there was a large pyre of blackened soldiers. They had been neatly stacked on top of wood and then doused with accelerant. Aside from crisp human forms, no details were recognizable.

The men with the Captain still approached with extreme caution. They had their medical packs securely fastened to their backs, and their rifles were in their hands. Only the Captain was unarmed. It was the last to step onto the shore, its weight sinking its boots into the sand. It surveyed the former battlefield with attention to every detail. There had been a last stand here, and it appeared that Oryan and his men were winning, at least for a while. The absence of any imperial uniforms and equipment was evidence that they suffered few casualties here.

The puzzlement to the Captain was the damage to the tanks. This had not been done by any of the ordinance that the Knights carried with them. It was too precise for grenades or even standard explosives. Not to mention that the bullet holes on the tank armor were too wide to be from a standard infantry rifle. Aside from that, the Captain knew that even the strongest of hand-carried weapons would merely scratch armor like this, and these blasts had penetrated clear through.

There was only one logical explanation: Jeckstadt and the Knights were dealing them a harder blow than they expected. When Nikroe saw that he might end up losing this battle, he made a desperate move. It was not like Nikroe to panic, but such an incalculable mistake on his part explained much. As a commander, knowing that his main defensive weapons were failing, he could not allow that force to get any further inland. In order to save the lives of his men, keep the fort in friendly hands, and to save the day from disaster, he called in an air strike with orders to kill or destroy everything that moved, friendly or otherwise.

The Captain began to move up the beach and into the palms. Here, too, there were signs of battle. There were fallen trees, a path made by explosives, and bullet shells littering the ground. It was also clear that there were soldiers from one army, perhaps both, scattering in all directions. The heavier weaponry provided by the air strike had made parts of the palm forest into desert. Here and there it could see weapons half buried by shifting sand or a few scavengers feasting on dead pieces of dismembered bodies. On the air there was a scent and a feel of death. It was not the presence of death that was unnerving, but the absence of life. Aside from the wildlife, nothing moved.

As it walked with the rescue team that accompanied it close behind, it could see the palms ahead thinning. The end of the first grouping of trees was near. It recalled the schematics from the briefing as well as its last encounter with this place. It and the Legion had not made it past this point.

The troops behind him were searching for survivors, but there were none. Since they had left the beach, there had been no whole bodies, even dead ones, at all. They were communicating with the rest of the rescue team who had just arrived on the beach. The Captain signaled them to spread out along the tree line and prepare for incursion.

The soldiers crawled to the edge of the trees cautiously waiting for resistance. The Captain watched their progress in disgust. They seemed to move in slow motion; they were undisciplined, and worst of all, they all reeked of fear. It watched them inch toward the clearing for what seemed like an eternity. Finally, its impatience forced it into action. It covered the distance between it and the closest soldier in a few long strides, then, grabbing him by his uniform, it threw the man from the safety of the trees into the open clearing. It listened intently for the sound of enemy fire.

The Captain heard the man stand up and shuffle loudly through fallen palm branches and sand. There was a long moment of silence before any more noises could be heard. "I, I think that whatever happened here is long over. There's ... well there's *nothing* here, sir," he said in a bewildered tone.

The other troops stood and walked slowly into the open sky. They spoke in amazement, their voices echoing a mutual sentiment of wonder and awe. As the Captain left the shadow of the trees, it was bathed in sunshine. It lowered its head to shield its eyes until they were accustomed to such a radiant light. Like the soldiers before it, it drew a sharp gasp inward when it beheld the devastation.

It searched its memory for the picture of what it had seen the last time. There had been palm trees as far as the eye could see in both directions. The forest in front looked as dense as the one behind. It recalled the firefight that had happened there between its men and the enemy. They would have been victorious had it not been for the air strikes and artillery. Now, the landscape was radically different. No trees remained. There were only burnt stumps where mighty palms had been. The sand was riddled with craters. This place looked like a tomb where nature herself was laid to rest.

The Captain looked ahead, past the desolation before him. It could clearly see the fort in the distance. Smoke rose in small pockets all around it, but at first glance from this distance, the fort seemed as dead as this stretch of land. It could hear no alarms as they would have most certainly been spotted by now. It heard no engines rumbling; no soldier of his was intercepting transmissions from inside. *What had happened here?* All of its previous assumptions had been wrong. Oryan had made it at least this far, and it looked as if he had made it to the very walls of the fort itself.

It signaled the men to advance, and it followed suit. They all stayed low at first, but by the time they were in weapon's range of the fort, they were fully upright. The scene at the walls was even more shocking than that of the path leading up to it. Even the Captain stood in its shadow, mouth agape. The ground before it was utterly black from intense fires, mass explosions, and scattered corpses. There was wreckage of all kinds scattered before the gates. The concrete walls were singed from fires and discolored from smoke damage.

As the Captain gazed upward, he once again found a shocking sight. There were men, or rather corpses of men, dangling from nooses strung from the top of the wall. Some of the bodies bore wounds from gunshots, some were without limbs from explosions, but each had a common thread. They were all officers, and none belonged to the empire. The Captain searched the faces of those who still had recognizable ones. There, hanging by his neck below the rest, was General Nikroe. His uniform was clean and neat; no marks from battle could be seen. His hands were tied behind his back at the waist. The General's face had become red and bloated, yet it knew who it was it beheld.

It traced the rope from the decaying general up to its source on top of the wall. There, it met a sight that shocked it most of all. Standing victorious once again above the corpse of the man who had defeated it just months earlier was the man it hated most of all. Standing alone on the wall, eyes fixed on it, was Captain Oryan Jeckstadt. It's black heart pumped hate through its veins.

"My Captain," Oryan spoke. "You seem surprised to see me. Lands that are rightfully the emperor's have been returned after long captivity in enemy hands. I humbly present to you the enemy fortification of General E. Nikroe. Long may you defend its walls and hold it against the wiles of the adversary!"

The speech was moving and patriotic. The soldiers who accompanied the Captain removed their helmets and saluted Oryan for his courage and honor. They were moved from a sense of duty, ready now to do their part no matter what that may mean.

The Captain did not share their sentiment. It glared at Oryan, grinding jagged teeth in anger. The two stared at each other for some time, trading nonverbal blows and contesting their wills against each other. In the end, it was the Captain who broke the silence.

"You present yourself at this victory and take claim for its accomplishment. Tell me, *Captain*, where are your men? Do they not also deserve to take part in this triumph for the emperor?" It was a weak attempt to degrade the character of Oryan, but that was all it could do. It loathed the man before it. In Oryan it saw everything that it could have been but was not. To add to that, where it failed, he succeeded. It had sent him here to die, yet he emerged alive. It would see him dead before its end; that much was certain. It would just have to wait a while longer.

"Did you not see them already?" Oryan retorted.

The Captain turned its head on a long, bent neck to see the men standing behind it. There were at least one hundred of Oryan's Knights forming a barrier to the tree ruin behind them. They all looked battle-worn, each with the look of murder in their eyes. Their clothes were tattered, muddy, and bloodstained. In the center of the gathering was Lieutenant Thomas.

At the same time, the remainder of the rescue team came running up behind the Knights. They were puffing for breath but glad to see their brothers-in-arms in no need of rescue. A cheer went up in praise of Captain Jeckstadt and his brave five hundred. The sound pierced the Captain to its center.

Oryan shouted from the walls, "Come! Enter! There is much to celebrate and much here to celebrate with!" The huge gate began to swing open, creaking once again on its hinges.

The Captain fumed at this unexpected turn of events. It had been looking forward to taking the report back to Kovac of the defeat of his new pet. Now, the tale of victory and heroism would come to its master's ears from Oryan himself. It would be sounded though the empire and broadcast on every net that the empire had won such a marvelous victory. It watched Oryan disappear from the wall and vowed to see him dead, whatever it took. It was time to take more drastic measures.

The men shouted their approval again and began to ask the Knights what had transpired. As they all ate in the mess hall of the fort, Thomas began to tell the whole tale of his captain, the Knights, of saboteurs, and legends on walls. Oryan remained silent for the recount of events past, but there was many a shout of, "*Knights!*" and other cries of approval and pride. They ate and drank and spoke long into the night.

The Captain did not attend. It remained outside the gate, awaiting the arrival of the reinforcements that had been promised to Oryan three days previous. As the sounds of happiness and drunkenness echoed behind it, black thoughts filled its mind. A call for blood and for retribution resounded in its ears. *Oryan survived today, but I control his future, and I grant no future to those who oppose me.*

And so the legend began and grew and spread. By the day's end, the whole world knew what had transpired here. There was a new kind of warfare coming. It had smashed conventional combat and tactics as a wave of a storm smashes ships upon rocks.

Across the empire went up a call for more men to come in service to their emperor. The Kentaurus Knights were a rallying cry for its army. If five hundred united men could deliver such a blow to the heart of their enemy, imagine what a united empire could do.

On the other side of the world, a kingdom wept. Vollmar held a silent vigil for their loss of land and men. The king himself shuddered when the news came to him. These Knights had dealt him a blow more severe than any other army could have. They gave no quarter and left no survivors. Mothers, wives, daughters, and sweethearts cried bitter tears knowing that their loved ones would never return home, even for one last farewell. He read the report and sat alone in his lightless chambers for many hours.

If this was the first battle to come, God save them all. This war had taken on a frightful change for the worse. Vollmar would never be the same. The course of the world's history was forever altered, and so was he.

Summoned

It was later called "The World's Coldest Winter" by many. Oryan's victory sparked the beginning of the largest invasion ever assembled. The kingdom of Vollmar, once the keeper of peace for the entire planet, was now engulfed in the bloodiest war ever waged. From the fort first captured by the Knights, Navarus continued to push across enemy territory. The attacks had come so quickly that Vollmar's response was ill-prepared and too late. When their defensive forces were finally assembled, their enemy's foothold in their land was already too strong to repel.

Vollmar tried in vain to launch a counter-assault on the empire, but Oryan and his Knights proved as efficient a defensive weapon as they had an offensive one. The reputation of the Kentaurus Knights grew from rumor to legend overnight. Dozens of battles were won based solely upon the ingenuity of Captain Oryan Jeckstadt. They were in constant combat. If the tide was turning unfavorably, the Knights were deployed. In six hours or less, they could be mobilized anywhere the war raged. The armies of Vollmar saw battle after battle go from certain victory to crushing defeat.

Captain Jeckstadt himself had become more a legend than the army he commanded, if such a feat were possible. His presence was daunting to anyone except his men. He was rarely seen except on the battlefield, where his prowess for killing was only matched by his lack of compassion. When he arrived, it meant death to any who opposed him. He personally killed over a thousand enemy soldiers, disabled thousands of tons of enemy war machines, and recovered volumes of enemy intelligence reports. He had even taken the life of one of Navarus's commanders who had put his men in unnecessary jeopardy. He took no prisoners, burning the corpses of the fallen. In time, he was being compared to the great General Kovac, and many considered him to be the more feared figure.

Oryan had left his lieutenant (who had become almost as renowned as he) at the barracks to train a new crop of Knights, filling the void left by fallen comrades. It was a prestigious schooling into which only the top one percent was admitted, and of that percent, very few completed it.

The impact that meant the most to Oryan was that of the effect his men had on the reputation of the Legion. Almost overnight, the Legion became a whisper. They were still used for covert and secret missions, but they were no longer the strong arm of the imperial fighting force. A commander for Vollmar remarked that given the choice, he would rather face the Legion. "Next to the Knights," he said, "they are kittens to the lion." The Captain and Oryan saw little of each other, but word was always sounding in the Captain's ears of the Knights and their exploits. Oryan, on the other hand, kept a close watch on the movements of the Legion. Even though the Captain had been warned to leave Oryan and the Knights alone, Oryan felt that the order from Kovac would not last. The Captain obeyed out of fear, but Oryan knew that it was beginning to fear him as much as its master. When the fear of him became more overwhelming than the fear of Kovac, Oryan may have to fight a battle on both fronts. For now, the Knights and the Legion were the greatest combination fighting force in history.

Over the course of one year, the shape of world powers changed dramatically. The empire's invasion slowed to a crawl when Vollmar won several crucial victories on their home front. Oryan and the Knights had been detained by an attack on imperial land. It was later determined that the foiled invasion by Vollmar had been a diversion to keep the Knights occupied while their main forces reclaimed strategic points on their home soil.

In the process of taking back those military strongholds, the armies of Vollmar gained not only land and victory, but also a major boost in morale. The lands they recovered had been defended by the Legion. The majority of the Legion had been killed in the attacks, and the Captain narrowly escaped with its life. Upon its return to the empire, it was denounced by the emperor as an unfit field commander and subsequently removed from duty. Control of the

Legion was turned over directly to General Kovac, who offered their ranks to Captain Jeckstadt. Jeckstadt refused. Kovac then promoted one of the senior officers to the command position, leaving him open to oversee the entire war rather than just a portion.

The loss of ground on Vollmar's front refocused Navaro, who once again realized he was facing a very determined enemy. Tamrus not only had the military might to oppose him, but the wisdom to direct them to not only opposition but to victory. Navaro knew he had the capability of winning this conflict, but the war was far from over.

He had offered Jeckstadt a higher command, but that offer had been declined. This man wanted to fight and wanted to do it his own way. For a time, Navaro had been offended by Jeckstadt's repeated disregard for the chain of command and his blatant disobedience to his emperor's will. Now, the emperor felt supremely confident that Oryan knew who he was fighting for. He allowed the Knights to be released from responsibility so long as battles continued to be won. Navaro never had a reason to regret the decision.

He was, however, concerned with Oryan as a man. He had nearly been defeated by his father, Armay, and that is what made him nervous. The emperor knew that Oryan had been raised by his father in the Slave Quarter, and that meant that some of his father's ideals had certainly been impressed onto the son. Oryan seemed far more proud than his predecessor, boasting with each victory and constantly searching for another stepping-stone to his legacy. Oryan wanted to be immortal, and so long as Navaro provided a means to that end, he was safe. What happened when the war slowed its pace? What happened when the last battle ended and the emperor was named ruler of all the world? Would Oryan then use his notoriety and the loyalty of the army to supplant him?

It was time to formally recognize this man for his accomplishments and his enormous contribution to the empire. This had to be a very significant reward, something that the whole of the empire would recognize and revere. He must curry favor with this captain before he found himself in the crosshairs of his most gifted killer. So, Navaro looked at his list of military leadership, but he knew that Oryan would not be bought by promotions. Wealth was also not a motivating factor, so money was out. Oryan was no politician, nor would he prove a worthy councilor, so administrative and staff positions were not appropriate. Aside from those facts, the emperor needed something more. These were all trivial titles designed for men with worldly aspirations. Like Kovac, Oryan had no use for temporal trinkets no matter how valuable. Despite all his power and influence, Navaro was at a loss.

He retreated to his studies, reading history, political satires, and religious superstition when a thought struck him that had not come to him before. The emperor paced the floor amongst his endless collection of history books searching for the right inspiration. He walked up and down the long isles for nearly an hour before a title finally caught and held his attention. He drew it from the shelf and examined its cover. *Warlords.* He leafed through the pages, skimming the biographies of the world's greatest military minds. As the pages turned, a name and a portrait caught his eye. The name before him was Mutrux.

Mutrux was one of the seven tribal leaders from earliest recorded history who was known for his prowess on the battlefield. It was written that he eliminated a majority of the smaller tribes single handedly. In a time when battles meant more than land or power, he was *the* survivor. It was he who eventually unified the seven tribes into one country with his inspired leadership. His reputation grew exponentially until, in the end, there was no other leader who had the courage to face him.

His domination of all warfare continued on in his son, who assumed control of this budding country. His son, being far more ambitious, doubled the size of his dominion. This heir also brought industry, wealth, mathematics, science, and logic to the pages of history. His name was Kentaur, and the country adopted that name as its own. Rather than distinguishing the position as king or emperor, Kentaur named his father the first warlord of Kentaur, and he was the second.

He left no heir, but a relative assumed control of the throne and from this bloodthirsty military warlord was born the original Kentaurus Knights. The country, though small by the standards of other kingdoms at the time, became the most feared military presence in the world.

This was just the reward that Navaro needed for Jeckstadt.

Since Oryan would not accept any existing advancements or titles, he would make a new one. It would elevate him from commoner to noble. His subordinates would no longer know him as *Captain*. After this, the empire would refer to him by his true title, the one that was meant for him from birth. He would be *lord.* The first Warlord of Navarus.

The next day, the emperor sent for his finest blacksmith. There was protocol here. He had no formal insignia or different uniform to award. There had never been a warlord before, and so he knew he must set the standard high. This had to be grand. He ordered a suit of armor made especially for Oryan. It was designed to mirror the armor worn by the Knights of old, but it was also designed with modern combat in mind. Instead of steel or iron, it would be composed of Tamrus. It was light and yet strongly reinforced. It could survive even the most severe of tests without a scratch. A special sword was made to accompany the armor, as well as a uniquely designed helmet. It was a helmet that combined modern technology and modern battle standards with the bold design of the ancient. The suit itself took three months of the blacksmith's time to forge, but the emperor paid well.

It had been a long time since he had seen the inside of this room. Now, he stood in the dimly lit entrance remembering how large this place had once seemed to him. After the Quarter and countless cheap, damp lodgings (courtesy of Ratajek), his barracks seemed a palace. However, after seeing almost half the world in less than a year, this room was small and stale.

He waved his hand over the door's electric panel. The lights brightened, and the door slid shut behind him. With the exception of the thin layer of dust that covered the whole of his room, nothing had changed. He had spent very little time indoors during training, yet this place was as close to a home as he had.

Oryan unbuttoned his dress jacket and hung it neatly in the closet. His field gear and uniform were all being inspected and cleaned for him. All he had with him was a small bag filled with a few changes of clothes and a few personal items. The console on his desk was still off, it being one of the few devices in his room that did not automatically turn on upon his entrance. The green light that indicated an awaiting message blinked methodically, but he ignored it in favor of the inviting appearance of something he had not seen in nearly a year: his bed.

He did not bother to change his clothes or even undress; he merely laid down in his dress uniform and closed his eyes. Sleep was what he was expecting, but sleep he could not find. Instead, he was recalling his many victories. From the first to the most recent, he saw them all in his mind's eye. The first had been flawed, and it had cost him many soldiers, but each time he led them into combat, his methods became more refined. In his last eleven incursions with the enemy, he had lost one man. That loss was the result of the carelessness of that soldier. He was a novice to the field of combat and failed to confirm a kill. As Oryan had taught them all, that was a mistake he would not live to regret.

He searched for his stars, which he had not done in countless nights, but he no longer needed them. He no longer needed the peace of the solace that his celestial icons used to bring. The stars that shone there were not to guide him; he had been wrong all along. Those points of light were there to *glorify* him.

As the stars at night only point you to the grandeur of the sun, so too were they pointing now to him. He had been wrong to focus on such minute and insignificant specks in the heavens. There was only one true light and one true glory, and that was the same one that brought life to the world. The moon only reflected its brilliance, and the stars themselves were but childish imitations of the wonder that was the sun. In all, every heavenly body that glittered in the sky was meant for one purpose: to draw one's eyes upward to see that which gives life.

So it was with him. Though he could not have enjoyed the success he had without his Knights, they were still only stars to the sun. He had set all the wheels in motion, and it was he in the end that kept them all alive and victorious. What he had wanted from the beginning had finally happened. He did not receive thunderous applause, but he was also not met with silence. He heard his name mentioned on the Net; he heard common people whisper rumors as he passed. When he entered military facilities, a reverent silence fell over everyone from the officers to the foot soldiers. He could not ask for more. The world over knew his name for good or ill. He was truly a legend.

Yet somehow, it was still not enough. As his mind tried to solve the riddle of his unrest despite his unrivaled success, he faded into a deep sleep, the likes of which he had not known for what seemed like a lifetime.

He awoke to the sound of a soft chime from his door. For some time, he was convinced that the noise was simply a fabrication of his dreams and it was in no way a real visitor wanting his attention. The chime sounded several more times before it finally startled him out of his slumber.

He rose from his bed, pressed his clothes with his hands as much as possible, wiped the sleep from his eyes, and then made his way to the door. He passed the clock, which informed him that he had been asleep for some ten hours. It did not seem that long, but perhaps it would pay dividends later. For now, he still lamented the loss of such a rare use of his time.

When he arrived at the door, he flipped on the small viewing screen that showed the face of the person calling outside. There was a face he had not seen in some time, but who was of the few that was worth waking up for.

"Lieutenant Thomas," he said, smiling. He turned off the view screen, turned on the lights, and pressed the release for the door. Oryan turned his back to his guest and slowly walked to his desk, expecting Thomas to follow him in. When he realized that there were no footsteps save his, he turned to face his friend once again.

"You're invited," he jested. Thomas still did not move. "Well, man, come in or at least tell me why you're here if it's not for a cordial visit!"

Thomas smiled. "Hello, sir. It's good to see you again, but unfortunately I'm here on official business." He stepped into the room but did not proceed past the entrance. "There was a message waiting for you on the Net, sir," he stated, looking at the small green light still blinking on Oryan's console.

"Yes, I know. Probably new orders, but even my Knights need a bit of leave every now and again. I thought I had made that clear to all concerned."

"You did, sir, and believe me, we are all grateful for the time away..."

"But...?" Oryan prodded him along.

"But this message isn't for the captain of the Kentaurus Knights. It is expressly sent to Oryan Jeckstadt. I don't think its orders, sir, judging from the envelope that it's in." He held up a very expensive letter.

Oryan studied the paper in Thomas's hand. It looked as if there was weight to it, even though it could be no more than a few millimeters thick.

"It was delivered this morning for you from an emissary who rode in a transport which carried the standard of Navaro himself. I had only hours before I learned you had arrived, so I had made my way back here. When I found you asleep, I sat down to wait. Shortly thereafter, the messenger came, and I felt you needed to see this."

"Why? Did you open it?" Oryan grew angry at the presumptuousness of this man. Though he was a trusted advisor and a friend, he was his subordinate.

Thomas was wounded at the stab but did not show it outwardly. "No, sir. I make this assumption by the fact that it was hand delivered by an imperial herald and that he seemed quite irritated that this message had not been received via the Net. Also, there's not much in this envelope. It feels like a card of some kind, but the paper that the envelope itself is made of would cost me more than I make in a week. Lastly, by the weight of the correspondence, I would say that whatever is inside is equally expensive."

Oryan let his anger subside, and he smiled at his very astute visitor. "Forgive me, old friend. I suppose that time in battle has made me forget my manners. You are very observant," he said, taking the envelope from Thomas. "But there are some things you failed to see." Oryan was pleased with how much detail Thomas had picked out of such little information.

Thomas smiled, seeing his friend had returned. That quick loss of temper moments before had sent many alarms through his mind. Though they seemed to subside as Oryan studied the envelope, he held in the back of his mind that this was most certainly not the same man he had left met just a year before.

Oryan began again. "My name on the front is handwritten. How often do you see that these days? Also, the pen used was no generic one either. See how deep the pen strokes etched the paper. There is no bleeding of the ink, and I'm willing to bet that it took someone nearly an hour to write it. Any guesses on where this came from before I open it?"

"We both know the Captain doesn't have any love for you. If he didn't have to, he wouldn't speak to you, much less send a graven invitation. Still, it has to be someone of wealth and class. Perhaps a nobleman, politician, or councilman trying to use your fame for there own agenda," Thomas speculated.

"A possibility, but then again, I think a politician or councilman would be here themselves. Most of them would want to use their silver tongues to curry my favor, not some invitation, no matter how formal it may be."

Thomas nodded. "I think we can eliminate a nobleman, as the transport would have carried their family crest rather than the imperial standard."

"So, what are our remaining possibilities?"

"My guess, though it doesn't seem his style, would be General Kovac. He is the only one with the resources and the title to call on you. Not to mention he's one of the few who knew where you would be right now."

Oryan agreed with his lieutenant's assessment but could not escape the feeling that it was not the General at all. Kovac was a blunt man. Highly decorated though it might be, this invitation was far too dramatic for him. If Kovac wanted to speak to him, he would either send the Captain or he would come in person. He recovered his dagger from his desk and slid it underneath the wax that held the envelope closed. He noted that the wax had the imperial crest embossed into the seal. Though the wax seal held the envelope firmly sealed, it pried away from the paper without leaving a blemish.

He reached into the open envelope to feel a very smooth, heavyweight paper. His fingers passed over similar pen marks as the envelope. Slowly, he removed the paper as Thomas leaned in to see the mysterious contents. The paper itself was small, only the size of a post card, yet it opened horizontally. Before Oryan opened it, the riddle was solved. The front of the card contained not the crest of the empire, but the emperor himself.

Thomas's mouth fell slightly open. Very few ever received even a message on the Net from the emperor much less a handwritten card. Oryan opened the paper and read silently what was there for him. When he finished, he placed the card back into the envelope, pressed the wax back into place, and set it on his desk. He remained silent, looking downward as if in deep thought. Thomas waited for a few moments but then could stand the silence no longer.

"Sir?" he asked. The query seemed to startle Oryan out of his trance. He looked at Thomas as if he had forgotten that he had been there all along. "What did it say?" he finished.

Oryan smiled wryly, and an air of arrogance passed over his face. "Pack your things," he said to Thomas.

Thomas stood up straight, ready to accept the order. "I'll inform the men," he said as his body fixed itself into the position of attention. Oryan's reaction was nothing short of shocking. He laughed; a deep rolling laugh of someone genuinely amused.

"No." Oryan still chuckled. "No, my friend, *you* pack your things. This call is meant only for me and my commander."

"What call? Where are we going?"

"To Obsidian, to the feet of *Navaro* himself."

The Warlord of Navarus

Obsidian was far grander than either of them had imagined. It was not built in a grid or block design like most major cities, but rather in concentric circles. There was a large outer wall, built thousands of years ago, that Navaro had fully restored when he took control. He had the planners and engineers working for almost three straight years to complete the monumental task, but it was a model of fortification. The walls were massive, thick enough to support three rows of battle tanks along the top and almost seventy feet in height.

There were only four entrances, one at each compass point, but the gates were large enough to sustain eight flowing lanes of traffic, four entering and four leaving. The gates themselves were considered a model of modern engineering, not only because of their size and bulk, but also the fact that they were as impregnable as a solid wall when closed. There was a constant military presence at each gate, both on top of the walls themselves and at stations just outside and on either side of the gates.

In the center of the circle stood Navaro's palace. It was constructed by the first ruler of Obsidian, and each subsequent ruler had made additions to make it what it was today. It stood high above the surrounding city and was surrounded by a wall of its own. That wall was not near the width or height of the outer wall, but it was made of the same materials, and its only gate was a smaller version of the ones on the outer wall.

In previous centuries, the rulers had designed the streets to join at different points so that no invading army had a clear road to the palace. In order to reach the center of the city, an army would either have to zigzag through main streets or destroy half the city to cut a clear path to the emperor. When Navaro's predecessor took the reigns, he completely uprooted the city to pave a broad and extravagant road that led directly to the palace gate.

It was on this road that Oryan and his lieutenant found themselves. They peered from the windows of their richly supplied and very comfortable transport at the glowing city around them. The city was built on a mesa, surrounded by what is called the Black Desert, aptly named for the black sand and rock that blanketed the area in all directions. The walls themselves were coated in a black finish that gave them the appearance of a black volcanic glass. However, the buildings and homes within the walls were built from a sturdy material that held an earthy red color. The only running water flowed from nearby mountains to form the southern boundary of the city, making this place a true oasis of civilization.

"I have never been inside the capital," Thomas admitted.

"Until today, I've never even seen the walls," Oryan responded.

Thomas looked back at Oryan, finally distracted from the city lights. He thought of his own home: a small, simple place, filled with humble people who worked every day merely to keep food on the table. The local lord was a fair and just man who was impoverished himself (for a noble), and so he treated the people as best he could. As Thomas watched the massive city streets roll by, he could not escape the idea that what they fought to defend was not the flashy world around them, but those who truly could not help themselves.

Oryan thought of his childhood and the harsh black and white world of slavery. He remembered that he was, for all intents and purposes, still in bondage. This thought was bitter to him. He had become free from everything in this world except his past. He was still just a slave, and until that changed, he would never be truly free.

The transport slowed to a stop, and the driver spoke. "Hey, Borden, I didn't know you got assigned here!"

There was a reply, but it was barely audible. "Yeah, I got me the genuine war hero that everybody's been talkin' 'bout. Here are the papers."

They listened to another stretch of silence and then more mumbling from the guard. "Yeah, thanks man," said the driver. "Hey, call me! It's been a while!"

The transport slid forward; the sounds of an intricate gate opening were heard.

"Well, this doesn't cease to amaze. Let's see if the architect is equally as impressive," said Oryan.

The mood shifted, and Thomas no longer felt himself disturbed by his commander's previous comments. The anxiety of this event returned. His stomach fluttered like a child about to receive a long-awaited gift. He checked his dress uniform again just for reassurance that everything was in its proper place. Oryan remained calm. If he was feeling even the slightest bit like Thomas, he did not show it.

The transport stopped, and footsteps could be heard outside the doors. There was also a dull roar of voices coming from outside. When the door was opened, the dull roar became thunderous noise. Reporters from every local media station had come to see the legends in person. A thousand pictures were snapped the second the door opened. Oryan and Ethanis had been unaware that this was intended to be a gala event. They ducked their heads and walked through the madness, led by several very large guards who were clearing a path across the yard and up the stairs.

The large and highly decorated palace doors swung open from the inside as the two approached. Once the doors were closed behind them, they were once again engulfed in silence. They looked at each other and then at their new surroundings. The main hall was enormous. Vaulted ceilings stretched high, supported by marble trusses nearly sixty feet overhead. There were two huge staircases on opposite sides of the room that wrapped up the side of the walls to the first balcony. Lush carpet was laid out in a single path from the door to the shadow underneath the balcony. There were elegant lights all around with a magnificent chandelier adorning the ceiling.

Each side of the carpet was lined with councilman, elected officials, nobleman, influential members of the black market, and those with enough financial or political status to be invited to the event. The stairs were lined with servants waiting for the pair to ascend to the balcony.

On the balcony was laid an enormous, elegantly decorated dining table with high-backed chairs on all sides. Standing on the center of the balcony, just behind the rail, was a commanding presence that Oryan was all too familiar with. The Lord General Lucius Kovac, dressed in a ceremonial uniform unlike any Oryan had ever seen, waited for them. Of all the faces in the crowd, the only one they both were missing was the one they both expected. Emperor Navaro was nowhere to be seen.

Oryan and Thomas stood in the entrance, trapped in the silence of the moment. The two of them were not used to formal gatherings, so the proper etiquette escaped them. Finally, a rather distinguished-looking man separated from the crowd and approached them. His pace was slow but steady; there was a slight limp in his leg.

He shook Thomas's hand first, then Oryan's. "Our salvation," he said as he bowed low.

A single clap was heard and then another. Soon, the ensemble at hand applauded and cheered loudly. Oryan was transported back to countless arenas, both grand and small, where he received similar praise. The two walked down the center carpet, shaking hands with the wealthy and influential. They were more than common foot soldiers and more than celebrities. They were true heroes. These people welcomed them with tears in their eyes. There was a feel of awe at their presence. They, the most powerful people in the empire, were starstruck by *them*.

The two men came to the shadow of the balcony, and the still cheering crowd parted on each side to allow them to pass to the stairs. Two beautiful women dressed in floor length, scarlet gowns came, and they each took one by the arm. Oryan was escorted off to the left and Thomas to the right.

Oryan noticed for the first time that large dining tables had been placed on either side of the carpet, behind the onlookers, to accommodate the host that was gathered here. The woman whispered in Oryan's ear with ruby lips the fantasies that she could make come true if he would find her after the ceremony. Oryan looked across to the other set of stairs to see a similar proposition being made to his lieutenant. Thomas seemed far more tempted by the offer.

The next time Oryan felt her breath against his neck, he stopped her. "My love, I'm not interested," he whispered to her. "However, you would do me much honor if you would be by my side for this." She blushed red from the compliment and held her tongue for the rest of the ascension on the stairs, but his modesty only fueled her desire for him.

They reached the top of the staircase where several high-ranking imperial officers saluted him. Upon his return of the salute, the woman on his arm showed him to his seat. He did not sit but rather stood beside his chair and waited for permission to be given. Oryan's attention was drawn curiously to the large object covered in black cloth in the center of the table. It stood almost three feet tall, and Oryan quickly discerned it had nothing to do with the meal. Kovac now stood next to a chair adjacent Oryan's. The noise of the crowd was silenced by a raise of his hand.

"Until the emperor arrives, I am your host," Kovac said to Oryan so that all could hear. "Until he comes, sit and enjoy the evening." With that, he sat down, and all the other guests followed suit. Kovac's suit was grayish silver. It was similar in design to the black military dress he wore more often, but much more lavishly decorated. It was most definitely designed to display the General's accomplishments with as much braggadocio as possible. Still, the tall, chiseled man looked regal in it.

Oryan was on one end, and he patiently sat his beautiful escort before pulling up his own chair. Thomas was seated at the far end, his beauty beside him. Judging the proximity between the two, Oryan calculated that it would not be long before they shared the same chair, especially when the alcohol was served and formalities forgotten.

The guests began eating and talking amongst themselves. Oryan fielded what questions were asked of him but otherwise remained silent. He studied all the members of the party at the head table while listening closely to Thomas whose tongue seemed to be loose this evening. It was apparent that his lieutenant was letting the fame and beverage go to his head. Oryan ate heartily but drank little. Tonight was anything but casual for him.

His female companion occasionally leaned over to him, putting her head on his shoulder or rubbing a soft hand across his thigh. Each time, he smiled at her but gently pushed her away. He was being watched. The true host of the party could not be seen, but he was here. Oryan knew that the emperor was watching from somewhere, studying his every move. *That's what I'd be doing.* Finally, growing weary of the girl's constant advances, he whispered something in her ear. She did not touch him again for the rest of the evening.

Oryan knew he was being scrutinized, so he wanted to make it clear that he could not be bought. Not for money, not for power, certainly not for a pretty face that promised lustful pleasures. It was then he noticed what he had not noticed before. There were small balconies located above the staircases that had seemed to be only decoration at first, but he became aware of a ghostly presence watching him from the one opposite his place at the table. The face was pale white but human. It ate and drank alone, only casually taking small bites of food or tiny sips of wine from a very tall crystal glass. He was barely noticeable, and Oryan doubted he had been noticed by anyone else.

Kovac had behaved much like Oryan that night, but now he noticed the great general glance at the same balcony and pause for a moment. Was Kovac unaware of the onlooker? Oryan watched the person in the balcony raise the glass and nod in salute to the General's glance and then disappear from view. Oryan understood now. Navaro had been dining with them all along.

After nearly two hours of dinner, food, and merriment, all the guests began to reflect on their lavish meal and surroundings. Many had never seen the inside of this palace before, so they leaned across to their neighbors asking questions of one piece of furniture or a rich-looking decoration. Oryan still maintained his composure, but Thomas had long ago succumbed to the pleasures of his companion in red. She now sat on his lap, silently rubbing her hand across his chest while he drank happily and shared stories of his experiences.

Kovac finally refocused the people's attention. He rose from the table and said, "Our host is regrettably detained; however, I feel it only proper, since the guests of honor are already in attendance, that we have a word from them. Perhaps Captain Jeckstadt could favor us, as I think his associate may not be able to keep all the facts straight."

There was a ripple of laughter from all except Kovac and

Oryan. Neither found it funny in the least. Oryan was not given to speeches, especially ones meant to cheer a crowd, but the sound of approval from those gathered forced his hand. He rose from his seat and approached the balcony's rail. As he passed, he caught Kovac's glance, showing his disdain for the General's choice of speakers. Kovac stared blankly in reply.

"This is the first time I've ever been asked to speak to such an … illustrious audience," he began. "Most of my words fall on the ears of your sons, brothers, friends, and neighbors. I have regrettably sent many of them to their deaths, and so I'm not sure what I might say that could be anything but a damper on your evening."

"Tell us of Nikroe's defeat!" shouted one voice from the floor.

"The Battle of the Red Naxela Pass!" cried another.

Oryan had tried to put a very harsh and negative spin on the war and his accomplishments in an attempt to retake his seat without a speech. He failed. He cast his gaze back at Thomas, who was obviously unaware of what was going on as his blonde friend had his attention. Oryan sighed. He closed his eyes, listening to the people chanting for tales of victory, naming specific battles or events. *Sheep*, he thought. He swallowed his disgust and opened his eyes.

He raised a hand to quiet the madness. "I believe that such tales are not meant for occasions …" He had planned on continuing with a short narrative of one of his more decisive victories, but his voice was replaced.

"But this most excellent soldier is far too humble to gloat over his own accomplishments," said a very masculine voice. Its rise and fall was harmonic, and all were almost immediately thrown into a trance by its melody.

Oryan was grateful for the intrusion and for the final appearance of his host. "Quite right, my emperor," he said, bowing to the presence that had appeared behind him as if from thin air. "For all glory is thine, your majesty."

The emperor came and stood next to Oryan at the railing. The crowd was once again on their feet, but this time in silence. Navaro placed a hand under Oryan's chin and raised his eyes to meet his own. His face was painted ceremoniously white with the exception of the black and red strokes of a skilled artist that formed a beautiful tapestry. It was as if the emperor was in fact a canvas and a masterpiece had been painted there upon. He wore silken black robes with red hems that were decorated with gold embroidery. The imperial crest was hanging on a golden chain around his neck. He had long black hair braided and shaped elegantly over his shoulders.

"I hope that you all have enjoyed your evening," the smooth voice continued. "As you all know, this night is more than just an occasion for celebration. We are here for more than rejoicing in our accomplishments. We are here tonight to honor a man who has done more for the empire since this conflict began than any other."

Oryan glanced at Kovac after that statement, but the General remained unmoved. Despite his affinity for the General, Oryan felt pride rise in his heart hearing those words from Navaro. Here, in front of every influential soul in the empire, he was elevated above the mighty Kovac.

The emperor carried on, naming from memory the history of Oryan's Kentaurus Knights, from their formation down through every battle they had won. Oryan remained calm and stoic on the surface, but inside he took note of every eye that looked on him as if to worship.

"To reward his greatness and his triumphs both on and off the battlefield, I offered him advancement. I offered him wealth and power. Such is the modesty of this man that even I, the emperor, was refused in favor of continuing his post as captain of his Knights," the emperor announced to the applause of the people. "I labored long to discover how to best accommodate such a rarity within the borders of my own empire. As he will accept no worldly offer, I had to find a gift worthy of his immortality."

Oryan listened closely. He thought he could see where this was going, but he had his reservations. Tradition held that the emperor was thought to be divine from birth. He was a walking deity whose destiny was nothing less than immortality in the highest circle of paradise reserved for only the great and noble emperors of the past. Some still practiced the belief and held to it, revering him for what they felt he was, and believed that his words were bound in the afterlife as well as in this world. Others felt it more just a tradition than a reality. Either way, his decree held more weight than any within his borders.

The emperor continued by a retelling of the history of the first Kentaurus Knights, of Kentaur and its tradition and dominance. He spoke of their contributions to the modern world. Then he began to highlight the lives of the great leaders who founded such a great civilization. "It was in this colorful and moving history that I discovered a reward fitting such a great soldier, a reward fitting of any Knight of Kentaur.

"It is said that when any Kentaurus Knight falls that his soul is lifted to the second circle of paradise, reserved for the greatest heroes known to the world. It was a bold claim then, and it is a bold claim now. In Kentaur, the only member of society guaranteed a greater eternity was their leader. To him was given the promise of the first circle of paradise, where only gods could inhabit. To him was promised glory and power to continue on through all generations of time. For it was his destiny to create life, to create worlds without number, and to have dominion over all that he created. It was to him, this king, this *warlord*, that these things were promised."

As he said the word *warlord*, his eyes became fixed on Oryan. Despite his rejection of other advancement, if this was offered to him, he would most certainly not refuse. His passion for history and for the history he had created overwhelmed his humility and disdain for temporary constructs.

A small cushioned kneeler was brought to Oryan's feet by an imperial priest, dressed as splendidly as was the emperor. "Kneel," said the hypnotic voice. Oryan knelt slowly. This was the perfect acknowledgment to all his accomplishments. If tradition was correct, he was about to be granted true immortality by the only person on the earth with the power to grant it. If not, it was still a reward that no emperor in the history of Navarus had bestowed on anyone before.

The emperor walked behind him and placed both hands on Oryan's head. "Here, before all of the empire and in the sight of all the world, I name you, Oryan Jeckstadt, *Warlord of Navarus!*

"Rise, Lord Jeckstadt. Greet your subjects."

Oryan rose, and the people cheered. He turned to the emperor, who bowed low to Oryan, and each person bowed lower. Nothing could be better than this.

When the emperor rose, he continued. "This is a new title in the empire, one that has never been bestowed before. You will set the precedent. As a man of noble right, I have arranged lands, title, and estates in your honor. May they serve you as you have served me until such time as I release the warlord."

Oryan still did not speak. Words were a waste. Instead, he bowed to the emperor, and the others once again followed suit.

"There is more," said Navaro. "Do you wish to continue your command in the field?"

Oryan composed himself quickly. "I would be unworthy of such an honor as this if I did not resume the post by which I earned it," replied Oryan.

The emperor smiled and bowed his head. "A warlord needs to be recognized on the battlefield as well as in these halls." He pointed to the object that remained covered in the table. Another priest removed the cloth to reveal a beautiful suit of armor. It was like nothing that Oryan had ever seen.

"You will find it as flexible as anything you have hitherto worn in combat. It was made for you. There is a similar design that awaits your captains," Navaro said, pointing to Thomas, who had now entirely forgotten his sensual partner.

The emperor turned to the masses, raised his arms, and proclaimed, "Honor and glory to Lord Jeckstadt, protector of my kingdom, defender of these lands!"

REVELATIONS

Oryan and Thomas spent more than a week at the palace. They were given every luxury that man could be permitted. Their voluptuous escorts from their arrival remained with them for the duration of the stay. Thomas did not stray far from his room, the warm flesh of his buxom friend, and all the alcohol he could drink. He saw little of his friend, and he was not at all disappointed by the turn of events. To him, a poor serf from half a world away, this was a fantasy come true.

Oryan, however, sent his escort on frequent trivial errands, leaving himself free to explore the palace. He spent most of his time in the palace library, where he found himself enamored of the emperor's vast wealth of knowledge. The library itself was as large as the ballroom where they had dined with the emperor and his guests, but it was much deeper. It held hundreds of bookshelves, standing twenty feet tall with books lining both sides. There were thousands of books that required a ladder to reach.

His time in the Slave Quarter had taught him to be a student of books, which was fairly archaic for these modern times as most information and literature were available on the Net. Still, the Net always felt impersonal to him, so here, in this hall of knowledge, he studied. He read history and military strategy. Oryan spent hours taking detailed notes on history's most epic battles. Each move was scrutinized, some proving a wise tactic while others, he deemed, were poorly conceived and executed worse.

On the last day he was to stay at the palace, he had compiled nearly two hundred pages of handwritten notes that most military minds could spend a lifetime studying. Long after his death, these two hundred pages were used as reference materials in military schools.

He had determined to spend every hour he had left in that library. For twenty-seven hours, he neither slept nor ate. A few of the servants came and went. They asked questions of him, but he ignored the queries. Some were more persistent than others, but in the end, his silence won over their duty to serve.

Though the time was agonizing for those chosen to wait on him, it passed all too quickly for him. So, when another presence took the seat across from him at his table, he took no notice. He was busy, and time was short. Eventually, whatever servant was there would leave. It was just a matter of not acknowledging them long enough for him to get the hint. Oryan busied himself about his studies until he realized that this new person was, in fact, reading.

For the first time in nearly ten hours, Oryan looked up. Before his brain could process the information, his body stood up from its seat and became rigid.

"My lord, forgive my rudeness, but I was under the impression that you were just another servant," Oryan apologized.

Emperor Navaro smiled softly and waved a hand to pass off the discourtesy. "Come, Lord. Sit with me," he said calmly. Oryan was still not used to the title, though coming from the emperor made it sound more official.

Once Oryan had sat down, the emperor continued. "I see you have found my library accommodating," said the calming voice. "Even more so than the room prepared for you."

Oryan studied the emperor's expression, tone, and, most importantly, his voice. "I prefer to keep my wits about me."

"Spoken like the true Warlord of Navarus. It would appear that you have not instilled this in your subordinates."

Oryan's jaw set. "They will do their duty. Right now, the only thing that need be on his mind is what drink to try. That is why he's not me."

"And never will be," chided Navaro.

Oryan remained silent. *There is only one, my lord.*

"As it should be. As there is only one emperor, so there should be only one warlord, and this is what makes you that man." He pointed to the notes stacked neatly on the desk in front of Oryan. "Writing your own histories, my lord?"

Oryan glanced at the papers and then at the emperor. "I'm no writer."

"Yet a volume of literature fills this table that did not exist in my archives before you arrived. And my servants tell me that you have rarely left here for several days. What keeps my warrior thus detained if it is not his own history?" The emperor smiled as he softly shut the book in front of Oryan and then carefully read the cover. "It seems to me that these ancient generals could have used your wisdom."

Oryan was becoming bored and intrigued by the conversation all at once. Speculative talk on what someone long dead could or should have done was nothing short of monotonous drivel to him. He felt a military debate with this man was not in his best interest. What piqued Oryan's curiosity was where this conversation was going. Why would the man with an empire to govern and a war to win spend his time in here? He leaned across the table. "Surely, my emperor, you have not come down here to discuss history—yours, mine, or anyone else's."

Navaro paused for a moment, not used to being dealt with in such a fashion. Then the smooth smile returned to his lips, and he spoke. "What I wouldn't give to be a soldier. You have no need for conversation or compliments, do you?"

"The only politics I know are at the end of a gun barrel or the edge of a sword. Words have little meaning to me." He paused listening to his own words. "My apologies, I know that I can seem very… abrasive."

"There is no need for apology. I came to bring you this." The emperor slid a small envelope across the table to Oryan. It was not elaborate, nor was it made from rich materials like the invitation to come to this palace.

Oryan studied it briefly and then looked back at Navaro as he picked it up. He removed the small knife that hung at his belt and slid it under the sealed edge. He removed the contents: a single folded sheet of paper. Immediately he noticed the emperor's handwritten signature at the bottom, but then he read the letter.

Each word was read carefully, and when he was done, he looked once more at the emperor.

"He said that you would understand why he could not deliver it personally. Lucius is a shrewd man," said Navaro.

Oryan suddenly felt disbelief and anxiety rise in his body. His senses heightened as if ominous tidings were certainly approaching. He glared from behind this new piece of news, unable to contain his disdain. "I have often been warned to beware the messenger whose lips drip with honey. It is said that the better the news, the worse the outcome. In one week's time, I have been given an honor that I could never have fathomed and now this."

Navaro was utterly confounded. "My lord, in order for one to gain such a position in this empire, he must certainly be free from all man's control."

"Except yours," Oryan added.

"The General felt that you had earned your freedom. Given your service, I wholly agreed to the proposal. When he came to me with the release letter, I joyfully endorsed it."

"I'm sure it was *his* idea. In one thing you are correct: Lord Kovac is a shrewd man. He would not so easily let his possessions go. He values control as much as you do, especially when it benefits him. Is this whole charade just a cheap way to turn my favor to you? I assure you, though I only now hold this paper, I have never been a slave. My allegiance lies with my men. I will not be bought or swayed by guilt-driven releases and cheap titles! Tell me again, *my lord,* why are you here? I can only hope that I have not so gravely misjudged you."

The decorative face paint served many purposes. He now held an air of infallibility as well as a creature devoid of emotion. He listened to Oryan's remarks as a man who was being stabbed through the heart with the dull edge of a rusty blade. His cheeks were flush with contempt though no one could tell.

Then he slowed his heart rate. Navaro knew that his new warlord had seen the slight breech in emotion. All it took was a twitch of an eyelid or a change in the rise and fall of his chest. Oryan was a careful student of men, discovering nearly instantly their strengths and vulnerabilities. Before now, he admired his champion from a far, considering him a most valuable asset. Now the game of psychological chess had begun, and he was already compromised. This asset had gone from a distant admiration to a powerful ally and now a genuine threat. Oryan, son of Armay, had broken his indifference.

Only Oryan noted the change. That was enough. Oryan now saw a weakness behind the statuesque façade, and he saw now, very clearly, that the being before him was, in the end, only human. A flawed, imperfect human. Navaro was no god, if only the two of them knew it.

"I can see that you are still suspicious of me," said the composed and smooth voice. "It is because you are not sure of my intentions. I assure you, Captain, my rewards have been out of nothing but gratitude to you. This is my way of thanking a man who will accept no thanks. It is true, I did present the idea of your freedom to the General, but he was not hard to convince. He feels little and says less, yet I think that he is thanking you too, in his own way.

"When it comes to your freedom, yes you are free from all men." He changed the subject. "I am curious. From the looks of your writing, you have been studying military history. That is only a fraction of my library. Did you venture outside those volumes?"

Oryan still felt alert, suspicion and doubt still vibrating through his bones. He allowed himself to relax outwardly again, intrigued by what was coming from this question. "Given my nature, my status in your military, and my newly bestowed title, I thought that was an appropriate choice for study."

The emperor nodded but looked down with an expression between understanding and pity. He rose from the table, and Oryan rose with him. "I have something to show you. Will you walk with me?"

They began to walk in a slow pace across the floor. The emperor's posture was perfect, his arms folded behind his back. The two remained in silence, Oryan wanted to say nothing to the man, and Navaro was searching for the right words. "I knew your father," he began. "It is courteous to say that I am the reason that you have had to be freed rather than being born that way. I am responsible for his captivity."

"And the loss of his eye," Oryan added.

The emperor acknowledged the remark with a slight nod and

continued. "I respected your father. You are much like him in your gift for strategy. He was among the most brilliant military minds I have ever known, and so I respected him as an adversary." They passed the first of the shelves filled with books. "But he was also a man of deep feeling. Though his body was in this world, his heart was in the next. In the end, he was defeated, but I knew where he was, and I checked in on him regularly, though he may not have known it. I lament his death."

Oryan was not sure what to believe. He only knew fragments of his father's rebellion from what Armay had told him and what clues he could gather from the Net. He was quite sure that Navaro did not lament the loss of the leader of a rebellion, but he could not detect even a hint of insincerity in his voice. Perhaps this was a man who respected his adversaries. Oryan needed to do more investigation.

They had come to a stop near the back corner of the library, a place that Oryan had never ventured to. Neither had given notice to the books around them as the conversation was causing serious reflection for both of them.

There was a long silence that followed the emperor's last statement. "Do you know what your father accomplished?" asked Navaro.

"I know enough to know that you checked on him from time to time, though he may not have known it."

Navaro allowed himself a slight smile. "Your father was the most successful leader I have ever seen. Had it not been for betrayal amongst his ranks, he may have been completely successful and never been brought to me for judgment. Armay defeated everyone, even the Lord General Kovac, though he will never surrender that information. I even still remember the name of the informant that finally gave him to us."

Oryan listened closely. This was a name he would not soon forget. There was justice to be reaped for the loss of a man's vision, both literally and figuratively.

"He was a tall man. His face was bright then. He was one of your father's commanders, as I recall. He came to us and revealed small plans at first, then, as he gained our trust, he told us where to find Armay and how to defeat him. He was a traitor from the beginning. And Seyah received a traitor's reward."

"What happened to him?" asked Oryan as indifferently as possible.

"As I told you, a traitor's reward. It matters little, as I am quite sure he's dead now," replied Navaro. There was something in his tone that led Oryan to believe that Navaro was not being completely forthcoming about this man. Not that he was lying as much as *protecting* him or his secret, whichever was more valuable.

At this point, Navaro withholding information was irrelevant. He had a name, and that was all he needed. He could piece together the rest himself.

"When your father was finally brought to me, I did what I could to convince him to serve the empire. Unfortunately, his vision was not mine. Before his sentence was carried out, I had an audience with him at his request. I will never forget that day.

"They brought him before me in chains; he was weary and ill. He came to the stairs of my throne and fell to his knees and remained there in silence for some time. I noticed tears drop from his face, but I heard no sobs. My guards motioned to me to remove him, but I would not have it.

"After a very long time, he cast his red eyes heavenward. His gaze finally met mine, and I was moved by the depth of emotion there. I was expecting a plea for his life, a last attempt to salvage what was soon to be taken from him.

"He made no such attempt. In a small but proud voice, he sued for the lives of his captains, his friends, and," the emperor shifted his gaze to Oryan, "his family. He spoke of his wife being great with child. He knew that I was aware of her, and he knew that my justice is only rivaled by my vengeance.

"I have heard such supplication before, but it was never like this. I was moved by this man, who, with all dignity stripped from him, still had only the welfare of others in his heart. So I asked him what he had to offer that could stay my hand. 'Nothing,' he answered. He made no speeches about mercy or respect for a worthy adversary, for indeed he was; he just lowered his head again and awaited my reply.

"I sent him away, assuring him that I would deliver my verdict in the morning. I thought on him all night; his expression and words would not allow me sleep. After I wrestled with this man and his request, I realized what it was that was troubling me so much. I am a god, yet I have never known what one might call *spirituality.* This man, this beggar at my feet, possessed something that I did not. Maybe it was the looming presence of his own demise that prompted it, but I believe that his was a lifelong knowledge of redemption in his life that moved me so. How noble! What a grand display of virtue and honor! There was I, emperor of Navarus, lord of hosts, a god who walked with earthly feet, being taught something of the nature of divinity by a beggar in chains before me!

"Then, thought I, perhaps he was only my enemy in his old life and his shame had given birth to a new one. Perhaps I was seeing something of what I might become, a creature full of grace and godliness. This man intrigued me so much that I almost rushed to the prison to be taught at his feet. Then I realized that, as the emperor, I must also demand justice, for mercy is powerful, yet it cannot rob justice.

"So, he received the punishment that you are familiar with. I could see no way to satisfy both mercy and justice. I banished him to the far corner of my empire. I took his eye, as a reminder that though he be alive, he would never be whole again. However, I gave him his woman from whence you came. The lesson he taught me that day was enough to warrant that gift."

Oryan had never heard such a tale before. In Navaro's eyes, there was no lie. Though he was leaving out Kovac's involvement in the sparing of Armay, he spoke his version of the truth openly, perhaps for the first time. Oryan loved his father and had known many eternal truths because of his wisdom. Suddenly, there was a deep swelling of guilt that rose in Oryan's heart. He only remembered Armay as a teacher of combat. As a hard, demanding man who was in a constant pursuit of perfection even if he could only achieve it vicariously through his son. But at the heart of the man was the truth that Navaro noticed from the first. The proudest of men could see who his father was, and he had not.

"Why are you telling me this?" he asked bitterly.

Navaro did not look at him but just looked at the books in front of them. "I want to show you something," he said as he reached for a shelf that was only slightly taller than he. To Oryan's amazement, he lifted the top off of the shelf, which released a lever. The shelf itself slid silently open, and there was a dark hallway beyond.

The emperor entered, and Oryan followed. Once they were both in, Navaro closed the bookshelf doorway behind them. It was utterly dark. "Light," the emperor said aloud to the darkness, and there was light. The hallway illuminated with a dim glow that seemed blinding to Oryan after the darkness. He was standing at the end of a wide hallway. There was a beautiful carpet that ran the length of the floor, and on both walls hung every trophy and prize imaginable from the corners of the world. Some were new, some very ancient. There were swords and armor, clothing, headwear, jewelry, artwork, and all the beautiful things crafted by the hand of man.

Oryan gasped as the weight of this chamber took hold. This was history. This was man's legacy long after they were gone. He walked in the middle, slowly taking in what he witnessed on both of the walls around him. Navaro followed, saying nothing, but observing and letting his guest observe. When he felt that his visitor had seen enough, he began to speak.

"What you see here is my accumulated wealth as well as the emperors' before me. There are artifacts here from the birth of the empire. I have kept the most beautiful thing that I could find from the countries that I have conquered. Much of what I have was gifted to me by kings, magistrates, and other rulers.

"Do you see that piece?" he asked, pointing to a small red necklace that hung on the wall. It shined like glass and was highly decorated with gold and other precious metals. "That is *doighter*, the rarest material in the world. That necklace represents eighty-six percent of all the doighter ever found. It also represents the largest amount of it in one place.

"Legend tells that the first emperor, my ancestor, brought it with him when he descended from the halls of the gods and explored mortality. It was he who created this empire from nothing, and it was he who secured its future as the center of technology and wisdom. That artifact could have financed the whole of my palace should I have sold it."

Oryan was impressed, but not by the necklace. He focused on the weaponry. There were pieces here that he had read about many times but he had never seen. As he gazed, he realized that his question of the emperor before they entered had never been answered.

"Why have you told me these things, and why did you bring me here?" he asked again, regaining control of himself and the situation.

"Light," Navaro said a second time, and a light brighter than all the rest shone at the end of the tunnel opposite the entrance. Hanging there alone was a military dress uniform. It was not ancient, but still many years old. It had been well taken care of. It was pressed, hung, and encased in glass. The underlay was green with gold lining around the edges. Though it was impressive and obviously designed to be the centerpiece of the collection, it was neither the oldest piece nor the most valuable. Oryan studied it closely to determine its significance, and then all at once it struck him.

He remembered his father sketching symbols in the Tamrus they worked on in the shops at the Quarter. That same symbol was lavishly embroidered on the sleeve of the jacket. As a child, Oryan had always considered them his mark, a signature of sorts that Armay used to brand his work. Now it all made sense. The symbols he had so carefully etched onto those pieces were neither his signature nor a brand. They were a silent pledge to his continuing loyalty to a kingdom long dead to all but him.

He raised a hand as if to trace the lines. He could picture Armay wearing it. He could see his head held high, the banners of Gondolin flying overhead. He could hear the horns signaling their men to their most valiant and brave leader. For the first time, he could envision what his father was meant to be. After long scrutiny, he turned to his host, unable to find the words.

"Each emperor chooses what he places at the head of this chamber. Traditionally it has been the artifact that he deems is of the most value. For me, that is what I hold most dear. It is a constant reminder of the lesson taught to me by the humble man in chains. Before your father, I was ready to be emperor. After him, I was ready to be a god."

Oryan nodded. Navaro's wisdom was his own. The truth that his father had taught him had been corrupted by ambition and greed.

The lust for power had defiled a truth that was altogether pure. "It seems to me the lesson is altogether lost on you. If all the world looks to you for your wisdom, it will be peopled with dictators and slaves."

Navaro remained unmoved. He looked at Oryan. "I have appointed you to be a god by my side. The day that I learned of your father's death I offered a prayer for him that he would receive all that he was meant to have. I know that he now sees my wisdom and harbors me no ill will. His spirit has reassured me of that from beyond the grave. In time, you will come to see the truth of it as I have. When you truly accept and understand your new title, you will see it too."

The emperor bowed and gestured back to the entrance. The conversation was at an end. Oryan bowed in response and walked past him to the door. He pushed it open, but before he could leave his father's legacy behind, the smooth voice spoke again.

"I am having the uniform moved." Oryan paused at the door. "I called upon my best servants to carry it to your new estate. May it find a place of honor in your halls as it has in mine." He bowed again.

This time, Oryan did not return the courtesy.

THE HUNT BEGINS

Oryan and Thomas left Obsidian the next morning. Though the emperor came to wish them both farewell, Oryan's last experience with Navaro had proven to be more than his fill. He said little to his lieutenant and nothing of the incident in the library. Mostly, he listened to his friend prattle on about what a wonderful experience it had been and how he would miss his beautiful companion.

His memory traveled to Celeste from time to time, but he pushed back the thoughts as they came. She remained the only beautiful thing in his world. If only he could find her, but it was still too dangerous to seek her out. He could not bring her up to anyone, not even now. His new title made him above the laws of the land, but Oryan still had many enemies.

Thomas had watched the palace disappear through the back window of their transport as they sped away. He had fallen in love with the lifestyle almost overnight. Going from a grunt of a soldier to a playboy living every adolescent's dream was almost too much to walk away from. He had drawn out, leaving as much as possible, but when the official call came from his captain, he knew that duty did not wait for him.

The two of them and the rest of the Knights had been granted a one-month leave. Oryan protested the idea, wanting instead to give them each half of that time. "One month is a long time for my men to rest while the enemy does not," he had told Alexander. Despite his opposition, the leave was still granted, and there was a part of him that was grateful they had denied his request.

He did not go to his new estate. Even when the coach came to take him there from barracks, he sent the driver away very disgruntled. Though he did not force his men to stay, many did, and so he spent the first week establishing a daily program for them to keep them honed. It was light work by comparison to their normal regiment, but it nonetheless served its purpose.

In a ceremony attended only by the Knights, he named Ethanis Thomas the first general of the Elite Forces unit. Once he had given his instruction to the leaders to carry on the routine for the remainder of the leave, he retreated to his quarters. There was business he had to attend to, and it required solitude.

He had been thinking on where to start since he left the palace, and he had decided that the best course of action was to start looking on the Net. He sat at his console and logged onto the Net. His ID and password gave him several levels above classified clearance, so perhaps he would have success where a layman would not. He found the empire's information database and typed in a name.

S-E-Y-A-H. The empire's database was extensive, but that name was fairly unique. It was a Gondolinian name to be sure, and a detailed census was taken shortly after the empire seized control, cataloging every person who dwelt within its borders. In Gondolin, only the female children were given last names; the males simply used their father's name for a second. That made the search fairly easy, especially when it only turned out two possible results from the inquiry. One was a dark-skinned man who was tried and executed for theft and murder more than thirty years before Oryan had been born. The other bore the face of a traitor; a dark and swarthy man with the look of both predator and prey. Oryan made his selection.

The console hesitated momentarily but then displayed some fifty pages of information, including a military entry photo taken more than twenty years ago. Oryan studied the face long and hard. He noted the dark eyes, the shape of the mouth, and any other features that would likely remain unchanged by the passing of time. Armay was in his mid-twenties when Oryan was born, and judging by the photo, so was Seyah. That would make him in his forties now, so Oryan saved the photo to do some more work with the military's facial aging programs later.

The first detail that caught Oryan's attention was the fact that the whole file was classified. Most soldiers have only their vital statistics and pedigree information hidden from public eye. Their service dates, duty stations, etc., were all public knowledge. Anyone with regular Net access could get them at any time. Not this man.

Oryan began to read the details. There was information regarding his birth and childhood, though not much. It seems that he was raised in a notable family, one close to the king of Gondolin. He received high marks in all his schooling and served for a time in the army, though it failed to mention whose command he was under. To Oryan, it seemed that anywhere his father could have been mentioned, there was an inconsistency in the text. It was as if there was a fact or statement missing that would link two or more others together. He deduced that those details were originally written but had since been omitted.

The document did speak at length of the surrender of Gondolin to Navarus, though its only mention of Armay's rebellion was to tie in Seyah's link to his imperial service. This is where Oryan was most interested. He knew enough of the details to know that he was not concerned with the first half of his life or even his involvement in the arrest of his father. It was what happened after that mattered.

Commander Seyah served in the battles of Doran, Stahele, and Fort MacKee. His ruthless tactics both on and off the battlefield earned him the nickname "The Butcher," and his superior officers quickly denounced him.

There was an interesting point. The man apparently was making swift enemies on both sides of the battlefield.

Shortly after Fort MacKee, he was relieved of field duty and placed into a counter-terrorism unit that specialized in the infiltration and elimination of traitorous groups and individuals. This unit eventually became Emperor Navaro's secret service unit known as Paladin.

That fits. The Paladin were the Legion of Navaro's law enforcement. They were above common law. When there was a disturbance that needed to be solved and they did not mind it becoming a public spectacle, the normal enforcement units were called in. However, if it was a lawbreaker who needed to be handled with unlawful methods, the Paladin went to work. Their subjects were referred to as "marks," and to be marked usually meant that you were shortly going to disappear and never be heard of again. If someone with contradictory opinions was speaking too loud or if those same opinions were gaining a following, if they were conducting business in a manner not suitable for "imperial standards," if they were causing any unwanted ripples, they became marks.

It was also the Paladin who acted as imperial liaisons to the black market. They kept tabs on the major underworld players, mob bosses, mercenaries, smugglers, and petty thieves. They were also the ones who never let anyone become *too* powerful in the syndicates.

To Oryan, those who joined their ranks were born traitors, so it was not surprising that this Seyah would be amongst the fathers. Though he was not disturbed by the news, a thought lingered in the back of his mind. He knew very well that there were only two people that the Paladin answered to: Navaro and Kovac. Oryan knew Kovac well enough to know that he would use these men as tools, but he would just as soon kill them as trust them. Why the gut feeling that the General had more involvement with this one? He read on.

As the founder of this unit, he once again demonstrated a natural ability to excel at his job performance. His subordinates achieved great success, and as a team they rooted out several notorious criminal organizations. It was largely due to his success that the emperor decided to fund the efforts of this unit full time and even adopt them as his internal investigations task force for national security.

There was a picture indenting the document here showing Seyah shaking hands with Navaro. It was a still image of the formal announcement of the formation of the Paladin. Oryan scrutinized the photograph carefully. He could see that the pair stood in the very same spot where he had been named warlord just a few weeks earlier. His new title suddenly felt cheap, and he felt filthy for accepting it.

There were people of note in the background. Most of them were the so-called nobility, but it was the very corner of the picture that caught Oryan's gaze. There, at the edge of the photo, was the beginning of a black dress uniform. All he could identify was the sleeve and a small portion of the jacket, but there were rank insignias and other decoration to be noted. This man was a general, that much was certain, but was it *the* General? Judging by the fact that this man's shoulder was at the height of most of the others' heads, Oryan concluded that it could be him. The General was at most of the more press-oriented events that the emperor held, so it was not uncommon to see him in the background, but there was just something out of place here.

The rest of the history documented his career as the head of the Paladin. It was mostly dates and incidents of honors received, medals won, and other events of note. Much to his chagrin, he noticed that he was quickly nearing the end of the document and he was no closer to an answer than he had been before. In fact, it seemed that the text was ending prematurely.

He began to read of his mysterious disappearance on a "rogue mission." The remaining paragraphs were about his involvement with an underground movement against the empire and of that rebellions flat failure. The last few words were chilling yet seemed very out of place.

Colonel Seyah Moranson was captured almost eight months after his disappearance. He was tried in the Imperial Courts and executed as a traitor to the throne.

It gave the date of his execution and ended with another classified symbol. Oryan jotted down the date and then moved on to the references for the text. It listed the military hall of records and Imperial Histories amongst others. It was a very standard list, until the last noted reference.

Excerpts from a journal found amongst the colonel's personal effects the day that he was executed. No confirmation on the author of the journal has ever been established.

That was it. That was the start he needed. Where to find the journal was another question. Although he would search the Net, he was sure that it was a document he would never see. Most likely that journal was destroyed by the House of Justice when Seyah was sentenced. Oryan still did not believe that the execution ever happened, but he knew that if they were going through all the trouble of erasing a man from public knowledge, they would certainly destroy all creditable proof of this cover-up. On second thought, the search for that journal was most likely a lost cause. Oryan looked at the list of nobles and justices who presided at the trial, and none of them were sentimental enough to keep such a trinket.

He pulled the actual recorded minutes of the trial and began to read all that he could about what went on that day. There were witnesses from within the ranks of the Paladin, as well as citizens who had seen his crimes firsthand. Like his history, it was apparent to Oryan that many pieces of the trial were omitted. The evidence was very strong against him, the witnesses were damning at every turn, and the final judgment was unanimous without any delay.

This bothered Oryan. It was too neat. He already had a feeling that the execution was a fabrication, but now it seemed as if the trial was as well. It was as if there was no dark secret left uncovered. There was no room for doubt. A man who had lived his life underground, hiding skeletons along the way, would not just do something like this so openly and so suddenly. There was no slow dissention into madness or betrayal. One day he was the silent threat for the emperor's lawbreakers, and the next he was a rebel. Yet, even the court proceeding detailed this as "insanity due to years of sustained overly stressful and violent situations."

Even stranger still, there was no audio recording of the trial. Most trials were not visually recorded, but there had been only a handful of trials on the books that did not contain an audio recording of the event. There were too many question marks here.

Near the end of the trial's written record there was another interesting discovery. Among those who attended the execution in person was Emperor Navaro. Some rulers would revel in attending the death of a traitor, but Navaro was not one of them. He was not one who delighted in seeing violence firsthand. He preferred to sway others to his cause and let them cover their hands in blood. If this was the truth, why was he there? If it was a fabrication, why would he allow himself to be listed as a spectator?

Unless *he* was the sentimental one! Maybe he could not resist putting his own brand of signature on this whole affair, real or not. The emperor himself stated that he collected what he found of value from those he had conquered. Mostly that meant artifacts, armor, sword, and other precious valuables, but what if he was not conquering a country or nation? What if he was conquering a man instead? He had kept something of his father's when he considered him a worthy conquest. What could be more valuable to take from a broken man than his identity?

The wheels spun in Oryan's mind. This was a long shot, but if that journal still existed, there was only one place it would be. The lost cause could become a holy crusade.

Minutes later, Oryan had transportation arranged back to Obsidian.

The transport came to a smooth stop in front of the emperor's palace. He had traveled nonstop for nearly two days. Oryan had not been idle in his journey. He had slept little, trying to gather as much information about Seyah, his associates, and major or minor players involved anywhere along the way. Most of the information on the Net had led to a dead end. Some took him in circles that led to no reasonable conclusion, and others simply contradicted themselves so radically that his suspicions continued to grow.

Mostly, he thought on where to start looking for this journal when he arrived at the palace. He doubted that he could gain access to the emperor's more private collection, but something told him that he would not have to look there. He made a three-dimensional map in his mind of the room in the back of the library filled with Navaro's spoils of war. Nowhere could Oryan recall seeing a book of any kind, and he would remember such a thing as it would be painfully out of place amongst the other treasure therein.

One of the emperor's guards robed in black and crimson slid open the door to let him out.

"Welcome, my lord. We are honored to receive you again so soon," said the guard.

He brushed passed the guard and headed up the stairs and to the slowly opening doors of the palace. As he entered, he noted the vastness of the room. There were no fanfares to greet him this time, just wide-open space. It had seemed grand to him the first time, with the massive room illuminated just right and the crowd buzzing from all directions, but now, he was looking at a dimly lit structure with only the echoes of his own footfalls to be heard. He stopped for a moment to soak in the complete silence that surrounded him. It was harshly apparent how small a place like this could make a man feel.

He traversed his way through the passages of the palace with hardly an upward glance, his feet knowing the way without his mind having to tell them which direction to follow. His thoughts were constantly on what course to pursue once he reached the library. Oryan felt certain that the book that he sought would not be categorized alphabetically or by author's last name. There were nearly a million volumes of literature in the emperor's library and knowing where to start would make this visit far more productive. However, he knew that he would go book by book if he had to.

Time slid past him as he walked and pondered. He gave no thought to his surroundings as he had on his last visit, and before he knew it, the hallway ended and he stood at the entrance to the library. A tall, slender man with the look of high society stood up from behind the desk just to the left of the doors. He straightened his expensive silk jacket and cast a sharp, prying glance at Oryan.

Oryan had come wearing his military dress uniform in an attempt to speed the process up by avoiding unnecessary questions and costly delays. It had worked until now.

"May I help you, *sir*?" asked the raspy voice between thin, pale lips.

"You can get out of the way," responded Oryan in a tone that would have prompted those who knew him to move quickly.

The man gave a menacing glare in return. There was an air of wounded pride and extreme offense in everything he said from that moment on. "I am sorry, sir, but I am the emperor's librarian and chief historian. No one enters this place without *my* express approval! You can only imagine that you will not gain such an offer any time soon."

"Do you know who I am?" asked Oryan, becoming more than annoyed.

"I believe the more important question is, do I care to know?"

Oryan grew weary of this game. "I am Oryan Jeckstadt, Warlord of Navarus. You will let me pass, or I will make sure that the emperor's chief historian spends the rest of his days dusting bookshelves for the guests. Do I make myself perfectly clear?"

The man drew back a step, realizing his folly, but his pride once again took hold, and he could not back down from this attack of his authority. "My lord," he began incredulously, "I have turned away everyone from princes to beggars. Your title means nothing here!"

This thin, proud old man knew not how close he stood to death that night. Oryan, however, maintained composure for at least one more attempt to settle the matter civilly. "Servant." He used the title as insultingly as possible. "Perhaps you would listen to the remainder of what I had to say. I am Oryan Jeckstadt, Warlord of Navarus, and I have a standing invitation by His Excellency to utilize the contents of this library at my whim. I was unaware that his decisions needed your approval."

The librarian tried to snap back with a blow more devastating than the one he had just been dealt, but he was foiled. Indeed, this soldier was arrogant and impetuous. He lacked all of those things that made a man noble. He was hot-tempered, rude, and above all, nothing but a common soldier. A grunt here to tell him how to do his job! However, that didn't stop him from being absolutely right. With a dark glare, the old man stepped aside and pressed the release of the doors.

Oryan stepped into the library, ignoring the old man's constant glare. The doors shut behind him, and the soft lighting of the room gradually illuminated the darkness. Wall after wall, shelf after shelf was revealed. It was then that the full weight of the task before him sank in. There were more volumes here than could be read in a thousand lifetimes. Here he stood, with only his hands and eyes to find a single book. And at this point, he was not even sure it was here.

Thirty-six hours passed. He had neither slept nor ate. He had begun his search on the libraries database, using, at first, the direct approach. He looked for anything that contained Seyah's name, and then he moved on to the literature about Gondolin, then onto recent court cases, Navarite history, and so on. In all, he had held some ten thousand titles to choose from.

Oryan remained undaunted, though he knew that he would have to rest and eat soon. Weariness was setting in, and he needed his mind to be sharp. This place was the emperor's after all, and he would need to think like that man in order to find what he sought. After some forty hours of searching, he found a secluded corner of the massive room, propped himself against a wall, and immediately passed into a deep sleep.

Armay had once told him that the best truths are found in quiet moments where one can be aloof from the cares and anxieties of the world. His father had been a man who spent many hours in solitude. Even though there was very little sacred in the Quarter, he always managed to step outside of himself and find what he referred to as "his center." Armay was a dreamer. That is to say, he believed that some dreams were forecasters or visions of what was to come. He felt that others were warnings of some upcoming calamity or of a choice that, if not made correctly, would spell doom.

Oryan had always heeded that ideal. For the most part, his dreams were forgotten by morning. He often dreamed of fame and success. More recently, his dreams had been dark. They had been full of memories he would rather forget: faces on the battlefield, scorched and burning earth, and things of that nature. For this reason, he slept little and light. Yet, it was his dreams that allowed him to recognize Celeste for who she was.

On this night, his mind was utterly focused on something more. He did not dream of battles or glory or love. He was driven, even unconsciously, to receive an answer to the question. It was the question that brought him here, and it was the question that bent all his will toward its answer. As it often did in his life, the solution came in the way he least expected it.

He had only been asleep a short while when he began to see himself walking up and down the isles of the library. It was as if he watched himself through some third-party point of view searching for a book. He could hear no sound, and he could feel nothing of his own emotions. The search was frantic, almost desperate, and his mind's eye paid close attention to the details. As the vision progressed, he could see himself running from shelf to shelf. As he watched himself, he became aware of the sweat that was beginning to form on his brow.

Finally, he saw himself slow and eventually stop at the end of one particular shelf. It was like all the others, many feet above his head and filled with books. Unless he saw more, this shelf would be impossible to distinguish from the others. As the vision continued to search, he began to look for more details. He looked for names of books, but none were clear. He tried to note sizes or colors of bindings, but again, no one book stood out more than the next. Then he caught a glimpse of brass. Most shelves in this library were inset into the side of the bookshelf that it rested upon. No extra brackets or support was needed. It appeared that this shelf had at one time been broken. Whoever repaired it simply fastened a brass-colored, L-shaped bracket underneath the shelf. There were bound to be very few of those patch repairs in this great place. It was the first real distinguishable detail that imprinted in his mind. The light gleamed off of the bracket until all he could see was white light.

He awoke. Instantly he was on his feet, traversing the isles of the bookshelves, slowly at first, taking note of each shelf corner; then his pace quickened until he was at a steady jog up and down the floor. His heart was racing, and his face was flush. He *knew* he was on the right track. It was all too real to have just been a dream!

Minutes passed like hours as he raced down the lanes. After twenty or thirty rows, doubt began to gnaw. Perhaps it was just a dream. It could be that he was just deluded by an overactive mind trying desperately to find some hope in this seemingly impossible search. This thought took hold, and he slowed his pace to a walk near the end of the row he was in. Finally he stopped, feeling that his efforts were futile.

He looked at the floor, trying to justify these efforts but finding there only frustration. *This is a waste. I was foolish to think it would be here!* If the book was still in existence, chances are no one knew its whereabouts. Oryan shut his eyes and let his head fall from its raised position. A heavy sigh escaped his lungs. The searcher felt defeat weigh down his head. It was time to go back to barracks.

His mind told his body to abandon the quest and head back to duty, but his heart held his feet firm. Something in the deepest corner of his thoughts tormented him and forced him to remain where he stood. It was hope. Small, dismal, and nearly extinguished, yet hope spurred him on. He shook his head again at the stubbornness that he possessed. Even on a seemingly fruitless errand, he could not give up.

A battle waged in his mind. Hope struggled with logic, and in the end, his sense of duty triumphed over hope's ambition. He turned to leave. But something caught his glance as he turned that gave hope all the fuel it needed to completely consume logic. The search was on again with renewed fervor. There was a glimmer beneath one of the shelves before him. It was small, and he had probably missed it a hundred times before while wandering these aisles, but now it was as good as a beacon on a stormy night. What he saw there was the reflection of brass beneath the shelf!

Oryan dashed to the reflection, hoping with each heartbeat that is was not his dream trying so desperately to become reality that it clouded his judgment. Nevertheless, there it was! The brass-colored bracket smiled at him like a child finally found in a game of hide and seek. His dream *had* been more than just imagination! In his elation for finding this thing, he nearly forgot what he had been searching for in the first place.

Even as he celebrated, reality crept from behind the joy and reminded him of the truth: the dream had ended there. There were no defining marks aside from this one. He stepped back and gazed at the sheer vastness of the world around him. The shelves and their contents loomed over him. This was as the dream had shown him, but he was no closer to finding the actual book than he was before. All he had identified was a small blemish on the otherwise perfect library.

As it had before, hope dwindled but did not die. One by one, he began to read the titles. He looked first at the smaller sized books as Seyah's journal was bound to be something he could have easily carried with him on his travels. Here there was little success. They were mostly about famous figures in history. This was not far from the place he had previously been when reading about Kentaur and its warlords.

As he scanned the row just above his head, he noticed a large, heavy, leather-bound book that seemed to stand out from the rest. Oryan could not place why as it was actually sunken behind the other books and, despite its size, could barely be seen from the floor. It had no title on the spine. In fact, there were no identifying marks of any kind. Still, Oryan reached for it. As his fingers brushed the leather cover, a wave of anticipation swept through him. He was drawn to this book as if it were calling to him from the dust. He gripped the sides and slid it from its lodgings. The book was surprisingly light for its size, as if the cover was the only source of weight. He examined the cover to find still no title.

There was only one thing left to do. Every book had a title page. It was a small matter of opening the cover and reading it, but as he placed his fingers on the edge, a warning sounded from his heart. It was a strange sensation. He somehow knew that he had found what he sought.

Once, a long time ago, he had felt fear creep into him. It was the fear of the unknown that haunted him on that rainy day in the Quarter. That day, even though he felt fear, he was not afraid. Through all the battles fought and won, both in the arena and on the field, he had never been afraid. To him, he had nothing to lose and so there was nothing to fear. Yet here, now, in this quiet place where there was no death to be seen or heard, he was afraid. More than fear, he felt sheer terror grip his lungs and freeze his blood.

It seemed to whisper. *Once you cross this line, there is no going back. Once you cross here, you may never be able to get back.*

His hands shook. With his left, he held the book, and with his right, he gripped the cover. His fingers were frozen and colorless. A cold chill crept down his back, his hair stood on end, and he was acutely aware of the drops of sweat dripping from his face onto the leather cover despite his chills.

He stared hard as if to burn a hole in the cover. His heart raced as his breath gasped forth in short ragged bursts. *Danger! There is danger here! Run!* The warning shouted again, and this time he heeded it. His professional indifference and soldier's calm left him entirely. Oryan threw the book as if it were hot coals in his hands. Before he could react, he was sprinting down the row, turning hard at the corner, and frantically looking to the exit. He reached the door, afraid to look back, fearful that some evil thing had arisen to destroy him.

As he desperately tried to recall how to escape, a familiar voice rescued him from himself. "Is there a problem, my lord?" it said through the comm on the door. It was the voice of the old man from the entrance. He had been watching Oryan very closely when he could and followed his flight from the books. His voice had been incredulous, as if to say, "Did the bad book scare the little boy?"

Still, in his state, it was the friendliest voice Oryan could have heard. He became aware of his surroundings again. He was not in a frightening place. It was quiet, calm, and serene here. There was nothing to fear. His heart slowed, and his breathing returned to normal.

"My lord?" the old man asked again.

"I'm fine. Surely you have something better to do than spy on me," he responded.

Oryan faced the library again. It seemed vast beyond imagining. He controlled his senses and mastered the irrational behavior that had taken him. Slowly, painfully, he began the slow trek back to the place he had once been.

The closer he came to where he had been, the more the sweat renewed its vigor. The steps became harder to take as, once again, the warning crept into his heart. Finally, he turned the corner, hoping somehow that the book would not be there. But there, lying exactly where he had left it, was the large nameless book. He closed his eyes, but no matter how hard he tried, he could not master this. Despite the warning, he stepped toward the menacing thing until, at last, he stood over it.

He bent down to get it, feeling the blood leave his fingers again. They crept underneath the cover, and Oryan watched as if from someone else's eyes as his own fingers gripped the book and lift it from the ground. It seemed so heavy to him. The weight brought him to his knees. Once more, he reached for the cover, but this time he did not run. With fear and trembling, he opened it.

Staring back at him was a title page. It read: "Traitors in History." This was it. He turned the page to find that the remainder of the book was not actually there. The pages had been removed and replaced by a frame of sorts whose edges had been carefully crafted to appear as pages of an old book. It was not elaborate, but it held in its center a small discolored, weatherworn book. Once again came the warning. *Walk away now. Put it back and walk away. Let the past stay buried.*

Oryan drew the book from the frame and placed its larger casing back on the floor. It seemed to him that the small book he held now weighed more than its disguise. Nothing had changed since he entered this place, yet he felt as if, should he proceed, he would lose something of such vast importance that it terrified him to do so.

He stood and slowly walked to the end of the row, his fingers studying the texture of this thing he held. *Put it back! Drop it and run!* Finally his thumb found the edge that opened the cursed thing. *Run!* His jaw stiffened, and his brow forced his eyes into a stern glare. It was time he knew the truth!

The cover opened stiffly, and Oryan read the first entry:

I have served in the army of Gondolin for nearly a decade only to see it fall without struggle into the hands of the empire. The king is weak. His general is weak. I, Seyah Moranson, am strong, and I will make the empire shake at my presence.

Oryan's heart became wrapped in icy fingers. Here was the name of the traitor in his own handwriting. His heart pumped the ice through his veins and up his spine. He would find Seyah. His time had come.

Rarely do people recognize great turning points in their lives, and so it was with him. What was lost in that room was not life as he recognized it, though life it was. What was lost, what died then, was the last trace of Oryan, the son of Armay, which was human. Where innocence had been, vengeance now dwelt. Where decency and compassion had once existed, hatred and rage extinguished their flame.

These things, if left unchecked, could consume a soul. Where these things were, redemption had no place and so cannot claim the creature. For such damned souls, all was lost. Yet try as he might to extinguish his light, others, both in this life and beyond, held claim on him still.

As he left that place, prepared to spend eternity in hell, others bent their will to him. They called to him with loving voices, urging him to come back from the brink. Such was the depth of his hate that he could not hear the call, yet they did not stop.

For as powerful as the darkness is, light, no matter how small, dispels the gloom. With light comes warmth and nourishment. The light of the stars sustains life on countless worlds. It carries in its wings new life, where old life had been extinguished. However, even the stars can die.

There is another force, which all life must have to sustain itself. This force conquers darkness and even death in a way that light cannot. It does not grow cold, it does not die, and it never abandons. In places where even light cannot reach, this force permeates.

Its name is love.

Distant Observers

The emperor had done his best to claim Oryan as his own. He had given him all that he could short of giving him his own crown. Oryan now had all of the wealth and influence that anyone could handle. However, Oryan had a destiny laid at his feet from the moment of his conception, and it was being monitored by others who carried a secret charge greater than any the emperor could comprehend.

Though Oryan knew nothing of it, his destiny ran deeper than titles, deeper than victories, medals, or even his own perception of glory. Deeper than his hate. It was the destiny of a hero. It was a legacy left by his noble father. Some destinies cannot be altered no matter how much the destined strays from the path.

His was the destiny of the Archide, and the foundations thereof had already been laid.

"Is he ready?"

"Does it matter? We need him now."

"Of course it matters. Look at him. *The Warlord of Navarus!* There is little we can do with a man who glorifies only himself."

"He is exceptionally skilled. He may be the greatest warrior who has ever lived. With what we've suffered recently, we need the best."

"No, we need the *right* warrior, not the best one. The wrong one and we are worse off than before. I don't think either of us is willing to risk that, even if he is the best."

"There is only one way to know if he is the right one. He must be summoned."

"And just how do you intend to accomplish that? No matter where that one goes, he's never alone. I need not remind you that we don't exist. To reveal ourselves in any way would be catastrophic. We would be giving our lives and everything we protect to the Phenex."

"All things happen for a reason. Perhaps we need not create an opportunity at all. Perhaps one will be made for us."

"Will we be able to recognize it when it comes?"

"Fame and popularity bring with them bitter enemies. They always do. It is the enemies from within that will give us our opportunity."

"Why are you so sure he's the one?"

"His lineage. I was not there for his upbringing, but I know the man who raised him. Whatever Navaro and the empire have done to him, somewhere, the seed remains—dormant though it might be."

"I knew Armay too, but it is the child who must nurture the seed. After all that we have seen of him, do you really think that he could succeed where even his father failed?"

"He didn't fail. He was stopped."

"Stopped by the same force that now controls the son."

"Coincidental. Remember, even in defeat, he revealed nothing."

"True, but if they knew who he was ..."

"They would not have known what to do with him. It is for that reason I believe he did not tell his son. That's a secret he could not force his little boy to keep. In the end, whether they knew it or not, Armay was a martyr, and his death was not in vain."

"He was so close. All our hopes were on him. He could have ended it all. What would we have done then, I wonder? What would the Guardians protect when the secret no longer needs protecting?"

"Is that why you're so against the son? Because you feel the father trampled on your dreams when you laid them at his feet? I suppose, when it's all over, we will no longer be needed. In that day, I will be content to partake of the fruit that we have worked so long to harvest."

"Until then, we must do what we have always done. Protect the Scrolls, find the Archide, and wait."

"We can't wait too long. Whoever the Phenex is, he gets closer every day. If we stand still, we will be easy prey for the predator."

"We are in the eleventh hour. I fear we may already be too late."

"Then why the hesitation?"

"What we protect means more than our survival. If we have indeed waited too long and the Phenex succeeds, then our knowledge dies with us. Light will diminish, but it will never be replaced by the darkness. If we choose the wrong man ... We have watched this Oryan for a long time, since his father was taken from us, but he is not his father. The secret would consume him, and all would be lost. If we reach for this man in our darkest hour, when despair and grief have taken their toll, will he be the one to save us? Is his heart strong enough to change the world?"

"He is not beyond hope."

"I feel he may be beyond our aid, and so we are beyond his. I fear he has already fallen."

"All men who fall reach for something to steady them. I believe he is the hero we need. Yet, even heroes need salvation. The question becomes, what does he need to steady himself before it's too late?"

"Perhaps the question is not *what* but *who*?"

"Perhaps. We need him to be *the* Archide. In order for him to bring salvation to us, perhaps we must first bring it to him."

"Our answers will not help him. In his state, they have only the power to condemn. We cannot save him."

"If a hero falls, can the heart of another bring him back? We may not be the answer, but *she* very well may be."

Old Friends and New Secrets

Two months had passed. Oryan had spent nearly every waking moment of life pouring over the journal. After leaving the palace, he had returned to barracks and locked himself in his quarters asking only to be disturbed by General Thomas, and even then only if it was absolutely necessary.

Thomas had only interrupted him twice. Both times were to notify him of active duty assignments. Oryan had gone on the first, but the battle had been decided before the Knights could arrive. The second he left to his general and the job was accomplished with the exactness of a surgeon.

Thus far, Oryan had followed the footsteps of a man he never knew yet took great interest in. He had studied maps and schematics of the lands and structures described in the journal. He read with infinite complacency of Seyah's bloodlust and desire for power. For Seyah, power meant fear. Those who served around him feared him, as did those he sought after. He performed radical procedures on those he captured, claiming to be searching for the right genetic formula for a superior human. All of his test subjects died.

The more the hunter read, the more twisted the journal became. Near the end, Seyah thought himself something other than human, a new stage of evolution far superior in both intellect and strength. His experiments became more gruesome. He tried to infuse others with his own blood in an attempt to give them some of his own genetic make up. When that failed, he would remove body parts, organs, facial features, and anything else he could to try and fashion them more like his own and then reattach them to the host. The female subjects were sexually violated before they were tortured and mutilated. Apparently some had become pregnant but miscarried due to extreme stress or as a result of the experiments themselves.

Although he learned a great deal about the *man,* Oryan was no closer to finding his whereabouts. The end of the journal spoke of a new assignment, which required his "unique skills." The text did not mention the name of the duty station or directions as (from what Oryan could tell) Seyah did not know. Still, he was clever enough to guess the destination, and so was Oryan.

The empire housed many different kinds of camps. There were work camps, those where people arrested for petty crimes, misdemeanors, etc., were sent. They were only for a short while, five years at the most, and the work was regulated for civil jobs that no one else wanted to do. These camps were meant only as crime deterrents. Most made it out alive.

The second was forced labor camps. This is where your more serious offenders were sent. They were there anywhere from six years to life, and the majority that made it out alive did not last long. Their work was brutal and the days long. Strictly rationed food and drink was given, and all labor was performed under the rod and lash of cruel wardens who delighted in nothing more than to see grown men cry. Seyah was a proponent and master of many of these.

The third were the Slave Quarters. Oryan was quite familiar with the third.

The last were the ones that fewer people were aware of. Most that found their way there never made it out to tell anyone else how to find them. That included the guards and those who ran the camps. There were no sentences pronounced, save one. These were called extermination camps. The empire kept them under dozens of levels of classification. To the public, they were rumors. Other nations had no idea they existed.

Nevertheless, they *were* there, and it was to the most notorious of these that Seyah was being sent. However, aside from a brief and somewhat deranged description of the journey to the camp itself, no other details were mentioned. The last entry was surprisingly clear. Someone or something was apparently giving him the freedom he had wanted the whole time. He was so elated, he could not even stay in character in his own journal. This struck Oryan since, if his end was what had been recorded on the Net, he would be anything but elated.

Oryan had done searching both through his legal channels and forging some illegal ones. He had gathered the names and locations of three extermination camps. One, known as Hunter's Ridge, was not far from him. It was settled into the mountain range just to the northeast of his barracks. The second, located on the opposite side of the empire, was called Shayes End. The last was located near the outskirts of a recently acquired territory. It was known only as The Pit.

The son of Armay knew that if he were to reach any of these places, he must do so completely under the radar and they had to be visited only a few days apart. If the empire found out that he was snooping around extermination camps, his search for answers would become increasingly more difficult, maybe even impossible.

He had arranged for his own personal transport. It was registered to the military, which simply made it another number in their books. The odds of them finding out who had that particular vehicle were slim, especially considering he did not have to see anyone to sign it out. There were no paper trails with his name on it.

He was packing very little. He wore his black military dress uniform and brought his new armor and sword with him just in case. Beyond that, changes of undergarments were all that existed in his bag.

It was while he was packing this small bag that General Thomas interrupted him for the third time. Thomas had been waiting outside his door for nearly ten minutes before he could muster the courage to press the button that would signal his presence to his commander. There was something different in him. Though Thomas could not put a specific name to it, he now felt uncomfortable around his old friend.

The door slid open. Thomas took a step inside the quarters and let the door slide shut behind him. The room had not changed. All of Oryan's personal effects were still organized and cataloged just as they had been from the start. The bed was still neatly made with clean linens as if it had not been slept on in months. There was a smell of disinfectants in the air. This place was sterile. Thomas felt some hope arise at this sight knowing that his leader was, if nothing else, still a disciplined soldier.

When he saw Oryan, his hope faded. The man was quickly packing. Were it not for a few defining features, he would have sworn he was looking at a different person. The man before him was old. His drawn face and pale skin made him look sickly. In their last battle, Oryan had been no less efficient or in control. He had been sharp and quick to deal death. Thomas knew that his commander was no less a machine of war just as he had been from day one. He may even be better at it now.

Oryan had allowed Thomas in but had otherwise ignored him. After a few moments of packing, he finally sat on his bed and looked at his general.

"Old friend, I trust you justify this visit with news of profound value," he said to Thomas.

There was levity to the comment, but forced levity. Thomas could sense the tension in his voice. He knew he was masking something. More than anything, Oryan wanted Thomas to do the talking. Thomas would not play along. "Lord, I have a message for you. It arrived only a few moments ago from a messenger on foot."

Oryan looked puzzled. "Who would be walking here? Did he give his name?"

"No, sir. And you misunderstand. He was running. It seemed by his appearance that he had been doing so for some time."

Oryan stood. "Is the messenger still here?"

"No, sir. He told me to deliver this message to you and you alone, and then he left the fort with the same haste that he had arrived in."

Thomas watched Oryan's features darken. He was trying to calculate who would be delivering such a message. Unannounced visitors and strange circumstances made Oryan revert into his emotionless mode. Thomas knew the look well.

"Let me see it."

Thomas handed him a small piece of folded paper. It was stiff and slightly discolored from the elements and sweat. Thomas watched his reaction. It was a short letter, but the general watched him study the words over and over. He fixed his gaze on Oryan's eyes. The usual brilliant blue was gone. They seemed soulless and empty. It was as if centuries of worry, stress, and life had somehow found their way onto a youthful face.

Thomas felt sorrow rise in his heart. He felt heartfelt sorrow for his friend and commander. There was sorrow, there was pain, and there was guilt. Could he have prevented this? Could he, even now, save him from the grip of this awful monster that wore away at his soul? He wanted to say yes, but he knew the resolve of this man. He knew that once Oryan had chosen a path, only Oryan could alter it.

Oryan's steely blue eyes traced the note over and over again. Ethanis Thomas could not handle the wait any longer. His usual knightly reserve was utterly spent.

"What does it say, sir?" he asked quietly.

Oryan shot a glance at his general as if he had just entered the room. For a moment, Thomas realized the precariousness of the situation. That note was something meant for Oryan's eyes only. If it had orders, it would have come through the normal channels on the Net and not by a personal messenger who would reveal nothing of himself or who had sent him. Perhaps he had asked too much of him in asking the contents of that letter.

A voice began to speak. It was not Thomas, and it was not Oryan, though it was he who was forming the words. The voice was thin and hoarse. Oryan read the letter: "*I know what you have been doing. I have answers. Come immediately. Tell no one.*" Oryan turned the tattered page to Thomas to read. Aside from those brief words, there was only a five-digit number.

"What do you suppose the numbers mean?" Thomas asked rhetorically, not realizing he had said it out loud. His mind was still on the mystery of the letter.

"Latitude and longitude," came the equally rhetorical answer from Oryan, who was still very apparently in another state of mind.

As always, he was right. "Where does it take you?" he asked, this time fully expecting an answer.

The shock and disbelief had worn away from Oryan's face. He had regained his composure, and the cold unfeeling shade of blue had returned to his eyes. "To answers. That's all you need know."

The tone of his voice snapped Thomas back into reality as well. Thomas handed him back the letter, saluted, and turned to walk away. He would not forget the numbers, however, and he would seek his own answers. As if his mind had been read, Oryan spoke.

"Don't look for me. All those who meddle in my past wind up with bloody hands."

Thomas paused and looked back over his shoulder. "With all respect, sir, it isn't just your past that bloodies hands." With that, he left his friend behind.

Oryan watched him leave and then returned to his final preparations. He did not need to change his arrangements, but the destination was certainly different. Although he had never seen those exact coordinates before, the location was not unfamiliar. Of the extermination camps he knew of, one fell within those coordinates. Shayes End.

Though he knew of no one that could have sent him that message, it did not feel threatening. The tone was one of urgency, but not of danger. His fame and notoriety had made him many unlooked-for allies, and perhaps this one was just what he was looking for. However, it could be bait to try and bring his search to a crashing halt. At that thought, he added an item to his bag. His pistol.

With that, he shouldered his bag, left his room, and headed for his transport. He placed his things neatly into the storage locker on the back of the vehicle and then entered himself. As he started the engine, a sharp voice of warning stabbed at him again. *It's not too late. Turn back now. Put the past behind you.* It was a familiar warning. The same as in the library, but as with his experience there, he shoved it aside and sped away from the barracks. Though he did not know it, he would never see them again.

It took nearly four days to reach his destination. He had stayed mainly on back roads; his choice of routes made the distance longer, so he drove fast, trying to make up for the lost time. As he neared the coordinates given to him in the anonymous letter, paved roads became harder and harder to find. Eventually, there were none at all. The positioning system in the vehicle was all that guided him. He drove on, seeing no civilization for miles. After many hours, doubt gnawed at him. This was a trap. It could be the emperor. It could be many people, for as his fame drew unseen allies, it also revealed many unseen enemies.

After many miles of empty grassland, he came to it at last. A fourteen-foot steel wall capped with razor wire. Slowly, he circled the structure, which enclosed an area some two miles in diameter. There was nothing extravagant about the wall. It was aged. There were signs of rust and neglect everywhere he looked. The grass around it was unkempt, reaching some two feet up the base. It was mixed with a tangle of ground-level vines and choking weeds.

In all, it took almost forty minutes to circle the perimeter. Nowhere on the wall did he see any entrances. There were, in fact, no defining marks of any kind. There were no names, signs, serial numbers or designation stamps. This kind of fortification was commonly used in the empire's military, but most bore at least some kind of identification. The abnormalities were beginning to make Oryan uneasy.

He stopped the vehicle and grabbed his blade. As he stepped onto the grass, he put the weapon back onto his belt. There was something wholly wrong with this entire area. Oryan had felt it when he arrived, but now it seemed to permeate his feet and creep up his bones. The chill ran through his whole person, standing hair on end and making even the gentle breeze feel harsh.

Every battlefield carried with it a sense of death. Those fields also carried a sense of honor, duty, and glory. Oryan reveled in those. This place, however, carried a sense of death unlike any Oryan had ever felt. This place was cold. It was evil. Unspeakable atrocities had happened here, the kind that made Oryan's flesh crawl and his stomach queasy. Innocent people had died horrible, gruesome deaths. Human experimentation, torture, and mutilation had all happened here. He checked his boots again, certain he would see blood seeping around them. This place was altogether unworldly. If there was an entrance, it was nothing less than the very gates of hell.

With the press of a button, the cargo hatch of his transport slid open. He reached inside his bag and removed his pistol. With the air of this place, it was no bad thing to be overcautious.

The wall seemed to tower over him, not because of its size, but because of what he feared lay beyond. As he stepped closer, the chill became more intense.

He reached the wall and began to look for ways to scale it. He had seen no entrance, so this seemed the only way. He was wrong.

From the corner of his eye he noticed a shimmer of red light from the ground to his right. Even as he noticed, the light became larger as a small portal appeared. An eerie red light shone forth. Oryan braced himself against the coming evil.

Nothing came immediately from the portal, though he was expecting some creature, some foul beast from the pit that he had only imagined in his nightmares. Such was the feel of this place. Seconds passed that seemed like forever. He was becoming shocked at his own senses. As his startled delusions continued to plague his fevered brain, a shadow broke the unearthly light.

Seconds later, three imperial guards burst from the portal. Their weapons were drawn, and despite his prowess, these men had taken advantage of his lapse of rational judgment and surrounded him. They had the edge now, but he was facing his favorite adversary: overconfident, under-trained, mortal men. His heart stopped racing, his brain calculated his enemies' demise, and he focused.

It was apparent they did not know who he was. "I have no quarrel with you, brothers, but if you do not lower your weapons, you'll all be dead men."

The soldiers did not move, though each traded glances with the other, wondering if this man was actually capable of killing all of them before they could kill him. They were wondering if he were supernatural. His sharp uniform and elegant blade was curious. Not completely foreign, but not completely familiar. Who was he? They did not wait long for the answer.

"It's best that you believe him," said a voice rising from the ground. "He has killed more men than even you can imagine; many of them far more skilled than you three!"

The guards lowered their weapons as Oryan loosened his grip on his. He turned to greet the new voice. He did not see the man's face yet, but that voice was all too familiar. It spoke to him as a voice from the ashes; whispering to him from a time long since dead. Oryan *knew* that voice, but he could not place it.

"Isn't that correct, old friend?" said the voice again. The stranger's face drew out of the shadows, and Oryan began to make out the details. This was a hard man, worn from years of hard labor. The flesh was lined with scars. It looked as if he had not shaved in days judging by the dark stubble that lined his chiseled jaw. Still, there was a lingering sense of stolen youth in this man that suggested to Oryan that though he worked in this place, it was not who he was. Despite seeing him in full view, Oryan could still not discern how he knew the man before him.

"Has it been so long?" asked the man as he approached. His eyes met Oryan's and then looked down in dismay. Almost rhetorically he asked, "Have I fallen so low?"

Oryan stared hard at him still. "I knew you in another life. You're not the man I was once familiar with. I am sorry, *friend*, I don't know you."

The man shook his head sadly and then looked to the sky as if asking some imaginary person very probing questions. "It's worse than I feared." He looked at Oryan with despairing eyes. "Come. There is much to discuss."

The guards and the officer retreated to the hidden entrance, but Oryan stayed where he was. If he followed these men now, he had to face the fact that his imaginations could be reality. Or worse, what he was afraid to imagine could be the reality.

The three guards had disappeared into the earth, but the officer's chest and head were still visible. "I know what you have been doing. I have answers," he said. Oryan recognized the words as those from the letter he had received at barracks days before. The man came back up from the portal and approached him. In hushed tones, he spoke. "I know you have doubts. Though you don't recognize me, I know you well. I'm only offering this once. I risk my life by aiding your quest. If you don't come with me now, you will never hear from me again. By my own choice or those of others, I will be silent. I go below. If you do not follow, good-bye to you; may God speed you on your journey."

With those remarks, he turned and retreated to where he had come from. Oryan hesitated only for a moment, but those last words had struck such a chord with him that before he had even made up his mind he was following this stranger into the abyss.

Once inside, Oryan noticed many things odd about his surroundings. The walls around him were all rounded, as if he were literally walking through a hole in the ground dug by an animal. The red lights had switched to the artificial white light that he was used to in most indoor settings, but they were harsh to the naked eye. The ceiling was low, so even the heat from the uncovered bulbs could be felt. Some of them flickered on and off while others were burnt out completely.

The man that had led Oryan into the tunnel had disappeared, but the tunnel did not fork, nor did it turn either right or left. After only a short while, Oryan could feel the floor beginning to ascend. He passed a series of burnt-out lights and then felt the tap of a metal floor beneath his feet. The curved walls disappeared, as did the low ceilings. Instead, there was a hum of electronic equipment and the dull roar of a generator. There were a few red warning indicators lit from which Oryan could make out a few details, but otherwise, it was darkness.

"Ah, forgive me," said the voice. "I'm so accustomed to this place I almost forget that you don't know where you're going." There was a click, and several more uncovered bulbs flickered to life.

Oryan's guess was right. There was a fully automated generator, in all stages of disrepair. This place did not see regular maintenance, but that was no surprise. It did not seem like they wanted much company, much less service calls. The warlord looked at his new host and then once again followed after him.

The man led him on past a few offices, what looked like barracks, and then into another long tunnel. This one was far different from the first. It was smooth metal sides with a translucent ceiling. There were subtle running lights along the floor, but a majority of the light came from the sun outside. They walked in silence for some time until the tunnel came to an end.

To his left and right, the tunnel curved back in either direction, but the man simply waited at the intersection. Seeing Oryan's curiosity, he spoke. "This tunnel network wraps around the perimeter of the installation. The building you came in through is the central hub. There are four tunnels like the one you just came through that each lead to a point on the outer tunnel ring, which acts as a kind of wall before the outer wall, as well as easy access for the men here. All of them are lined with explosives should things *go wrong.*"

The last words sent chills down Oryan's spine.

"In case of rebellion," Oryan stated.

The man nodded. "Or invasion."

If the empire were to be invaded, they would want no evidence of this place. It was designed to incinerate at the touch of a button.

The man let the short conversation sink in. "Well, let us walk a bit. I'm sure that you still have many questions."

Many I fear to ask, thought Oryan.

The man waved a bracelet that he wore along the small, lighted strip that ran waist level around the outer wall of the tunnel. There was a beep and a click as a section of the tunnel displaced, and the man pushed it up and open.

They stepped back into the dismal light of the cloudy day. Before them was a courtyard stretching some fifteen meters to the outer wall and wrapping completely around the tunnel network. The grass beneath their feet was slightly tall, but it appeared, unlike most things, well kept. However, the air was still. The walls blocked all hope of a breeze. What was worse was the absence of sound. *Silent as the grave* was all too literal a phrase. How many corpses lay beneath his feet? He choked back the thought.

"I come here often," said the man. "This is the only place that I can find some measure of peace. I even keep the grounds as well as will be kept." He gestured to the grass. "It helps."

He began walking toward the outer walls and away from the tunnel. Oryan walked a few paces with him so he could still hear his voice, but not too close. Even though his so-called friend did not seem dangerous, this place had eyes and ears, none of them living and all of them hostile. When they reached the outer wall, they stopped.

"I have been here nearly eleven years. In that time I have seen the outside of these walls six times, including today. It sickens me to call this place home, but I scarcely recall anything else."

"So leave," said Oryan, suddenly feeling some sympathy for him.

The man smirked and chuckled slightly. "This place does not exist, so neither do I. You cannot leave that which does not exist. Besides, what would I leave to? There's no life after this. I have sent many letters in eleven years and no one has responded."

"I did."

"Yes. Yes, you did."

Oryan still could not place where he knew this man, but it was becoming clearer with each passing moment. His mind was trying to place it, coming ever so close, but not close enough. "Why did you send for me? You said you have answers; who said I had questions?"

The smirk stretched across his face again. "To answer the second question first, *you did.* Simply by being here, I know you seek information."

"Yet you sent *me* the summons first."

"Quite so. I guess that leads us to the answer to the first question. I sent for you because I know what you're seeking. Or shall I say, *whom* you are seeking." He gauged Oryan's response, but in typical fashion, Oryan was like stone. He slowly walked toward Oryan, stopping only a few feet from the warrior.

"The years have aged you well. Though I see life and cares have made their mark. It's etched into those creases on your brow and the lines on your face. They leave scars more obvious than the one on your chest. My god, boy, did they get to you too?"

And there it was. Like a sharp slap of cold rain in his face, Oryan knew the man before him. A few scars, the facial hair around the lips and on the chin had thrown him off, but it was clear now. Those eyes, though they bore horrific images seared into them, were still the same. He remembered them filled with tears of pain and then again with sparkles of laughter. Armay had saved his life once, even though he was a slave and this man one of his captors. This was the last friendly voice he had heard before he left the Quarter a lifetime ago.

"*You . . .*" he whispered.

The man stood up straight. "For the first time, let me introduce myself. I am Colonel Nathan Larson. I summoned you because I owe you a life. Your father gave me this one, whatever it is, and since I can never repay him, I owe his son the same favor."

Oryan was still in awe. "How did you find me?"

Larson laughed loudly. "My boy, you have *not* been hard to keep track of! The *only* undefeated champion in history. Leader of the finest troops the world has ever seen. These things bring with them a certain amount of notoriety. The world is too small a place for the son of Armay to vanish."

"How do you know who I was looking for?"

"For someone who came here with no questions, you certainly ask many!" the colonel mocked.

The remark snapped Oryan from his state of shock back into reality. There were more important questions to be asked than the ones he had been asking.

"Do you know who I seek? If you have information, I want it," he said, sounding as authoritative as possible.

Larson looked coldly back at him. "Beyond these walls, you are my superior. In here, I am the law. I know that I'm no threat to you, but I didn't bring you here for you to intimidate me. I'm not afraid of you because I'm already dead! I was snuffed out of existence years ago when they sent me here!" Rage and hatred rose in his voice. His wrath was not aimed at Oryan, but he let his venom loose all the same.

Then he composed himself. "Besides, I *do* have information, so it would be pointless to kill me before you know what I know. I've dealt more torture than you can imagine, so even that would not pry the information from my lips. I offer it to you freely because, as I told you, I owe that much to *him*."

There was a tinge of guilt that struck Oryan. He was used to getting what he wanted, and so that was his normal first approach. "I'm sorry. I meant no offense."

He looked at Oryan incredulously at first and then almost lovingly, as a father might behold his child. "You seek the man who betrayed your father. Don't ask me how I know; just realize that I do.

"Do you see these walls? They were built by the man you seek. Think, Oryan. *Shayes End*. See the letters and think." He stopped for a moment as the emphasis calculated into this boy's mind. When he saw the information register, he continued. "Yes, Shayes End becomes *Seyah's* End.

"This was his last duty station. He made this place on the broken backs and torn flesh of the very people he then mutilated and murdered. He was a sick, twisted, evil man—if you can call him that.

"They say that he was tried in the court systems for "crimes against humanity" and then executed, but you and I both know better. His last log entry in the systems here are dated some three months after his publically held execution. If he's dead, it did not happen as they would have you believe."

Though this confirmed Oryan's suspicion, the information was nothing new to him. "If he was not taken by the courts, where did he go?"

Larson shrugged. "No one knows. This place, my friend, is where the trail goes cold. It was only slightly traceable to here, but whatever happened to him, it's as if he was truly erased from history. If you want my suspicion, he's buried right here with the other wretched corpses in this place.

"There is a medical log that speaks of one of his experiments going very wrong. He was developing a highly corrosive acid that only became active when it came in contact with human flesh. Apparently, one of his *subjects* was not properly fastened down and smashed a vile of it against his face. It seared deep into the tissue; but what was worse was that the fumes he inhaled from it were not only toxic, but equally corrosive to his throat and lungs.

"A medical team reported here and operated for weeks to save him. No records are kept after that, which around here means that they failed and he is just another unmarked grave somewhere in this giant cemetery."

Oryan's blood went cold. He saw no lie in Larson's eye. It was apparent that the colonel had done at least as much research into Seyah as he had, with the advantage of being here for eleven years. "You brought me here at the risk of life and limb for this?"

"Fool." Larson shook his head. "This information isn't the deadly kind. What have I told you that you had not already surmised? I told you I had information, and I do. But it's not about the man who betrayed your father. It's about the man who *killed* your father."

Oryan once again stared blankly. He did his best to show no emotion, but his flushed cheeks gave away more than he could hide. "I was under the impression he was killed by an outbreak of JEJ."

JEJ was the abbreviation for a new strain of virus that was being found in isolated areas where sanitation and medical conditions were less than satisfactory. JEJ stood for *Julian e Jekkar*, which, being translated, means "the walking dead." It was a terrible way to die. It was fast-acting in the sense that the infected were usually dead within three to six months, but for the sufferers, death could not come soon enough. The virus rotted flesh from the outside and mutilated organs on the inside. The abscesses that formed on the skin were worse than any boil. As the body tried to force out the infection, it only made matters worse. The large amount of open sores made other infections common. It ate holes in lungs, heart, and kidneys. It also thinned the lining of the stomach so that the person's own acids would burn through the tissues resulting in extreme pain and eventual death.

There was no cure as of yet. Physicians could slow the spread of the infection, even lessen the pain, but they were helpless to stop it. Most that contracted it were herded into camps where they stayed as to not infect the healthy population. Once their time had come, their names were cataloged, their bodies heaped into a pit, and then burned. Detoxification teams came after to cover the charred corpses in a harsh, yellow sulfur-based compound that prevented the infection from going anywhere else.

Larson shook his head again. "And you believed that? You found your information from the same sources that told you Seyah was publicly executed, and you believed them?"

Oryan was confused. "Then tell me why the government would use an outbreak of JEJ to explain the dismantling of a forced labor camp. They could have just as easily called it a riot or rebellion, slaughtered everyone in the place, and brought in a new crop. There's no reason for a cover-up."

"There was a perfectly good reason. *You.* And who told you it was the government?"

Oryan tried another guess. "The military?"

"Half right," the informant said. "Not the military as a whole, just one man who stood to lose a lot if anyone were to find out your true origin and the one man who stood in a place to carry out the extermination of an FLC. He just had to do it in a way that no superior officer would question and no one would be willing to follow up on."

The deduction quickly set in. "Halgren."

"Correct. You see, Halgren was and is a black market slave

trader, as you are painfully aware. It would be detrimental to his little enterprise if anyone could identify him as a direct link in the pedaling of the empire's slaves.

"After you left, he became increasingly interested in your father. He did his homework on the man. When he learned who it was he had stolen a child from, he was more than a little concerned.

"He approached your father some two weeks after your fight with the boys at the gates. He told him that, despite their best efforts, the knife wound you had received had proven fatal. Armay did not believe the news. He beat Halgren to near death before the rest of the guards got there. I was among those who restrained him, but it was ironically Halgren who spared his life, or so I thought.

"At that time, I was made lieutenant and put in command of the guards at the gate. I was babysitting a group of men more interested in drinking and gambling than their actual duty. After all, a forced labor camp such as ours was not exactly a soldier's dream.

"Halgren left the camp shortly thereafter, checking in from time to time, mostly by teleconference, just to make sure that his command was running smoothly while he was off becoming rich from of your newfound success. After a while, your name reached even my ears. Shortly thereafter, Halgren returned.

"He stayed in barracks, daily checking on the status of the workers. He said little if anything at all to anyone, just observed the comings and goings. He made all of us uneasy. No one could tell why he was there or what he was hatching, but we all knew something was going to happen. You could feel it in the air. It was electric, almost like the day you fought at the gate."

Oryan was transported back to that day. He remembered the feel and the thickness in the very air he breathed. The elements knew, as did his soul, that the world was about to change. Thousands of memories—sights, sounds, and smells—poured through his brain. Unlike this place, which reeked of death, his camp had been home to him for most of his early life.

And there was Armay.

The memory of his father stung worst of all. The warrior choked back the tears and held his breath so as not to release even the smallest sob.

Larson continued. "When we all gave up trying to figure out

what he was doing, it happened. One morning, a detox crew arrived on base with Captain Halgren. They were suited up in white, running in and out frantically, and did so for the rest of the day.

"I wish that I would have put two and two together sooner. First, they didn't come in a detox vehicle. They wore no IDs, they carried no medical equipment that I could see, and what was more obvious was that they were screening none of the men stationed at the camp. They simply went into and out of the gates saying nothing to anyone. We were all so curious as to what they were doing, everyone overlooked the discrepancies to normal detox procedures until it was too late.

"That night, Halgren told the company that an outbreak of JEJ had been found in the camp. We all believed him, especially when he had signed emergency transfer orders sending a majority of the men to other duty stations. They all left that night. He kept a handful of the officers, myself included, to make sure the camp was properly closed down and the virus contained.

"Why he chose me, I do not know. Perhaps he saw something in me that I didn't know about myself. Maybe, he just really didn't know me at all."

Larson's eyes were glued to the ground. There were no tears. Oryan sensed that he did not have tears left for all he had done. Whatever he had done there seemed to be the beginning of what he was doing here. Though he did not speak up, with every ounce of his energy, he was begging him to continue.

Larson said nothing for some time. His lips moved as if he was going to go on, but they were quickly closed again. His jaw shifted tensely. His mind searched for the words to try and make this next news be anything but what it was. Finally, he told a truth he had not uttered since the day it had happened.

"We were led into the camp the next morning by the false detox team we had seen the day before. It was not long before we realized that they were not a detox team at all. Once we were all out of sight of the gate, they removed their suits. Maybe they were just degenerates that Halgren kept close by to do his dirty work. To this day, I don't know.

"They went from house to house, moving the residents out to the edge of the camp, near the tree line where you and the other boys used to box and play sports. The day before, Halgren's men had not been idle. There was a pit dug some fifty feet long and twelve feet wide. I knew immediately what that meant.

"I watched them bring the women and the children to the edge of the pit. I couldn't move. I was ... *frozen* knowing what was about to happen. It was only when I saw your father that I stood up to the abomination.

"I tried to get them to stop. I tried to run. In a last attempt, I ran to your father, trying to free him, *if only him,* from what was coming! Maybe things would be different now," Larson lamented. "Yes, things would be different. I would have been dead long ago.

"But, I didn't. I was so scared! They beat me so much that I couldn't stand. Then they would drag me to one of the prisoners and smash their faces with rods and rocks until they were unrecognizable. I was *covered* in their blood! It ran down my face, with my own! I wanted to look away, but no matter which way I looked, there were people being massacred.

"I saw children holding onto their parents' mutilated bodies as Halgren and his men severed their fingers to loosen their grips. They screamed. Oh, God, they screamed!" Larson stopped, choking back countless emotions.

"After a while, the world was black. I awoke hours later to the smell of burning human flesh. The bodies had been piled into the pit and were burning. I was lying in a pool of blood and vomit. I couldn't tell if it was my own or not, but I know that it made me throw up again at the stench.

"When I could see again, I could see two men dragging a man between them to me. It was Armay. His hands were tied behind his back. He had been beaten, but from the sound of things, he had given as well as he had received. I learned later that he had killed three of Halgren's men before they were able to restrain him properly.

"They threw him at my feet. My right eye was swollen shut, and my jaw was broken, so I couldn't speak. I wanted to beg for his life, but I could only mumble. He got to his knees and shook his head. 'Don't,' he told me. 'You find my son and tell him what happened.'

"Halgren walked up behind him and spoke to me. 'You breathe a word of this to anyone, and I promise you your fate will be worse than these people. You ever mention the name of Oryan again, and I will find you. I'll finish you and everyone you have ever known or loved. And when I'm done, I will make sure that you are found guilty for it all.'

"He grabbed your father by the hair and yanked his head back so that he could see him. 'And you, General. Know that your son is my pet. And rest assured, you one-eyed freak, he'll be mine forever.'"

There was a pause again. Still, Larson shed no tears, though the well of emotion was painfully clear in his trembling frame.

"He took his knife and stabbed him in his eye. I desperately tried to get my hands on him, but my leg was shattered by the club of one of his goons. I don't remember anything until I woke up in the hospital nearly a month later."

There was silence now. The whole world had changed for him. A thousand thoughts raced through his head. He was seeing the faces of the people he had once known and called neighbor. They were all gone. Their voices, their lives, and their stories had been wiped from all knowledge because of him. This was the reward of his fame.

"Why didn't he just kill you?" Oryan asked. "He could have blamed it on anything and passed it off. Why would he leave a living witness?"

"You of all people should know that a wounded officer means an incident report filed by his commanding officer," said Larson.

"A dead one requires a formal investigation by members of the Imperial Military Command," finished Oryan, putting the pieces together without any more prompting. An investigation was something that Halgren couldn't afford.

"Correct. He could beat me as badly as he wanted as long as there was still breath in my lungs. I wish, for more than my sake, he had beaten it all out of me."

"Why didn't you come out with it? Surely he's not capable of all that he said he was."

Larson stayed quiet for a moment. In his mind, he searched for the right words, but no answer he could give seemed good enough for the son of the man he failed to rescue. "Aside from my leg, the slowest part of me to heal was my jaw. It took two surgeries and four months for me to speak again. Even the eye," he ran his finger across the scar on his face, "was quicker to heal. In that time, I had nightmares. Whether from the stress or the drugs or the coma, I couldn't tell. After a while, I couldn't separate reality from fantasy.

"By the time I was 'myself,' it all seemed like some horrible dream. For a while, I doubted even my own senses. What I could still remember perfectly, however, were the words of Halgren. I remembered the threat. What was worse, in my mind's eye, *he* was right. It *was* my fault that all those things had happened. It *was* me who was responsible for those people's death. I couldn't be sure.

"I was moved from duty station to duty station, even the front line for a very short time. I was deemed unfit for duty due to mental instability. I woke up screaming and babbling on about these things that I'd seen, but they were passed off only as delusions.

"After a while, they put me in a psych ward to try and calm my dreams. Doctor after doctor gave me pill after pill to get rid of the nightmares. I was catatonic from the different medications. I don't remember much from then either.

"Finally, I was ordered to go in for a testing series designed to bring to light repressed memories. The doctor I worked with was kind and patient, and it was he who first realized that my 'nightmares' were much more than that. Eventually, he wrote up a formal report about the atrocities that I'd witnessed. It was never sent or published. To my knowledge, he never made it home after he finished it. He was reported missing the next day.

"However, his therapy had made me confront my demons. Though I was anything but stable, I came to grips with what I had seen and what I had failed to do. I tried suicide. I failed three times. Once my last attempt failed, ironically, I was promoted and sent here. Suicide is common here. Here, my horrific stories of your camp are commonplace. The men here laugh and share memories like that over lunch. After a while, I became numb to the whole event; though, I kept my eye always on you and your career. I knew, eventually, I must answer for my sins."

With that, Larson said no more. He slowly calmed his heart and stopped his body from shaking. Warmth returned to his fingers, and he once again came to some kind of peace with his life. "And since that day, I have become the very monster I beheld," he said under his breath.

All this time, Oryan had been after the wrong man. Seyah's deranged experiments had led to his own demise. It was, however unsatisfying, a fitting end to the villain. He had died slowly and painfully, and there was still hell to look forward to. Oryan had been so wrong. Who he should have been hunting all along was Halgren.

"Why did you wait until now to tell me?" he asked.

"I could give you reasons. Your youth. Your innocence. You've been so caught up in your own legacy that I wasn't sure you even cared to know. It was as if you were trying to bury your past with the momentary glory of the present. It wasn't until you began to face your past that I began to seek you out.

"Perhaps it was just me trying to make sense of it all. Maybe it was just me trying not to admit to anyone that I was too weak to save him. Maybe it's all of these.

"Whatever the reasons, I'm here now and I have repaid my debt. Good-bye, Oryan, son of Armay. I'm sure that you can find your way out. News does not travel through these walls, so I'm sure that no one here knows you at all.

"Good-bye, and we will never see each other again."

Oryan looked at Larson for a short while. He was standing erect, hands behind him, clasped at the small of his back. Oryan turned to go, but something caught his eye. There, on the wall behind Larson, was a faded smear of blood. As his eyes focused, the grim truth became a reality. Within the stain were the impressions of fingers forever driven into a steel wall. Someone had nearly escaped and had marred steel in the attempt. The feel of this place came back to him, but this time, Oryan welcomed it. He knew what he was about to do. He turned his back on Larson; he turned his back to mercy and forgiveness. He left the sane and civilized world behind and plunged into the violent world of revenge.

Larson watched as Oryan disappeared through the tunnel. The door sealed behind him, leaving the colonel alone in the green courtyard. Slowly, he reached down and untied the laces of his boots. For the first time in more than eleven years, he felt the touch of grass on his bare feet. It was cool and soft, as refreshing as the cool water of a running river on a summer's day.

He closed his eyes. A single tear welled in his eye. He raised his right hand, which now held the grip of his pistol, and placed the muzzle against his temple.

"It's done."

A heartbeat later, he lay lifeless in the grass, his last tear falling silently to the earth.

Lies and Deceit

General Lucius Kovac sat in his quarters. In front of him was a glowing red holographic image of terrain maps. Under his right hand was a simple control panel that allowed him to shift the units on the terrain map from one point to another. He had a certain amount of ground troops, some tanks and other light armor vehicles, and a small air force. He placed his available forces in strategic areas and then rotated the entire image in front of him so as to place the rest. Once he had his forces in place, he reached up with his left hand and touched the green round button just to the left of the holographic controls.

The terrain map rotated so that he could see the battlefield from a completely omniscient point of view. He was watching the soldiers move from above the map. The computer began to move the opposing force that he had pre-set into its memory into its own strategic positions. As time elapsed, the battle waged. The computer would advance its forces, and Kovac would counter. Flashes of light erupted from the battlefield as tanks or aircraft would be obliterated from the field.

Kovac swiveled the controls, and the map rotated again. From this point of view, he moved a company of troops into the void that was left from a destroyed vehicle. Another quick rotation and a few commands and his aircraft cruised into battle, destroying critical enemy advances. This game of gain a yard, lose a foot continued until eventually the computer was defeated.

For most, this would be a game too fast-moving and challenging for them to grasp, much less attempt. Kovac had designed the software and pioneered the technology. It was the most advanced battle simulator invented; yet only he possessed it. What made it even more effective was the fact that it was completely moldable to whatever terrain he wanted, whatever units he wanted to give for himself or against.

This day, it was no game at all. He had downloaded the terrain maps from the military database for a patch of earth that was soon to become a battlefield. He read the intelligence reports of the empire's forces and Vollmar's. Then he uploaded that information into his simulation and ran the program. The island of Akon was displayed in such detail that the General felt he could walk the terrain blindfolded should he ever venture there. The computer was designed never to try the same attack pattern twice, and so he had been staging these combat simulations for nearly thirteen hours. In that time, the forces of the empire had only lost once.

It was in this way that he perfected his strategy and sent the organization of troops and the plan of attack on to his field commanders. It was a key battle, one they could not afford to lose. Though he was thousands of miles away, he was in complete control. He knew as long as that was the case, his forces would emerge victorious.

He was slowly rewinding the details of the last simulation to view any correctable mistakes he had made. He felt confident that the only variable that existed was the unpredictability of men when faced with defeat.

It was then that the chime rang from his door.

"Come," he said, slightly annoyed at this interruption.

The door slid open and slid closed, but he heard no footsteps or a voice announce their presence inside.

"Captain," he acknowledged without turning around. "I didn't call for you. Why are you here?"

The Captain felt dejected, as if it had been slapped in the face. It was not used to being treated like an unwelcome guest. "My master," it began, "I have received no order in some time. I thought, perhaps, I should come to see if I could be of service."

Kovac was even more annoyed at his creation. It was as if this thing could do nothing without his command. There were times that his Captain was far too much like a child for his liking.

"Lies do not become you, Captain. You are here because you want to know if I'm sending the Legion into battle and if I will let you lead them." Kovac was not a subtle man and aimed to knock the Captain out on the first punch landed. This was not a time for playing sadistic cat and mouse games. Besides, the Captain had long proved to be anything but a challenge to manipulate.

It glared through dark eyes and hissed out a breath of discontent. There was more on its mind than that, but its dark thoughts were just as transparent to the General. "Yes, Lord. That is why I've come."

Kovac stood out of his chair and faced the Captain. He held one hand behind his back and placed the other thoughtfully around his mouth. "Are you still seeking vindication for the performance of Warlord Jeckstadt and his Knights? Since this war began, they have more than proven the sharper edge of the blade. How many times has *your* Legion been defeated to date?"

The question was rhetorical, of course, meant to agitate and remind the barely human thing who indeed its master was. "Perhaps you have outlived your usefulness. After all, every legacy eventually has its end. This war is unlike anything we have ever seen. On a larger scale than any war fought before in the history of the world. Maybe you and your men were meant for smaller incursions.

"Akon is crucial, and I will need my best. So, Captain, in your judgment as a commander and loyal servant to the emperor, which of the two units should I send?"

This was not rhetorical. Kovac wanted his intruder to answer this question.

The Captain thought black thoughts. It bent its hate toward this new tormentor. If it could move quickly enough, it could cut out his tongue. He could no longer utter such lies without that or perhaps his ears as a lesson in humility. The vengeful thoughts raged, but its feet stayed firmly planted. It clenched its fists and ground jagged teeth, but still did not move.

"As a loyal servant to the emperor," it spat through clenched teeth, "send the more *experienced* force."

"Do you consider your men the more 'experienced' force simply because they have been in the emperor's service longer? Or, by experienced, do you mean the force that has been *proven* by their experience thus far in this war? Each interpretation presents a different conclusion. So, whom do I send?"

It gathered up its cloak in its left hand and drew it up close to its chest. It craned its head on the bony neck on which it sat but turned its face away, trying to avoid direct eye contact. It was sure that the General could somehow read its unholy thoughts if he was looking directly into its eyes. These thoughts it could not afford to be read.

It was true, the boy Oryan had proven more than a match for it in the beginning, but as a careful student of war, it had watched him and observed how he fought. It had watched Oryan win countless times. It had sent him into impossible odds where this cocky young upstart would surely be killed, only to see him emerge victorious time and time again. *Warlord Jeckstadt!* It spat at the title. He was an arrogant son of a slave! He was not worthy of that post!

It was jealous through and through, knowing that in all the areas it failed, he succeeded. More than jealousy and more than hatred, it felt fear. Fear that it could so easily be replaced in the eyes of its master. Since the day that Oryan and his men had defeated it in open combat, Lord Kovac had seemed less and less interested in its success. It yearned for the approval of its master but was always met with scorn. Even its victories in the war had paled by comparison to those of the Knights and their immortal commander. It had watched and waited, but for all of its scheming, it was still no closer to dispatching its enemy. If they did meet again, *when* they met again, it still knew it was not the better soldier. All of this ate at its mind like a cancer and stoked the embers of hate in its blackened heart.

"Fear not, good Captain," the General spoke at last. "You and your men shall be on this battlefield when the fight commences. I know what you have done for me and for the emperor in the past, and it has not been forgotten, nor overlooked."

The Captain's eyes met the General's. There was some approval there. Not as it had once been, but there it was. "A humble thanks, my lord. I assure you, Legion has not outlived its usefulness. We will make of it a victory to challenge even the great Warlord Jeckstadt and his Knights!" it said in a thin, raspy voice.

"You misunderstand," the master spoke. "You and Legion will be there and so will the Warlord and his Knights. He will command his forces and lead the main attack. You and your men will handle the smaller incursions and prevent the enemy from taking any flanking positions."

The fire blazed in its chest. The flames burned so hot that they danced behind its cruel eyes. *Villain! Deceiver!* It hated its master all the more. Hated him for dealing it such a cruel card. Hated him for lying. Hated him for building up its hopes only to shatter them again. As it watched the shards of its pride scatter across the floor, it realized why it hated him the most. It hated him most of all because, in the end, it could not hate him.

The General watched the Captain squirm with this news. He knew what a blow that was. Still, there was no sympathy for it. It was what it was, and the General had outgrown his fondness for it. It was easy to trick, easy to taunt, and that made for a blunt tool. Much like a child who watched the insect struggle after he had removed its wings, Kovac watched the Captain. He had made his point, but he was not through yet.

"Oryan is seeking Seyah," he said clearly.

The writhing Captain stiffened. Its hunched back became rigid. That was a name it had not heard in a long time.

"Oryan is seeking Seyah, and I have no doubt that eventually he will find him." Kovac continued to twist the knife.

"Seyah is dead," the Captain sneered.

Underneath the calm exterior, Kovac smiled. "Quite so, and the informant told him just that; nonetheless, even the informant did not know the details that surrounded his death. Right now, the predator seeks other prey, but I know him well enough to know that was not the end of his search."

"Put out the *informant's* eyes and make him suffer. Make him wish he had never heard the name of Oryan Jeckstadt!" interjected the Captain.

"There is no need, as you would only be desecrating a corpse. The informant shot himself in the head shortly after delivering his message."

He chose the easy road. He must have known what was coming! Coward!

"Why does Oryan seek Seyah?" it asked.

The General stared long at the Captain. "You already know that answer, just as I do. Or have the long years made you forget who he was? Surely you must remember that Seyah had many enemies, not the least of those closely intertwined to Oryan. Did you think he would never ask those questions?"

"What do we do?" asked the Captain.

Kovac watched it squirm more. "You seem to have forgotten all about your wounded pride and bruised ego. Do you not wish to ask me why I am sending both Legion and the Knights into the same battle? Or did the mention of *that* name make you forget?"

The flames began to grow hot once more. They were momentarily dimmed by the long-unheard name from its past, but now the rage consumed the creature again. It could bear no more. "My lord's wisdom is undeniable; his decree is beyond contest. I need no further explanation," it muttered as it turned to leave.

Kovac let a dark smile cross his lips. He waited for the Captain to open the door. Once it slid open, he spoke. "In answer to your question, it is not a question of *we*. What will *you* do, Captain?"

The silhouette disappeared into the other shadows, and the door slid closed. As it slithered down the hall, its mind raced. It hated the very air it breathed and most of all Warlord Oryan Jeckstadt. Its neck twitched, head rocked, and teeth snapped at the very thought of him.

So, it was he that the General preferred. So much so that even the memory of Seyah was not sacred nor spared from this boy's cruelty. It must end Oryan at all cost, before he discovered too much. It must do this before he did the same to it.

It resented the very thought of fighting on the same side as that sniveling worm. This was a disgrace to it and its men! It was an insult! It was ... an *opportunity*. It stopped in its tracks. This could not be more perfect. This was a chance to show them both who was the best. A jagged, grim smile creased the ragged flesh of the Captain. The time for revenge was at hand.

In the General's quarters, Kovac sat before a large holographic projection of a battlefield soon to be red with blood. But which war was to be decided and whose blood would be spilled was the question.

This simulation had been run a thousand times in his head, and now the time was at hand. Fate and time itself had been a straight road leading to this moment. For the second time that night, the great general smiled.

Predator and Prey

Oryan sipped water from a small glass. The ice clattered against the bottom as he placed it back on the table. He sat back in the wicker chair and let his shoulders relax. His white hair had been shaved, and his bare scalp was hidden under a short-brimmed hat, which hung just over his dark sunglasses. A loose, button-down shirt was on his back, though it was not fastened in the front. He would not wear one at all were it not for the distinctive tattoo between his shoulder blades. He wore a pair of comfortable shorts and sandals that he discarded when he walked along the beach. He sat alone.

Across the open patio sat an off-duty military officer. Although his clothing was far less vacation style than Oryan, his actions were not. In front of him was a tall glass of some alcoholic beverage, and there was a buxom, scantily-clad woman to his right and left. Their names were Celia and Alayna, Oryan had discovered. Across from the officer sat one of his executive officers, one Lieutenant Lance.

Aumakua was anything but a difficult duty station. For most enlisted men and their officers, it was more a tropical paradise than an assignment. It was a weekend getaway in which every day was a weekend. Somehow, someway, Captain Jonathan Halgren had paid up with the right people and made his way here, no doubt to spend his vast wealth acquired from Oryan's success.

Finding Halgren had not been difficult. Unlike Seyah, his service record and current assignment were a matter of public record. Oryan had even discovered that he was considering retirement, and what a perfect place to do so.

Oryan could understand why Halgren had wanted to come here if retirement was what he was considering. He had been here nearly a week enjoying the clear blue skies and the bright yellow sun. Even he had managed to develop an even shade of bronze. His trip here was strictly business; yet, he rather enjoyed those times when his target ventured out to the beach or into the sea. The last time that Oryan had looked at any large body of water, it was as black as the night sky above it. When he arrived here, he was able to see the bottom of a crystal-clear ocean.

He had to travel keeping a low profile. His name was still a household word, both for his exploits as a Centauri and now as a military figure. Everything from his transportation to his lodgings has been paid for in cash and registered under several different aliases. He wanted no one to know he was here.

Halgren had been utterly predictable. Perhaps it was his status as an officer in the Imperial Army that made him so flagrant, or perhaps it was his arrogance that made him feel untouchable. He flashed large sums of money so that anyone who cared to notice could see that he had far more than a captain's pay. He found a new girl every night, taking them to only the most luxurious hotels. Were the military to care, he could be discharged, fined, and thrown into a forced labor camp for many of his actions. By this point, Halgren had realized that he was in some sense above the law.

Oryan had made careful notes of where he was at all times, tracking his movements even down to the bathrooms he used. He was on base very rarely and had left most of the responsibility of running the company to his subordinates. Most of his time was spent in the local casinos where he spent lavishly for very little return. It made the casino owners happy as they provided every luxury at their own expense. For the hunter, this was a very easy target to track.

But there was a down side. Oryan was trying his best to stay out of the public eye, and that was the only place that Halgren wanted to stay. He needed to get his prey unaware and alone. This was not an easy task. It needed to seem as if he simply disappeared. He had been formulating a plan for several days, and as he placed his glass on the table, the last pieces of his plot fell into place.

He tilted the glass so that a sharp glare shone from it. He angled it until it caught the eye of the woman who was sitting alone several tables away. When she located the source of the light, he gave her a smile and a slight wave of a hand filled with a stack of large bills. It did not take long for him to find himself no longer alone.

As was customary with this sort of transaction, she came and sat comfortably on his leg, wrapping her slender arms around his neck. She bent close to kiss him, but he turned a cheek in a sign that he was less than interested. She brushed her blonde hair away from his face and began to stand when he reached for her. With a firm, but gentle grip, he let her know she was not to leave.

"I called you over for business, but not for my own," he said softly to her.

"Who says I'm for sale, honey?" she replied.

Oryan smiled and pulled her closer, letting her know that he meant business. She was startled by the strength in his hands. He looked strong, but not like this. He could hurt her easily if he wanted. This was not the person to question, she decided.

"I want your number. I want you to show a friend a good time, but only when I call." He flashed a few hundred between them and then slipped it into her top.

"What if I'm busy?" she asked.

"Then make yourself available," he replied. "You do this for me, and you'll be very happy you did."

She did not know him and in her line of work, she distrusted everyone. Typically, her clients paid in full in advance. The money he had given her was more than enough to cover her services, but this was a bit of a strange request.

"When will you be callin'?"

"Soon."

"Who's the friend?"

Oryan smiled again. He had her.

After his meeting with the woman who called herself Miley, he visited a few of the casinos that Halgren was known to frequent. Using a few forged documents and some smooth talking, he checked Halgren out of his hotel and cashed out all of his winnings and withholdings. To the casinos involved, they thought nothing of it. Mr. Halgren came in, withdrew his money, and left the premises.

When the real Mr. Halgren arrived to find all of his money and his room already gone, he was less than pleased. He cursed and spat, telling them all that he would visit them all soon. His threats took a very pleasing turn for Oryan as he was removed from each place by security and banned from the establishment. That went better than he hoped.

By the time the sun sank behind the trees, Halgren had crawled into a local pub with his officer friend who was apparently riding the coat tails of his captain's wealth. When Halgren was ousted from the hotels and casinos, so was he.

Once inside the pub, Halgren began the process of quickly intoxicating himself. He had no money available to flash at the women, so he spent his time brooding over glass after glass. It was only after a woman who called herself Miley took Lieutenant Lance away that he decided to find his way back to barracks. He was in no condition to seek revenge currently, but he was sure to find the bastard who had ruined his week, and when he did, God have mercy on him because he would not. For now, he needed some sleep.

Halgren staggered outside to find his shuttle occupied by the very nude bodies of Lieutenant Lance and his new friend. He was not one to interrupt a friend enjoying the finer things in life, so he poured the last of his drink down his throat and began to walk. He knew the city like the back of his hand. He knew the shortcuts and the back roads, and that is what he took.

The captain muttered to himself as he walked the dark streets. All around him, he could hear the sounds of people enjoying this place. He could hear the distant chimes of the casinos. There was music and dancing at the clubs and even some of the bars. On nearly every street corner was a beautiful woman who wanted his attention. Normally, he would oblige, but he had already lost more money than he could spare that day.

The more he realized he was missing, the more he became incensed. He stopped in a dimly lit alley, noticing a recruiting poster hanging on the wall. The edges were torn and frayed, and it was barely clinging to the wall. This was the poor part of the city, and many of the boys here grew up to be soldiers. The recruiters came down here often, but never alone. This neighborhood was rough.

There was a young man slumped over on the opposite wall from him. He seemed as if he was suffering from the same disease as Halgren. In his hand was a bottle of alcohol, and his head was bowed. He looked dirty, as if he had been there for days, but Halgren did not recall seeing him when he first entered the alley. Of course, he was pretty drunk, so it was not out of the question that he simply missed the stranger.

"Do you see that?" he said to the other man, pointing to the poster. "That's an old poster. That poster was hanging on the wall the day I signed up."

The man lifted an eye to acknowledge his new company. "Must have worked."

"Not what I said, you drunk!" Halgren chuckled. "I said it's what I remember seein' *after* I signed up! No lousy poster could convince me to join the army. No lousy father, either! I got drafted.

"Still," he said as he positioned himself to urinate on the poster, "musta gotten some damn fools. It's still here, ain't it?"

There was no response. "What's your story, brother?" He kept relieving himself and turned his head to see the other unfortunate degenerate who suffered from an excess of the hard stuff. The man was gone. All that was left was the nearly empty bottle of whatever drink he had. "Must notta liked the conversation. Maybe the same guy screwed him that screwed me. He better hope that he gets to him first. I guarantee he'll be nicer."

Halgren finished his business and fastened his pants. "I guarantee he'd be nicer," he mumbled as he turned to leave. That's when he noticed him. At the end of the alley, silhouetted against the streetlight, stood the grim figure of a man. The figure did not move even as Halgren came walking toward him. "Somethin' I can do for you, stranger?" he asked. There was only silence. As he drew closer, Halgren could make out the same tattered clothes he had noticed on the man sitting in the alley. "Is that you, friend? Was I borin' ya'?"

Still no movement and no words.

"Listen, you better get to answerin' me soon, or I promise you you'll regret it," he said, drawing his pistol. No sooner than he cleared the weapon from its place than the shadow disappeared.

He stopped in his tracks. Both hands gripped the pistol now as he inched forward. He blinked hard, as if that would fix his slightly blurred vision. He was regretting his excessive drinking now. Sweat crept from his brow, falling in slow lines down his face. "Oh, I know who you are now!" he said, summoning up his arrogance and courage. "You must be the same lousy bastard who took all my money! Still afraid to show your face, you coward?"

"You know who I am," said a voice from behind him. He spun on his heels, drawing pistol to the ready. He scanned the alley seeing nothing but empty space. He blinked hard again, thinking that something would appear. The sweat soaked his collar now, his breath was coming hard, and his invincible façade was quickly fading.

"Then come on out! If I know you, you've got no reason to hide! We can be just like old friends!" he said defiantly.

"Like old friends," came the chilling repeat. The voice was everywhere. He spun, looking both ways to find the source, but still there was only the alley. His back found the wall, nearly startling him at its proximity. His heart was racing, forcing the alcohol through his blood at a furious rate. It was dulling his senses and altering his reality. "Who are you!" he shouted to the darkness.

There was cold, sickening laughter at first from the left, then the right. Next it was above him and then right in front of his face. Whoever was here for him was getting closer, and he could not see them. He heard a shuffle of gravel to his right. He snapped that direction and fired a single shot at the noise. There was nothing there. The bottle on the ground where the stranger had been fell on its side behind him, the sound of the glass hitting the pavement echoing between the walls. He turned one hundred and eighty degrees and fired a single shot again. The result was the same.

He began to back up slowly, step by step, from his apparitional attacker. He was painfully aware of each grain of dirt under his boots. He felt the crunch under his toes and then his heel. Finally, when alcohol and madness seized his quaking frame, he turned to bolt from the alley, but it was blocked. Less than a yard in front of him was the shadow. Hope was abandoned, as was reason. The gun fell from his hand. It seemed to him at that moment it would do no good.

His breath was coming hard and heavy when it came at all. Each inhale shook his chest, and each exhale became shorter. The shadow moved in his blurred vision. There was a terrifying scream coming from the very depths of a damned soul. It seemed to come from some unseen world, but it was as real as this wraith before him. The noise buckled his knees and sent him to the ground. It was only then, as the shadow enveloped him and his world went black, that he realized the scream had been his own.

He awoke hours later in a room he had never been in before. His shirt was gone. His hair, his face, and his chest were drenched with water. There were tight braces that held his wrists and ankles firmly against the chair in which he sat. His tongue felt swollen inside his mouth, which was dry and sticky. His vision was still blurred, but he doubted it was from the alcohol. His head swam even as his brain pounded against his skull. Every inch of his body ached from his encounter and was compounded by his hangover.

There was a single light above him. It was hung from a chain in the ceiling and dangled several feet over his head. There was no cover, and so the naked bulb burned his sensitive eyes when he tried to look around.

After a few minutes, as each part of his body made its complaint, he noticed a different kind of sensation. As he shifted his shoulders, trying to rotate stiff joints and stretch cramping muscles, he felt something on his chest. It was not painful at the moment; rather, it simply pulled at the skin. The strange sensation shot a warning to his spine that although it did not hurt yet, it could change its mind at any time.

He looked down to see the source, but his vision was still blinded by its sensitivity to the harsh light. Still, he kept staring, this being the only discomfort that he could not explain. As he regained his vision, a more horrific reality than he could have imagined sunk in. There were pieces of tape on his chest above his heart. There was a clear tube running away from his chest, but the tape was not holding it on. *The tape was holding something in.* There was dried blood around the area that his renewed sweat was causing to run down his chest.

What was happening here? Where was he? A thousand possibilities raced through his head, each making the intense fear he was already feeling worse.

"Welcome back," said a voice from the darkness beyond the light. It was the thing from the alley. The events became painfully clear in his head.

"Who are you? Where am I? What are you going to do to me?" he asked, not sure he wanted to know the answers.

"You are in no position to ask questions, Captain," said the voice, which seemed to be coming from in front of him. "I, on the other hand, am in a position to do so, and I will. But, as I am in a generous mood, I will answer a few questions for you though they are not the ones that you've asked."

Halgren could hear malice in the voice, but it was controlled. He knew it was going to hurt him, but for what and why, he did not know. He could not place the voice. Now that he was not in the alley, he recognized the tone and the inflection, but it did not seem like it was from *his* past. It was a male voice. An officer in the military, or just some person he had offended without even knowing, he could not tell.

"You have already noticed the lead in your chest," he continued. "What you do not see is the needle that I have placed into your heart. It's not fatal, I assure you, merely a precaution.

"If you have not felt them yet, there are two additional leads in your body. One is in your left arm and one in the right. There is also a patch on your arm, which relays your vital statistics to the equipment those leads are attached to. Should your heart rate rise dramatically, the lead in your left arm will pump a sedative into your body that will slow your heart down and keep you from going into shock. I can't have you missing this, now can I?"

Dear God, what is he going to do to me?

"The lead in your right arm will continuously pump antibiotics into your system to make sure than there are no infections taking place. I won't let anything so simple take this away from me.

"Lastly, should your heart rate fall, the lead in your chest will pump adrenaline directly into your heart. I can't have you falling asleep on me either; though, I doubt that will be a problem.

"Now, for another answer to a question. You know very well

who I am, as I told you in the alley. Think hard, my friend. The last time you saw me in person was probably from several hundred feet away."

Halgren was coming to himself. He had his senses about him, and each time he felt his heart race through fear, the clear fluid in the tube drained into his arm and he felt the invisible hand of soothing slow it down. That voice was familiar. It was slowly taking shape, but he could not put it all together.

"When last you heard my voice in person, I was a child. You have heard my name a thousand times since. Do you know me yet?"

It was right there on the tip of his tongue and the front of his mind!

"Of course, you may have shut me out of your mind. After all, your friend stabbed you in the back pretty good. I suppose, in the end, that's what you get for dealing with the likes of scum like Ratajek."

The last piece snapped into place. The world stopped. Of all the possibilities that he had imagined, this was not one. At first, he felt as if pleading for mercy and pinning his sale on Ratajek, but then another revelation: *He was not here to avenge himself.*

"Oh my God," he said in a small voice.

"Oryan will suffice. Now, I will begin asking my questions. I want you to be completely honest with me. Maybe honest with yourself for the first time as well. I can promise you that the more honest you are, the less this will hurt."

Oryan appeared from the shadows and stood at the edge of the light. Halgren could make him out now. He had watched that boy end careers and lives all to line his pockets. The sight of him used to fill him with pride; now it filled him with dread.

"Captain, after I left the Quarter, how long before you began looking into my past?"

As the captain dug through memories long buried, Oryan tightened the straps around his ankles and wrists and applied new ones to his waist, his head, and upper arms.

"When your career started to take off. When I realized how valuable you were to me. I had to see if anyone else would recognize you," he said nervously.

"Good. That wasn't so hard, now was it?" asked Oryan as he

leaned over Halgren. His face was inches away from his captive's. His hands were on Halgren's. A smile crossed his lips. Halgren felt his breath come in quick, ragged gasps again. There was a twist of Oryan's wrist followed by a sharp snap and a scream. As Oryan stood, Halgren saw his middle finger snapped at the knuckle and bent backward over his hand. He wanted to scream more, but the sedative traced through his veins. The pain was intense, but he could not react to it as he should.

"Next, how did you learn who my father was?"

"Camp records," he gasped out. "I researched them and then went on to military archives!"

Oryan came closer. The vitals sensor beeped louder and faster to signify a rise in heart rate. The pump quietly went to work to correct that. The crack of bone was heard two more times followed by two more screams and the incessant beep of the sensor.

"Now, tell me truly, perfectly honest, when did you decide that he had to die?"

Halgren was gasping for breath; a cold sweat covered his body. Tears involuntarily ran down his face. Three fingers were now completely useless. The flesh around them had begun to swell, intensifying the pain. He could barely hear his tormentor past the pounding of his own heart in his ears.

"Make an effort to answer now," Oryan said calmly.

"I didn't make that call. I was just—" His hurried answer was cut short.

"Ah, now there we have it. I asked you to be honest with yourself, not just me. Perhaps, this will help to jog your memory." Oryan came into the light again carrying a scalpel. He started from between the collarbones and made an incision from there to the bottom of the rib cage. Several horizontal cuts were made intersecting the first incision at the top and bottom. Screaming filled the room, drowning out all other noises.

Oryan made his cuts and stepped away, the sound of Halgren's screams playing like music in his ears. When he stopped and the sedative had done its work, he came closer again. "This can't get in the way," he stated to himself as he removed the needle from Halgren's chest.

Halgren watched with tear-stained vision as Oryan carefully set the adrenaline needle aside. Oryan thumbed the edge of the flesh that he had just cut and with infinite complacency peeled it back off of the breastbone across the ribs. More screams. Halgren fought against his bonds, forcing blood from his ankles and wrists. Blood mingled with the sweat from beneath the leather strap that held his forehead still.

Oryan reveled in it. He studied the muscle and tissue as he exposed it as if he were carving a cadaver for research. Over the next thirteen hours, he kept his victim alive. He asked his questions, dealing small damage for truthful ones and further dissecting him for those he felt were not what he was looking for. The open wounds were cauterized, and blood was given to keep him alive as long as possible. When he got what he wanted from this man, when he saw the last seconds of his life slip away in his blood-soaked hands, he smiled and breathed the fire out of his lungs. His nostrils were filled with the metallic smell of human blood, and it was a sweet savor.

It was logged at the base that Captain Halgren reported in the following morning, looking very drunk. He staggered to his quarters and was never seen alive again. Three weeks later, a group of soldiers found his headless, mutilated carcass strung between two trees while on a routing exercise. The military began an investigation as it always does, but the outrage over his death was quickly silenced and the investigation stopped when the skeletons were removed from the captain's closet. With so many suspects and so many motives, the case was quickly abandoned.

Halgren's father received a package on his doorstep. There was no return address and no other way to identify the sender. There were no fingerprints, no hair, and no evidence of any kind that the authorities could find. Inside the package he found the head of his only son. Both eyes were removed and placed into the mouth, which was sewn shut. Both ears were missing. Across the flesh of the forehead was carved four words: *Sins of the Son.*

Betrayal and Desolation

It had been two weeks since Captain Halgren had been abducted from the alley at Aumakua. His hunter had learned many useful pieces of information from him during the last few hours of his life. He had learned the names of those who had helped him in the genocide of the camp. Most importantly, he had discovered that the good captain was *given* the idea for the false JEJ outbreak.

From what he could gather, an unknown source had been sending him detailed information on how to handle an actual outbreak of the disease for months before he faked his. The source, though they remained anonymous, appeared to be someone with very high security clearances. All the messages sent to Halgren were classified and encoded. Also, each time Halgren had tried to respond to the communications, he was only given further details about the disease. Near the end, they had begun to suggest the falsifying of an outbreak and even showed him the loopholes to avoid investigation and suspicion. Oryan should have known that he was not clever enough to come up with that on his own. But who sent the messages was another question. He would have to do further investigation.

As for those who aided in the murder of his father, there were only five. Halgren kept them close. Like Halgren, they were easy to find. Each had been dealt with in their own fashion. It had been slow and cruel, but the orchestrator of the slaughter had received the worst.

For Oryan, to add six more names to the body count he had accumulated was of no concern, but what surprised him was the lack of closure he felt after this handful had been dispatched. He felt no remorse or guilt for their deaths. His revenge had been sweet, but now that it was over, he did not feel satisfied. In the end, he still did not have his father back.

He had finished his business in short order, killing all six men in just over a week. Once he had concluded his affairs, he was headed back to the barracks when he got the call.

There was a battle coming soon. From the intelligence reports, it was a critical fight. It was a remote location called Akon. It was just an island in a chain of islands. Unlike the one that he had left, this one was cold and covered in snow. Were it peace time, this place would be of no real significance. However, each of these islands had been dearly fought over in the past six months. Only one remained unclaimed by the forces of Navarus. This island chain was located just to the north of the kingdom of Vollmar. It was a perfect location for an enemy who wanted to launch continued attacks against the kingdom. Akon was also the last in a chain of islands that made a near land bridge between Vollmar and Navarus.

Oryan had studied the terrain maps in depth. The location of the battle to take place was a large valley in the middle of the island. It was straightforward in its strategy. There were no real pitfalls to it. What confused the warlord was not that he and his Knights were being called in, but the Legion was activated as well, with command given back to the Captain. General Kovac himself was in command of this operation, and it did not seem a logical move. The Knights could win this incursion by themselves.

This must have been a request of the emperor's. Navaro was not a tactician, but his lust for power and control was unquenchable. This island would solidify his control of the entire western hemisphere of the globe. Only Vollmar and a few independent countries would remain. With this tiny patch of earth, that was not a far-off goal.

Still, Oryan felt a presence far more sinister at work. He did not trust the Captain, and mistrust in your allies was the first sign of a weak front. Weakness was unacceptable. Something was compelling them together, and it was deeper than Navaro and his power struggle with Tamrus. Despite his misgivings, duty called.

He slid his personal transport into the garage near his camp. Once he had collected his things, he headed straight for the briefing room. There was no time to waste. He had to get his Knights up to speed and soon. Before the night fell this day, they would know the details of this assignment as well as he did.

The briefing room was silent when he arrived there; most of the men were not even aware that he had arrived, and so they were not waiting for him. A few emergency lights were on, enough for the commander to see the edges of the holographic table in the middle and the bleachers around it. Everything was in black and white. He let his pack slide to the floor as he reached for the main lights. One by one, the dull thud of electricity firing fixtures to life could be heard. Oryan pulled the data chip from his breast pocket and slid it into the holographic table. Another thud and a constant hum brought the images to life.

He was transported into battle. While Kovac used computer simulations to determine the results of future battles, Oryan completed the same task all in his mind. He twisted the images in his brain, calculating the best placement of his men, the Legion, and the main bulk of the empire's forces. Within minutes, he was completely absorbed in imaginary combat.

"I see you're back," said a familiar voice. "I trust your business was successful."

Oryan did not turn from the rolling three-dimensional map in front of him. "My good man, my business is always a success; otherwise, it would not be mine."

Thomas stood behind Oryan, studying the map for a few moments with his commander. He was aware of the mission and had already reviewed the material, but he too was working things out in his mind. However, he had not come here to talk rank or study terrain maps with his friend.

"Do you remember Foley?" Thomas asked.

Oryan lost his focus on the hologram for a moment in reflection. He stared past the soft blue glow to the void beyond. "I remember it was a blood bath," he said after a moment's contemplation.

"I remember that too. Do you remember what we found in that prison?"

The memory flashed through his mind like a photograph he should have never seen. It had been a black op to rescue some key military leaders taken prisoner several months earlier, but the weapons that the Knights used had some regrettable consequences. A man half burned but still alive holding his two children in his arms in much the same state.

"Yes, I remember. There was nothing that any of us could do for them."

"I know. I don't hold you responsible, but it's been on my mind lately."

There was a lack of tone in Thomas's voice that made Oryan turn. "What else is on your mind, General?"

"It seems like a long time ago now, but I still remember your voice before that mission. I remember the rain and the anxiety. Most of all, I remember your words. I remember the talk of immortality. It haunts me to this day."

"Don't misunderstand, my lord, you have shown us all what it is to be invincible. There isn't a man in this unit that feels he couldn't take on an entire army by himself. Our victories have truly solidified our place in history. We are all, in some way, immortal."

There was a long pause. Oryan did not understand what had spurred this conversation, but there was a strange feeling rising in the pit of his stomach. It was not unfamiliar, but it seemed a feeling he did not want to rise any further. Still, his friend's words were keeping him silent. There seemed little he could say that would alter the mood.

Thomas seemed to be collecting his thoughts as if this speech had been prepared for months but was only now falling drastically short of the mark. Presently, he began again. "Thirty years from now, people will sit in their homes or at their jobs telling stories about this war. They'll compare where they were and what they were doing the day the first shots were fired. They'll reminisce about their feelings and how it forever altered their worlds in some way."

"Then they'll come to me. They'll ask me what it was like to have been there. To have *seen* it all happen in person. They'll listen intently, marking my every word as I tell them the tales. They'll thank me for my bravery and courage, or they will condemn me for my devotion to the evil they opposed. They'll applaud me for being a hero and tell me they will never forget my name or my sacrifice. Or, they'll let me rot in some prison for my crimes.

"Inevitably, they will ask me about you."

The feeling rose from Oryan's stomach to his heart. It wrapped cold fingers around the beating organ, making the warrior want nothing more than for this man to stop, but he was powerless to stop him.

"I'll tell them how I watched from my barracks as you defeated Agrion in that arena. I watched the events unfold as you became the greatest champion in history, setting records still untouched.

"I'll tell them about the first time I saw you in person and how you truly were larger than life. How every word from your mouth inspired men to be greater and do greater things than they could have ever dreamed. They'll picture in their minds the sight of Captain Jeckstadt on the wall, bringing an entire army to its knees. I'll tell them of the magnificent Warlord of Navarus. The foe of the wicked, defender of the empire. The man who shook nations. They will hear, and they will be amazed.

"But when the lights fade and the questions cease, it will be only me left with my memories. It'll be in that time that I remember Oryan Jeckstadt, the man. I'll remember how much, at first, I wanted to be like him. I'll remember the sweet savor of victory, knowing that I never had to taste the bitterness of defeat.

"Then I will see those faces at Foley. I will see those innocent eyes staring at me under charred eyelids, and I'll remember doing the only humane thing I could think to do. Suddenly the grandeur of immortality will come crashing down. In that hour, I will remember just how mortal I truly am. In that hour, I will pray to God that He can forgive me what I've done."

The feeling wrenched Oryan's heart. His friend's words pierced him to the soul. The faces of those at Foley seared his eyes. The faces of the men on the wall weighed him down as if he was asked to carry the world on his shoulders. The twisted face of Halgren filled him with bitter pain. Did they deserve the fate he had dealt them? Who was he to deliver judgments with such finality? With all that he had done in the name of duty and justice, did he not deserve the same?

It was anger and revenge that came to his rescue. The thought of his father on his knees and the blade that ended his life washed over the guilt. Halgren was a murderer. That man's hands were bloodier than his own. He had never killed a man that would not have done the same to him.

Then there was Agrion…

The anger burned through him. "Only soldiers who have done something they are ashamed of have to feel that way. For me, if I make it through this war alive, there will only be the cherished memories of my fallen comrades. I need no forgiveness from *God!* What has God ever done for me?"

"God is everything, my lord. Without Him, your victories would never have come to fruition, and without Him, the lives of your brave men would be for naught. Perhaps your words are spoken out of turn," countered Thomas calmly, despite the rage rising in his commander's voice. "When the cheers are over, when people are done calling on you, when your men no longer chant your name, what will *you* have?"

Oryan's wrath knew no bounds. He forgot his friendship with this man, the way he had always stood by him, no matter the consequences, and the way he was his brother when the world around them wanted his blood.

"Ungrateful peasant!" he shouted, rising from his seat. "*I* have given you everything! *I* granted those men immortality! Their reward after this life was forged by *me!* As is yours! Perhaps it is you who has spoken out of turn, *General!*"

Thomas rose. He would not back down from Oryan, even if it meant his life. He knew he was right, and deep down, he knew that Oryan knew it.

"You forget yourself, *my lord!* Only the guilty take the truth to be hard."

Oryan reached for Ethanis. His strong hands groped for his throat and quickly closed like a vice to squeeze the life out of his friend turned tormentor. He drew his face close to his own. With blind hatred, sheer venom, and anguish of soul, he spoke. "I loved you, trusted you, like my brother!" Thomas struggled for breath. "I've given you everything! You condemn me, and you don't know me! Who are you to pass judgment on me?" His grip loosened, his eyes lost their focus, and the anger left his voice. He dropped Thomas to the floor and sat heavily beside him.

"You don't even know me." Oryan's voice was small and weak.

He was a man tired of carrying so much hate, but he feared that should he let it go, he had nothing left. "Where have you gone, brother? Where are you now?"

Thomas was on his hands and knees, rubbing his neck. His breath was returning slowly, but each intake of air burned down temporarily crushed windpipes. He had expected the attack and was surprised he lived through it, but that did not change the pain he felt.

"Oryan," he said finally when he could master his breathing. It was the first time he addressed his commander by his first name. "Oryan, I have been and always will be your friend. If I don't say these things to you, who will? Or will you go throughout the rest of your life thinking that the world owes you everything? You and I both know, in this war, there are no innocent men."

Oryan looked at his humble general. The rage had subsided, but he was not certain how to react. He did not want to reach for Ethanis, but he longed to help him up. He loved and hated him in the same moment. What confounded him, what he could not place, was where the hatred came from. Did he truly hate his friend, or did he just despise himself?

General Thomas raised himself from the floor. He stood up straight and straightened the uniform now creased from the attack. He extended a hand and lifted Oryan to his feet. "I know why I fight. Do you? Whatever demons you have, I hope that you're not still fighting against them. We can't change the past, but we *can* alter our futures."

Thomas saw the battle-hardened killer weigh his words in the balance. He watched as the years of death and war faded. Then, at last, he was left with the innocent boy who left his father and his home a lifetime ago. The sparkle of repentance and forgiveness replaced the smoldering ashes of rage in his eyes. It was Oryan again.

To Oryan, Ethanis Thomas was a tormentor. He saw his friend become a beacon of light that burned him even as it purified. He felt guilt and sorrow rise in him as he had never felt before. The consuming fire of revenge had burned so hot for so long that it could no longer be maintained. Like the star that shone too brightly, the heat died quickly and was replaced only with the cold void of empty, lonely space.

"Ethanis," he said in a voice barely above a whisper. "I … I'm …" he trailed off without knowing what to say.

"I know," Thomas replied. "I shouldn't have said anything, but I've felt a sense of urgency in that message. I don't know why. When I learned we were activated and that you were on your way back, I've thought of nothing else. If it was the last thing I ever said, I had to say it." He paused for a moment. He drew a deep breath and brought himself back to the task at hand. "Well, it's said. Now's not the time. I notified the men of your arrival. They'll be here in less than an hour. For now, let's look at these terrain maps together. It's best we were on the same page. There is a battle to win, and we have a reputation to uphold."

He composed himself. He gazed at his friend and fellow soldier with awe and wonder. His message had struck a chord and not just of anger. Ethanis had not only survived his wrath, he had also earned his admiration. Since his father, Oryan had admired no one. After a few deep breaths, he placed the words of Ethanis Thomas in the back of his mind and summoned the strength of the greatest lord of men the world had ever known.

They filed in and filled the bleachers around the projection. He watched them, filled with gratitude at their sacrifice and dedication. They were the most finely tuned instruments of war in the world. He would be proud to lead these men into battle, even to death.

Once they were all seated, he began. "Gentleman, I've said it before, and for those of you who are still alive and have been with me from the beginning, you're about to hear it again. For you newcomers, this is the most important message I have to give.

"Yesterday is gone forever. Tomorrow may never come. Today is here. What will you do with it? Everyone had the same twenty-four hours. It is the only fair constant in this world. There is only now. If we don't make the most of now, yesterday means nothing. If we don't learn from yesterday, tomorrow will most certainly never come.

"A few days from now, we may all be dead. We may never

return from Akon. Thus, we have two choices. We can dwell on our impending doom and do everything we can to run from it, or we can square our shoulders to the task and meet it as Knights. I, for one, would rather die on my feet than live running from what may come.

"Make no mistake; death may come swiftly to us all, ready or not. Tomorrow or fifty years from now, we are all dead men. All I ask is that if it's our time, we make sure that we give the man next to us every chance we can to ensure that it's not his. Do that, and you'll all be legends."

Two days later and thousands of miles away, Oryan stood on the top of a hill that surrounded the field where, in the morning, the battle was to commence. He had left the camp, his men, and the safety of the army behind and sought solitude amidst the driving snow. He was fully dressed in his battle armor.

The climb had been difficult. Normally, a hill of this size would have been nothing more than a long hike, but the quickly deepening snow, which covered an inch of ice, had made the journey more treacherous. He did not mind. The warlord was in no mood for a pleasant stroll or even a peaceful walk. The words of Ethanis Thomas still rung in his head, making him unable to sleep. And so, he climbed.

Now, the journey behind him, he gave heed once again to his thoughts. The snow fell heavily, making everything in the world seem black and white. Somehow, it seemed appropriate.

His thoughts had been final, as if he could see the end of his quest at hand. Before he had left the barracks, he had written a last will and testament and left it in his quarters, as well as many other treasures he had come to value. A sealed box contained what few journal entries he had kept, his notes on military strategy, history from the emperor's library and, of course, Seyah's journal.

He made sure everything was in proper order. His clothes were neatly pressed and hung. His home, the one that he had known for the longest time since he left the Quarter when he was sixteen, was pristine. Despite all of those things, he felt that adequate preparation for this had not been made. He felt, as it was with the last day at the Quarter and the first day at the barracks, that his life was going to change. He would never see that place again.

He was twenty-two years old now. He had spent two and a half years as a Centauri and the rest as the leader of the Kentaurus Knights. He was one of only two undefeated champions in the amateur circuit and the only undefeated champion in the professional arena. He was equally undefeated on the battlefield—to date, successfully completing forty-three of forty-three missions. He and his men had killed over twenty-five thousand enemy troops; destroyed a combined total of over one thousand five hundred enemy vehicles, including ground, air and naval units; and captured sixteen critical enemy military structures. He was the most successful commander in history.

He was the Warlord of Navarus. His accomplishments had raised him to such a pedestal that a new position was created, putting him second only to the emperor in both political and military power. Not even Lucius Kovac could make that boast. In some circles, he was considered one of two men in the world destined to become a god.

He had achieved more than any ten men had in their lifetimes, and he was less than a quarter of a century old. He had lived, by all who chose to look, a much-fulfilled life. Yet for all of his glory, he reflected on what he had. He owned a massive estate in the heart of the empire, yet he had never even seen it. He had servants, butlers, chefs, and maids that he had never met. All that he truly owned in the world rested in a tiny room thousands of miles from here.

He had no family. His father was brutally murdered by the very man who set him on the path to becoming the legend he now was. Though justice had been served, it was not enough. He had no one to look to for wisdom. He had no one to lean on when times were rough. There was no home to look forward to when this war was over.

Ethanis had been right. His accomplishments were not his own. They were the result of others playing him on cruel puppet strings to achieve their own ends. He was, in the end, utterly alone. The God he had long since abandoned had done the same to him. He could have looked to Him hundreds of time for peace and solace, but instead he simply turned inward and relied on passion, hate, and pride to fill the void. Though they covered his sin and his vain ambition, he was never satisfied. Each step he took with them only took him farther away from what he really needed.

What he needed was *her.*

The very thought of her made him ache more than even the thought of Armay. She was the only good thing he had ever known. Fate had dealt him blow after blow, and then there was her. He had not thought of her in a very long time. Her memory was bittersweet. He could live a thousand lifetimes and suffer a thousand times what he had if only her memory was there to hold on to.

That night with her had made him feel whole again. It had made him feel as if he had a clean slate again. She was the first spring rain that brought life from death. As he thought about the taste of her, his mind was filled with guilt. She *had* been his chance, and since he had known her, what had he done with the gift she had given him? He loved her, but she was ripped from him like everything he loved in his life. And after all he had done and couldn't undo, how could she still love him? He was filled with guilt for his sins, with pain for his transgressions, and sorrow for the life that he was given and chose to forsake.

In the end, he was alone.

"It never ceases to amaze me how quiet the world becomes when the snow falls," said a familiar voice from behind him.

For a few moments, Oryan did not respond. He was focused on the scene before him. However, since their last conversation, he had begun to take careful note of what his friend said. As if for the first time, Oryan soaked in the muffled silence the snow cover provided.

"It is the calm before the storm," he said as he pointed to the clearing at the base of the hill. "Do you see that, General? Less than a year ago, children played there. They had their games and their lives, and nothing else in their world mattered. There *was* nothing else. This conflict was a world away.

"Tomorrow, we'll bring it here. Tomorrow, we'll shed men's blood here. We will color the white snow red, and this silence we enjoy will be replaced by the last sounds of dying men. There will be prayers and good-byes and screams.

"When it is over, maybe not tomorrow or a year from now, or ten years from now, children will return here again. They will play on the grass made green by the men who died. The sounds of laughter and life will return. They'll run through the field on clearer days, and life will continue much as it was before we came.

"By then, the blood spilled here will be forgotten by all but a few. You speak of legacies, my friend. You spoke to me of what people will ask you about in the years to come. I don't think you'll ever have to worry about telling your tale from a prison or in your home. I think the world will know already. As for answering for me…" Oryan had still not turned to face Thomas. He remained focused on the vision of children playing in the field before him. Ethanis did not find any solace in his words though he knew that Oryan meant them.

"Someone has to, old friend. In the end, who is answerable for their own actions other than themselves?"

Oryan remained unmoved. "We see things very different, you and I. I don't feel the touch of God in my life anymore. Whatever hope I had of joining my father is gone. For me, there is only here and now. The world will judge me, and so I have my reward. Hero, or villain, all I look forward to is death."

Thomas had never heard Oryan speak of his father or any relation. Normally, he would not pry into his past, but if he did not ask now, there would never be another chance. "You loved your father, and he is gone. Did you die with him?"

There was a pause. The wind sprayed the falling snow back into their faces. Oryan's head fell ever so slightly, and his breath curled away from his face in thin clouds.

"No. I chose my own death." He looked at Thomas. "There is a thing that I must do. It may cost me my life, but it must be done. I have to find her, living or dead. When this battle is over, the Knights are yours. This is my last order to you."

Thomas watched as Oryan began the slow march back down the hill to the camp. He had known him for years, and yet this was the first time he had seen anything more than a commander. Somewhere in him, there was humanity. There was light and honor that had not been stolen by the emperor or the war. Even if it was small, there was hope. Whoever *she* was, perhaps she could save him.

The Kentaurus Knights stood on the front line of the empire's forces. Oryan had ordered that armor be made for each man, resembling his, for the battlefield. Once a man made it through his initial training as a Knight, he received several different variations of the armor. One contained deep forest green fabric with black armor. Another was crimson armor with black cloth, and the third was all white with black trim for just such an occasion. They were an impressive sight, truly looking like warriors from a forgotten time. They filled their enemies with fear as front line soldiers and caused sheer panic and pandemonium for any one or any one group of people discovered they were being hunted by them.

After so many victories, Oryan had discarded the usual battle-dress uniform in favor of the armor. True, it was less subtle, but it was still light and flexible. All the tactics of modern combat could be performed and accomplished, perhaps not by another group of soldiers, but certainly by the Knights. Besides, no matter what they wore, the presence of the Kentaurus Knights was anything but subtle.

The Knights were organized into four rows of one hundred and twenty-five men each. The front line consisted of Knights who carried only small arms on their waist and swords on their backs. In their hands they held five-foot-tall, broad, Tamrus-plated shields. Any frontal assault by enemy infantry was futile. Their bullets were merely turned aside by the wall of shields.

The second line consisted of Knights with no shields, but rifles slung on their shoulders. They maintained their pistols and swords, but it was they who returned the volley of gunfire during open-field combat.

The third line was composed of soldiers ready for anything. They were the death dealers, should the fight become too close for rifles to be an effective offense as well as defense. When the enemy reached the front line, the rifle-bearers took a step to the right while the sword-wielders took one to the left. Then they plunged into the enemy lines and did what they did best. Oryan was among that line, as was General Thomas.

The last line consisted of the heavy arms-bearers. They carried rocket launchers, portable SAM launchers, and other, more stationary weapons. It was their job to keep the front three lines as free as possible from enemy tanks and air forces.

This tactic had proven deadly efficient, even when the enemy tried to adapt to the new style of combat. It had made Oryan an even greater military genius in the eyes of the empire, as well as Vollmar. Combining the strategies of ancient combat and modern was brilliant given the advent of certain new technologies.

Typically, the lines were only one-hundred-men wide, as the remaining twenty-five from each line were used as a separate force, implementing guerilla tactics while the line formation did its work. Today, however, there was no need. Behind the Knights stood five thousand soldiers of the Imperial Army and the Captain with the Legion.

Oryan had avoided the Captain at all costs, save to discuss its role in the operation. All he needed them for was to fan out, both right and left, to keep the enemy from flanking the main force of the empire. It was a simple task, but one that Oryan felt the Captain could handle.

Their forces had arrived on the island after the armies of Vollmar, but the men, driven by their warlord, established their position on the field first. Just as they found themselves ready for combat, the rumble of tank treads could be felt under their feet. Oryan had anticipated that they would use their heavy equipment first rather than send their men into slaughter, and so he had prepared for just such an event.

From the coast of the island controlled by the empire, warships readied their artillery. Upon the signal from Oryan, they began to bombard the enemy line. The shells were not meant as exact weapons, but rather a diversion for the attack to come.

The tanks of Vollmar rolled along confidently, avoiding the random blasts from the cruisers. Once they made visual contact with the enemy, their cannons boomed. However, visual range did not mean weapon's range.

General Thomas watched closely as the shells landed closer and closer to the lines. When several landed too close for comfort, he ordered the launch of a newly designed weapon. A single missile fired high into the sky above the battlefield. Surface-to-air missiles from behind the tanks streaked through the sky. As one closed in, the missile detonated before it could be destroyed. There was a brilliant, bright red explosion, and bits of shrapnel rained from the wreckage, landing amongst the tanks.

Impervious to the initial impact of the shards, the bulky weapons continued their progress. At first, it seemed as if the new weapon had been ineffective until one of the tanks rolled a great tread over a piece of hot metal from the fallen missile. Another explosion erupted, this time from the ground. It lifted the right half of the tank two feet into the air. The treads and some of the wheels shattered into dust, and the armor on the belly of the beast lay exposed. A half a second later, the ground lit up as the heavy vehicles found the highly explosive mines left from the missile. Dirt, snow, fire, and metal shot in hundreds of directions.

A cheer went up from the Imperial Army, seeing their foes primary attack dispatched so quickly. The Legion and the Knights kept their reserve. True, no more heavy armor was coming from that direction; however, this was most certainly not the end of the fight.

A few tanks still remained, and the empire's stationary turrets and rocket launchers made short work of them. Coming on the heels of the tanks was the infantry. They marched at first in rows, then split into smaller and smaller groups until they had assumed their positions. Oryan quickly surveyed the situation and surmised that these were not just ordinary foot soldiers. Their efficient dispersal and excellent use of the snowy terrain made him believe that these were Special Forces units. They were called the Night Hawks, and they would be more than a match for the Legion, but the Knights were still the superior force. Nonetheless, he braced for the fight to come.

He ordered the army behind him to disperse and set up a wide perimeter that would effectively neutralize the threat of an attack from the rear. He did not send the order to the Captain yet to take up flanking positions, as he wanted that to be a surprise.

Following the Night Hawks came the marines. They came in formation, twenty men across and twenty men deep. Oryan's intelligence reports showed him that this was only half the total force. Still, numbers do not win battles.

Once the marines passed the tank wreckage, Oryan turned to his men. "Knights! Advance!"

The front line moved forward, shield wall intact. All at once, it started. The marines began their charge, breaking ranks and firing thousands of rounds into their aggressor. The sizzle of super-heated metal instantly melting snow could be heard through the blasts of weapons and the roars of men. The second row of Knights returned the volley, striking any place the armor was weak. Hundreds fell, but where one lay, two more arose to take his place. They would advance three yards and lose one. The Knights lost but a few and continued their steady march forward.

A few remote aircraft had been detected coming from the shores, and the empire responded in turn. Their carriers launched their squadrons, and even as Oryan's Knights waged war on the ground, the sky was alive with combat of its own.

The battle waged hot in the field. The gap between the two forces had been closed, and so the third row of Knights had begun their work. They cut their way through the enemy lines, taking nearly thirty enemy troops for each Knight who fell.

In the center of the carnage was Oryan. Each stroke he made took another foe with it. It was he who led the charge, and it was his efforts that weakened the center of the attack and opened the field for further Knight advancement. At his back was his general. The two fought together as one. They flowed like music, each performing in perfect harmony with the other. Together, they finished off whole companies.

When the first wave of marines was waning thin, Oryan fell back and let his men continue their slaughter. There was one thing left to do to secure this day. Though he had been in the thick of the fighting, he had not forgotten the Night Hawks. They were still out there and probably waiting until Oryan and his men finished off most of the first wave before they would spring their attack and then send in the second wave and overwhelm the enemy. Oryan checked the tree lines and signaled the Captain.

From the start, the Captain had resented this battle. It was nothing short of insulting what it and its men were being asked to do. To have been reduced from the most deadly fighting force in the world to clean-up for this arrogant little child in such a short time was horrific.

Still, this battle presented a unique opportunity. Its master, the great Lord and General Kovac, fueled that hate. It was only recently that it realized that its master was doing all of this for nothing more than his own amusement. For too long it labored for the recognition of its master to be the center of his attention and twisted affection. The Captain had been his star pupil at one time. Now, however, it was replaced by this scum that had not even learned at the feet of the master.

Oryan was a plague. He was the disease that was rotting the core of its fragile existence. Oryan infected everyone around him with his dreams of self-aggrandizing glory! In the end, he would take everyone with him. The Captain knew it, even if no one else could see him for what he was. However, Oryan was far more lethal than any normal virus. His infection was far more subtle and many times more deadly. He was altogether attractive, convincing thousands, even millions, to follow him to destruction. Oryan served no master, no higher purpose than himself! Men like him brought death and nothing more.

Even its master had fallen victim to the sickness. Kovac watched him and studied him with envious eyes. The empire saluted him and praised him for his victories. What they did not realize was that those victories truly only belonged to him. He did not care about the greatness of this regime!

There was, however, a cure to this virus. Like all plagues, it had to come to an end. Like all diseases, someone or something was smarter than it. Like the end of all things, it simply needed a catalyst. It was the right person at the right place and the right time.

Now was that time. The Captain was that man. This would be that place. It would save the empire and its master even if it meant its death. Even if it meant that all had to suffer humiliation. At the end of this day, its master would know who it was who saved the empire. It would once again win the prestige it deserved and take it from the thief who slithered into its world and shattered everything it held dear!

It was time for vengeance. It was time for the cure. It was time for mutiny.

Then, the signal came.

There was silence on the comm. Oryan signaled again and waited. There was again no response. Though Oryan was not at the front lines, he was still in the thick of his men and could not see past them. It was apparent that the Captain had abandoned his post. That traitorous wretch had fled at a crucial moment to reap its petty revenge! Now, the chances of his survival dwindled and diminished. The odds suddenly took a dramatic swing in favor of his enemy. Though small, there was still a chance for victory here. There was still a chance that his Knights could see home again. That chance, however small, was all he needed.

He raged through the lines back to the front line and found his general again. Once again, they began their great slaughter. Oryan fought harder, abandoning all thought of his own safety. Dozens of the enemy fell every minute at their hands. The Knights were spurred on by the surge from their commanders. They fought harder, taking lives with each move.

All around Oryan, the screams of dying men in front of him swelled. Behind him, the roar of his own men, vitalized by the look of fear in their enemy's eyes, became louder than the cries of the dying. It was as he had grown to expect. Despite the Captain's betrayal, there was victory still to be had.

It was then that the Night Hawks sprung their attack. Gunfire blasted into their sides, and now the battle waged everywhere but their backs. For his men, that meant good odds. The enemy had been clever and fast, but not thorough. They had attacked too early. With the Captain gone, their rear was completely exposed. The main bulk of the empire's army waited to be called into action. Had the Hawks waited only a few more minutes, there would be a considerable distance between the Knights and aid. Luckily for them, the enemy did not know that. Still, the battle raged hotter. Knights began to fall in greater numbers, and their lines were constantly being reformed.

Oryan was rushing from place to place, wherever the tides were turning, to make sure that he still had the upper hand. It was desperate, but he was determined. An explosion threw Knights in every direction. The air battle had been decided, and Vollmar had proven superior.

Oryan listened to his communicator and then to the carnage around him. Slowly, there came a sound that made the situation fall from short odds to none. He had been so wrong. He had underestimated his enemy. This foe was smart and cunning. It was patient, deadly, and, despite his initial thought, had waited until just the right moment. The horror grew and gripped him to the core. He and all his men would never leave this field.

The call of his men behind him had changed. No longer did they cry with the thrill of battle. Their screams had become those of men betrayed. Oryan heard, with chilling clarity, the sounds of his men being slaughtered.

The Captain had not left. It had not run. It had not fled in an attempt to isolate the Knights. It and the Legion were still very much in the fight. They had advanced to the back of the Knights, drawn their weapons, and started killing those with whom they were there to fight. Like a spider awaiting the fly, it had waited, and Kovac had given it the opportunity. Oryan had been set up all along.

Knights fell all around him. Blasts from the Legion as well as those from the enemy overwhelmed them on all sides. The Knights fought gallantly, taking hundreds with them even as they fell. Those in the rear had turned to face their betrayers, dealing death as it was delivered unto them. With the screams of his own dying men all around him, Oryan felt for the first time in his life the bitter sting of defeat. It was then, when all hope was being stifled like a candle in a storm, Oryan heard a voice that brought him back from the brink.

He did not understand the words, but he knew what they meant. The voice belonged to General Ethanis Thomas, who was still alive, despite the carnage. His general rushed to his side, shouting cries of glory beyond death. Oryan sheathed his sword and grabbed a rifle from the ground. He shot at anything that was not a Knight, moving madly through the crowd. He charged to the rear, Thomas just behind him, tearing through all enemies as if they were only imaginary.

The lines of his men no longer existed. The enemy was everywhere. They were through on all sides, intermingled with the Knights. Thomas and his commander dispatched Night Hawks, marines, and Legion with equal indifference. They had both now abandoned their rifles in favor of their blades and pistols.

They fought together in harmony again, an invincible force unto themselves. No poet could give word to the grace, elegance, and lethal perfection that they were. They were the battle. They were the beginning, and they were the end.

Deep into the lines of the Legion they raged, shoulder to shoulder, back to back. Oryan did not even need to see his general to know that he was there. In that moment, the two of them together could take on the whole world.

There was a pain in Oryan's side as if he had been punched hard just above the hip. He fought on, only giving it a second's notice. There was no time for pain. He and Ethanis slaughtered the Legion, watching several abandon their campaign and flee rather than face the two warriors. The world was in chaos and Oryan the agent thereof until the world went quiet.

There was a gunshot that somehow rung louder than the rest. Then there was the last sound of a dying man. The last sound of a fallen comrade. The last sound of the only friend he had in the world.

He spun around hard, desperate to save the life that hung in jeopardy. It was a life that he could not lose. It was the life that had called him from the ashes of revenge and given him hope. The voice that spurred him on to fight to the last. That voice was already extinguished.

On the ground at his feet lay the broken body of Ethanis Thomas. It was as if the sun was gone. A great light in this world of darkness was extinguished. Now, no one would be able to ask this hero to hear his tales. No woman would call him her own. No children would call him father. The zeal for battle and lust for death left Oryan. None of it mattered. The Knights were dead. Thomas was gone. All was lost.

He sank to his knees. There was another blow, this one to his back, but once again, he gave it no heed. He felt his strength leave, and he nearly surrendered and accepted the fate that belonged to him. He could think of no greater tribute than to die by the side of his brother. But, it was not his time. Through the tears welling in his eyes, he saw a vision that called him back from the gates of death. There, observing the madness, was the Captain.

Suddenly, the embers of revenge that his dead friend had

quenched blazed into life. They raged hotter and more consuming than ever before. This man, this *creature*, before him was the source of his pain. It was the personification of all that haunted him. *You have taken everything!* His heart screamed a blood-chilling cry that rang from his lungs and filled the air.

His eyes, blind with hate, could only see the Captain. He did not know how many fell in his wake, but nothing could slow the vengeance that gave him wings. There was another stinging blow to his shoulder. It rang through his arm and wrenched the sword from his hand. Finally, the distance closed as the Captain fired desperately to save its own life.

Oryan lunged, bare hands grasping the throat of the villain and wrenching his whole body to the ground. There was no sound from the Captain. Oryan's strong hands had severed the oxygen supply instantly. In his ears, Oryan could only hear the sound of his own racing heart as he squeezed the life from the devil. The Captain kicked and fought, flailing wildly. It pierced Oryan with its blade, but he felt no pain. Oryan felt the bones in the neck give way and crack. The flailing stopped and turned to spasms, the throes of a dying man. Under his thumbs, Oryan felt veins, wind passages, and muscles collapse. Blood trickled from under his fingertips. Still he held fast. There was a sharp blow to his back, but still he would not release. Even after all life was gone from the body, he squeezed harder, pressing his fingers through the flesh.

All the fire and all the hate were being unleashed. If this was to be his end, this was to be the end for this thing as well. He could not bring his friend back to life, but he could do him this one honor before he too passed through the veil of mortality. He had forgotten completely the war around him. Nothing in the world existed except him, the Captain, and his hate.

There was a sudden sharp blow that knocked his helmet from his head and sent a shudder to his whole frame. His grip loosened as his world faded to gray. Suddenly he realized how tired he was. Each muscle in his body ached. There were centers of pain all over him. The world blurred as he straightened his back. He was now kneeling over his victim. The white snow fell softly; each snowflake came in and out of focus before his eyes. There was no color. He looked down at his hands. They were visions in a gray-scale world save the scarlet blood that lined the creases and pooled in his palms.

It is over. Father, I am dead. I have failed you. Ethanis, my brother, I am as dead now as I have been to you for so long. You will never know my sorrow.

Celeste. My Celeste. I never told you. There was so much I wanted to say. I love you.

There was another blow to his head. He slumped to his back on the snow, the regret of a wasted life torturing his last moments. Despite his armor, he felt utterly exposed. The eyes of a vengeful God pierced his soul and laid him naked before the heavy judgment of a jury composed of those he had wronged. Here, in his last moments, he felt the anguish of a man damned. He could not cover his sins. He wished to be forever crushed out of existence as if he had never been born.

Just as the whole world faded to black, a shadow appeared above him. It had no form or detail. Just a shadow, some emissary from hell come to collect its prize. It spoke, but it sounded only like the distant echoes of language. Oryan surrendered to his fate. He let go the hope for redemption and succumbed to the full weight of justice.

My God, I am dead!

He closed his eyes and remembered no more.

Shortly after his fall, the battle was over. The remaining forces of Navarus were so demoralized they retreated, surrendering their positions without a fight. The Hawks pursued, giving as they had received and taking none hostage.

When the smoke cleared and the wounded were being cared for, the commanders of each force reported the battle's outcome to their superiors.

Two messages were sent.

One was sent to Emperor Navaro and General Lucius Kovac. It read:

> *The battle is a total loss. Ninety-eight percent casualties. The warlord is dead.*

The other was sent to the halls of Tamrus in the heart of Vollmar.

We have taken the field. The Kentaurus Knights have fallen. The Legion and their Captain are dead. Oryan Jeckstadt has been taken alive.

To Be Continued…